Beauty
To Die For

The Cosmetic Consequence

Judi Vance

Beauty To Die For

The Cosmetic Consequence

©1998, Judi Vance

Published by:
ProMotion Publsihing
3368-F Governor Dr.
Suite 144
San Diego, CA 92122
1(800) 231-1776

ISBN 1-57901-035-0

The views and opinions expressed herein are solely those of the author and are expressed for the purpose of stimulating thought and discussion. This book should not be construed as providing medical advice to any reader or recipient of the information.

Printed In The United States

This book is dedicated to the wise women of the world who, through their own determination to create a more healthful body, are educating themselves and consequently their families

Acknowledgments

Very special thanks to:

Cathy Miceli for her unwavering belief that this book must come to fruition. My appreciation for her countless hours of sorting through technical jargon and transcribing it into a language that everyone would understand is immeasurable. Thanks Cathy!

Tom Mower for inspiring me to write about this emotion packed subject. Thank you for your perceptiveness, encouragement, and most of all, for the challenge to "learn what you know."

Dr. Ted Clarke, my life-long friend, for the fine editing he did on the book. His experience with editing and his scientific eye allowed for additions and changes that are greatly appreciated.

Rowan Hamilton, for his complete review of the book. Thank you for your sincere comments.

All the women (and some men) who shared their health and skin care problems with me. Your confusion and frustrations corroborated the need for a book such as this.

My father and mother who left me the legacy of not having to be perfect and teaching me to have the courage to stand in my own light.

All the rest (but too many to mention) who have helped to bring this endeavor to the world. Your faith in me has been unwavering and words cannot express my gratitude.

Table Of Contents

Introduction: Introduces Judi Vance, background on her past illness and what led her on this journey and investigation into personal care products. Also touches on inadequate testing, labeling laws, marketing and cost factors in industry.

Hair Care Products: covers commonly used including; shampoo, conditioner, dye. Also touches briefly on wave solutions, sprays, fixatives and gels.

Face Products: covers all products commonly used on face including; moisturizers—wrinkle creams, exfoliants (AHA's, Retin-A) exfoliant—scrubs, soaps and cleansers.

Face Makeup: Color cosmetics including foundation, blusher, lipstick;

Eye make-up—liner, shadow, mascara.
Special Section: Mouthwash and Toothpaste - Fluoride.

Body: Body creams and lotions, talcum powder, sunscreens, fragrances—neurotoxins, antiperspirants/deodorants, depilatories (hair removal cream).

Nail Care Products: Nail polish and nail polish remover. The hazards of artificial nails.

Baby Care Products: Powder, bubble-bath and shampoo for babies, touches on new trend of kiddie cosmetics and fragrance.

Foreword

When my product development company in Britain researched the market for a new skin care technology, the results were outstanding.

We went to a wide range of subjects to find out about their skin problems. Everyone in hair salons was or had suffered from contact dermatitis, especially those washing hair every day. We found that they had tried every product on the market for help with their hands, including prescriptions from their doctors. The list of occupations where skin problems were a daily hazard grew— from the aircraft industry to chemical workers and car wash attendants. The stories came in from people with no contact with industrial hazards. Problems with shampoos (which we had met in the professional hair salons) facial creams, body lotions, colored products and baby products filled our files. People were even sensitized to water.

Then, as if to add a final note to this list of misery, we discovered the statistics for eczema and dermatitis in Britain— 16% of the population. Recent research showed that 3% of the natural composition of our skin is now hydrocarbons from atmospheric pollution.

The message was clear. The majority of people lived and worked in a toxic environment.

My own work as a clinical herbalist and cosmetic scientist showed me the health needs of my clients and a source of many skin conditions—the very products they apply to their skin. At the most basic level regular soaps are made from caustic soda; detergents from sulfuric acid.

Soon after coming to Canada in 1996 I met a fellow crusader, Judi Vance. During the conversations we have had we recognized in each other common values and a common quest for the sources of debilitating toxic and overload conditions we have both suffered and fully recovered from. My response to my experience was to begin a twenty year career in natural medicine. Judi has been on a

i

tireless quest to bring education and information to a public bewildered by illnesses they cannot understand.

Judi has behind her a career in the cosmetic industry. This was the foundation for the Cosmetic Health Report, a journal giving clear and vital information about the chemical and health issues surrounding the multi-billion dollar cosmetic industry.

Last year, Judi gave me a copy of the book that has come from all these years of work. It is factual, detailed and informative about the many health hazards of cosmetics, shampoos, perfumes and other personal care and toiletry products. She explains what the problems are, what causes them and why. A vastly profitable and largely unregulated industry is making us sick. Judi Vance tells us how. Her references are the industry's own information, journals, medical texts. The bibliography is exhaustive and impressive.

Concise and powerful. This book can awaken society.

Rowan Hamilton, Cosmetic Scientist and Herbalist

Preface

This book was written to provoke change. It is not intended to cast blame or suggest misconduct but to simply propose the re-evaluation of the ingredients in personal care products. There is a judicious need to analyze and, if necessary, modify the existing formulations should they be found to contain potentially harmful ingredients or suspected carcinogens.

This population, the one that dictated buying trends from the ridiculous (pet rocks) to the sublime (surgical enhancement) has flatly rejected the aging process. Not merely looking toward a more youthful appearance, these baby-boomers are looking toward prolonging life—and the quality of it. We have become conscious about taking responsibility for our own bodies and the state of our well-being. We are trading information almost as fast as it is printed. Starting with personal networking through to the international exchange of information on the internet, intercommunication is expanding this generation's understanding of their bodies. They demand accurate information—recent research, reports, articles— and want to know the credentials of the people writing them.

A magnetic-like force draws these like-minded individuals together. The focus of introducing positive changes in lifestyle links them on their pilgrimage to wholeness. The quest to reunite the mind, body and spirit and the willingness to accept personal accountability to achieve this end is their common denominator.

It is a courageous passage out of a world that was once thought of as the protector of humankind, an establishment to safeguard individuals against the propagandizing of unconscionable product sales or services. We envisioned a great sentinel surveying all new products and services and forcing them through meticulous methods of scrutiny. Obviously, this is not the case. A plethora of new chemicals are introduced each year and it would be near to impossible for the agencies to test everything that comes to the marketplace. There are too few employees and departments to address all concerns regarding product labelling and safety.

iii

Clearly, the necessary studies required on ingredients is a long way away. In the meantime the public sector will have to rely on their own networking to collect the information they require to make sound personal choices.

How do we make an informed decision on something that we know nothing about? How do we obtain accurate information on an industry that is built upon illusion in the first place? Personal care products (cosmetics) have long been shrouded in a mysterious veil of intrigue. Patented formulas became the norm and ingredients were purposefully absent from the packaging. You can't even call the manufacturer and find out what is in it! This generation wants to be informed and manufacturers should sell on the basis of effective ingredients versus the mystique of secret formulas and magical transformations.

We are no longer complacent about what we are breathing, ingesting, or absorbing. Something that is put directly on or in our being should be painstakingly analyzed for adverse effects to body chemistry.

Why have these seemingly benign ingredients been overlooked? In the technologically advanced environment that we live in, wouldn't we expect some advances in methods of testing for product safety? I believe it is long overdue that we ask for accountability in an area that can profoundly affect our health. It is imperative that we establish testing parameters based on the human being that exists today—not the one from 70 years ago when these ingredients were grandfathered into the system. Our bodies have become increasingly overburdened with each generation since then and it is totally unjustifiable to use testing methods that were founded three or four generations ago. We must become aware of the fact that what resides in our bodies may also reside in the bodies of our offspring as well.

I'm a visionary who believes that a conscious effort towards cleansing ourselves physically, mentally and spiritually will ultimately provide us with the level of health we crave. The inner harmony that once presided in the body can be re-created. We weave our own tapestry. It is our own choosing as to what ingredients we decide to put on our bodies. Again, where do we find accurate information?

We need to ask the question, *What are the systemic and long-term effects of these chemicals?*

No longer can we relinquish our own health responsibilities with *what we don't know won't hurt us.* We must become aware of all exposures to the body. We must stop the assault in as many areas as possible and personal care products seem to be an excellent place to start.

To set the record straight, I must say that I love cosmetics. Passionately! I am the only person that I see on my morning run that has her face on, right down to my lipstick. Cosmetics are as much a part of my life today as they were when I first entered the beauty industry at the age of fourteen. Working part-time after school, I studied under the tutelage of an outstanding pharmacist/chemist whose words are still with me today. "Buy the pretty containers if you like but remember you can buy the same cream from behind the pharmacy counter at a fraction of the cost."

And I did just that. For years I bought expensively packaged beauty products that sat on my bathroom counter for all my peers to see while the creams that I actually used came from the little brown jars stowed away in the drawers. However, I bought all the latest colour cosmetics according to what the ads told me were the *in* colours of the season. I was a collector and had drawers full of pencils, eyeshadows, lipsticks and blush. Each day, as I left for work, my face was painted in hues that matched my outfit.

The only time that I was forced to forego my ritual was at age 36 when my life came to a grinding halt. In 1984, following a general anesthesia for a minor surgery, I awoke to a vast collection of bizarre symptoms. Fatigue, muscle aches and pain, headaches, intense burning from the mid-chest area to the knees, allergies, and sensitivities to odours, light and noise were new to me. Seizures, low grade fever, joint pain, swollen lymph nodes, severe muscle weakness, anxiety, heart palpitations, night sweats, neurological symptoms including brain fog, memory problems, and poor concentration were a part of life. Depression, mood swings, sleep disorder, skin rash, cold hands and feet, and an irritable bowel soon followed.

For six years I journeyed from one medical specialist to another. The fact that each specialist gave a different name to my mysterious illness—everything from lupus to arthritis to allergies to fibromyalgia to an unknown immunological defect—catapulted what was left of my intelligence into finding my own answers. The conflicting information, half answers or no answers was almost overwhelming. I gradually succumbed to the realization that I had to count solely on myself to find the answers. I began doing my own research.

This was no easy task when I couldn't read a page of written material without all the words on the page blending together. I used a piece of cardboard with a slot the size of one line cut out of it. Line after line my research progressed. My trial and error, self-prescribed rituals taught me a great deal about my body. Some things seemed to be working and others weren't. Some things made me feel worse and some things made me feel better. The self-administering brought a reduction in symptoms but any stress, whether it was physical or emotional, plummeted me to the depths.

I lived on the edge and one step off the path could lead me into trouble. My health was fragile.

By 1991, my only remaining symptoms were neurological (memory problems, mood swings, forgetting what I was saying in mid-sentence) and I finally found an internist who provided me an appropriate label for my mysterious illness. The unlikely name of the culprit was myalgic encephalomyelitis, more commonly known by the misnomer Chronic Fatigue Syndrome. As lacklustre as its name infers, there is no doubt that this is one syndrome that you will want to stay away from.

I had come a long way! Yes, it was scary but it was also challenging. It was an adventure that proved fruitful at the end but was terrifying as I lived through it. Now, I'm at a level of health where I've never been before. I have educated myself about my body and emotions and they have educated me. If I had to go through the whole thing over again, I would—as long as I also reaped the wisdom.

So how did I break the hold of this syndrome and turn my life around? Consider these questions. Why am I feeling like this, what is wrong with me? Why are our children born with asthma? Why does arthritis hit us at such a young age? Why does cancer wipe us out before our time? Why do we have to go through life feeling the pits? Ask questions such as these and more and more people will search for answers. When we stop accepting *not feeling well* as a part of life and we start changing our ingrained lifestyles and habits we discover the vitality that is inherently ours.

Although I believe that feeling bad helps us move through some of life's valuable lessons, I also believe that we are entitled to have optimum health.

The US Public Health Service, a decade or so ago, listed an amazing number of care services provided each year in the US: 50 million treatments for allergies, 110 million for digestive disorders, 70 million Americans for obesity, 10 million patients suffered poisoning owing to pharmaceutical prescription. In conclusion, the report estimated that only 2 percent of the population enjoyed fairly good health. (Andre Passebecq Ph.D., M.D., Human Plasma and Marine Plasma.)

Astounding numbers. These figures don't even reflect the new syndromes that have popped onto the scene like Chronic Fatigue Syndrome. As a society, we are tied to poor health, our lives revolve around it. It is socially acceptable to be sick and to some, it actually plays a beneficial role in their lives. It takes a lot of courage to examine ourselves and our illnesses and to examine our patterns and lifestyles. But... that's what's happening. People are tired of being sick.

Our fast paced lives, coupled with nutrient-deficient convenience foods has set the stage for many of today's disorders. Many of us cannot rid our bodies of toxins the way we could when we were younger. Assuredly, it was my cessation of many common toxins, my total body cleansing and rebuilding that brought me to the incredulous state of wellness that is mine today. If it worked for me, can it help others who are suffering?

When my symptoms first began, I read practically every medical book that I could get my hands on. The only book that appeared able to build a relationship between the seemingly conflicting symptoms was a book on poisons. There, I could find a correlation between my physical and neurological complaints. A book on poisons is not a typical book that a sick person would peruse. Because the illness followed a minor surgery I was looking for an association between the anesthetic and my symptoms.

An immunological defect showed up in one of the many tests performed on me. This led me to extensively learn how the immune system functioned. Before long, I became convinced that if I could take some of the burden off my immune system, lighten the load which it had to deal with, then perhaps it would strengthen and repair.

Trying to figure out what the load was in the first place was a feat in itself. Knowing that my immune system was on constant surveillance meant that I needed to know what it was watching and how it handled what shouldn't be there. With a brain that could barely function I attempted to write down all my possible exposures on a given day. I had to chart it all; the drugs, the cleaning supplies, the food additives, the water, the air, the carpet off-gassing, and last but not least, my personal care products.

My artificial, acrylic nails seemed suspect. I had no idea what chemicals were in them but I did know that the fumes were so horrible that I always left the nail salon with a headache. My questions about their safety opened doors that soon led me to question the chemicals in other personal care products as well. Was the aluminum in my deodorant causing my brain dysfunction or was it the toluene in my nail polish? Was my perfume causing my chest pain or was it the fragrance in my lipstick? Was my sunscreen causing the rash on my body or was it my body lotion?

Generally, it made me realize that I didn't have the answers nor did anyone else. We were indiscriminately applying these chemicals without any idea as to their safety.

All through my illness I was always intrigued by the fact that more women than men would succumb to what are now being referred to as "environmental illnesses" and I was puzzled by the fact that the auto-immune diseases affected so many more women than men.

Arthritis and related disorders affect the lives of about 4 million Canadians. Women comprise 60 percent of the cases of rheumatoid arthritis and fibromyalgia and 90 percent of lupus.

The US quotes rheumatoid arthritis as affecting 2.5 million, with female sufferers out-numbering males by three to one. Between 500,000 and one million Americans have lupus and 90 percent are female. Some 250,000 to 350,000 people have multiple sclerosis and two thirds of the cases are women.

So what do the medical experts say about these auto-immune diseases affecting women at these rates? It's our hormones. You know, those mischievous little devils that get blamed for practically everything that goes wrong with a woman. John J. Condemi, M.D., clinical professor of medicine at the University of Rochester School of Medicine and Dentistry in New York said, "Estrogen somehow allows the auto-immune illness to occur more readily." (When the immune system goes awry, Nancy Monson, *Glamour*, Jan. 1994. p. 20.)

Interesting, though, as we now start to look at how some pesticides, dioxin, PCBs and some petroleum by-products can actually mimic estrogen in the body. Several hormone-related human disorders, including low sperm counts, testicular and breast cancers, and endometriosis have arguably been on the rise in the decades since DDT, dioxin and the like entered the food chain (TIME, September 19, 1994). The average (mean) concentrations of PCB's, DDT, and DDE were 50 percent to 60 percent higher in the women with cancer. (*RACHEL'S Environmental & Health Weekly* #279, Peter Montague, April 1, 1992.) Endometriosis, a formally rare condition where the cells that line the uterus are growing outside the uterus, now afflicts 5 million American women!

In 1978, when Israel banned the use of DDT, Lindane, (which, incidentally, is used in lice shampoo) and benzene hexachloride, the breast cancer rate, which was double the rate found in other industrialized countries, fell by eight percent. (*The London Free Press*, Sept. 29 1994.)

Our outdoor air exposes us to dioxide, methane and chlorofluorocarbons. Our indoor air subjects us to fumes like tetrachloroethylene, styrene, phthalates, methacrylate, methyl naphthalene and "outgas" from our computers, copying machines, paint, carpeting and furniture, along with pollutants such as radon, chloroform, formaldehyde, benzene, toluene, xylene, hexanes, alkanes, nitrous oxide, carbon monoxide and asbestos.

Our drinking water is contaminated with benzene, trichloroethylene (TCE), polychlorinated biphenyls (PCBs), mercury, fluoride and inorganic chemicals such as arsenic, cadmium, lead, barium, and chromium.

The US food supply has been contaminated with over 21,000 pesticide products including PCBs, methyl bromide, dieldrin, aldrin and endrin. (Gary Null, Ph.D., *The 90's Healthy Body Book.*)

So we ask, what harm do all these chemicals do? My grandfather lived to the ripe old age of ninety and they didn't bother him! We're not talking about the same world that our grandfathers were brought up in. They were brought up without the heavy pollution and on food that was eminently more nutritious than the diets of today.

Many chemicals that we are exposed to such as benzene, toluene, phenol, trichloroethylene, styrene and formaldehyde, for example, are hydrocarbon based and take up residence in the lipids (fats) in the body and most have an affinity for the brain. There they cause symptoms of depression, inability to think straight, exhaustion, anxiety, dizziness and headache. Sound familiar? How many people do you know who are taking medication for symptoms such as these?

Fragrance, for instance, uses up to 5,000 hydrocarbons (Richard H. Conrad, Ph.D. *Perfume Expose*). A 1993 Brain Spect Scan report showed bilateral temporal hypoperfusion (diminished blood flow) following the inhalation of a popular brand of perfume. The Brain Spect Scans on patients with Chronic Fatigue Syndrome (CFS) showed 71% of patients had either unilateral temporal hypoperfusion (65%) or bilateral temporal hypoperfusion. (I. Mena, MD and J. Villanueva-Meyer, MD, *The Clinical and Scientific Basis of M.E./CFS*).

Dr. Anthony Komaroff, a CFS researcher, clinician and principal investigator of a National Institute of Health—funded CFS research centre, reported on the serious damage to the brain found in patients with CFS, apparently causing many body systems to malfunction. (*Townsend Letter for Doctors*, Aug./Sept. 1995, p. 20)

So...was it my perfume or was it the fragrance in my lipstick?

In another study reported in *The Medical Post* on September 27, 1994, propylene glycol, a common humectant in moisturizers, was found to produce an increase in beta activity in the brains of chemically sensitive people. Beta activity increases are seen in high anxiety states.

So...was it my moisturizer that was causing my neurological problems?

No matter what the cause, it is clear that my body had become overburdened with toxins.

In a very simplistic manner we will take a look at what happens when a toxin enters the human body. First, toxic molecules enter the body by one of three ways; inhaled, ingested or absorbed. The body, recognizing the toxic substance, usually makes an effort to make the substance less poisonous so as not to damage organs as it passes through. It does this by either adding an electron, removing an electron, or by removing hydrogen from the original or parent compound. In certain instances this is all that is required to remove the now changed substance through the kidneys and out through the urine.

If the kidneys are overloaded, a secondary system makes the offending molecule bigger by attaching to it a protein, or portion of a protein called an amino. In this form the substance becomes more water soluble, is easier to excrete through the bile and pass out through the digestive tract. Each chemical has a dozen or so choices as to what compound it can be changed into and sometimes the body makes a mistake and makes a toxic substance even more poisonous.

At a glance, it would appear that the body has the absolute propensity to keep us uncontaminated. But, it isn't that simple. Sometimes, the *detoxification pathway* is temporarily blocked or is busy with another substance that got there first. In some instances, the pathway may be permanently damaged. Genetics play a part by equipping us with the necessary constituents required for the detoxification process. This is why some people react to a substance and others don't. They are born without a specific enzyme that is required to make the toxic chemical harmless. (Sherry Rogers, MD, *Tired or Toxic?*)

But, it's not all genetics and toxic overload that get us into trouble. A lot depends on our lifestyles. Some of the enzymes required to make the poisonous substance harmless require specific vitamins, minerals, amino acids and essential fatty acids to carry out their function.

Simply stated, we cannot change what we inherited but we can change the rest. We can limit our exposure to toxic substances and we can upgrade our eating habits.

Some things in life we can't readily change; for instance, it is impractical for us to go around wearing gas masks to purify the air we breathe. But, we can drink safer water, we can make changes in our indoor environment to decrease the chemical off-gassing, we can eat less-contaminated foods, and we can switch to healthier personal care products.

If we are to be responsible for our own health, which essentially is the only way we can work our way through this state of unwellness, then we have to make changes. We need to start educating ourselves and making the changes necessary for optimum health.

Let's get our heads out of the sand and start taking a good look at what we are doing in the name of beauty.

Introduction

No one really knows when we humans first started painting or otherwise adorning our bodies. Perhaps it is a practice as old as humankind itself. Archaeologists and anthropologists have uncovered evidence that ancient peoples used mixtures of animal fat, vegetable and mineral dyes to paint themselves and decorate their dwellings. We can only speculate on the reasons for the use of such primitive cosmetics. They may have been used for ritual religious ceremonies or simply to alter appearances in order to conform to an *ideal* look of the day. Whatever the reason, the practice of changing how we look has lived on in many forms through the eons to this day.

In 1938, by passing The Federal Food, Drug and Cosmetic Act, the US government created a legal definition for cosmetics. Cosmetics were then defined as products for "cleansing, beautifying, promoting attractiveness, or altering the appearance." Health and Welfare Canada, the Canadian counterpart, offers a similar definition: A cosmetic includes any substance or mixture of substances manufactured, sold or represented for use in cleansing, improving or altering the complexion, skin, hair or teeth and includes deodorants and perfumes. Soap is considered to be included as well as products for animals. In both the US and Canadian definitions, a cosmetic is defined "in terms of its intended purpose rather than in terms of the ingredients with which it is formulated." (*Consumer Health and Product Hazards/Cosmetic Drugs, Pesticides, Food Additives, Volume 2 of The Legislation of Product Safety*, edited by Samuel S. Epstein and Richard D. Grundy, MIT Press, 1974.) In other words, a cosmetic's definition is more a statement of what it does than what it is.

If we take a look at the long history of cosmetics we can see that there have been some pretty scary results from the use of cosmetics containing unknown or unsafe ingredients. In Elizabethan times women powdered their faces with a mixture containing white lead called ceruse, and colored their lips with a reddener containing fucus—red mercuric sulfide. Nasty stuff and they knew it but they continued to use these poison palettes to paint their faces until well into the 18th century despite the fact that it caused hair loss and it literally destroyed the outer layer of skin. Why? Probably because it was more important for these fine ladies, and some gentlemen, to look the ideal beauty than to be healthy or even to survive.

We can all sit back and smugly tsk, tsk at our misguided ancestors but don't tsk too soon. Take a look around you today. How many things do we put on to our sophisticated selves? The average woman will use at least 10 personal care products on herself before she has even left the house each day. Ah, but that's different. We're not talking about lead or some other scary mercury concoction—these products are safe—we've come a long way since then! Besides that, you may argue, our government would never let any product on the market that was not proven safe for our use. Don't be so sure! As David Steinmen, author of *Diet For a Poisoned Planet* and *The Safe Shoppers Bible* once said to me . . . "The government is not our parent, they're not there to protect us on every little thing. We as consumers are not children. We are adults responsible for looking out for ourselves."

In other words we've got to be responsible for ourselves on this one and, although the authorities do protect us from some of the really big scary things out there, there are a lot of things they can't protect us from. One of these areas of personal responsibility concerns the products we put onto our bodies—our cosmetics and personal care products.

Like many of you, I too once believed that it was impossible that any unsafe or even questionable product could find its way into the marketplace. However, innocence was soon lost. What I discovered through years of research changed my whole way of thinking—fast!

Whereas a new drug must go through long testing and exhaustive examination before it can be used on the public, cosmetics and cosmetic ingredients are considered unregulated. It is not required that they be tested by the FDA or any other government department and they do not need to be approved by these agencies. The fact is they are *tested* on the public—a sort of shoot now, ask questions later approach to testing. A manufacturer need not even release its formulas to the government agencies or report any adverse reactions caused by its products in testing or even once it has been released on the public. Most cosmetic ingredients have not even been thoroughly tested for their long term effects, let alone their short term effects, such as rashes or irritations.

I remember a conversation that I had with a cosmetic chemist a few years back. His area of concern was clearly in the texture of the cream. After we debated back and forth on various cosmetic ingredients he finally said in exasperation, "What I don't understand is what you have against glycerin. It's what gives the cream the glide." Looking closely at his face I replied, "I am not concerned with what makes a product glide, I am concerned with what the ingredient is doing once inside a woman's body." His mouth dropped open, indicating to me that he had never considered where these chemicals go once they are in the body.

Well, apparently someone out there had some of the same questions regarding the toxicity of cosmetic ingredients. In 1980, in the US, the National Toxicology Program, along with the National Research Council (NRC) and the National Academy of Sciences, conducted a study in order to determine two main principles:

1) To determine toxicity testing needs for substances to which humans are exposed so that the federal agencies responsible for the protection of public health will have the information needed to assess the toxicity of such substances.

2) To develop and validate uniformly applicable and wide-ranging criteria by which to set priorities for research on substances with potentially adverse public-health impact. (Toxic Testing: Strategies to Determine Needs and Priorities, Washington DC: National Research Council (US) National Academy Press, 1984).

They considered 65,725 substances of which 3,410 (cosmetic ingredients) were approved for use. A random sample of 100 were then selected based on the presence of some toxicity information. After examining this sub-sample they were led to the conclusion that in a great majority of the substances, "data considered to be essential for conducting health hazard assessment were lacking." When judged against standards for toxicity-testing 92% were found to be inadequate. Of the 18 standard tests used, only one was judged adequate. More rigorous testing in the areas of chronic studies, inhalation studies, neurotoxicity, genetic toxicity, and the effects on a fetus were found to be needed. Finally it concluded: "This report shows that of tens of thousands of commercially important chemicals only a few have been subjected to extensive toxicity testing and most have scarcely been tested at all." (*Toxic Testing: Strategies to Determine Needs and Priorities*, Washington DC: National Research Council (US) National Academy Press, 1984.)

Well you say, what harm is done, after all it's only cosmetics. We're only putting them on our bodies, we're not ingesting them like we would a drug or food additive. At one time that argument would have held water. Not today; it's as leaky and porous as our very skin which is not the impregnable barrier we once thought it to be. The fact that today seasick sufferers and wanna-be non-smokers can enjoy the high seas and a tobacco fix through a patch that delivers medication through the skin has shot holes in the argument that there is no potential hazard of poisons entering our bodies through skin absorption. Why is it that industrial and pesticide chemical labels warn in case of an accidental spill, where the skin is in contact with the chemical, that the very first thing to do is to "thoroughly wash the chemical off the skin?" Absorption of the chemical through the skin is implied to be as dangerous as if it had been ingested. Anything we apply to our skins should be considered safe enough to eat. (*Tired or Toxic?* Sherry Rogers, MD, Prestige Publishing, 1990, page 39.)

Still you insist, just because this stuff is capable of being absorbed, and just because these products may or may not have been properly tested or approved by the guys at the capitol, it still doesn't mean it can hurt you. Well this is where we take off the gloves, stop pulling punches, get out the big guns and set the record straight on consumer safety and cosmetics. This little book is here to tell you what neither your mother, nor your government and particularly not your friendly personal care product manufacturer will tell you about the everyday, seemingly innocent collection of bottles, jars, and tubes on your bathroom counter!

How it works . . .

It would be nearly impossible to do a comprehensive study of every cosmetic ingredient in existence. There are several good books on the market that offer complete ingredient descriptions. This book will take you beneath the skin and examine the effect that some standard ingredients have on your health. Let us take a look at some of the most commonly used products and their components starting at the top with our hair and working our way down. Each section will cover a different body region and the products commonly used for that area. In addition there is a special section for babies who rely on you to make the right decisions on their behalf. At the end of the book you will find a glossary of terms and ingredients. This book is only to get you started. Personally, I will always be involved in the never-ending process of learning and educating myself about the products that I am in intimate contact with every day. My advice to you is to read all you can on this subject and then act on it. To this end I've provided a list of suggested reading and some information on the current labeling laws in United States and Canada as they pertain to cosmetics. I have also composed a sample letter to manufacturers requesting information on specific ingredients you may be concerned about in your personal care products.

Claudette Colbert, a famous actress of the 30's and 40's, once said, "It matters more what's in a women's face than what's on it." In this case it should matter just as much what's on it!

When makeup guru Charles Revson was asked what he was hawking he replied, "Hope." Jack Mausner, senior vice president of research and development for Chanel, agrees with Revson and said, "Hope, yes, absolutely, but the hope that exists is on the part of the consumer. I would say the most important fault lies with the consumer. The consumer wants immediacy of effect, and if she gets angry because she doesn't get it, she comes after us." (*Why Women Believe in Miracles*, *Allure*, October, 1993, page 90.)

So...it's our fault that we have such high expectations! But where did we get the notion that this cosmetic potion would alter our appearance in the first place. Was it a dream we had or was it the advertisement in a magazine or on television? Do we really believe that a fifty dollar bottle of cream can erase a lifetime of wrinkles or have we fallen into a pervasive sales trap perpetuated by the cosmetic industry which is the largest advertiser on television and in magazines.

"As species go, women are a soft touch for a pretty package, and cosmetic companies know it...60 to 80 percent of the cost of the average tube of lipstick comes from the container." (*The Trouble with Packaging, Allure,* August, 1991.)

There is frequently a huge percentage spread between cost and sales price in cosmetics. When Procter & Gamble bought the cosmetics firm Noxell Corp. for $1.3 billion the industry speculated that friction would develop because "the approach to marketing at a big packaged goods firm and a cosmetics company were worlds apart. Tide really does get your clothes whiter, Dawn really pulls the grease away from your dishes. These are things we can see," said a P&G marketing veteran.

The product benefits in cosmetics, however, are psychic rather than rational. In terms of ingredients and formulation, there is little real difference between one brand of cosmetics and another. The product advantage to the consumer is how it makes her feel about herself. (*Culture Shock*, Michael McDermott, Cosmetic & Drug Marketing.)

In 1992, US consumers spent 3 billion dollars on skin care products, 4 billion on fragrances, 2.39 billion on shampoos and conditioners, and 1.5 billion on antiperspirants/deodorants. (*Drug and Cosmetic Industry*, June 1993, page 30). Today, the cosmetic industry is a 20 billion dollar business.

one

Beware of Hair Care

There's no denying the importance our hair plays in our self image. We've all heard or used the expression, "I'm having a bad hair day." It has become the catch phrase for all the little stuff that can go wrong on an average day. It's not surprising that sales for shampoos and conditioners were 2.39 billion dollars in 1992. (*Drug and Cosmetic Industry*, June 1993, page 30.) We spend a lot of money and time grooming our locks, fretting over hair loss, coloring, moussing, gelling, conditioning, cleaning and spraying our way to perfection or, as the saying goes, not a hair out of place. It's a huge part of our culture. We use our hair to express ourselves, to indicate who we are and how we feel about ourselves.

Not that long ago hair care consisted of washing it with a bar of soap and brushing it to a sleek natural shine. Then along came the first pomade type conditioners. Colors such as natural henna used by the ancients were eclipsed by coal-tar based dyes. The curling rods of our grandmothers were replaced by permanent waves. The hair care industry took off with a vengeance. Today there is a plethora of hair care products currently on the market across North America. These are used at home and in the burgeoning hair salons across the United States of America and Canada.

Shampoos need to come clean on their ingredients! What most of us don't know about that wonderfully creamy, fragrant, frothy stuff we pour on our heads everyday during our morning shower ritual is what's in it. Shampoos are generally composed of a mixture of about 50 percent sodium lauryl sulfate, some sodium stearate and about 40 percent water. Most liquid type shampoos may contain

the following tongue-twisting names for detergents—triethanolamine dodecylbenzene sulfonate, ethanolamide of lauric acid, along
with perfumes, dyes, and a host of other syllabic names to create
the desired consistency and performance. Add to that, glycerin
and sorbitol, conditioning agents, and preservatives that may include
p-hydroxybenzoic acid and sodium hexametaphosphate. Don't
panic over these big names, we'll give you the dirt on them in the
glossary.

Shampoos are among the most frequently cited in complaints to the FDA. Reports include eye irritation, scalp
irritation, tangled hair, swelling of hands, face and arms,
and split and fuzzy hair. (*A Consumer's Dictionary of
Cosmetic Ingredients*, Ruth Winters, MS, Crown Trade
Paperbacks, 1994.)

One of the big culprits in shampoo seems to be sodium lauryl
sulfate (SLS). SLS is a surfactant, or wetting agent, which means
its purpose in the formula is to lower the surface tension in water
thus allowing the shampoo to spread out and penetrate more easily.
There are four categories of SLS: Anionic, Nonionic, Cationic
and Amphoteric. The last group, Amphoteric are deemed the
mildest. Anionic and Amphoteric are the types found in most
shampoos, conditioners and other cosmetics such as lotions.
Anionics are the most widely used bases in shampoos because of
their foaming properties and lower cost and the amphoteric group
are used in addition to these bases because of their hair conditioning
properties. (*Harry's Cosmetology*, Chemical Publishing Company
Inc., New York, 1982, p. 432.) Mild in comparison to their brothers (Nonionic group used in spray-on oven cleaners) there are still
many problems with SLS that, as a consumer, you should be
aware of.

A study cited by the *Wall Street Journal* (November 1, 1988)
linked SLS to cataracts and nitrate absorption. The nitrate absorption occurs when the SLS becomes contaminated with NDELA
(N-nitrosodiethanolamine) during processing. This contamination
comes about as a result of SLS coming into contact with any
number of chemicals including triethanolamine (TEA), which as
you will recall is a commonly used ingredient in shampoos as a
detergent. Put simply: SLS + TEA = NDELA (a nitrosamine and
a recognized carcinogen).

It doesn't Stop there . . .

In September, 1992, John Bailey, director of FDA's Division of Colors and Cosmetics, while addressing the Dermal Clinical Evaluation Society, reported the discovery of another reactant chemical contaminant that seemed to be showing up in cosmetics, specifically in shampoos and bubble baths. Excessively high levels of 1,4 dioxane, a substance found to cause liver cancer in lab animal studies conducted by the National Cancer Institute in the 1970's, seem to be occurring in products that use non-ionic ethoxylated surfactants in emulsion products such as conditioners. It was also noted that shampoos for children use higher levels of ethylene oxide to decrease the irritancy factor. In fact the higher degree of ethoxylation the more likely the occurrence of 1,4 dioxane.

(John Bailey) expressed concern that levels of 1,4 dioxane found in recent samples of baby shampoo and conditioners were not significantly lower than when original FDA analyses were performed over ten years ago. 1,4 dioxane has been determined to be an animal carcinogen and may be a human health risk. Most common human exposure to this compound occurs in shampoos formulated with sodium or ammonium laureth sulfates or other ethoxylated surfactants." (*DCI*, November, 1992.)

The question of absorption of these chemicals through the skin is even more critical in the case of shampoos. A study performed at Oak Ridge National Laboratory in Tennessee found that absorption was affected by structural factors of the skin such as hairiness. Skin is not a uniform barrier. There are a lot of holes in our skin including hair follicles, sebaceous glands and sweat glands. By examining the role these easy access holes have in absorption of two different chemicals, the researchers found that in one of the chemicals, benzo[a]pyrene (BP), "4.4 to 9.4 percent of the BP penetrated the skin from hairy mice—two to three times more than was absorbed through the hairless-mouse skin." (*Science News*, Vol. 133 June 25, 1988, page 407.)

Another factor affecting the absorption rate is metabolism or the ability to change one thing into another thing. Healthy skin can alter chemicals, changing their structure and allowing them to be more easily absorbed. Fat-seeking chemicals will be attracted to areas of higher metabolic action such as hair follicles and sebaceous glands. So even chemicals that are not easily absorbed because of their structure, are given an opportunity to *get in* because of the passport they receive at special locations on the body including our head covered in hair follicles.

There are many factors that can effect the absorption of chemicals through the skin. One factor to be considered is the base the chemical or substance is mixed with or dissolved in. Different bases effect the rate of absorption through the skin. Sodium lauryl sulfate, a surface active agent and a common surfactant used in shampoos, was found to increase the absorption of certain chemicals. Simply put the SLS in your shampoo could be increasing the rate of skin absorption of other chemicals in your shampoo and conditioner which may include preservatives, fragrances and color additives. (*Cosmetics and the Skin*, F.V. Wells, Reinhold Publishing Corporation, New York, 1964.)

Sodium lauryl sulfate can actually damage the outer layer of the skin, the stratum corneum, causing dryness, roughness, scaliness, fissuring, loss of flexibility and a reduction of the barrier functions of normal healthy skin. The lipid dissolving action of some detergents, including SLS cause damage to the moisture retaining ability at the cellular level resulting in water loss and loss of water-binding ability. (*Cosmetic Science*, C. Prottey, 1978.)

I recall a chemist at a convention saying that they learn in their first year of chemistry that SLS denatures protein. I can only wonder at this since SLS is used so widely in our skin and hair products. Did they also teach first year chemists that skin and hair have protein components?

The Latest on Shampoos...

Recently a University of Ottawa researcher found that estrogen can make common breast cancer tumors resistant to chemotherapy.

(*Vancouver Province*, September 13, 1995.) There have also been studies linking estrogen to increases in some forms of cancer including cancer of the endometrium or uterine lining. (*Time*, June 26, 1995 p. 36.)

Estrogen has also been pointed to as a possible explanation why more women than men are afflicted by auto-immune diseases such as lupus and multiple sclerosis.

Scandinavian researchers have recently made a startling connection between a decline in sperm quality in many countries in the last few decades and chemicals that mimic estrogen. The chemicals known as alkyl-phenol ethoxylades are used in the production of shampoo. "'Boys exposed to such chemicals before puberty could suffer disruption of their hormonal processes,' says Jorma Toppari of the University of Turku in Finland." (*Vancouver Province* September 28, 1995). In this same article, Jorma Toppari states that "We know that these compounds are hormonally active, and we know that you can influence sperm counts by exposing a child or a fetus to hormones that act like these compounds." This gives a whole new meaning to the words..."I'm gonna wash that man right outta my hair!" (Rogers and Hammerstein)

And last, but far from being least, SLS is a mutagen! This means that it is capable of actually changing the information in genetic material found in cells. SLS has been used in studies to induce mutations in bacteria. (Masako Higughi, Shinpei Araya and Masataka Higughi, School of Medicine, Tohoku University, Sendai 980, Japan).

Other Nasty Stuff in your Hair Care Products...

Formaldehyde. Yes, the same stuff used to preserve dead tissue is a common ingredient in some shampoos. It is a disinfectant, germicide and fungicide and is used in shampoos as a preservative. In 1983, researchers from the Division of Cancer Cause and Prevention of the National Cancer Institute recommended that it be further investigated since there is a suspected link to some cancers. It was found to cause DNA damage and inhibit repair. It causes lung cancer in rats and potentiates (increases the effect of) the toxicity of x-rays in human lung cells.

Summing up . . .

Studies are ongoing in this area. SLS is cheap and available and cost is definitely a factor when manufacturers are deciding on their formulations. The irony is that we as consumers rarely see any of this saving and pay high prices for products that contain the same cheap ingredients as a lower priced product that doesn't have the benefit of a well known name and a huge advertising budget. There are safer products on the market. There are safer alternatives to SLS but they can cost up to ten times more than SLS. One manufacturer said to me, "I know it's not a good ingredient, but everyone uses it."

To Dye or not to Dye...

A few years ago the headlines screamed across the nation. *Hair Dyes Linked to Cancer*. It was pretty unnerving to think that the use of hair coloring could effect our chances of getting cancer. Then, almost as fast as it erupted, it was over with the publication of a study that seemed to contradict earlier findings. Those of us who colored our hair breathed a collective sigh of relief and returned to the use of hair dyes. If you read the articles dispelling all previous findings, you may remember coming across very low-keyed cautions, usually near the very end of these articles. This barely whispered caution concerned the use of black hair dyes and very deep red dyes as they were a suspected link to non-Hodgkin's lymphoma. The main reason for concern is well founded in years of previous studies linking coal tar colors, a major ingredient in hair dyes and other cosmetics, with many forms of cancer in animal studies.

A study done at The University of California found that cosmetologists and manicurists had four times the usual rate of multiple myeloma. The article published in the American Journal of Industrial Medicine, stated that "The number of cases of multiple myeloma was found to be excessive for females in the occupation cosmetologist, hairdressers and manicurist," and further goes on to say, "People in this occupation have potential exposure to a number of chemicals that produce mutation in bacteria." (*Multiple Myeloma in Cosmetologists*, Sylvana Guidotti, William E. Wright,

John Peters, *American Journal of Industrial Medicine*, 3:169-171, September, 1982.)

What were these mutagenic chemicals? A list of the worst offenders that cosmetologists are exposed to on an everyday basis include:

Shampoos: sodium lauryl sulfate, sodium laureth sulfate, DEA, propylene glycol, formaldehyde.

Hair dye: 2,4 diaminoanisole, 2,4-diaminotoluene, n-nitro-o-phenylenediamine, 4-ethoxy-m- phenylenediamine, H_2O_2

Permanent Wave Solutions: ammonium thioglycolate, alkaline sulfite

Nail Products: acetone, ethylacetate, toluene, butyl acetate, ethyl methacrylate, benzoyl peroxide.

Make Up: talc, mica, various dyes.

Hair Sprays: isobutane, methylene chloride, alcohols.

Colors to Die for?

In 1978, a New York University Medical Center research reported that comparing 129 women with breast cancer with 193 women without breast cancer showed the likelihood of developing breast cancer was higher among those who used hair dyes. (*A Consumer's Dictionary of Cosmetic Ingredients*, Ruth Winters, MS, Crown, Trade Paperback, 1994.)

A 1988 study published in the American Journal of Public Health summarized its findings stating that the "use of hair dyes in this case-control study was associated with elevated risk of leukemia and lymphoma, and risk increased with extent of exposure." (*Hair Dye Use and the Risk of Leukemia and lymphoma*, Kenneth P. Cantor, et al., *American Journal of Public Health*, May, 1988, Vol. 78, No. 5.)

Sheila Zahm of the National Cancer Institute conducted a survey of 500 men and women suffering from cancer. She compared this group with 1400 healthy people. Her conclusions were that people who said they frequently used hair coloring products were more likely to develop non-Hodgkin's lymphoma and multiple myeloma. (*Allure* magazine, November, 1992;

American Journal of Public Health, July, 1992, Vol. 82, No. 7.) From this initial survey she went on to work with the FDA to design a more detailed study of hair dyes.

In 1992, the National Cancer Institute (NCI) published findings in the American Journal of Health that showed almost double the risk of multiple myeloma in men who used hair dyes. (*Hair Dye Use in White Men and Risk of Multiple Myeloma*, Linda Morris Brown et al., *American Journal of Public Health*, Dec. 1992, Vol. 82, No. 12.)

As far back as 1906, legislation (US) was put into place to control the use of artificial colors. A list of so called *safe* colors was established and since then has been constantly changed and updated as problems arise. Today, there are only nine safe colors permitted to be used in cosmetics. Many of the colors used in cosmetics today, however, are coal tar colors. These color ingredients are derived from petroleum by-products and have a spotty past as far as safety is concerned. The special attention given to coal tar colors is reflected in the FDA regulations that require every batch of coal tar dyes to be certified and carry a registration number. Certain coal tar dyes are to be restricted to external use only and should not be used on lips where there is the possibility of a consumer ingesting small amounts. Similarly, some of the coal tar dyes are unsafe for use around the eyes.

Why with so many cautions built into the system regarding coal tar dyes, should we feel their use in hair dyes is safe? Obviously by the amount of studies that have been done and are currently under way there are some doubts as to their safety.

The latest information available through the NCI, after the completion of a huge study involving half a million women from the years 1982 to 1989, found no increased risk for women using hair dyes except for those who are using permanent black hair dye for more than 20 years. (*FDA Consumer Updates*, May 1994). Still there is a noticeable sense of caution here as consumers are none the less warned to avoid prolonged contact with dyes, to wear gloves and if you are getting your hair colored in a beauty salon make sure the person who is applying the color is qualified to do so.

More Cautions...

NCI data shows that at least two major hair dye components cause cancer: 2-nitro-p-phenylenediamine and 4-amino-2-nitrophenol.

Six other commonly used ingredients tested positively as mutagenic when the AMES test was applied. The AMES test screens for genetic damage in bacteria treated with a chemical. Testing positive is considered to be a signal of a potentially mutagenic substance. (*A Consumer's Dictionary of Cosmetic Ingredients*, Ruth Winters, MS, Crown Trade Paperback, 1994.)

Here's a list of the other coal tar dyes that are known or suspected carcinogens:

4-EMPD (4-ethoxy-m-phenylenediamine)

4-MMPD (4-methoxy-m-phenylenediamine)

4-MMPD sulfate (4-methoxy-m-phenylenediamine sulfate)

2,4 DA (2,4 daminoanisole)

2,4 DA sulfate (2,4 daminoanisole sulfate)

2-nitro-p-phenylene diamine (listed above)

4-amino 2-nitrophenol (listed above)

2,4 TDA (2,4-toluenediamine)

phenylenediamine

(*Being Beautiful*, Center for the Study of Responsive Law, Washington, DC, 1986.)

Books published specifically for the education of hairdressers recognize the dangers of some hair color dyes and include warnings such as, "Laboratory tests on rats, bacteria and certain insects show that some components of permanent and semi-permanent hair dyes can cause changes in cell nucleus structure." (*Complete Hairdressing Science*, O.F.G. Kilgour, Marguerite McGarry, Heinemann Professional Publishing, 1989.)

Another explains that although no hair color agent possesses all the qualities in a given list, it goes on to say that modern permanent dyes give a most reliable color, though they tend to cause dermatitis and some are suspected of causing cancer. (*Hairdressing Science*, F. Openshaw, B.Sc. M.I.T., Longman Group Limited, 1978.)

If you are wondering how these suspect coloring agents are able to be used in consumer products it is because although they are subject to government regulation, i.e.; each, batch must be certified by the FDA, they are exempt from the Cosmetic Act because they are deemed irreplaceable.

At the writing of this book the controversy over the safety of synthetic dyes for hair still rages on. Let's leave this topic with a few final words of caution:

1. ask your stylist to carry safer colors;

2. always do a patch test as described in the manufacturer's instructions on how to use.

NEVER, NEVER use hair dye to dye eyelashes or eyebrows!

two

Saving Face

The average woman may use 8-10 cosmetic products on her face every day. In this section we'll be taking a look at seven of the most commonly used products; moisturizer, foundation, blush, eyeshadow, mascara, eyeliner and lipstick.

A Wrinkle in Moisturizer Creams

Baby boomers are reaching middle age and are starting to notice the signs of aging in their faces. What to do? Reach for that miracle cream you purchased that promises you'll look years younger. The commercial and print ads all show beautiful young women with supple skin and nary a line in sight. Look closer! Some of the actresses and models you see advertising those modern miracles are probably years younger than you to begin with! It's the same sad story all over again—our constant search for love, happiness, youth, success ends with a trip to the cosmetic counter and the purchase of that little jar of hope. The fact is there is no product on the market today that can reverse the effects of time. So, short of signing up for a face lift, the lines and wrinkles you have now are yours to keep. In the past there have been hundreds of so called miracle creams and lotions. They were sprung on the consumer, mostly women, and touted as the latest scientific marvels. Try for a second to look at these claims realistically. Do you really think the foremost scientific minds of the day are spending countless hours in their laboratories to come up with a little jar of cream so we can all lie about our age or ask, "how old do you think I am?"

Unfortunately, as with many cosmetics, these miracles in a jar have slipped past the rigorous testing procedures afforded to drugs and food additives when, in fact, if they actually did what they claimed they could they should have by definition been regulated as drugs. One case in particular involving a product containing hormones resulted in near tragedy. The users experienced miscarriages, abnormal menstruation, and since then the product has been linked to breast cancer. The product was eventually removed from the market but not before considerable damage was done. (*Being Beautiful*, Center for the Study of Responsive Law, Washington, D.C. 1986.)

Since then there has been wave after wave of miracle creams and potions each new *discovery* claiming to be the last word on skin rejuvenation. Here's a brief run-down.

Tretinoin (Retin-A) is a vitamin derivative. It was used as a prescription drug for the treatment of acne. Later it was found to plump up the skin and eliminate small wrinkles. Several manufacturers jumped on the bandwagon and began promoting the inclusion of vitamin A in their formulations claiming it was producing similar effects as Retin-A. Studies in the 1980's showed there were some subtle changes to skin with tretinoin. (*Allure* magazine, Nov. 1991, *Journal of American Academy of Dermatology*, August, 1991.) Others disagreed with findings saying that the reason it seemed to work was because it literally irritates the outer layer of the skin to such a degree that it swells or puffs up, reducing wrinkles. As John DiGiovanna, a dermatologist and scientific investigator for the National Cancer Institute says regarding its appeal . . . "Medicine's involved here so the implication is that Retin-A is doing something magical." He also noted that, "If you said sandpaper had the same effect, no one would care." (*Allure* magazine, November, 1991.)

The latest thing to hit the market are the fruit acids or Alpha Hydroxy Acids (AHA). In 1990, there were 5 AHA products on the market, one was by prescription. By 1993, there were 50 and by 1994 over 200 new products were on the market. In January and February of 1995 alone there were 32 new products containing AHA introduced into the marketplace.

AHA's claim that by gently removing the dead skin cells our skin will look healthier and feel smoother. When Dr. John Bailey, acting director of FDA's office of Cosmetics and Colors, spoke at the Sixth Annual Spring Seminar of Society of Cosmetic Chemists in New York, in April, 1994, he warned that AHA had clearly stepped over the boundary line between what is considered a drug as opposed to a cosmetic. His concerns were with the application of the higher percentage solutions being used today, as much as 50 percent by non-professionals and people with less than adequate training.

Once again the specter of a substance being tested on the public showed its ugly face. Bailey's biggest concern "is the absence of sound scientific data about long term effectiveness, sensitization and allergy reactions. Also lacking was information about topical absorption, whether the apparent wrinkle smoothing was caused by surface irritation and what percentages if any produce accelerated cell turnover." With regards to the lack of hard data on AHA's already on the market Bailey later added "the public is the test subject here." (*DCI*, May, 1994.)

From a Drug and Cosmetic Industry (DCI) article published in January of 1995, Dr. John Bailey again expressed his concern about AHA's long term use and whether the regeneration mechanism may in fact be thinning out the stratum corneum (outer layer of the skin) causing an increase in sensitivity in the skin. It may perhaps even be causing subtle changes in the protective qualities of the skin, reducing its effectiveness as a barrier against absorption of other chemicals in cosmetics. Bailey also cited evidence that fibroblasts cease to respond to accelerated turnover after 50 to 60 cycles or treatments with AHA's. A fibroblast is a specialized cell, one of the most common cell types found in growing connective tissue. This means that after repeated treatments the cells are not responding in the normal manner or as they were after the initial treatments.

As of 1993, the FDA didn't require companies to list percentages of concentrations of fruit acids in their products. This additional information on a label may however be of no use to the average consumer since if, for example, a product contains a 10 percent solution but is buffered with ammonium hydroxide so it won't sting, it may only produce the result of a 6 percent solution. (*Self*, June, 1993, page 164.)

Okay, okay, so what the AHA proponents are saying is remove the outer layer of the skin to decrease signs of aging and to give skin a general appearance of smoothness, right? But what about the people that say that very same outer layer of skin is what protects us from moisture loss and signs of aging. If you are confused about this you're certainly not alone. In a recent article in *Self* magazine on moisturizers and your skin, the first part of the article states that new moisturizers with lipids that mimic your own skin's lipids are beneficial because they build up and bind skin together forming a protective barrier against moisture loss. Lipids are actually described as the "glue that holds the skin together." Next comes a section on AHA's that say they're beneficial because they act as an exfoliant and dissolve the "intercellular glue" between dead cells, peeling them away to reveal softer, smoother skin. (*Self*, August, 1995, page 107-108) Wait a minute! Isn't that the same protective barrier we just glued together to prevent moisture loss? It seems everywhere we look a different group is telling us to do something different to our skin.

Have you ever wondered why men seem to age more gracefully than women. Their skin is less likely to suffer from over cleansing and drying because they do not as a rule buy into these skin care fads. Perhaps it is not just the so-called differences in our skin structure. I was always told men had thicker skin. Perhaps it is what we have been doing to our skin that is making the biggest difference in both its structure and ability to stay healthy and young looking.

Soaps

Most of us have used soap every day of our lives since babyhood. Soap in one form or another has been around for a long time. Our grandmothers saved animal fat and wood ash to make a big batch of soap to be used for everything from bathing to laundry. Soap has changed very little since our grandmother's days. Bar soap is still generally made with a mixture of fats, either animal or vegetable, and caustic soda or lye. Soaps that claim to be neutral are more likely to be alkaline with a pH level of about 10 compared with the natural pH level of about 5 or 6 for human skin. Most soaps cause drying and some skin irritation. One of the main reasons for soap's drying effect is improper rinsing.

Soaps work by breaking down the bond between the skin and grime attracting natural oils or sebum, hence dirt is able to be removed. Unfortunately the oil that soap is removing is that same oil that provides a natural moisture barrier. As soap removes the oil it can also damage the outer layer of our skin and reduce its effectiveness as a protective barrier.

Liquid soaps and gels often contain SLS which as stated earlier can also cause damage to the outer layer of skin. (See section on SLS in shampoos.) Cleansing bars that are marketed as non-soaps contain synthetic detergents which may include SLS.

Soaps that claim to be rich in emollients may contain mineral oil and other pore-clogging additives. These soaps are difficult to rinse off and often residue can build up, smothering the skin, thus preventing good epidermal respiration.

Soaps that are designed for oily skin contain less of these emollients but are often too harsh, causing dryness and irritation. If you use a soap or cleanser that leaves your skin feeling very dry and stretched right after you wash with it, your skin actually feels oilier in just a few hours. Stripping the natural oils will produce more oils and sebum and, since the protective barrier has been eliminated, these oils and the dirt they attract will cause more irritation and infection (acne) than before.

Since soaps are composed of fats they are an ideal breeding ground for bacteria. To solve this problem many manufacturers have added an anti-bacterial agent to many soap formulas. These agents may include:

Cloflucarban

Captan - Also used in agriculture as a fungicide

Dichloro-m-xylenol

Glyceryl monoglyceride - Fungistatic agent effective against molds and yeast and lipid-coated viruses

Irgasan DP 300 - A biphenyl derived from coal tar

Triclocarban - Considered unsafe for use in maternity units or on infants (Aubrey Hampton, *Natural Organic Hair and Skin Care*, 1987.)

Finally, soaps that are designed for sensitive skin may contain less fragrance and other additives that produce irritation but there are no guarantees that they will not cause irritation at all.

Exfoliants - Facial Scrubs

Whenever I hear the word *exfoliant* I think of a lush tropical rainforest with a perfectly balanced ecosystem whose life and moisture giving trees have been destroyed leaving a dried up wasteland prone to erosion and desertification. I know our skin isn't a rainforest, and I know the term I'm confusing exfoliation with is defoliation, but I can't help drawing comparisons here. Exfoliants are products that by mechanical or chemical processes scrape off the outer layer of skin. Marketers will have you believe that this process is beneficial and will reveal the healthier skin below the so-called dead skin cells on the outer layer.

Skin is a living, breathing organ that is constantly renewing itself. The average turn around for skin cells is about 28 days. A skin cell starts its life deep in the inner layers of our skin. It is round and plump and full of moisture. As it ages it migrates to the outer layer, flattens out a bit and eventually sloughs off naturally. While it is a part of the outer layer it helps form a protective moisture barrier for its younger brothers still in their infancy and adolescence. Exfoliants disrupt the natural order of things when they remove these adult skin cells and leave those below open to premature exposure to the environment. Without their big brothers the immature cells can dry out and age more rapidly than is natural.

Once again I feel as if we women are being sold a bill of goods that is not only unnecessary but may be harmful to our health. Irritation caused by improper use of exfoliants can lead to damage to the protective skin barrier resulting in moisture loss and increased susceptibility to absorption of other harmful chemicals found in cosmetics. The fact that these scrubs cause our skin to dry out and lose moisture and then require a moisturizer, makes it all seem like a vicious circle created by the cosmetic industry. If there isn't a need on the market, create one and then provide a solution that creates another need and so on and so on.

Why do we Moisturize?

Why do we need moisturizers in the first place. Just ask any woman and she will tell you emphatically that she has dry skin. In a study conducted by C. Prottey, Unilever Research Laboratory, it was proposed "that treatment of the skin with lipid solvents dissolved the lipids of the semi-permeable membranes, thus allowing the hygroscopic substances to be leached out and lost. Moreover, Middleton (1969) suggested that certain detergents (e.g. sodium lauryl sulfate) could dissolve these lipids and allow intracellular hygroscopic substances to escape, with resultant loss of water-binding ability. (C. Protty, *The Molecular Basis of Skin Irritation*, *Cosmetic Science*, 1978.) In the March, 1992 issue of *Self*, Joe DiNardo was quoted as saying, "Once you break the lipid layer, you can't retain water in the skin. You've broken the seal, and water evaporates."

Sounds to me like the surfactant not only sets the stage for the necessity of moisturizers but also paves the way for the ingredients to enter. The protective lipids take hours (sometimes minutes) to replenish. (*Self*, February, 1992 page 147.)

What's in our Moisturizer?

Some of the worst things in your moisturizer may include petrolatum, mineral oil, isopropyl myristate, trietholamine, glycerin and propylene glycol. All of these ingredients may clog your pores and smother your skin's respiration; and in no way do these ingredients benefit your skin.

Propylene glycol - This is the most common moisture carrying vehicle in use in cosmetics. It's cheap and available. It has also been suspected of causing sensitivity reactions. It in fact absorbs moisture from your skin (See section on body lotions.) propylene glycol is also used extensively in industry as a component of brake fluids and anti-freeze preparations. It's also used in the production of varnishes.

Isopropyl myristate - This fatty compound that has been shown to clog pores and cause blackheads and pimples also has a more sinister hidden danger. As discussed earlier there are some ingredients in cosmetics that when in contact with one another can create contaminant reactions. This is true with isopropyl myristate. When it comes into contact with either a Di- or triethanolamine (another common ingredient in cosmetics as a buffer, and as a detergent) the result is a nitrate compound such as n-nitrosodiethanlamine, a suspected carcinogen. Moisturizers for the face and body are applied over a large portion of the skin and remain there for several hours. This exposure is significant.

Glycerin - Although this ingredient is used in moisturizers to help the cream *glide*, it is detrimental in that it draws moisture from the skin and holds it on the surface, effectively drying the skin from the inside out.

A few Last Words about Moisturizers . . .

Any product that makes a claim that it contains "an active ingredient" is no longer considered a cosmetic but a drug. A product that makes that claim must prove it. Most over-the-counter moisturizers and wrinkle creams do not make such claims. They can not penetrate the skin to cause any changes in the outer or inner layers. They do not reduce the signs of aging. The most they do is provide your skin with a moisture barrier and any fatty oily cream will do that, including the oil you use on your salad!

My research shows that there are some beneficial and effective ingredients for the skin. The manufacturer, though, has no way of telling the consumer about the ingredients or the research supporting them. This is because these ingredients fall somewhere between the definitions of drugs and cosmetics. Known as skin rectifiers, they have been shown to be effective in actually changing the structure of the skin. Manufacturers, aware of these studies, choose not to make these claims in promoting their products because if they do their product, previously deemed a cosmetic, will be classified as a drug and therefore will have to undergo 10-12 years of testing at a cost as high as $230 million. The claims of structural changes must be proven by the manufacturer. This creates a real quandary for both the manufacturer and the consumer. A product may contain an *active* ingredient yet it will not be used as a claim or promotional aspect on the label or in the advertisements. This is truly a gray area in labeling laws that needs to be examined. Perhaps a separate classification can be devised that covers ingredients that are more than cosmetic but less than drugs. In this instance it seems once again that new legislation is needed to catch up with technology.

In one such instance, I recall trying to find the studies on an ingredient called Cross-Linked Elastin (or more specifically

Desmosine and Iso-Desmosine—two amino acids) (Efficacy survey on wrinkle treatment products for Narhex Australia Pty. Ltd., Dr. Vyt Garnys, Ph.D., Cetec Pty. Ltd. Consulting Enterprises in Technology.) The company producing the product could not supply me with any information. The reason was that the FDA would consider the company as making a claim merely by providing the research. So I went on a paper chase to France. By pure chance, I read an article in *Vogue*, October, 1991 which mentioned that a dermatologist was involved in a double blind study involving a form of elastin. The chase led me to Australia where I eventually got a copy of the study. Another ingredient, which is often called Yeast Cell Extract, was just as hard to find research on. Once found, I was able to make an informed decision to use it.

Personally, I search for products that contain these types of ingredients and am prepared to pay for the ingredients but not a designer name or class-act package. However, the moisturizing cream that contained the Yeast Cell Extract that sells for over $285,000.00 per pound cost less than most brands of moisturizers.

For more information on moisturizers see the section on body creams and lotions. Surprise! They're made of virtually the same ingredients in that little costly jar you are buying at your cosmetic counter or from your beautician.

The Great Make-up Cover up!

Foundations, blushers and lipsticks - Many of the liquid foundations on the market today contain some of the same ingredients listed in the section on moisturizers, such as mineral oil, isopropyl myristate and propylene glycol. They contain fragrance and also color agents. Of these color agents many are made from coal tar dyes.

In the 1960's, Dr. Benjamin Feingold conducted studies on artificial colors and found links between these colors and behavior and learning problems in children. The Feingold Association, a non-profit organization for the chemically sensitive, today estimates that one out of every ten people are affected. Symptoms range from headaches and nausea to life threatening asthma attacks. The artificial colors found in make-up along with a host of other chemicals can be absorbed through the skin. (*Let's Live*, November,

1992, page 76.) When you consider that a woman may wear make-up for over eight hours, with touch-ups to her blusher and lipstick, that's an incredible exposure rate to a group of questionable substances and mixtures of substances.

Another note of caution is to realize that many of the colors used in foundation make-up are approved for general cosmetic use, not to be ingested and you should be particularly careful when applying around your eyes—they are not colors approved for use in the eye region. Does this make sense to you since we in fact use this all over our faces including the eye region and around our mouths and lips?

Foundations - These may contain bentonite or kaolin. Bentonite is white clay found in the US and western Canada. It is used to put out forest fires because it has the ability to smother the flames. Similarly it can smother your skin and prevent necessary respiration needed for health. Kaolin, also known as China Clay, is used in foundations as well as oil absorbing powder, face masks, liquid and cake powder and dry blusher.

Alumina or aluminum hydrate is also a white coloring base or extender used in foundations. It is a natural or synthetic form of aluminum found in bauxite and corundum. This chemical can be irritating to the respiratory tract if inhaled and although there is no known skin toxicity, aluminum has been linked to Alzheimer's disease.

Your foundation may also contain mineral oil, propylene glycol, alcohol, waxes, perfumes and preservatives.

Lipsticks - The group of colors used in lipsticks are more controlled than in foundations because it is recognized that small amounts can be ingested inadvertently through regular use. The colors certified by the FDA fall into seven categories. One of these categories, the xanthene group, is used most widely in the production of lipsticks since it contains very brilliant colors.

If you look at your lips you'll notice a difference from the surrounding skin of your face. The color of your lips is due mostly to the capillary blood vessels that lie close to the surface covered by translucent tissue.

Lipsticks are used to color and protect lips by providing them with a moisture barrier. Many lipsticks are composed of castor oil and dye, fatty alcohols and various glycols and esters. Too much oil in a lipstick will cause it to *bleed* so formulas often contain a wax such as carnauba or beeswax. They may also contain fragrance. (See section on fragrance.) Since the area of application is literally right under our noses, a manufacturer may add a heavier amount of fragrance than any of your other cosmetics in order to mask any chemical smell.

The color in your lipstick is either a dye or a pigment. Dyes actually stain your lips and last longer than pigments but they are limited in that they are only available in a small amount of hues. This is due to strict regulations by the FDA regarding the use of dyes that may be ingested. In 1985, a public interest group, Public Citizen, sued the FDA in an attempt to have them determine the safety of 10 dyes widely used in lipsticks as well as in other cosmetics and foods. Six of those dyes, including D&C Red #3, #9, #33 and #36 and D&C Yellow #5 and #6, were found to be in most lipstick brands tested at the time. Public Citizen's studies showed that the dyes were found to cause cancer in animals.

Pigments are opaque, unlike dyes which are transparent. They come in a wider range of colors and can cover areas uniformly. Pigments in lipsticks are derived from the same compounds as red and pink paints. Some lipsticks contain both pigments and dyes which is why the color may change after it has been on your lips for a while. The opaque pigments may be licked off leaving the staining dyes. (*Consumer Reports*, February, 1988, page 77.)

Lipsticks may contain aluminum hydroxide. Aluminum hydroxide is used to give water-soluble pigments staying power. It is used particularly in the vivid pinks and reds. Although the amount in lipsticks is very small, we have the right to know which products to avoid if we want to eliminate any contact with the trace element.

Your lipstick may also contain preservatives such as formaldehyde and anti-oxidants such as BHA (butylated hydroxyanisole) both of which are listed in Ralph Nader's *Center for the Study of Responsive Law* list of ingredients that are either known or suspected of causing cancer.

Blushers or rouges - Rouge is one of the oldest forms of cosmetics. At one time the use of rouge was equated with being loose and easy—hence the expression *painted ladies*, referring to the stereotypical saloon girl, read prostitute. Today blushers and rouges are not stigmatized and are used widely by many women to achieve that fresh healthy glow. The problem is that the ingredients that mimic a healthy glow could actually be harming your health.

Powder blushes contain lake colors. Lake colors are created by precipitating a soluble color with a form of aluminum, calcium, barium, potassium, stronium, or zirconium making them insoluble (the inability to be dissolved in a solvent). This simply means that they are made by a process where a color that was once soluble or easily dissolved in a solvent becomes insoluble. Powder blushers also contain talc. Talc is a mineral and non-biodegradable. If inhaled it can build up in the lungs causing similar health problems to those associated with asbestos inhalation. For more information on talc see the section on talcum powder further along in the book.

Cream blushers are composed basically of the same things that are found in lipsticks and since they may also contain humectants such as propylene glycol, preservatives and moisturizers they can cause allergic reactions and clogged pores.

Eye makeup - shadow, eyeliner, mascara - Since these products are applied to an area that is extremely sensitive and there is a higher danger that the make-up will come in contact with the eye, there are more regulations regarding the colors allowed in their production. With few exceptions only inorganic pigments (lake colors) may be used in eye cosmetics. The main coloring agents used include ultramarines, iron and chromium oxide pigments and carmine NF. Iridescent colors are achieved by adding pure aluminum.

Despite the fact that these color formulations are deemed safe by the FDA for use around the eye, the ingredients themselves can pose significant health risks due to the fact that they contain heavy metals and can be absorbed into the bloodstream, and build up in the internal organs. The long term effect of such exposure has never been fully tested nor has the effect of such a variety of chemical substances on our bodies over a lifetime of use.

One real and known danger found to exist in eye-liners and mascara are the bacterial contaminants found on the applicators and in the product. Exposure can lead to severe eye damage and even blindness. There are several cases on record in the US. that indicate that these are not a few isolated cases. In one instance, in 1982, a woman was applying mascara and inadvertently scratched the surface of her eye. The mascara being used was a refill for which she was using an original applicator. The deal was that when the original container was empty the consumer needed only to buy a refill and use the same applicator. Pseudomonas bacteria had accumulated on the old brush and her eye became infected when the brush came into contact with the eye. The result was severe corneal damage and the eventual need for an cornea transplant. (*Lankford* v. *Fashion Two Twenty Cosmetics*, NC, Sept. 21, 1982.) The plaintiff argued that for four cents more the manufacturer could have included a new brush in the package with the refill. In a later case a plaintiff won a substantial award because the manufacturer failed to properly test the preservative in the mascara and warn consumers to discard applicators after 90 days from purchase, or sooner if there was a change in the odor of the product. (*Rilenge* v. *Noxell Corp*. US. District Court, S.D. Ind. No 1P-81-1046-C August 25, 1983.)

Mascara and eye-liner are composed basically of the same ingredients. Eye-liners may contain alkanolamines as solvents which are composed of alcohols from alkene—a saturated fatty hydrocarbon and amines—ammonia. They may also contain polyvinylpyrrolidine (PVP) a solid plastic resin also used in hair sprays and lacquers. Ingestion can produce gas, fecal impaction, and damage to the lungs and kidneys. PVP may last in the system for months. Inhalation of PVP from air sprays has been linked to thesaurosis (foreign bodies in the lung). As with mascara there is a problem with bacterial contamination in eyeliner despite the addition of preservatives such as methyl paraben.

Nothing to Smile about...

Mouthwash and toothpaste - In 1991 the National Cancer Institute released news of a study that showed that using a mouthwash with a 25 percent or higher alcohol content increased the risk of oral (lip, tongue and mouth) and pharyngeal (throat) cancers. After taking into account the use of tobacco and alcohol by the participants in the study, it was found that women who used higher alcohol content mouthwashes had a 90 percent higher risk, men a 60 percent higher risk, of developing these specific cancers. Shortly after the release of this information, Warner-Lambert, manufacturer of Listerine (26.9 percent alcohol) announced a new version of the product with significantly less alcohol. (*Wall Street Journal*, April 23, 1991 p.B1, Ron Winslow.)

Some of the other ingredients in mouthwash may include sodium bicarbonate, methyl salicylate, propylene glycol and resorcinol. There may also be artificial colors and flavors which can cause allergic reactions in some people. Known or suspected carcinogens that may be included in your morning gargle could include ethyl carbanate—a solvent, formaldehyde, methenamine and phenol—antiseptics, and sodium saccharin—a sweetener.

Despite what the manufacturers claim, all toothpastes or dentrifices are composed of basically the same ingredients. Sound familiar? They inevitably contain mild abrasives, sudsers, humectants, flavors and colors. Some may contain sodium fluoride: the ingredient that since its introduction to the world in the 60's, has been the cause of countless commercial kids to run joyfully towards the camera shouting "Look mom—No cavities!"

In 1991, the US Public Health Service released a review of the benefits and risks of fluoride. The study showed an *equivocal* (ambiguous) risk of cancer from fluoridated water. Other possible risks listed in the report include bone tumors, bone fractures and genetic mutations. (*Health Freedom News*, February, 1992.) The report also noted an increase in dental fluorosis (mottling of the teeth) with the over exposure of fluoride. Fluoride can be toxic. Every time you brush your teeth with a fluoridated toothpaste it is likely that you will ingest fluoride. Children using toothpaste should be cautioned to rinse their mouths and spit out any residual toothpaste. Sodium fluoride can cause nausea and vomiting if swallowed and can even be fatal depending on the amount.

A 7oz. tube of fluoride toothpaste can contain enough fluoride to kill a small child. (*The Fraud of Fluoridation*, review by Jule Klotter, *Townsend Letter for Doctors*, Aug/Sept., 1995, p.119-120.) Fluoride in higher doses is very poisonous and there are several sources parents should be aware of besides that tube of toothpaste, including fluoridated gels and some mouth washes.

Fluoride at low levels (as low as 1ppm) may interfere with the enzyme actions that help break down food, produce energy and build new tissue. (*The Fraud of Fluoridation*, review by Jule Klotter, *Townsend Letter for Doctors*, Aug/Sept. 1995, p.119-120.) It has also been shown that fluoride can inhibit the immune system. There have been several studies in laboratory mice and rats that link exposure to fluoride with increased risk to some types of cancer.

In 1965, at the University of Texas in Austin, a study was done that concluded that 1ppm of fluoride in water increased tumor growth in mice. (*Health Freedom News*, February, 1992.) In 1977, Congress ordered the US Public Health Service to examine any possible links between fluoridation and cancer. The National Toxicity Program of the USPHS contracted the Battelle Memorial Laboratory to conduct animal studies to answer the question once and for all. In 1988, Battelle released the findings of their studies. It was found that high doses of fluoride resulted in bone cancers in male rats, oral cancer in both male and female rats, and the occurrence of a rare form of liver cancer in both male and female rats. Although much of the findings were downgraded by the NTP as being *equivocal*, an independent evaluation of the findings conducted by Dr. Calabrese, Professor at School of Public Health, University of Massachusetts disagreed. Dr. Calabrese states: "A study which displays a statistically significant increase in malignant bone cancers by a chemical is simply not consistent with what most people would call equivocal" He went on to say "The information available indicates that NaF (sodium fluoride) is a bone carcinogen for the male rats." In all fairness it is important to realize that too much sun can cause cancer just as too much time in the bar can cause cirrhosis of the liver. These studies were based upon high doses of fluoride, however, there is little question that each of us should be aware of the potential health risks associated with fluoride consumption and make the necessary alterations as they pertain to our own personal needs and lifestyle.

Fluoride proponents will have us believe that this industrial waste by-product used as a rat poison is the best thing since sliced bread. The pro-fluoride camp will tell you that it not only prevents cavities but it is also being used experimentally to help prevent osteoporosis—the loss of bone mass in post-menopausal women.

Early studies showed that yes, subjects that received large doses of fluoride did increase their bone mass but the bone laid down under the influence of fluoride was undermineralized. "Although fluoratic bone is sclerotic, in the sense that there is more of it than normal, it is not as strong, weight for weight, as normal bone, nor as highly mineralized, and spontaneous fractures are common." (*Fluorides in Caries Prevention*, 3rd Edition, J.J. Murray et al, 1991.)

Fluoride may also be a factor in repetitive strain injury or RSI. RSI is a fairly recently recognized syndrome in people who use the same group of muscles and joints repeatedly such as a typist. Samples of bone taken from patients suffering from RSI were found to be higher in fluoride concentration than those who did not have RSI. In some patients symptoms were dramatically lessened when they decreased their exposure to fluoride. (*Fluorides in Caries Prevention*, 3rd Edition, J.J. Murray et al, 1991.)

Although it has long been believed that fluoride in our water played an important role in preventing tooth decay, there are some studies that suggest otherwise. In a 1986 article in the *British Journal Nature*, Australian researcher Mark Diesendorf reviewed 24 studies from eight different countries. He found that the rates of tooth decay had declined equally in countries that had fluoridated water and those that hadn't, suggesting that this source of fluoride did not have any impact at all on the prevention of tooth decay. (*Don't Drink the Water?* Sharon Begley, *Newsweek*, February 5, 1990, p.61.)

One of the sudsers found in most toothpaste is our old friend sodium laurel sulfate. The known or suspected carcinogens found in toothpaste include ethanol, formaldehyde, PVP (Polyvinylpyrrolidinone) and sodium saccharin. (*Being Beautiful*, Center for the Study of Responsive Law.)

three

Body Beautiful

Moisturizers - Next to soaps and toothpaste, hand lotion along with shampoo, mouthwash and talcum powder are purchased in the highest volume accounting for 22 percent of cosmetic sales each year. Somehow this is not too surprising. It seems we have a different moisturizer for every part of our bodies—hand cream, face cream, cream for our dry elbows and legs, foot cream and all over body cream! A moisturizer is a mixture of oils, fragrances, waxes, and preservatives that make your skin feel softer and smoother. Although many claim to contain special, new ingredients designed specifically for a certain region of your body, basically most consist of the same group of compounds and chemicals. Their main purpose is to hold moisture in the skin and prevent it from drying out.

All moisturizers contain humectants. As the name would suggest, humectants attract and hold moisture from the surrounding environment. They also draw moisture up from the underlying dermal layer. Some of the humectants you may find in your moisturizer include glycerin, lecithin, propylene glycol, urea, lactic acid and glycolic acid, sodium lactate, butylene glycol, pyrrolidone carboxylic acid and hyaluronic acid.

In this chapter we will focus on the most commonly used humectants.

Propylene glycol is one of the most common humectants. It is used in many cosmetics including liquid foundation makeup, spray deodorants, baby lotions, emollients or moisturizers, lipsticks and suntan lotions. It is less expensive than glycerin and has a better permeation rate. It has also been linked to sensitivity reactions—

local irritations, allergic reactions. This would not be news to the manufacturers of propylene glycol. If you were to purchase a drum of this chemical from a manufacturer he is required to furnish you with a material safety data sheet (MSDS) and it may alarm you to find that this common, widely used humectant has a cautionary warning in its MSDS that reads, "If on skin: thoroughly wash with soap and water!" What? Aren't we putting this stuff on our skins daily, sometimes in copious amounts over long periods of time?

It's no wonder propylene glycol has been linked to many severe health problems including contact dermatitis (irritation), autotoxicity, kidney damage and liver abnormalities. It has been shown to be toxic to human cells in cultures. (*Bulletin of Environmental Contamination and Toxicology*, Jan. 1987.) In fact, in tests conducted over the years propylene glycol has been shown to inhibit skin cell growth in human tests and cell respiration in animal tests. (J. Pharm. Belg. Nov/Dec 1989). It was found to cause skeletal muscular damage in rats and rabbits (*Pharm Res* Sept. 1989). It is reported to directly alter cell membranes (*Humuan Reproduction*, Feb. 1990) to cause thickening of the skin (*Contact Dermatitis*, 1987) skin dehydration and chronic surface damage to skin (*Derm. Beruf Umwelt* Jul/Aug. 1988.) It was also shown to increase beta activity (changes found in anxiety states) when inhaled. (*The Medical Post* Sept. 27, 1994.)

Propylene glycol is a known irritant and sensitizer causing dryness, erythema (abnormal redness) and even blistering. (*Safety Evaluation of a Barrier Cream*, Contact Dermatitis, 17: 10-12, 1987.)

Despite its record, propylene glycol continues to appear in our everyday products. It was originally developed for use in industry as an anti-freeze, brake fluid, airplane de-icer among other applications and it's doing a good job there. How it got into our cosmetics 30 years ago is anyone's guess but it's time it was taken out of our personal care products and kept off our bodies!

Other ingredients you may be applying to your bodies may include petrolatum, a petroleum derivative. It is used in creams to make them smoother. It can cause allergic skin reactions and there have been studies linking petroleum products with cancer.

Phenol carbolic acid is obtained from coal tar and is a general disinfectant found in many moisturizers. It can cause vomiting and nausea if ingested even in small amounts. As well, it can cause more serious consequences such as circulatory collapse, paralysis, convulsions, coma and death as a result of respiratory failure. There have been reports of deaths from the ingestion of as little as 1.5 grams and phenol can also be readily absorbed through the skin. (*A Consumer's Dictionary of Cosmetic Ingredients*, Ruth Winters, MS, Crown Trade Paperback, 1994, also *Chemical Hazards of the Workplace*.)

Potassium hydroxide, an emulsifier, can cause skin irritation and is corrosive if ingested causing pain, bleeding and could lead to death. In animal studies tumors resulted when moderate amounts were applied to the skin of mice.

There is no doubt that we as a population use a lot of moisturizers. We use them all over our bodies sometimes leaving them on for several hours such as in the case of body lotions and suntan lotions. We've been told that moisturizers protect and relieve our dry chapped skin. We haven't been told what's in these creams, lotions and moisturizers we are applying liberally and frequently. Because of this we were unaware of the potential damage we were doing with each application. Ingredients like propylene glycol and the others do not belong on our skins or in our cosmetics.

Talcum powder - The main ingredient in talcum powder (bath powder, baby powder) is talc. Talc comes from the mineral magnesium silicate which is ground up to a fine powder. Talc makes powders and creams feel smooth and slippery. The danger with talc is that its fine particles are similar in structure to those of asbestos. Like asbestos, talc particles can easily be inhaled and build up in our lungs. Talc alone was not found to cause tumor growth in the lungs but when it was introduced with benzo(a)pyrene, diesel emissions, it was found to induce tumors in 80 percent of the animals treated. (*Cosmetic Talc and Ovarian Cancer*, D. L. Longo et al, *The Lancet*, August 18, 1979.)

Another danger to be aware of concerning talcum powder concerns the practice by some women of using powder as an aid to feminine freshness by sprinkling it in their panties, on their panty liners and sanitary napkins. The danger lies in the discovery that the talc particles are finding their way into the women's bodies and eventually making their way into their reproductive organs. "Studies have shown talc granules in ovarian tumors suggesting more research needs to be done," says Carolyn D. Runowicz, M.D., Director of gynecologic oncology at Albert Einstein College of Medicine and Montefiore Medical Center in New York. (*Redbook,* Vol. 184, March, 1995, p.86.)

In another study at Boston's Hospital for Women, Division of the Brigham and Women's Hospital, 215 women with ovarian cancer were compared to a control group of the same number, relative age and ethnic background. Of the 215 women with ovarian cancer, 32 had previously used talcum powders in the above described manner. The conclusion of the study showed that the risk of developing ovarian cancer was 3.28 times greater for those using talc powder than for those who didn't. (*Ovarian Cancer and Talc, A Case-Control Study*, Daniel W. Cramer et al, *Cancer,* July 15, 1982.)

An unrelated study traced the presence of talc particles in post surgical patients. Talc was used on surgical gloves for decades and researchers were starting to see evidence that the talc had been inadvertently deposited in surgical patients via the surgeons' gloves. One woman however had never had any abdominal surgery yet had talc deposits. The mystery was solved when it was discovered that her husband used a brand of condoms coated in talc. The talc particles had worked their way upward through the fallopian tubes. We are not recommending you stop using condoms to protect yourself and your partner from STD's or unwanted pregnancies. We would, however, recommend you ensure your condoms are not talc coated.

Talc is strongly linked to ovarian cancer, "Talc was observed in a number of ovarian and uterine tumors." (*Journal of American Medical Association*, March 15, 1995, Vol. 273 No.11, page 846.)

It has been suggested that using powder made with food grade cornstarch appears to be a safer choice. Still others simply recommend practicing good hygiene as the safest of all choices.

Sunscreens - For as long as we can remember the sun has been our friend. We long for those sunny days of summer and we despair when the weather man tells us we won't see our sunny friend. Vacations, days on the beach, relaxing by the pool are all wonderful images that come to mind when we think of fun in the sun. Dark tans have long been associated with the rich and famous. It wasn't that long ago, however, that it was perceived quite differently, only the working class were *tanned* from outdoor labour while the upper class went to great lengths to protect their milk-white complexions. Times change, fashions change and we are swept along with that change. Today tans are not always viewed as healthy. With the ozone scare and more information about the aging effects of the sun the trend seems to be reversing once again. If we look back at the history of tanning and tans as a status symbol we can see that as the fad for dark tans grew so did the reports of cases of malignant melanoma (skin cancer).

Malignant melanoma rates have increased 1,200 percent since 1930, faster than any other types of cancer (*Self*, July 1992, Page 125.) Then along came sunscreens and we all said, yea! We headed back to the beach. We felt invincible as we lathered on our protective shield so we stayed out longer and longer. Gone were the days of suffering from those lobster red burns. The sunscreen protected us from the UVB rays responsible for sunburn. What we didn't realize was that we were exposing ourselves to greater dangers than ever before because although we were safe from the UVB rays, the more deeply penetrating UVA rays were unaffected by the sunscreens and since we were spending more time out in the sun our exposure was drastically increased. UVA rays penetrate into the deeper layers of the skin, down to the melanocytes, the cells that can turn cancerous and lead to malignant melanoma. Without the built-in warning system of the sunburn we were at the mercy of the solar rays.

On top of that there are some studies that suggest that while these sunscreens block the UVB rays and let the UVA rays through to damage our skin they may also be doing us another serious disfavor. Two epidemiologists from San Diego, Cedric and Frank Garland proposed that the use of UVB blocking sunscreens can hinder the body's production of Vitamin D. Vitamin D has a hormone-like effect in our bodies that seems to interfere with the growth of tumors. (*Suppression of in vivo Growths of Human Cancer Solid Tumor Xenografts by 1,25 Dihydroxyvitamin D3*, John Eisman, et al, Garavan Institute of Medical Research January,

1987). We get Vitamin D from milk and cold-water fish but most of our body's supply is produced when we are exposed to UVB sunlight. So in blocking the UVB we are decreasing our *in vitro* levels of Vitamin D. "Sunscreen blocks absorption of the sunlight spectrum responsible for the cutaneous synthesis of Vitamin D (Ultraviolet B)" (*Chronic Sunscreen Use Decreases Circulating Concentration of 25-Hydroxyvitamin D*, Lois Y. Matsuoka, M.D., et al, Department of Dermatology Medical College, April, 1988.) The controversy over the link between Vitamin D and cancer is ongoing as is the debate over the benefits of using or not using sunscreens. It is interesting to note that some doctors are now recommending that women increase their Vitamin D intake to 800 mg a day.

Studies have been conducted that draw parallels between how we use sunscreen and a laboratory test that exposed mice to a succession of UVB, then UVA, then UVB rays which produced some evidence of increased cancer rates. (*Carcinogenic Effect of Sequential Artificial Sunlight and UVA Irradiation in Hairless Mice*, Bent Staberg, MD et al, Arch Dermatol - Vol. 119, 1983.)

Other studies suggest that UVA can act as promoters of tumors that may have been initiated by UVB exposure. The use of "sunscreens has allowed individuals to increase the length of time that they spend sunbathing and as a consequence, they may be exposed to massive doses of long wave UV radiation (UVA, 320-400nm). There is now much evidence to suggest that UVA acts to promote tumors that have been initiated by UVB." (*Long wave Ultraviolet Radiation and Promotion of Skin Cancer*, Mary Steidl Matsui, Cold String Harbour Laboratory Press, Jan, 1991.)

Many of today's cosmetics contain a sunscreen or a UV inhibitor. Many of the most commonly used sunscreens have been found to cause allergic reactions, photo-sensitivity, and contact dermatitis or skin irritation. In a two year study of 280 patients tested with common sunscreen agents, 5 percent had allergic reactions. The most frequent contact allergens included: hydroxy methoxy methyl benzophenone (Mexenone), isopropyl dibenzoylmethane (Eusolex 8020/8021), octyl dimethyl para-aminobenzoate (Escalol 507), butyl methoxy dibenzoylmethane (Parsol 1789), amyl dimethyl para-aminobenzoate (Escalol 506), ethoxy ethyl-p-methoxy cinnamate (Givtan F). (*Sensitivity to Sunscreens*, J.S.C. English, et al, *Contact Dermatitis*, 1987:17 159-162.) If you should have an allergic reaction to your make-up or body lotion, it could be the sunscreen additive in the product.

A study done by the National Toxicity Program reported a link between hydroquinone and some types of cancer. Animal studies suggest that exposure to some sunscreens can cause more serious damage than skin allergies. The study concluded that "in rats and mice there was clear evidence of carcinogenic activity of hydroquinone for male F344/N rats (dose levels of 25 or 50 mg/kg in water) exposed to hydroquinone, as shown by increases in hepatocellular neoplasms, mainly adenomas. (*Sunscreens and Hydroquinone, Scientifically Speaking*, Anne Wolven Garrett, DCI March, 1989.)

It's also interesting to see that since the introduction of PABA (para-aminobenzoic acid) in the early 60's the rate of melanoma has increased at the same rate as the sales of sunscreen. (*Mother Jones*, May/June, 1993.) Sales in 1991 were 380 million dollars, twice as much as a decade earlier. When PABA is exposed to sunlight it can produce genetic damage. Perhaps we had better return to using our natural built-in warning system to protect us from the sun. Wear a hat and cover up and stay out of the sun during the hours of 10 am to 3 pm. If you choose not to use a sunscreen remember, just because it doesn't look like you are burning, doesn't mean you're not getting burned.

Something Stinks in the Fragrance Business!

"When I was a child our family went on car trips to visit relatives. These family outings usually took place on Sunday afternoon. We'd all pile into the car, Dad at the wheel, Mom riding shotgun and kids in the back seat. Mom came armed with an extra douse of perfume applied just before our departure. We'd be on the road for less than a few miles before I'd start feeling queasy. Then inevitably I'd be sick to my stomach ruining my dress, the car's upholstery and everyone's day. I was labeled as being prone to car sickness and despite every attempt to remedy this affliction, including attaching chains to the back bumper and taking motion sickness pills before the trip, I kept getting sick."

Now this is clearly just an anecdotal story with no scientific backing but the person telling the story feels sure that if her mother hadn't used perfume in those days, she would not have been car-sick.

> Being enclosed in a small space with some perfume manufacturers idea of feminine scent compounded with a pine or lemon scented air freshener dangling from the rear view mirror for all to enjoy—I was doomed from the instant I climbed into the car!

There have been no studies done linking childhood car-sickness with the use of fragrance by mothers but there have been plenty of studies done that do link the use of fragrance with many other mysterious illnesses.

The fragrance business is a multi-billion dollar industry. Don't be fooled by slick ads with movie star names and images of romance beyond our wildest dreams. The perfume industry is a dirty one with just one thing running it—profit! You'll notice I've referred to it as an industry. That's what it is, employing industrial chemicals, over 4000 of them, to tantalize our sense of smell and create wonderful illusions. One ad in particular comes to mind: the ad showed a woman spraying herself with the product in the morning. Later that day a man catches a whiff of her on the street and risks life and limb chasing her down to present her with a bouquet of flowers. The ad then asks, "does this ever happen to you?" As if applying this product will make one irresistible to passing men. The message was so clear. I recall it vividly to this day although it was aired several years ago.

The facts are a lot less attractive. First of all, the perfume industry is the least regulated of all the cosmetics. There are no agencies anywhere that can protect the consumer. A manufacturer of a scent can keep his formula from the authorities and from you by claiming it as a trade secret. That little spritz of irresistibility isn't like the Colonel's secret herbs and spices. It may contain 200 or more highly volatile, mostly petroleum derived chemicals that undergo no testing for their individual or combined toxicity.

Neurotoxins - Neurotoxins are chemicals that poison the nervous system. (*Neurotoxins: At Home and The Workplace,*

Report to the Committee on Science and Technology, US House of Representatives, 1989). Our nervous system is the communication network responsible for directing and maintaining normal bodily functions. Neurotoxins affect us in different ways. Some attack the peripheral nerves found in our extremities, including hands and feet, affecting motor co-ordination and loss of feeling. Others can attack the myelin sheath (fatty coating surrounding the nerve fibers) causing irreversible damage to organ functions and motor ability. Others also cause chemical imbalances in the brain that can lead to neurological dysfunction. Children and the aged are most susceptible. Exposure can occur from contact through the skin or by inhalation as well as from ingestion. (*Neurotoxins: At Home and The Workplace*, Report to the Committee on Science and Technology, US House of Representatives, 1989.)

Every day millions of people are exposed to neurotoxins at work and home. They are in solvents, pesticides, drugs, food additives and cosmetics. Symptoms of exposure can include dizziness, nausea, muscle weakness and blurred vision. This is just the tip of the iceberg. Some irreversible damage is being done to our nervous systems, our brains and our motor functions. Neurotoxins have also been linked to several neurological diseases including, ALS (Amyotropic Lateral Sclerosis—Lou Gehrig's Disease), Parkinson's Disease, Multiple Sclerosis, Lupus and Alzheimer's.

According to a report done by the Office of Technology Assessment (OTA) toxins found in many commercially used chemicals, including those used in cosmetics, can poison the nervous system. This report has caused concern that exposure to these neurotoxins might be linked to a variety of neurological diseases. (*Science*, Vol. 248 May 25, 1990, Sarah Williams). This is a huge problem considering how many chemicals the average person is exposed to every day. Dr. Peter Spencer, a neurotoxicologist from the Oregon Health Sciences University, who chaired the OTA's Neuroscience Advisory Panel, found that the testing of chemicals for their potential neurotoxicity is inadequate and inefficient. Worse there doesn't seem to be any strong mandate by government agencies to set test standards.

Musk AETT (acetyl ethyl tetramethyl tetralin) and Musk Ambrett used in fragrances have been proven to be potent neuro-toxins. These two raw chemicals used in the fragrance industry were tested and found to be dangerous. The perfume industry took the test results for Musk AETT to the FDA and voluntarily removed it from the market, but the FDA chose not to regulate this compound, so it can be used in the future. "In all, there are 850 known neurotoxic chemicals. Regulatory standards exist or have been recommended for only 167 of these." (Dr. Spencer, US Committee report.) Dr. Spencer's concern regarding the number of neurotoxic chemicals used in the industry may be fueled by the nature of the damage caused by some of these chemicals. "Nerve damage can be irreversible: the nerve cell is unable to divide like a liver cell or blood cell . . . if one loses a nerve cell, that's it. As one depletes these nerve cells, it is suspected [that] throughout a lifetime of chemical exposure eventually the result is expressed either by subtle behavioral changes or more frank neurological deficits." (Lynn Lawson, *Staying Well In A Toxic World*, p. 280.)

The conclusion seems obvious—there is a definite need for more testing and more control over what goes into products released to the public.

In 1991, the EPA analyzed the Volatile Organic Compounds (VOC's) given off by 31 fragrance products and sampled the air in 15 different commercial and residential environments for VOC's. They found 150 chemicals present in everyday products. Linalool, considered highly toxic, was most commonly found. In the study of 15 locations they found 100 chemicals including toluene, xylene methylene chloride and 1,1,1-trichloroethane, all known to be toxic in animal studies. This quote, "Toluene was most abundant in auto parts stores and in department stores' perfume sections." from Lynn Lawson's book *Staying Well in a Toxic World*, sort of sums up my feelings about the chemicals employed by the fragrance industry.

The public is becoming aware of the potential dangers, not to mention the annoyance, of the flagrant use of fragrance on the public. In the US, there are new laws disallowing perfume samples that aren't contained in a specially sealed manner to be included in magazines. The implication is that unwilling exposure to perfumes via this method is no longer being tolerated by the general public. In other instances *no-scent* policies have been initiated in fitness centers, churches, offices, and public meeting places. In San Francisco demonstrators rallied outside a Cosmetic, Toiletry and Fragrance Association Convention to protest against perfumes. Just as non-smokers have protested against second-hand smoke, non-scent advocates are angry that their air space is being taken over by fragrant fumes.

Reports show that thirty minutes after inhaling a perfume some patients display diminished cerebral blood flow.

Perfumes are volatile chemicals designed to broadcast into the surrounding air. Referring to the use of perfume, Julia Kendall, Co-Chair for Citizens for a Toxic-Free Marin had this to say, "It is dangerous for anybody who is wearing it, and it is really dangerous to us." Kendall has compiled the following list of toxic chemicals commonly found in perfumes.

THE TWENTY MOST COMMON CHEMICALS FOUND IN THIRTY-ONE FRAGRANCE PRODUCTS

1991 EPA Study

Reference: Lance Wallace, Environmental Protection Agency

Phone (703) 349-8970

Excerpts from *Health Hazard Information*

Compiled by Julia Kendall, Co-Chair

Citizens for a Toxic-Free Marin.

Phone (415) 485-6870

Reference: Material Safety Data Sheets (MSDS)

ETHANOL -a principal chemical in perfume, hairspray, shampoo, fabric softener, dishwashing liquid and detergent, laundry detergent, shaving cream, soap, vaseline lotion, air fresheners, nail color and remover, paint and varnish remover) - EPA Hazardous Waste List: fatigue; irritating to eyes and upper respiratory tract even in low concentrations. Inhalation of ethanol vapors can have effects similar to those characteristic of indigestion. These include an initial stimulatory effect followed by drowsiness, impaired vision, ataxia (loss of muscular coordination), stupor.

LIMONENE - a principal chemical in perfume, cologne, disinfectant spray, bar soap, shaving cream, deodorants, nail color and remover, fabric softener, dishwashing liquid, air fresheners, after-shave, bleach, paint and varnish remover. Carcinogenic. Prevent its contact with skin or eyes because it is an irritant and sensitizer. Always wash thoroughly after using this material and before eating, drinking...applying cosmetics. Do not inhale limonene vapor.

LINALOOL - a principal chemical in perfume, cologne, bar soap, shampoo, hand lotion, nail enamel remover, hairspray, laundry detergent, dishwashing liquid, vaseline lotion, air fresheners, bleach powder, fabric softener, shaving cream, after-shave, solid deodorant) Narcotic. respiratory disturbances, depressed frog-heart activity. In animal tests: ataxic gait, reduced spontaneous motor activity and depression...development of respiratory disturbances leading to death. Attracts bees.

BENZYLACETATE - a principal chemical in perfume, cologne, shampoo, fabric softener, stick-up air freshener, dishwashing liquid and detergent, soap, hair spray, bleach, after-shave, deodorants) Carcinogenic (linked to pancreatic cancer); From vapors: irritating to eyes and respiratory passages, exciting cough. In mice: hyperemia of the lungs. Can be absorbed through the skin causing systematic effects. Do not flush to sewer.

BENZYL ALCOHOL - a principal chemical in perfume, cologne, soap, shampoo, nail enamel remover, air freshener, laundry bleach and detergent, vaseline lotion, deodorants, fabric softener) "irritating to the upper respiratory tract, headache, nausea, vomiting, dizziness, drop in blood pressure, Central Nervous System (CNS) depression, and death in severe cases due to respiratory failure."

BENZALDEHYDE - a principal chemical in perfume, cologne, hairspray, laundry bleach, deodorants, detergent, vaseline lotion, shaving cream, shampoo, bar soap, dishwasher detergent) Narcotic. Local anesthetic, CNS depressant. Irritation to the mouth, throat, eyes, and skin, lungs, and GI tract causing nausea and abdominal pain. May cause kidney damage. Do not use with contact lenses. Sensitizer.

A-TERPINEOL - a principal chemical in perfume, cologne, laundry detergent, bleach powder, laundry bleach, fabric softener, stick-up air freshener, vaseline lotion, cologne, soap, hairspray, after-shave, roll-on deodorant) highly irritating to mucous membranes. Aspiration into the lungs can produce pneumonitis or even fatal edema. Excitement, ataxia, hypothermia, CNS and respiratory depression, and headache. Prevent repeated or prolonged skin contact.

A-PINENE - a principal chemical in bar and liquid soap, cologne, perfume, shaving cream, deodorants, dishwashing liquid, air freshener. Sensitizer (damaging to the immune system).

ACETONE - a principal chemical in cologne, dishwashing liquid and detergent, nail enamel remover EPA, ZRCRA, CERCLA Hazardous Waste Lists; Inhalation can cause dryness of the mouth and throat; dizziness, nausea, incoordination, slurred speech, drowsiness, and, in severe exposures, coma. Acts primarily as a CNS depressant.

ETHYLACETATE - a principal chemical in after-shave, cologne, perfume, shampoo, nail color, nail enamel remover, fabric softener, dishwashing liquid. Narcotic. EPA Hazardous Waste List; "irritating to the eyes and respiratory tract, may cause headache and narcosis, defeating effect on skin and may cause drying and cracking, may cause anemia with leukocytosis and damage to liver and kidneys. Wash thoroughly after handling."

g-TERPINENE - a principal chemical in cologne, perfume, soap, shaving cream, deodorants, air freshener. Causes asthma and Central Nervous System (CNS) disorders.

CAMPHOR - a principal chemical in perfume, shaving cream, nail enamel, fabric softener, dishwasher detergent, stick-up air freshener. Local irritant and CNS stimulant, readily absorbed through body tissues, irritation of eyes, nose and throat, dizziness, confusion, nausea, twitching muscles and convulsions. Avoid inhalation of vapors.

METHYLENE CHLORIDE - found in shampoo, cologne, paint and varnish remover. Banned by the FDA in 1988! No enforcement possible due to trade secret laws protecting chemical fragrance industry. EPA, RCRA, CERCLA Hazardous Waste Lists; Carcinogenic. Absorbed, stored in body fat, it metabolized to carbon monoxide, reducing oxygen-carrying capacity of the blood. Headache, giddiness, stupor, irritability, fatigue, tingling in the limbs.

1,8-CINEOLE

a-TERPIOLENE

NEROL

OCIMENE

b-CITRONELLOL

b-PHENETHYL ALCOHOL

b-MYRCENE - unable to secure MSDS.

More facts on fragrance - Toluene, used as a solvent in many cosmetics was found present in every fragrance sample collected for a 1991 EPA report. Toluene is suspected to be cancer causing (US Fredrick Cancer Research Centre). It can cause liver damage, skin irritation and respiratory tract irritation. It was also found to trigger asthma attacks. It is listed in California's Prop 65 (Proposition 65, California's toxic control law enacted in 1988) as a birth defect causing chemical. See nail care section for more on toluene.

In the 1991 EPA study that looked at 20 of the most commonly employed chemicals from 31 fragrances, it was found that 14 out of the 20 occur naturally in essential oils. Among these 14, three are known allergic sensitizers and two are suspected carcinogens (Richard H. Conrad, Ph.D., Environmental Consultant, 1994.) Again, just because it is natural doesn't mean it's safe.

In an article in *Chemical Marketing Report* dated June 21, 1993, there is mention of at least two chemicals (xylol and ketone musk) used in the perfume industry that despite their known toxicity are still in use. Others like nitrocyclic musk, have virtually been abandoned by all but a few producers due to its instability and toxicity. It is still used in lower line soaps and detergents. (*Chemical Marketing Report*, Matthew Gallagher, June 21, 1993.)

Phthalate esters (used in perfume industry) were placed on the list of toxic chemicals under the Emergency Planning and Community Right to Know Act. An EPA spokesman reported that waste water discharge levels for three phthalate esters, including diethyl phthalate are under reconsideration. Industry observers are expecting a zero tolerance level for phthalate esters in waste water. (*Chemical Marketing Reporter*, May 8, 1989.) It seems these chemicals are considered dangerous toxic waste.

One Last Word ...

Remember! There are no agencies that regulate the fragrance industry. There have been some moves within the industry for self-testing and voluntary removal from the market of any product found to be a problem. More testing is needed, especially in the area of neurotoxicity.

Formulas can remain undisclosed by the industry. Perfume formulas are closely guarded secrets.

It's a multi-billion dollar industry that uses raw chemicals that cost pennies per pound. What we seem to be paying for is a package, a name, an image and a whole lot of advertising.

We all have the right to breathe fragrance-free, fresh air.

Anti-perspirants and deodorants - Anti-perspirants and deodorants are actually classified as over the counter drugs, not cosmetics, since they affect the function or structure of the body. Anti-perspirants and deodorants are among the top selling cosmetic products. It is estimated that 9 out of 10 women and 8 out of 10 men purchase and use anti-perspirants or deodorants (Margaret Morrison, US Dept. Health and Welfare, FDA, 1979, HEW Publications.)

How they Work ...

Anti-perspirants are formulated to actually retard the flow of perspiration by lowering the pH level in the areas when they are applied. This inhibits moisture. Deodorants, which may contain some anti-perspirant, are used to control the odor produced by bacterial action as they interact with sweat and other chemicals. It's not sweat that makes us stink, it's the action of billions of bacteria on the sweat. Killing bacteria will solve half the problem. That's why many deodorants and anti-perspirants contain anti-bacterial chemicals—see formaldehyde as well as fragrance. (*American Health*, Dec. 1990, p.16.)

The anti-perspirant agents that affect the flow of perspiration are metal salts, most commonly salts of aluminum. In the late 1970's a group of researchers found that the brains of Alzheimer's patients contained abnormally large concentrations of aluminum.

Daniel Perl, a neuropathologist at Mount Sinai School of Medicine in Manhattan, and a group of his colleagues, began to make a connection between the high levels of aluminum in the brain and Alzheimer's Disease. In Alzheimer's patients' brains aluminum was showing up in huge quantities, up to 50 times the normal amount in some cells (*Discover*, September 1992, Peter Radetsky.) Perl and many other researchers believe that there is a real connection.

There is evidence that aluminum is poisonous to the nervous system but it's unclear how aluminum is getting into the brains of those suffering from Alzheimer's. Once again the camps are divided. Some researchers believe that the higher levels of aluminum are caused by the disease while others believe the higher levels are factors in causing the disease. Most agree though that Alzheimer's is a multifactorial disease—many causes and as yet those causes are unknown (*Harvard Health Letter*, Lisa Poniatowski Easley, Oct. 1990).

There is evidence however that does suggest that aluminum is a major factor in the disease. Aluminum is not readily absorbed by the body when ingested. Most of it is filtered out by the kidneys and liver in a normal healthy body. As we age our kidneys and livers slow down and their ability to filter our blood of toxins like aluminum is decreased. (*Public Health Reports* Nov./Dec., 1993.)

Ingestion is only one way that aluminum can enter the body. Inhalation is quicker and more dangerous. Dr. Perl believes we can breathe in aluminum. "The olfactory system is the only place where nerve cells in the brain are exposed to the environment." (*Discover*, Sept. 1992, Pg. 89, quote from Daniel Perl in article by Peter Radetsky). In animal studies, aluminum compounds were traced from the nasal passages and tracked to the brain. The aluminum traveled along neuron pathways to the brain. By entering the body in this way the aluminum bypassed the bloodstream, avoiding the filter system of the kidneys and liver, and found its way to the brain, causing neurological damage to the area affected in Alzheimer's disease.

In 1990, a University of Washington study found that people who used anti-perspirants containing aluminum had a slightly higher risk of Alzheimer's disease than those who didn't. (*Discover*, Sept. 1992, Pg. 89.)

We are surrounded by aluminum. It is in our water, food additives, cosmetics, and over the counter drugs such as antacids. It is the third most common element on earth. (*University of California Berkeley Wellness Letter*, April, 1993.) There are still a lot of unanswered questions regarding the role of aluminum in Alzheimer's and other chronic diseases. To avoid any unwanted exposure to aluminum it has been recommended to avoid using spray deodorants that contain it. Fortunately, since anti-perspirants are considered drugs, they must list ingredients on their labels allowing you to make an informed decision.

Hair Today – Gone Tomorrow: Depilatories

These vile smelling lotions used to remove hair from parts of our bodies we want to have hairless do come with plenty of cautions. Complaints to the FDA regarding the use of these products include skin irritations, headaches, scarring, skin rashes and burns. Most lotion-type depilatories contain, as their active ingredient, calcium thioglycolate, a stronger relation to chemicals found in permanent wave solutions. Since hair is composed of tissue similar to skin, these chemicals that are designed to dissolve unwanted hair can also damage skin in the process. If they are left on the skin too long they can cause severe burns and may result in scarring. (*The 90's Healthy Body*, Gary Null, p. 129.) Calcium thioglycolate is also used to tan leather and its use has been linked to thyroid problems in animal studies.

Shaving would seem to be the safest method for the removal of unwanted hair.

four

The Nail Story

Sometimes when I see women with outrageously long, gaudily painted nails, I wonder how they manage to get anything done! Besides the amount of time it seems to take to maintain these things and the fact that they serve no purpose in our ability to carry out our daily tasks, it seems artificial nails also present a huge risk of exposure to some very toxic substances.

Artificial nails and nail products in general are made from chemicals, some of which are dangerous solvents. Different products contain different chemicals but most products can be classified as acrylics, gels, fiberglass, porcelain tips and wraps. Although different brands, they basically contain the same ingredients and therefore pose similar health problems.

Chemicals in your Nail Products

Solvents - used to keep artificial nail products liquid, to remove or dilute products. These chemicals can be easily absorbed into the body either through the skin or through inhalation. It should be noted that they can affect the nervous system (neurotoxins) and some have been linked to birth defects in animal studies.

Glycol ethers - These have been linked with birth defects in animal studies. They have caused damage to the male reproductive organs in animal studies and exposure to glycol ether has lowered the sperm count in human males. The damage occurred at very low exposure rates without the usual warning symptoms such as nausea and dizziness. Recently The Wall Street Journal (October 13, 1992) reported that IBM, Digital Equipment Corp., AT&T, Texas Instruments and many other large corporations were raising awareness among their employees about the health hazards of working in areas where glycol ethers are present. The reports linked exposure to these chemicals with higher than normal rates of miscarriages.

Acetonitrile - Acetonitrile is used in the removal of artificial nails. It is highly toxic and has caused birth defects in animal studies. It can easily be absorbed through the skin. According to the National Institute of Occupational Safety and Health (NIOSH) the target organs are kidney, liver, CVS (cardiovascular), CNS (central nervous system), lungs, skin and eyes.

Methyl methacrylate was banned by the FDA in 1974 because it caused irritation and allergic dermatitis to customers and manicurists. MMA is still being used illegally. In 1982 and again in 1986 it was found to be present in artificial nail products and in the air of some nail salons. As recently as three years ago, when I attended an artificial nail training class (with the purpose of snooping) I had a look through the MSDS sheets and lo and behold!, there it was. It was still in their product.

Ethyl alcohol is also a solvent. Exposure can be through inhalation or accidental ingestion. EA is an irritant of the eyes and mucous membranes. It can cause central nervous system depression displaying symptoms such as lack of concentration, somnolence [drowsiness] and fetotoxicity in animal studies. (*Chemical Hazards in the Workplace*, Nick H. Proctor, Ph.D., James P. Huges, MD F.A.C.P., Michael L. Fischman, MD, M.P.H., 1989, Van Nostrand Reinhold.)

Potassium hydroxide (Caustic Potash) - Used as an emulsifier in hand creams as well as cuticle softeners it is extremely corrosive and may cause irritation of the skin. If ingested it can cause bleeding, collapse and death. In animal studies it was applied to the skin of mice in moderate amounts and was found to cause tumors. (*A Consumer's Dictionary of Cosmetic Ingredients*, Ruth Winter, M.S. Crown Trade Paperbacks, New York, 1994.)

Methylene chloride - a solvent considered by NIOSH to be a potential human carcinogen. It is a mild central nervous system depressant. It can cause eye, skin, and respiratory tract irritation and it was found to cause cancer in animal studies. People with cardiovascular disease may be at a greater risk because of induced hypoxia (a deficiency of oxygen reaching the tissues). Prolonged contact with the skin may cause severe burns. It was found to be a fetotoxin in animal studies, and is linked to lung and liver adenomas and carcinomas.

Benzoyl peroxide - an additive in self-curing plastics. Inhalation can cause irritation of mucous membranes. There have also been animal studies that indicate benzoyl peroxide may act as a cancer promoter on mouse skin. (*Chemical Hazards in the Workplace*, Nick H. Proctor, Ph.D., James P. Huges, MD F.A.C.P., Michael L. Fischman, MD, M.P.H., 1989, Van Nostrand Reinhold.) You may recognize this chemical as also being a main ingredient in many acne preparations.

Formaldehyde is used as an antibacterial, was shown to be carcinogenic in two strains of rats. Squamous cell cancer of the nasal cavity was observed following repeated inhalation of about 14ppm (parts per million). An excess of deaths from cancer of the brain has been noted in professionals, such as embalmers, anatomists and pathologists, who are exposed to formaldehyde.

Toluene - a solvent that can cause central nervous system depression, headaches, depression, nausea and can create feelings of intoxication. Long-term exposure of workers has been linked to minor abnormalities in neuropsychological tests. Repeated and prolonged skin contact can cause drying, fissuring and dermatitis. Some animal studies link exposure through prolonged inhalation to reduced fetal weight and slowed skeletal development. (*Chemical Hazards in the Workplace*, Nick H. Proctor, Ph.D., James P. Huges, MD F.A.C.P., Michael L. Fischman, MD, M.P.H., 1989, Van Nostrand Reinhold.)

Toluene exposure can cause serious long-term health problems. A study that examined workers exposed to toluene found that two years after the exposure there was still some evidence of chromatid-type aberrations (changes in genetic material). (*Chromosome changes with time in lymphocytes after occupational exposure to toluene*, Mutation Research, 142 (1985) 37-39, Elsevier, E. Schmid et al.)

Before you get your nails done at a salon ensure there is proper ventilation, and the manicurist is using safe ingredients—ask to see a Material Safety Data Sheet for the products and chemicals being used.

five

Oh, Baby, Baby

If you've ever walked past a hospital viewing room lined with new-borns you know that those precious little lives arc all beautiful, delicate and full of potential. Nervous, first-time parents will attest to the fact that they don't however come with owner's manuals and their upkeep can be the cause of many a sleepless night. Today there are so many products on the market to help parents in their task of maintaining baby. Creams, lotions, oils, powders, soaps and shampoos designed just for baby can be seen by the shelf-load in every drug store and supermarket. Some of these products should, however, come with a warning label because, just like products geared to the adult market, there are some serious notes of caution when it comes to the ingredients employed.

Baby oil usually contains a mixture of petroleum products and mineral oils. They may also contain chlorobutanol, an antioxidant. Chlorobutanol is a central nervous system depressant and in the past was used medicinally as a hypnotic.

Baby lotions are similar in composition to body lotions used by adults. Sometimes the only difference may be a slightly altered scent and perhaps a *baby* color and of course a different package. As with adult moisturizers, baby lotions will contain humectants such as propylene glycol. As you will recall, propylene glycol and most humectants actually pull moisture from the skin and therefore have a drying effect. They may also contain anti-microbials which may cause allergic skin reactions. Baby skin is very sensitive to many allergens and even if the product claims to be gentle or hypoallergenic it will still contain some dyes, perfumes and other chemicals that can cause skin irritation.

Petroleum jelly or petrolatum is a mixture of semi-solid hydrocarbons from petroleum. Petroleum derivatives have been linked to cancer and are known to cause allergic skin reactions. They can also trap moisture against the skin thus promoting a breeding ground for bacteria.

Talcum Powder - The main ingredient in talcum powder (bath powder, baby powder) is talc. This subject was covered before. The hazard is the inhalation of talc particles which can build up in the lungs. This can be resolved by using corn-silk or food grade cornstarch.

Bubble Baths and Baby Shampoos - Adverse reactions to bubble baths have been noted since 1955. Injuries include rashes, skin irritations and genital/urinary tract disorders. The detergent ingredients in bubble baths remove the protective coatings from the skin thereby allowing infection or inflammation to occur. Considering the amount of time a child or baby can spend in a bath and the frequency of bathing, the exposure to these potentially hazardous ingredients is a major concern.

Bubble baths usually contain a wetting agent such as sodium laurel sulfate as well as triethanolamine (TEA). As was mentioned in an earlier section of this book, the combination of the two can create nitrosamines which are known carcinogens.

The nitrate absorption occurs when the SLS becomes contaminated with NDELA (N-nitrosodiethanolamine) during processing. This contamination comes about as a result of SLS coming into contact with any number of chemicals including triethanolamine (TEA) which, as you will recall, is a commonly used ingredient in shampoos and bubble baths as a detergent. Put simply: SLS + TEA = NDELA (a nitrosamines and a recognized carcinogen).

SLS is particularly dangerous to young children since it can cause severe damage to the surface of the eye if it is accidentally splashed on the face. It can easily be absorbed and retained in the eye. Studies done show that the uptake of SLS is greatest in younger eyes. The same study found that penetration wasn't limited to the eyes but included systemic tissues such as the brain, heart, spleen and liver.

From Chapter on Hair Care...

In September of 1992, John Bailey, director of FDA's Division of Colors and Cosmetics, while addressing the Dermal Clinical Evaluation Society reported the discovery of another reactant chemical contaminant that seemed to be showing up in cosmetics, specifically in shampoos and bubble baths. Excessively high levels of 1,4 dioxane, a substance found to cause liver cancer in lab animal studies conducted by the National Cancer Institute in the 1970's, seem to be occurring in products that use non-ionic ethoxylated surfactants in emulsion products such as conditioners. It was also noted that shampoos for children use higher levels of ethylene oxide. In fact the higher degree of ethoxylation, the more likely the occurrence of 1,4 dioxane.

He expressed concern that levels of 1,4 dioxane found in recent samples of baby shampoo and conditioners were not significantly lower than when original FDA analyses were performed over ten years ago. 1,4 dioxane has been determined to be an animal carcinogen and may be a human health risk. Most common human exposure to this compound occurs in shampoos formulated with sodium or ammonium laureth sulfates or other ethoxylated surfactants. (John Bailey, DCI, November, 1992.)

Bubble baths may also contain alcohol, alkyl benzene sulfonate—a detergent, and sodium chloride (salt) all known to have a drying effect on the skin.

Recently there has been a disturbing trend towards *kiddie cosmetics*. Wall Street Journal, January 28, 1993 reported that sales of children's toiletries amounted to 260 million dollars in 1992. By age 13, 71.6 percent use blusher, 84.9 percent use lip gloss, and 94.1 percent use a hair conditioner.

At this point it may be important to note that virtually all baby care products come in packages that are not child-proof. Ingestion of bubble baths can cause gastrointestinal disturbances and stomach distress. Since these and many baby care products contain chemicals that are potentially toxic if ingested, it would seem prudent to package them in containers that would prevent accidental ingestion rather than the pretty, easily accessible packages seen on the market today.

Almost all baby products contain some form of perfume and most contain dyes as well. These ingredients are unnecessary and possibly harmful to the health of your baby.

The European launch, by a leading manufacturer of perfumes, of a line of baby fragrances marks a new and disquieting movement in the industry. Not happy with the booming adult market, the industry is now targeting the baby market. The new lines, introduced to the market in the spring of 1994, were created for new-borns to three year olds. Other fragrances are aimed at toddlers to seven year olds. Is it really necessary to scent our children and contribute to their life-time exposure to chemicals that may be neurotoxins? Perhaps the best you can do for your baby is practice *less is best* when it comes to the personal care products and chemicals.

six

Hormonal Hazards

A group of scientist and physicians world wide were becoming increasingly concerned with the apparent effects of so-called "hormone disrupters" in our bodies and in our environment. Following a workshop held in Erice, Italy, November 5-10, 1995, 23 of these same men and women of science put forward a profound statement on the topic which has now become known as *The Erice Statement*. (See *RACHEL'S Environment & Health Weekly* #499 in bibliography for complete list of scientists and physicians who signed the statement.)

Let's step back a bit and start at the beginning with a few basics. Hormones are, very simply put, chemical messengers in our bodies. They travel through our blood steam like tiny couriers delivering critical messages that turn on or off our bodily functions. They control growth, our development and behavior from the time we are but a single cell—our mother's egg or our father's sperm—to the time we die. There have been 100 different hormones identified in the human body. The tissues and organs that produce and respond to these hormonal messengers are collectively called the endocrine system.

Hormones play a major and critical role in life, and not only human life but in other organisms on this planet including other mammals, birds, fish, reptiles and amphibians. These finely tuned systems of messengers and responders are so sensitive that even a small disruption can be catastrophic to our species and in fact to all life on this planet as we know it.

Now, back to Erice, Italy, and the Erice Statement . . .

The statement begins:

Research since 1991 has reinforced concerns over the scope of the problems posed to human health and ecological systems by endocrine-disrupting chemicals. New evidence is especially worrisome because it underscores the exquisite sensitivity to the developing nervous system to chemical perturbations [disturbances] that result in functional abnormalities. Moreover, the consequences of these perturbations depend upon the stage of development during which exposure occurs and are expressed in different ways at different times in life, from birth through to advanced age. This work session was convened because of the growing concern that failure to confront the problem could have major economic and societal implications.

The group went on to lay out specific concerns in the form of a consensus statement. The consensus statement can be covered with the following simplified nine points.

1. Hormone disrupting chemicals can negatively effect neurological and behavioral development and therefore will effect the potential of individuals. The exposure can start in utero. The result of exposure can have long term and wide reaching consequences.

2. The endocrine system is an easy target for disruption due to its natural and necessary sensitivity. Unlike the naturally occurring hormonal messengers, many of the man-made compounds and by-products of manufactured agents are persistent and can undergo bio-magnification in the food web. This means they can be collected and stored at each level of the food chain. Those eating higher up the food chain have the potential to be exposed to greater levels of disrupters.

3. The disrupters are wide-ranging—across all continents and oceans—in every population from the arctic to the tropics. They can also be passed from generation to generation because of their long-life and ability to be stored in the body. Endocrine disrupting chemicals are found in living tissues in concentrations millions of times higher than the natural hormones. Some of the manufactured chemicals can be found in living tissues at levels barely measurable yet even

still they are at levels considered to be biologically active, meaning they can effect changes and disruptions.

4. Exposure of fetus is not limited to gestation (or as in the case of birds and reptiles the incubation period), but can be contributed to through the mother's life-long exposure to disrupters. The chemical burden of the mother and father can potentially damage the unborn.

5. There are narrow windows during which exposure to the endocrine disrupters can cause permanent damage to the developing fetus. Exposure levels that would not adversely affect adults can cause irreversible brain abnormalities during development of the unborn and very young since they do not as yet possess any natural protective mechanisms.

6. Normal brain functions are in part the result of essential hormones such as thyroid hormones. Disruption of the thyroid during developmental stages of life can result in abnormalities in the brain and behavioral development. Abnormalities as a result of the disruption of the concentration of thyroid hormones can include motor dysfunction such as cerebral palsy and may also include other abnormalities ranging from moderate to severe mental retardation, learning disabilities and attention deficit-hyperactivity disorder.

7. Man-made hormone disrupters also have the potential to disturb normal brain sexual development. Studies of wildlife exposed to chemicals known to have disruptive properties have exhibited disturbances in sex hormone production and/or action.

8. There are commonalities between species when it comes to the mechanisms of hormones and their disrupters and therefore what is affecting the birds, reptiles and other mammals is also taking a toll on the human species.

9. It's not yet known how many chemicals fall into the category of *endocrine disrupters* but compounds known to have effects on the endocrine system include dioxins, PCB's, phenolics, phthalates and many pesticides. Any compound mimicking, antagonizing or altering the endocrine system is potentially part of the group.

Exposure is World-Wide

This is true and there isn't too much we can do to escape exposing ourselves since, as we read, the endocrine disrupters have been found on every continent and in every ocean. We can, however, take real steps in limiting our exposure by making wise decisions in our lifestyle choices, what we choose to put into our bodies and, as this book advocates, what we choose to put onto our bodies. The Erice Statement talks of vast consequences on a global level. We want you to first consider your own internal world.

This is where we bring the focus back to our main topic—the cosmetic consequence. As you may remember, I mentioned in our chapter on hair care the study linking shampoo to decreasing sperm levels. Shampoo, like many other personal care products contain man-made chemicals capable of altering or disrupting the endocrine system. These chemicals fall into the notorious category known as xeno-estrogens or estrogen mimickers. Many of the chemicals in your personal care products are derived from petro-chemicals, which are known to be xeno-estrogens. Petro-chemicals are fat-soluble (stored in fatty tissue), non-biodegradable and are toxic to our body's natural hormonal system.

In the preface I quoted John J. Condemi, MD, clinical professor of medicine at the University of Rochester School of Medicine and Dentistry in New York as saying, "Estrogen somehow allows the auto-immune illness to occur more readily." Are the hormone mimickers doing the same thing?

Testing, Testing, 1, 2, 3 . . .

Another cause for alarm found among the participants at the conference in Erice is that there is frightfully inadequate testing for endocrine disrupters in products. Most manufacturers believe testing for a product's skin irritation potential is as far as they have to go. As more evidence comes to light, will they continue to ignore it and blithely go on producing harmful products in pretty packages? Not if we continue to demand better and safer products, more effective testing of those chemicals and combinations of chemicals already on the market and a moratorium on the introduction of any new chemicals onto the market. There are an estimated 70,000 chemicals currently in commercial use. Every year about 1,000 more are added. The task of testing the chemicals currently in use is astronomical. The job is even more greatly magnified when you take into account that not only should the existing chemicals be tested individually but they should also be examined in combination with other chemicals they may possibly come into contact with in our bodies and in our environment. It has been estimated that it would take 100 laboratories, working 24 hours a day, seven days a week over 180 years to test just 1000 chemicals in unique combinations of three. That would require at least 166 million different tests! The reason for such combination testing is obvious because in the real world, outside the sterile laboratories, we are constantly exposed to any number of chemicals. This happens the minute we step outside our door, pesticides, car exhaust, air-fresheners in the car . . . the list goes on all day!

What can we do?

The best information and advice is to first of all avoid any petro-chemically derived products on your body. If you have trouble identifying a petrochemical ingredient, you can check out the glossary at the back of the book or visit your local library where you will find lots of resources on this topic.

Secondly, make it a point not to purchase any personal care products without ingredient lists either on the package or alongside the product, as is the case with some specialty stores.

Thirdly, make it known to the retailer that you refuse to purchase items that don't have labels with ingredients.

The only way change will come about, in an industry that for so long has been selling illusions, is if we force them to see the truth and tell the truth.

seven

Animal Testing

Not that long ago a movement that started small and grew to international proportions changed the way people thought and dressed. I'm talking about the movement against the fur industry by animal activist groups. This movement actually changed the thoughts of men and women and created a new *politically correct* idea of fashion and beauty. At the time it seemed impossible that a relatively small group of people could make any headway against a huge, multi-million dollar industry. Furs were status symbols and much sought after by those climbing the social ladder. Now a new wind is blowing and wearing fur has lost its glamour. The industry is seen as a tainted one by a growing number of people. What drove this movement was a public outcry against cruelty to animals. The same public outcry is starting to be heard on another front. This time the focus is on the use of animals to test consumer products such as cosmetics.

Animal testing is outmoded, inefficient and cruel. The only thing it has going for it is that it is cheap and relatively easy.

Here are the Facts

Biomedical research accounts for only 27 percent of all animals currently being used. The remaining 73 percent of animal experiments fall into the categories of product testing and education.

Animal testing is no guarantee that a product is safe. Every year products are released onto the market that are toxic to humans despite tests done by manufacturers. A perfect example of this are the hair dyes which require labels warning consumers of their dangers.

Animal test and cruelty free alternatives - The Draize Eye and Skin Irritancy Test was introduced 45 years ago by toxicologist John H. Draize. It is used to measure the harmfulness of chemicals by observing damage to eyes and skin of test animals. Rabbits are the most common animal used in these tests because they are abundant, cheap, easily handled and they have large eyes, making signs of irritation easy to observe. They are also used in skin irritancy tests. Their fur is shaved, their skin is then abraded and then the test chemical is applied for observation. All test animals are killed at the conclusion of the tests.

Rabbits are not people. There are some glaring physiological differences that should be considered when using them as test models for human reactions to chemicals. For instance, the eye of a rabbit does not have tear ducts. There are alternatives that are more efficient and cruelty free.

And... the Alternatives are...

In vitro technology can provide accurate testing without the use of animals. The Eyetex system, a chemical assay test, is effective in screening new ingredients, monitoring production and product stability testing. Epipack system uses sheets of cloned human skin cells to test for skin reaction to ingredients. There are also tissue culture systems and mathematical models available as alternatives. Computer programs can actually predict the toxicity of ingredients as well as test for skin and eye irritancy. In comparison these tests make animal testing seem like something from the dark ages. Isn't it time manufacturers of personal care products at least came into the 20th century, considering we are now on the brink of the next millennium?

Most of the testing on animals today is designed to look for local irritations, i.e. eye and skin reactions. As noted in an earlier section of this book, systemic testing, particularly in the area of neurotoxicity, long-term chronic health effects and fetal toxicity is greatly lacking. The problem lies in the fact that the industry can use animal tests to look for the visible effects of a single ingredient on a surface level and that seems to be the extent of the testing being done in most cases. There is a need to develop cruelty-free tests that can look at how chemicals interact in the human body or with other chemicals. Animal testing is literally only scratching the surface of the problem.

Like the fur movement of a few years ago the industry will have to make changes as we the consumer demand them. The *price* of wearing cosmetics shouldn't be subsidized by the lives of the animals being used in their testing. It's a decision we all can make. The time has come for a change. If you would like more information about animal testing and alternatives you can contact your local Anti-vivisection Society.

eight

Labeling Laws

Thankfully, Americans have ingredient labels on personal care products. When Canadians finally obtain the same courtesy, here's a trick you can use to read and understand the labels better. As you may have noticed, the labels on food products list ingredients in descending order from the most to the least: the ingredient occurring in the highest percentage will be at the top of the list and the ingredient occurring in the smallest percentage is at the bottom. A cosmetic chemist in the U.S., trying to decipher another chemist's formula, often uses the *1 percent rule*. Generally, ingredients occurring at about 1 percent will be found somewhere in the middle of the list. Those ingredients above the middle can be assumed to be about 1 percent or more and those below the middle will be below 1 percent. Using this very simple scale a chemist can guesstimate the percentages of the other ingredients and so can you.

Easy markers to determine the 1 percent mark are usually color additives, preservatives and fragrances. Where you find these items you can generally assume that ingredients above will be over 1 percent and ingredients below will be under 1 percent. (Rebecca James, *Let's Live*, Jan. 1994.)

More Simple Tips to Figure out what's in your Cosmetics

As I said earlier in this book it would be impossible to talk about every ingredient in your cosmetic product and even what we have covered may seem a little overwhelming to some. There are some simple ways to decipher the cosmetic jargon on labels.

When an ingredient starts with the letters COC, LAUR, MYR as in cocoyl sarcosinamide DEA, lauric acid, and myristyl myristate it means these chemicals come from a coconut source. Coconut oil has long been used as an emulsifier in many cosmetic products.

STEAR and GLY, found at the beginning of a chemical name, mean the ingredient's purpose is to add that *rich-feeling* to a product and it can be derived from either a plant or animal source. Two examples of these are stearic acid and glycosaminoglycans.

Ingredients derived only from petroleum include mineral oil, paraffin, isopropyl alcohol, microcrystalline wax and carbomers. Ingredients that are partially petroleum based will include syllables such as ETHYL, METHYL, BUTYL, PROPYL, OCTYL, PVP, ENE and ETH.

Alcohols include METHANOL, ETHANOL, PROPANOL and their many modifications including, SORBITOL, BUTYLENE GLYCOL, RETINOL (Vitamin A) and PANTHENOL (Provitamin B-5). Basically all ingredients ending in -ol and some ending in -yl are alcohols.

Alcohols are used in a wide variety of personal care products for a wide variety of reasons from solvents to anti-bacterials to humectants as in the fatty alcohols such as CHOLESTEROL and CETYL ALCOHOL.

Esters are the end product of mixing fatty alcohols with acids and removing most of the water from the mix. Esters are emulsifiers and essential stabilizers found in creams and lotions. They give lotions a less oily, more emollient feel. An easy way to spot an ester in your product is by looking for ingredients where the first word ends in -yl (a fatty alcohol), and the second word ends in -ate (a fatty acid) such as in isopropyl palmitate.

Vitamins may be included in the formula for your cosmetics but there is no evidence that they can be absorbed by your skin for any beneficial purpose.

Vitamin E or tocopherol is an antioxidant which preserves fatty components in creams and lotions.

Preservatives-parabens - The most common of all cosmetic preservatives include: methyl, propyl, butyl and ethyl parabens.

Formaldehyde-releasing preservatives include: quaternium-15 (tradename Dowicill 2000), imidazolidinyl urea (Germall), diazolidinyl urea (Germaben), dmdm hydantoin and 2-bromo-2-nitropropane-1,3-diol (Bronopol). (*Cosmetics*, Rebecca James Gadberry, *Let's Live*, March, 1995.)

The Label Game

Here's a little true and false game that could teach you about some of the label myths. Test your label skills by answering true or false to the following questions about common claims you may find on your cosmetic labels.

Hypoallergenic means that the cosmetic will not cause any allergic reaction. True or False?

False! Hypo (less) allergenic means it is less likely to cause an allergic reaction but it doesn't guarantee that it won't. Most of the allergic reactions from cosmetics can be traced to fragrance additives. That doesn't mean, however, that if a product is "fragrance free" it doesn't contain a fragrance additive. Since all of the chemicals used in cosmetics have some odor, some of which are unpleasant or undesirable, manufacturers hide or mask the chemical smell with a masking fragrance. So even if there is no discernible fragrance, chances are there's a fragrance present.

A product that claims to be non-comedogenic will not clog pores therefore will not cause acne breakouts. True or False?

False! Once again a product that makes this claim can't guarantee it. The manufacturer can choose to not employ chemicals that are commonly known to block pores such as mineral oil, cocoa butter, propylene glycol among others. This still does not guarantee that all of the ingredients used will not contribute to blocked pores and acne.

I can feel safe when a product says it has been tested by dermatologists. True or False?

False! If just one dermatologist tested one individual with one product this claim can truthfully be made. It does not have to mean that the product or the ingredients in the product have undergone any long-term testing for safety or benefit.

Products labeled *cruelty free* or no animal testing, have not been tested on animals. True or False?

False! Even if the product itself has not been tested on animals the ingredients used in the product probably have. Most formulas used in the cosmetic industry are old, some haven't changed in fifty years. These same formulas have in the past been tested on animals. If a company uses one of these standard formulas, gives it a different name, puts it in a new bottle and claims that they have not been tested on animals, they are not being truthful.

Higher priced personal care products contain better ingredients. True or False?

False! The ingredients are basically the same in high end and low end products. Price is not a deciding factor in choosing your products. Ingredient costs are the smallest, proportionally, in the whole cost of a product. The most costly part of your product will inevitably be the container. The cost of the actual ingredients will be just a few cents whether you are paying two dollars or twenty-five dollars for a bottle of shampoo. The only way you can justify a higher cost in any personal care product is by knowing what the ingredients are. It's not surprising we don't have labels on cosmetics in Canada for just this reason. Manufacturers don't want you to know that when you buy a so-called premium product, and pay big bucks, that it contains the same ingredients as a product you can buy in your grocery store for a fraction of the cost. In some cases the ingredients do cost more than the average products ingredients. In our list of alternative and safer products you may find ingredients that can cost thousands of dollars a pound. The fact that most manufacturers choose not to use these higher priced ingredients even though they know them to be safer, again indicates where their priorities lie—a better bottom line.

Cosmetics labeled *natural* are better than those that are not. True or False?

False! Natural doesn't mean better. A cosmetic or personal care product may contain a natural ingredient such as aloe vera but that doesn't necessarily mean that it will be in any way a benefit. Often a product will contain only a minute amount of some popular or recognized natural ingredient and yet to read the advertisement you'd think it was chock-a-block full of the stuff. Also, natural ingredients are no better or worse than some synthetics. Next time you see an ad for a natural personal care product or cosmetic, check the label if there is one, see how much of this ingredient is in the product. Check what else is in the product, because if there are any ingredients that aren't natural is it being truthful about being a natural product?

Sodium lauryl sulfate is made from coconuts therefore it can be considered natural and safe. True or False?

False! SLS is in fact a synthetic detergent. If it is present in a shampoo or conditioner that product cannot be labeled as natural.

Behind the Scenes - The Industry

As stated earlier, the manufacturing of personal care products is big business. A multi-billion dollar business. Very few manufacturers got into the industry for the betterment of mankind. They saw the potential to earn big bucks.

Many of the *salon formation* products have been developed by hairdressers-come-formulator/manufacturer. Various health food store personal care products formulators have the same credential history and may be developed by an herbalist or other health care practitioner without a scientific or chemist background. They simply follow some of the suggested recipes in the cook book of cosmetics, *The Cosmetic Bench Reference*, or they produce formulas suggested by the chemical manufacturer; not exactly great science considering that some of these chemicals are absorbed into our bodies.

Don't be afraid to ask if there is a chemist or scientist formulating the products, although this isn't always foolproof. One woman who attended one of my seminars called the manufacturer of the product line she was presently using and asked why they were using potentially harmful ingredients in their products. A few days later, during a conversation between myself and their chemist, he asked where I was getting my information.

"Through medical and scientific research," I replied and asked where he got his.

"From the CTFA." he said.

Well, folks, that is the Cosmetic, Toiletries and Fragrance Association and I'm hard pressed to believe that they would publish something derogatory about what they wanted to sell.

Another manufacturer that I spoke with said that he realized that some of the ingredients being used were perhaps harmful but said "everyone was using them." Well, herein lies the problem. Changing an apparently harmful ingredient to a safer one costs money. With shampoo for instance, the cap on the bottle generally costs more than the ingredients. Switching from sodium lauryl sulfate to a safer alternative can drastically alter the price.

Marketing is the name of the game in cosmetics and personal care products. For a transition to occur, the emphasis must be placed on the quality of the ingredients in the product, not the quality of the marketing.

Summary

Canada labeling laws - In Canada labeling a cosmetic involves few guidelines. One of the curious aspects of government concern involves the wording used on labels to describe the intended use of a product. Remember cosmetics and drugs are defined in terms of their intended use, not in terms of their ingredients. A cosmetic cannot technically be perceived as an instrument of change or healing or else it would be considered a drug. Therefore the use of verbs like *protect* must be applied very carefully by the manufacturer. In the case of a lotion, deemed a cosmetic, the label can say it protects against the drying effect of the wind but it cannot say it *protects* against sunburn. Neither can it make a claim such as it will *heal* a condition, because healing implies that it is actively charged or possesses active ingredients and then would be considered a drug. So the woe-begotten manufacturer must promote his product very carefully around a maze of semantic guidelines. All of this said, there is little the government can do to stop manufacturers from using vague terms that may or may not be misinterpreted by the average consumer. Clever label writers get around this by saying the product will "reduce the signs of aging." Wrinkle creams are notorious abusers of misrepresentative labeling. If a cream claims it will make a physical change in the structure of your skin, i.e. eliminate wrinkles, it will be classified as a drug.

I phoned up Health and Welfare Canada and requested information on labeling laws. A few weeks later I received a copy of a set of guidelines produced by the Canadian government regarding the labeling of cosmetics. The guide, though only a thin booklet, contained a considerable amount of information on the required dimensions of labels and the proper use of quantity denomitations. I was beginning to think I had receive the wrong booklet since, as I neared the end, I had yet to see any information on the labeling the ingredients on a product for sale as a cosmetic.

When I reached the section on "Avoidable Hazards" in the labeling laws, I thought—at last, some hard and fast regulations laid out by the government to protect me, but it did little to make me feel safe. In fact it brought home all too clearly how alone we all are out here in the cosmetic jungle.

Avoidable Hazards and Cautions

With respect to the use without danger of cosmetics, the Act (F&D, Section 16) and regulations (Cos., Reg. Section 24) prohibit, in a very comprehensive manner, the sale of a product which presents a hazard to the health of the user. When the hazard is considered an avoidable hazard the product can be sold on condition that the label warns in an adequate fashion how to use (not to use) the product in order to eliminate the risk. The combination of instructions for use, cautions, and symbols all in English and French, would satisfy this requirement. (*From Health and Welfare Canada Guide for Labeling Cosmetic*, 1988.)

For example, the label for a hair dye containing coal tar dye or coal tar dye intermediate (see section on hair dyes for dangers) must, by law contain the following warning:

CAUTION: This product contains ingredients that many cause skin irritation on certain individuals and a preliminary test according to accompanying directions should first be made. The product must not be used for dyeing the eyelashes or eyebrows. To do so may cause blindness.

By including this caution and further instructions on how to carry out the prescribed testing, the manufacturer has fulfilled his obligation—nothing else need be said as to what exactly is in the product and the onus is now on the consumer to be the tester of the product for their own personal use.

Initially, when I phoned Health and Welfare Canada asking about the requirements for labels on cosmetics, I was informed that they could send the appropriate forms which I could fill out and send back to them so they could have a permanent list of ingredients in their files. If any problems arose with the product they would be able to pull the file and check the ingredients. They do not pre-approve the ingredients.

As mentioned earlier in this book, my research shows that there are some beneficial and effective ingredients in cosmetics but the consumer has no way of knowing which products contain these ingredients and the manufacturer has no way of telling the consumer about the use of such ingredients. Any claims of structural changes must be proven by the manufacture through the same approval course that a drug must undergo. This creates a real quandary for both the manufacturer and the consumer. A product may contain an *active* ingredient yet it will not be used as a claim or promotional aspect on the label or in the advertisements since such claims must be proven and that takes time and money.

Personal care products sold in health food stores and salons usually have labels showing the ingredients. Also, some specialty stores will have a book with a list of ingredients for all their products that you can ask to see.

What we need to do

In the United States, the FDA requires that labels on cosmetics list all ingredients. In 1973, ingredient statements on cosmetics were required under the *Fair Packaging and Labeling Act*. Before that time the US consumer (like Canadians in the present) could only guess at what was in their cosmetics. Now they can find out about the ingredients listed by checking the *International Cosmetic Ingredient Dictionary* published by the Cosmetic, Toiletries and Fragrance Association. This dictionary contains a list of the most widely used cosmetic ingredients, their definitions and their trade names and is available in many public libraries.

Despite this there is still some concern about the consumer not being able to decipher the ingredients on cosmetic labels. Many ingredients listed won't always be understandable to the consumer even with the help of the *Cosmetic Ingredient Dictionary*. They may be trade names yet to be included in the dictionary and may bear little or no resemblance to the actual chemical name. What's even worse is that manufacturers can still claim an ingredient or group of ingredients as trade secrets.

Over 20 years have gone by since the *Fair Packaging and Labeling Act* was enacted in the US and still Canada has no similar legislation. Canadians must demand ingredient labels so they can make informed decisions about their personal care products. Cosmetic and personal care product labels are seen as a low priority by Health and Welfare Canada. This must change. These products are used extensively everyday by practically the entire population. They are, in my opinion, and the opinion of many independent researchers, not adequately tested for their use on and in the human body. Change will only come as we, the consumers, demand it. Clear and honest declarations of what is in our products is the only solution. Take care when buying your cosmetics. Be aware of what the industry is selling!

Write to the FDA or Health Canada and demand that a thorough investigation of cosmetic ingredients take place immediately. Your voice needs to be heard. Let it resonate with others until it becomes louder than thunder. And, rest assured that the storm won't pass until this atrocity is halted completely and permanently. Remember, the cosmetic industry has been selling images, illusions and hope because we've been giving them permission to do so. Let's make the industry do an about-face on their labeling, marketing and ingredients.

nine

Where Do We Go From Here?

We now know the hazards of some of the ingredients in our personal care products. What do we do now? Make intelligent alterations in lifestyle to help create a more healthful future!

Thankfully, we have choices. This chapter will help explain the options available to us in accordance with our own needs and desires. As concerned consumers, I believe it is up to us to let the industry know exactly what our desires are. If it is our wish to have more healthful personal care products then we can show that by the choices we make. Manufacturers are in the business to make money and if they see us opt for the healthy products of the competition they should follow suit by producing them. In the meantime, we need to become investigative shoppers, analyzing ingredients for their beneficial properties and questioning others for their potentially harmful effects. Unless you have ascertained that you are using completely safe, therapeutic, quality products, you are well advised to use cosmetics sparingly and infrequently. Take time to learn about each ingredient on the label. If the ingredient isn't listed in the glossary of this book, go to the library or search the Web. Write to the manufacturer if you have questions regarding the formulation. No response? No buy!

Some of us may wish to choose products that are 100 percent chemical free, while others may simply want to avoid ingredients deemed carcinogenic, mutagenic or toxic. Whatever our choice, we have the power to select what is right for us as individuals with unique requirements.

The beauty ritual is too deeply ingrained in culture for me to suggest that you halt your regimes entirely. You could simply plead ignorance and continue with whatever products you are presently using. One day though, you may regret that you didn't make the changes when you could. Too many of us have to bottom out before we are willing to look at our lifestyles and make appropriate changes. Don't be of the "wish I could have, would have, should have" mentality. Act now!

Pure and Simple

The safest, albeit least welcome, method of skin care would be to use purified water and nothing else. This method is often adopted by men who use electric shavers. They seldom, so they tell me, use any soap on their faces unless the shampoo dribbles down from their hair. Some women do the same. The *au naturelle* women who shuns cosmetics of all kinds, could possibly get away with this method. A damp face-cloth, or a splash of water, and away they go. Their natural lipids and dead skin cells are protecting them as nature had intended.

What about our hair. Do we just let it mat into dreadlocks? Or, do we walk around with stringy, greasy ringlets? Just take a look at the oldest picture you can find (look in a history book if you can't find an old photo) and you will probably see that hair before the chemical era was clean and shiny. The first recipes for soap were inscribed on clay tablets by the Sumerians over 6,000 years ago. The soapwort root has been in use since the Egyptian times and was widely used by Native Americans as a gentle, sudsing cleanser. The Hopi Indians used yucca while those in Southwest America used a species of the lily family called chlorogalum. England produced their first soap in 1641 and years later Spain introduced an olive oil soap called Castile.

Yes, we survived without chemicals. Nevertheless, times changed. The population grew, conditions altered, and the need for convenience products blossomed. Production of ingredients became necessary to fill the demands of the masses. The chemical era came in at just the right time to help fulfil the needs of human-ity. Natural was out and chemicals were in. Then we started to find out that some of the chemicals in use actually produced derogatory health ramifications. All of a sudden, aware individuals were determined to go back to the way things were. They demanded natural ingredients. Today, however, most of the seemingly natural products are still affected by chemicals. The great majority of essential oils are extracted with propylene glycol or other solvents, synthetically produced, or are adulterated, which means that they may be cut with synthetic oils or diluted with nut oils. The "from coconuts" or "plant derived" ingredients use chemical processes to extract the material out of their present form. This makes it difficult for the savvy shopper to know whether or not their choices are pure and of benefit to the body. Talk about a rock and a hard place!

Pure Castile soap, for instance is made by combining a base (sodium hydroxide, sodium carbonate or potassium hydroxide) and an acid (vegetable oil or animal fats). The reaction between the two is called saponification. The yield is soap. Or, as it is described on the wrappings of the soap, all natural soap.

Reviewing sodium hydroxide in the glossary will indicate that it is extremely toxic. One drop of this on your skin can cause layers of tissue damage. Caustic soda, as it is often called, is the most widely used and available chemical. Most caustic is produced as a co-product of chlorine through electrolysis of sodium chloride. The electrolysis cells used are of the diaphragm, mercury, or membrane type; and this type of production cell has a significant effect on the kind and purity level of the end-product. *And, they call this natural?*

Understanding the complexity of chemistry isn't easy. As you can see by the above description, the reaction of a highly toxic base with an acid actually changes the compound. Now, as castile soap, it only causes mild skin irritation, although not in everyone that uses it. Most formulators are aware of this problem and counter it with skin soothing essential oils or herbs. What is unknown, though, is what happens when it penetrates the body.

As I said earlier, labelling laws prohibit a manufacturer from making any claims regarding the effectiveness of the ingredients. This is a double edged sword as far as I'm concerned. While the regulatory systems pay little attention to toxic substances entering the body through absorption, they are concerned with something safe and natural actually penetrating into the dermis or hypodermis layers of the skin. As we all know, you cannot patent a plant!

The widely used prescription hormone, Premarin, is a good example of the manipulation of something natural. For the pharmaceutical company to get a patent on the hormone (which is derived from the urine of pregnant horses) it had to change the molecular structure to demonstrate that it was unique and therefore patentable.

So what happens to these naturally occurring plant substances when the authorities decide to classify them as drugs? They will be removed from the market and probably brought back on as drugs via the pharmaceutical companies.

Can a lemon make a change in the body? Of course! It was used years ago by sailors to prevent scurvy and it contains a substance that can dissolve gallstones. Does this mean that lemons are drugs? That depends on how far the regulatory systems intend to go with this nonsense. On a global basis, our herbs and vitamins are undergoing a political takeover by the pharmaceutical interests. The natural, restorative and healing substances, so beneficial in cosmetics, may one day be prescription only (and look out—so might be lemons).

Becoming Ingredient Wise

If absolute purity is your desire and you want entirely chemical-free products then ask manufacturers for documented proof that their raw materials are indeed free of chemicals. If we start asking the right questions and turn our backs on those who do not provide sincere answers, we will change their present *modus operandi*. After all, they are in the business of making money and when it starts to dry up, they will make a change. Don't buy into the *proprietary rights* or *trade secret* jargon. It is merely a smokescreen and any company that hides behind it has their best interest—not yours—in mind.

As I said earlier, natural substances cannot be patented. Only the process of extraction, the manipulation of the natural molecule, the addition of a chemical, etc., can be trademarked or patented. Manufacturers of the so called "natural" products, therefore, provide a complete disclosure on the ingredient label. Nothing to hide—except the chemicals used in the extraction or reaction process.

Beware of ingredients that say they are from a natural source. Sodium benzoate, for instance, is often referred to as coming from benzoin gum. It's not! It is synthetically produced. Cocamidopropyl betaine is referred to as a coconut derivative. It is not—it is a amphoteric surfactant that is synthetic.

Does it really matter as to whether or not an ingredient is naturally derived with the absence of chemicals? Let me tell you about the castor oil story.

Castor oil has been used throughout history in ancient India, China, Persia, Egypt, Africa, Greece, Rome and in the Americas. Reports show that physicians used it in the 17th century both internally and externally for a wide variety of ailments. In recent years, castor oil drenched wool or cotton flannel packs have been strategically placed over the abdomen as an aid to draw out toxins. Many holistic health practitioners recommend the packs to their clients to reduce the overall toxic load in the body. Dr. Jacqueline Krohn writes in her book, *The Whole Way to Natural Detoxification*, that castor oil has a drawing power as deep as four inches into the body.

As I was attempting to find more information on this subject I decided to check the internet. I entered into the domain of the *Positive Health News* where I discovered that many people with AIDS were using and reporting on the effects of the castor oil packs. I was amazed to learn that the packs had significant effectiveness in increasing the white blood cells. With AIDS patients monitoring their white blood cell counts quite often, they were able to chart the improvement. Alas, some people reported that they received no improvement whatsoever. As editor Mark Konlee noted, they initially had no idea why the discrepancy. Then they discovered that all the people who received positive results had used a cold-pressed castor oil. Adulterating the castor oil with heat or chemicals rendered the oil inert of it's healing capacities.

So if it is healing, cleansing or restorative activity that you want out of your products, choose ingredients that are naturally derived, cold-pressed, distilled, and any other processes that do not alter the vital life force of the substance.

This is not to say that every chemical is bad. Some, providing they do not irritate or penetrate the dermis or hypodermis layers of the skin, may actually provide some benefit. The silicons—dimethicone, dimethicone copolyol, and cyclomethicone—are examples of silicons with a very large molecular weight. These silicons replace the more hazardous petroleum chemicals such as mineral oil. They lay a mesh-like pattern of molecules across the skin and allow the respiration of the skin to continue. They also allow the moisture in the skin to be retained. A simple test to determine whether or not a skin care product is suffocating your skin is to apply a thin layer of the cream or lotion to a piece of cardboard. Place one drop of water on top and wait five minutes. If the water is absorbed into the cardboard it probably won't seal the skin completely.

The grade of raw materials, i.e. pharmaceutical grade, is also not disclosed to the consumer. Manufacturers using pharmaceutical grade ingredients may pay up to five times the cost of the crude form that other companies use. Special resin filtering systems can also be used to remove contaminants. Another process is vacuum stripping. The problem here is that so very few companies go to this extent to produce safe products. Why? Too costly.

Formulating is another consideration when analyzing a product. Butyl and methyl parabens are particularly problematic when used in a formulation that has a pH under 4.5 or over 5. A few manufacturers ascertain the safety of their parabens by keeping the pH within the proper ranges. The problem here, of course, is how do you know which manufacturers do this unless you ask and they are gracious enough to give you the answer?

Now that you are wondering why all the chemicals are used in cosmetics in the first place, I'll share a few reasons—the first being cost. Chemically extracted plant derived ingredients and synthetically produced cosmetic ingredients cost less and therefore keep the price of the product in a competitive range. The second reason they prefer to use the chemical counterparts is for performance and ease in formulating. All the emulsifiers—alkoxylated alcohols, alkoxylated amides, alkoxylated amines, alkoxylated carboxylic (fatty) acids and fatty alcohols—are in the product to hold the oil-based and water-based ingredients together so they don't separate in the finished product. Lecithin, a natural alternative, is more expensive and requires more know-how to create a stable product.

We purchase products for the first time based on the packaging or based on promised performance. Creams that glide smoothly, lotions that smell favourable, shampoos that leave the hair feeling clean, conditioners that repair damage, toothpastes with appealing taste and sunscreens that prevent burns are what create repeat sales. The chemicals are there to insure that the texture, scent, and feel meets with your approval.

I will never forget the first time I made my own shampoo. Following a recipe, I decided to eliminate a chemical that I deemed unnecessary in view of the rest of the plant materials I was using. Within days I discovered why the ingredient was in the recipe. With hair that resembled the fluff on a pollinating dandelion, I realized that the ingredient prevented static electricity.

Are these chemicals beneficial to the skin? The argument between the two forces, natural and synthetic manufacturing, needs to be addressed on what each is trying to accomplish. *Synthetic* manufacturers strive hard to create skin care products that closely imitate the protective layer of the skin thereby retaining its natural moisture content. *Natural* manufacturers promote their products as being therapeutic and therefore nourish, heal, restore or otherwise improve the function of the skin. A third (rare) type of manufacturing exists, however, that goes well beyond the first two. This, to coin a term, is referred to as a *cosmeceutical.* This is where science meets skin. Judging from the research I've accumulated, many skin rectifying substances have shown tremendous promise to actually regenerate the skin at a cellular level. One such study (shown to me after I signed a non-disclosure statement) detailed how a compound found in a certain species of plant was almost identical to a constituent found in human skin. Although this was a good find, it was useless in skin care products because the size of the molecule was too large to enter the skin. The science, therefore the patentable process, was the discovery that the molecule could be made smaller by mixing it with another plant substance. This is called fractionating the molecule.

To understand ingredients and how they work, we need to take a quick journey into the physiology of skin. Take a few moments to really examine this drawing and refer back to it as each component is discussed.

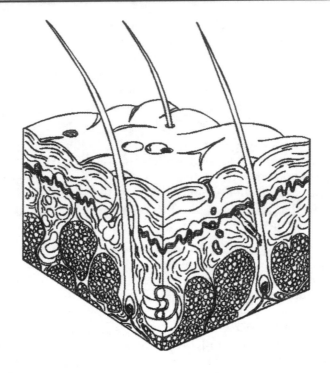

The skin's overall function is to protect the body from heat, damage and UV radiation. It also safeguards against microbial assault and some chemical penetration. The skin performs a number of functions: sensory detection of pain, heat or cold; temperature regulation, adjusting moisture-loss according to temperature and atmospheric conditions; elimination of metabolic waste, hormones and enzymes along with sweat and sebum (oils); and lastly, it is part of our eminently complex immune system.

Our personal concern is not the inner workings of the skin but rather, what makes it *look* better. A little working knowledge in the structure of skin will aid you in determining what types of ingredients you require for your particular skin care needs.

Amazingly, one square inch of skin contains 650 sweat glands, 65 hair follicles, 234 feet of nerves, 57 feet of capillaries, 19,000 sensory cells, 94 sebaceous glands, 1,250 pain receptors, 13 cold and 78 heat receptors, plus Langerhans (immune) cells.

The sweat glands are part of the temperature regulating system. When the sweat mixes with the oily secretions from the sebaceous glands it forms a protective mantel which has a pH between 5.6 and 6.6.

Underneath this protective mantel we have three layers with specific functions which we will talk about individually.

The Epidermis

The epidermis is made up of five sub-layers. The bottom layer is aptly called the germination layer. Next are the mucosum, granulosum, lucidum, and the more familiar corneum layers. This is the layer that is responsible for the look and feel of the skin. This is where your glow and youthfulness comes from. The Langerhans cells, which are responsible for the immunity, and the melanocytes which are responsible for skin colour, are in this layer.

The epidermal cells are formed in the germination layer and migrate towards the surface ending in the corneum layer where they are shed. It takes approximately 28 days to complete this process when we are young and extends to about 37 days after the age of fifty. Large amounts of water are held within the spaces between the cells. As we age, the skin's ability to retain water diminishes.

The Dermal Layer

The dermis is the layer that offers the structural support of collagen and elastin protein fibres. The collection of capillaries and blood vessels provides the route for nutrition to reach the cells. It is also composed of connective membrane, lymphatic vessels, nerve fibres, hair follicles and sweat and oil glands. The collagen is, however, the main constituent of the dermis and is chiefly made of amino acids. The collagen and it's precursor, procollagen, are responsible for binding to water, maintaining a high moisture content. The space between the collagen and elastin fibres is filled with glycoproteins known as glycosaminoglycans and fibronectin. Mucopolysaccharides are a component of the glycosaminoglycans.

The Hypodermis Layer

In this final layer, fat cells act as shock absorbers protecting the blood vessels and nerve endings. It is here where the muscle joins with the skin and where the fibrous and elastic bundles extend.

What is the Purpose of Skin Care Products?

From the consumer's point of view, we purchase them to counteract aging, alleviate blemished skin, moisten dry skin, soothe irritated skin, improve sensitive skin, and protect the skin from the environment. Can skin care products provide the proficiency that each of us is looking for? I believe there are ingredients which do help in the repair and rejuvenation process. Some manufacturers have provided me with research papers on some ingredients and, according to the studies, they do indeed provide benefit. However, as stated earlier, the manufacturer cannot tell you whether or not a product actually *does something* because that would be making a claim.

If an ingredient is absorbed or penetrates the first layer of the skin, the epidermis, it is considered a cosmetic. If it penetrates the dermis or hypodermis it is considered a drug. These rulings are presently being modified with a new classification—cosmeceuticals. However, the manufacturer is still not able to make a claim regarding the ingredient's performance.

Although the skin serves as a barrier against foreign material it also, under certain circumstances, allows the entry of it. Whether through the pilsebaceous pores, sweat gland ducts, hair follicles or through the intercellular channels that bind cells together, ingredients can penetrate. Many factors affect the penetration—the general health and hydration of the epidermal layer; high environmental humidity and high temperatures; vigorous exercise.

Manufacturers can employ specific methodology to enhance the absorption of ingredients. By sealing the skin with an occlusive agent the skin becomes more hydrated and permeable allowing for easier penetration of the active ingredient. To penetrate through the lipid (oil) containing intercellular spaces, an oil carrier is used to assist in the transportation of the therapeutic ingredient. Also, there are ingredients which are specifically developed as carriers.

Liposomes, for instance, are such carrier. As Nikolaus J. Smeh explains so well in his book, *Creating Your Own Cosmetics— Naturally,*

> They are phospholipids which are essential for the formation of every living cell. Phospholipid molecules consist of one part that attracts water (hydrophillic) and two more parts that are attracted to lipid substances (lipophillic)—very similar to an emulsifier. Nature has used this unique structure to form the outer membrane of the cells of every living thing.

> The attribute of phospholipids to allow the formation of membranes spontaneously outside of a living system have made this substance an ideal ingredient to nourish the skin, to act as a true anti-aging treatment by preventing the formation of early wrinkles, and to smooth the skin by strengthening and repairing the epidermis by topical application. These spontaneously formed membranes are called liposomes. One reason that this substance has not found wider application in cosmetics today is the relative high cost of the purified compound and the difficulty in formulating stable products containing liposomes.

> Under certain conditions phospholipids form sphere-like cellular structures of very small size called liposomes. When these liposomes are formed in a solution of bio-active substances in water, these bio-active substances end up inside the hollow spheroids enclosed by the phospholipid membranes. These liposomes readily pass through the epidermis and into the dermal layers of the skin. There, phospholipids are readily absorbed and shed the soluble active ingredient to be used by the skin structure. As an example, natural anti-oxidants (like vitamin C) can be enclosed in liposomes and carried into the skin to counteract skin aging through free radical formation.

> Phospholipids from plant sources have a very high content of essential fatty acids (70 percent linoleic acid and 6 percent linolenic acid for PC). The study also shows that phospholipids, being a natural component of the

membrane system, are hygroscopic and hold water in place inside the skin where an increased level of hydration is needed. Topically applied hydrolyzed proteins (collagen, placenta, etc.) cannot penetrate the skin barriers and perform this function. Even if they could get inside the skin they would be immediately attacked by the immune system. Phospholipids, on the other hand, have shown no adverse effects in the almost thirty years of use in medicine and now in cosmetics.

Many researchers have shown that topically applied liposomes increase the hydration of the epidermal layer and actually replace lost or damaged phospholipids of the keratinized cells throughout the epidermis.

Liposomes may be listed as lecithin or modified lecithin on the label.

This is a great discovery but it also has it's pitfalls. If the products are not contaminant free, you run the risk of carrying the toxins into the deeper layers of the skin and may in fact deliver them directly to the blood supply.

Obviously, purity is an issue when it comes to applying products to the skin. The need for contaminant-free products is much greater than the need for regulating claims. Thankfully, I'm an educator not a manufacturer. I can therefore report these findings to you by way of my website www.cosmetichealthreport.com.

The confusion over ingredients isn't simply that the ingredients themselves are toxic. In other words, the contaminant may be a by-product of the ingredient. When the FDA tested 54 ethoxylated cosmetic raw materials they found that all of them contained 1,4 dioxane. Another study showed that 40 percent of the products containing TEA were contaminated with nitrosamines, a very carcinogenic compound. My goodness this gets difficult. How do we, as lay-people, know whose products are clean?

Well, we consumers are getting smarter. Hulda Regehr Clark, author of *The Cure For All Diseases*, invented a simple little device that signals when the frequency of a toxin is detected in a product. When one of her associates tested a few of the cosmetics that I use, they were completely free of carcinogens and solvents. I am assuming that the tester and machine were accurate. This tells me that a standard of quality exists but it also says that the majority of manufacturers choose not to incorporate these costly methods.

Choosing the Right Ingredients

The primary ingredients that you should consider in any formulation are the ones that are supposed to *do something*. If a skin care product, for example, is devoid of any real benefit then you are merely wasting your money (not to mention your skin). Solely applying ingredients that are of value to the cream and not your skin isn't what you had in mind I'm sure. But, if you look up the ingredients on the label (remember, you should only buy products with the ingredients listed) in the glossary, you should be able to see if the product is strictly made up of emulsifiers, emollients, buffers, texturizers, binders and preservatives that are obviously there for devising a satisfactory cream or a protective mantel for the skin. If what you are looking for is repair and healing, then only the natural, plant extracted ingredients will serve that purpose. After all, the reason you are buying skin care products in the first place, is to reduce the signs of aging and combat dry, irritated or blemished skin.

Even preservatives can be natural. Recently, a magazine reported that one of the scientists working at one of the top cosmetic companies found, through testing with the industry's standard microbiology test, that grapefruit extract was a very potent preservative. In fact, they found that they could use 100 times less of this natural compound. Current regulation states that all cosmetics must contain one percent preservative.

So, what are we are looking for in a good skin care product? First, define what you want a skin care product to do and choose the ingredients under that heading.

Aging Skin

Alchemilla Extract

Aloe Vera

Artichoke Extract

Avocado Oil

Benzoin Essential Oil

Centella Asiatica

Clary Sage Essential Oil

Cornflower Extract

Cross Linked Elastin

Fenugreek Extract

Ginseng Extract

Glycoprotein

Glycosaminoglycans

Glycosphingolipids

Green Tea Extract

Horse Chestnut Extract

Horse Tail Extract

Hyaluronic Acid (low molecular weight)

Hydrolyzed Mucopolysaccharides

Hydrolyzed Vegetable Protein

Karite

Kukui Nut Oil

Lecithin

Linoleic Acid

Liposomes

Live Yeast Cell Extract

Macadamia Nut Oil

Meadowsweet Extract

Myrrh Essential Oil

Neroli Oil

Niacinamide

Oak Bud Extract

Oat Extract

Palmarosa Essential Oil

Panthenol

Pantothenic Acid

Papain

Phospholipids

Phytosomes

Pine Essential Oil

Pineapple Enzyme

P-Methoxycinnamate

Polyglucan

Inflammed or Irritated Skin

Alchemilla Extract

Allantoin

Aloe Vera

Arnica Extract

Artichoke Extract

Avocado Oil

Barberry Extract

Barley Oil

Benzoin Essential Oil

Bilberry Extract

Bisabolol

Borage Oil

Calendula Extract

Centella Asiatica

Chamomile Extract

Cornflower Extract

Echinacea Extract

Eucalyptus Essential Oil

Fenugreek Extract

Gotu Kola Extract

Juniper Extract

Kukui Nut Oil

Lavender Essential Oil

Lecithin

Linoleic Acid

Liposomes

Mallow Blue Extract

Marigold Extract

Marshmallow Extract

Meadowsweet Extract

Myrrh Essential Oil

Neroli Oil

Nettle Extract

Orange Flower Oil

Palmarosa Essential Oil

Passion Fruit Extract

Phospholipids

Phytosomes

Plantain Extract

Polyglucan

Dry Skin

Aloe Vera

Artichoke Extract

Avocado Oil

Clary Sage Essential Oil

Ginseng Extract

Glycoprotein

Glycosaminoglycans

Glycosphingolipids

Horse Tail Extract

Hyaluronic Acid (low molecular weight)

Hydrolyzed Mucopolysaccharides

Hydrolyzed Vegetable Protein

Jojoba Oil

Kukui Nut Oil

Lecithin

Linoleic Acid

Liposomes

Live Yeast Cell Extract

Macadamia Nut Oil

Panthenol

Phospholipids

Phytosomes

Polyglucan

Sensitive Skin

Allantoin

Aloe Vera

Avocado Oil

Balm Extract

Bilberry Extract

Chamomile Extract

Clary Sage Essential Oil

Horse Tail Extract

Jojoba Oil

Liposomes

Mallow Blue Extract

Myrrh Essential Oil

Phospholipids

Phytosomes

Blemished Skin

Allantoin

Arnica Extract

Artichoke Extract

Biotin

Birch Essential Oil

Burdock Extract

Calendula Extract

Eucalyptus Essential Oil

Juniper Extract

Lavender Essential Oil

Liposomes

Mallow Blue Extract

Melissa Essential Oil

Neem Extract

Papaya Enzyme

Peppermint Essential Oil

Phospholipids

Phytosomes

Plantain Extract

Beneficial Ingredients in all Formulations

Alginate

Ascorbyl Polypeptide

Beeswax (unbleached)

Cyclomethicone

Dimethicone Copolyol

Lecithin

Linoleic Acid

Liposomes

Myristic Acid

Oleic Acid

Orange Essential Oil

Polyglucan

Polyglucoside

Propolis

Protein

Raspberry Extract

Reticulin

Retinyl Palmitate Polypeptides

Rose Hip Seed Oil

Rose Hips Oil

Rose Essential Oil

Rose Water

Rosemary Essential Oil

Rutin

Sage Essential Oil

Seaweed Extract

Selenium

Shea Butter

Silk Proteins

Soap Bark

Soapwort Extract

Sodium Alginate

Sodium PCA (NaPCA)

Sorbitol

Sorrel Extract

Sphingolipids

Spirulina Extract

Spruce Essential Oil

Squalane

St. John's Wort Extract

Steroyl Lactylate

Sucrose Cocoate

Sugar Cane Extract

Sumac Extract

Superoxide Dimutase

Sweet Almond Oil

Tea Tree Essential Oil

Thyme Essential Oil

Tissue Respiratory Factor

Titanium Dioxide

Tocopherol

Triglyerides

Veronica Extract

Vitamin A Palmitate Oil

Vitamin B2 Powder (Riboflavine)

Vitamin B3 Powder (Niacin)

Vitamin B6 Powder (Pyridoxine)

Vitamin C Powder (Ascorbic Acid)

Vitamin D

Vitamin E

Vitamin E Acetate Oil

Watercress Extract

Wheat Germ Glycerides

Wheat Germ Oil

Wheat Protein

Witch Hazel Distillate

Xanthan Gum

Yarrow Extract

Yeast Extract

Ylang Ylang Essential

Stearyl, cetyl, oleyl and lauryl alcohols

Sorbitol, glycerin, and mannitol

Although plant derived substances are natural and more readily available to the body, please take into account the following precautions when purchasing products with essential oils in them. Purchase a good book or take a short course in aromatherapy to learn how to use the oils properly.

Pennyroyal, Aniseed, Mugwort, and Wintergreen, although rarely used, can be highly toxic unless precisely formulated.

Cedarwood, Birch, Cassia, Eucalyptus, Cinnamon, Clove, Thyme, Fennel Lemon and Orange can become increasingly toxic if used repeatedly over a period of time.

Pennyroyal, Clary Sage, Juniper, Rosemary, Basil, Hyssop, Marjoram, Myrrh, and large amounts of Peppermint should not be used during pregnancy.

Sage, Fennel and large amounts of Hyssop or Rosemary should not be used by people with epilepsy.

All essential oils should be used with caution by people who have asthma or environmental sensitivities. Use small amounts to begin with and gradually increase the amounts if there is no adverse reaction.

Furthermore, you need to check with the manufacturer to make sure that the oils and extracts are in a pure, unadulterated form. This means that they were not extracted with propylene glycol or solvents. Most of the products that I have checked are still loaded with contaminants even though the formulation looks fairly innocent. Many of the products on the market simply add a few of the natural ingredients to make them appear healthful. Just today, I requested an ingredient list from a product line that keeps sending me flyers on their presumably healthy shampoos and conditioners. The fax arrived and moments later the phone rang asking if I had received the fax. Well, I must admit I didn't spend much time with the gentleman on the phone. When I said I wasn't interested in the product because it had a high level of a mutagenic ingredient, he replied that he knew that but the chemist with the manufacturer informed him there wasn't any other way to make shampoo! Excuse me, but I think the chemist needs to go back to school. Or, perhaps he needs to learn not to be a blatant liar.

Here's what you want to Avoid

You can weed out a good 95 percent of prospective brands simply by avoiding these ingredients:

Synthetic Fragrance - Look for products that use herbal extracts or essential oils, to scent their products. Avoid any product that lists "fragrance" on the label as they are synthetic hydrocarbons.

Colour Additives - Look for products that are colored by the natural hues of the herbal extracts or natural colourants. Avoid any product that uses FD&C or D&C colours.

Petroleum Derived Ingredients - Look for products that contain natural ingredients such as shea butter, phospholipids, or hydrolyzed protein. Or, select products with the large molecular weight polymers instead (dimethicone, dimethicone copolyol, and cyclomethicone).

With this book in hand, you can further taper your list of prospective brands by looking for beneficial ingredients in accordance with your own individual needs. It doesn't leave a whole lot of brands to choose from. It will, however, save you time, money and—possibly your face. A magnifying glass may be a good accompaniment to view the tiny print of the ingredient listings. In the shopping aisles let's remember the catch phrase from *Hill Street Blues*, "Let's be careful out there."

Our Choices

During my workshops, I teach people how to make a facial cleanser and skin emollient so that people walk away with a visual sense of the function of each ingredient used in the formulation. Just like making a white sauce—and just as easy too—you make a base (butter, flour and milk) and add other condiments to it (cheese, herbs, flavoring) to enhance. Cosmetics start with a base and have other ingredients added to enhance the scent, texture, color or performance. Once you know the basics of formulating, deciphering labels becomes an easy art.

Many people wish to continue making their own cosmetics while others choose to make smart purchases. I have included some simple recipes at the end of this chapter for individuals who want to insure safety while researching the best products to use. The *Cosmetic Health Report* Website will continuously update you with exotic and therapeutically sound recipes that will be similar in texture and performance to the commercially made products.

Products that are safe do exist. The problem is that the great majority of stores do not carry them. This obviously makes it difficult for the shopper desiring safety. Health food stores carry some products which are certainly safer than many of the off-the-shelf brands. Do not think for one moment that because it is in a health food store it is safe. This is not always the case. Read the ingredient label. Small boutiques, aromatherapy shops, beauty spas, a few hair salons and a few companies that sell directly to the public appear to have the safest ingredients. Investigate yourself. Reliance on a salesperson's pitch can lead you down the wrong path. I am constantly amazed when someone calls me offering information on the product line which they sell. Most are touting their toxic products as being "safe and environmentally friendly" and their customers are "looking years younger."

There is hardly a person on earth who isn't aware of the benefits of proper nutrition. Statistics show more than 45 percent of adult Americans take nutritional supplements daily. Women take calcium and Vitamin D to maintain strong bones and take boron when pregnant. Men are rushing out to buy saw palmetto to vanquish their prostate problems and take vitamin E to strengthen their heart. Coenzyme Q10, beta-carotene, zinc, magnesium, amino acids, selenium, and a wide variety of herbs are used not only for prevention but to rectify the underlying dysfunction. We know they help regenerate the body, heal disease, build strength and stamina and keep our bodies healthy. We know this.

Now go into your bathroom and read the ingredient labels on your cosmetic products. What ingredients do you see that will help regenerate the skin cells, heal inflamed skin, build tissue strength, and maintain the health of the skin? I rest my case!

Making Your Own Cosmetics

These recipes are easy to shop for, simple to make and they give you an opportunity to test the waters as to whether or not you wish to continue making your own products. All the materials are available through health food, grocery, drug, herb and aromatherapy stores. If you live in a rural area, or don't have access to the aformementioned stores, you can check your local library for the names of herb suppliers.

Pure Shampoo

½ ounces soapwort root

6 ounces distilled water

¼ teaspoon sea salt

2 teaspoons *cold-pressed* castor oil

6 drops *pure* Rose Geranium essential oil

Contents of one vitamin E capsule 400 I.U.

In a stainless steel pot, simmer the finely chopped and crushed soapwort root with the water for 15 minutes.

Let mixture cool down then strain it well. Pour into a well-sterilized jar or bottle. Add the salt, put on the lid or cap and shake well. When the salt is completely dissolved, add the castor oil and the essential oil. Empty the contents of the vitamin E capsule into the mixture.

Keep the shampoo in the refrigerator and shake well each time you use it. It does not have high foam and works best if you apply the shampoo to both hands and run your fingers through your hair. Soapwort root is a natural sudsing agent and will clean in a gentle fashion. The cold-pressed castor oil, especially if applied to a warm scalp, will assist in the drawing out of toxins and will aid in immunity. Leave on the scalp during the duration of your shower and follow with the conditioner or rinse just prior to getting out. The Rose Geranium oil assists in balancing the scalp oil glands and is said to possess qualities that can heal and regenerate. It also acts to lift your moods—science actually shows that it is mentally soothing and reduces the stressful feeling. Rose Geranium oil contains compounds that are anti-fungal and anti-bacterial and lends its preservative qualities to the formulation. If you are planning to make larger batches, you may want to freeze some of the formulation for later use. You can also omit the vitamin E from the mixture and add one ounce of pure grain alcohol or 100 proof vodka to the formulation instead, if you want to preserve it longer. Inquire with the liquor licensing agency in your area to see if special licensing is required to purchase grain alcohol.

Hair Rinse

8 ounce apple-cider vinegar

1 ounce 100 proof vodka

1 teaspoon cold-pressed castor oil

1 ½ oz dried herbs or 4 ½ oz fresh herbs

To Make The Herbal Solution

Choose herbs that are organically grown, pesticide-free and fresh. If you do not have a local supplier see the source list in the appendix.

Sterilize a wide-mouthed jar with a tight fitting lid and pour in the vinegar and alcohol. Next, chop the herbs of your choice and shake well to mix. If you are using any fresh herbs be sure to wash them carefully and gently and dry quickly by blotting with a clean towel or unbleached paper towels. Shake the jar every few days and store in a cool dark place. In two weeks you can strain the solution through a cloth and then a paper sieve, removing the small particles of herbs.

Add to the solution, 1 teaspoon castor oil. This solution does not require refrigeration; it will keep at room temperature for a considerable length of time. You can vary the herbs you use. There are many books on the subject of herbs and you can refer to the appendix at the back of the book for a listing of some titles.

Keep an empty bottle or jug in the shower or other area where you wash your hair. Add 1 tablespoon of the herbal solution to a quart of warm water and rinse your hair.

Herbal Solution For Normal Hair

Use 1 ½ ounces of any four herbs in equal parts. If you are using fresh herbs you will need about 4 ½ ounces. Choose from Calendula, Burdock, Nettle, Rosemary, Clover, Birch or Horsetail.

Herbal Solution For Light Hair

Use 1 ½ ounces of any four herbs in equal parts. If you are using fresh herbs you will need about 4 ½ ounces. Choose from Chamomile, Rhubarb root (squashed), Marigold, Burdock, Nettle, Clover, Birch or Horsetail.

Herbal Solution For Dark Hair

Use 1 ½ ounces of any four herbs in equal parts. If you are using fresh herbs you will need about 4 ½ ounces. Choose from Burdock, Nettle, Sage, Black Walnut hulls, Bay leaves, Clover, Birch or Horsetail.

Herbal Solution For Dandruff

Use 1 ½ ounces of any four herbs in equal parts. If you are using fresh herbs you will need about 4 ½ ounces. Choose from Rosemary, Coltsfoot, Sage, Chestnut, Burdock, Nettle, Calendula, Clover, Birch or Horsetail.

Herbal Solution To Promote Hair Growth

Use 1 ½ ounces of any four herbs in equal parts. If you are using fresh herbs you will need about 4 ½ ounces. Choose from Stinging Nettle, Panama Wood bark, Sage, Bay leaves, Rosemary or Birch.

Deep Conditioner

3 ounce sweet almond oil

1 ounce jojoba oil

1 ounce wheatgerm oil

10 drops of Rosemary essential oil

10 drops of Sage essential oil

10 drops of Ylang-Ylang essential oil

Contents of 1 vitamin E capsule 400 I.U.

Shake all the ingredients gently together in a sterilized glass jar with a tight fitting lid. Saturate a cotton ball with conditioning oil and apply to scalp area. Next, apply the oil to the ends of your hair. Wrap your head with plastic food wrap or a plastic bag cut open. Cover the plastic wrap with a hot towel straight from the hot water rinse/spin dry cycle of your washing machine. Leave on for 15- 25 minutes then rinse thoroughly.

The Rosemary essential oil will improve the skin metabolism and circulation in the scalp. The Sage will regulate the sebum production in the scalp and aid in the prevention of hair loss. The Ylang-Ylang has a similar effect as the Sage.

Essential Oil Fragrant Rinse

Fill a dark colored, glass spray bottle (to prevent inactivation by light), to top with distilled or purified water. For best results follow the chart below for proportions. If you are choosing two oils divide the number of drops between the two oils. For example, 1 drop of frankincense and two drops of patchouli equal the required three drops.

Add 3 drops of one (or two) of the following:

Frankincense essential oil

Patchouli essential oil

Oakmoss essential oil

Sandalwood essential oil

Vanilla essential oil

Peru essential oil

Add 6 drops of one (or two) of the following:

Ylang-Ylang essential oil

Neroli essential oil

Clary Sage essential oil

Rose essential oil

Tuberose essential oil

Rose geranium essential oil

Add 12 drops of one (or two) of the following:

Mandarin essential oil

Bergamot essential oil

Verbena essential oil

Lavender essential oil

Cedarwood essential oil

Chamomile essential oil

Fill the sterilized spray bottle with purified or distilled water. Add in the essential oils and shake gently to mix. Give the bottle a little shake each time you use it. Spritz on your hair and body and in the room if you like. Use caution when using it around other people as some individuals are sensitive to the chosen scents of others.

See Jean Rose's book, *The Aromatherapy Book*, for more details on essential oils and what mixes well together. Understanding their ability to work on both mind and body makes learning this ancient methodology a welcome gift, especially in today's world when our emotions can run amuck many times throughout the day.

You can create your own spritzers to lavishly spray around yourself throughout the day and evening. I have two favorites. One works with my body to create a more energetic environment. I use it to inspire myself into doing housework. It's a blend of Lemongrass, Grapefruit and Petitgrain. My other favorite does just the opposite. The combination of Sandalwood, Ylang-Ylang and Neroli soothes and relaxes me. Investigate your options with these wonderful creations of nature.

Body and Face Wash

For any woman that wears make-up (especially mascara), it is difficult to find a satisfactory facial cleanser that actually cleans the skin without damaging it. The ones that appear to remove the grime (not to mention mascara) always contain some sort of oil. Or, they contain ingredients that you wouldn't want on your face, such as borax or liquid soap. Prepare the recipe for Pure Shampoo and add in the essential oils that are suited to your particular needs.

Skin Tonic

1 tablespoon Marsh Mallow flowers

1 tablespoon Horsetail

1 tablespoon Plantain

1 cup distilled water

¼ cup Witch Hazel

¼ cup 100 proof vodka*

In a stainless steel pot, add the water and herbs. Bring to a boil then reduce the heat and simmer for five minutes. Strain when cool and put into a sterilized jar. Add the witch hazel and vodka. Apply to the skin after cleansing with a cotton ball.

Vodka is used as a natural preservative. If you have access to grain alcohol it is better yet. Without the alcohol your hand-crafted products would spoil within a few days. Essential oils can be used as a preservative in some products.

Skin Moisturizer (for normal skin)

1 ounce sweet almond oil

1/3 ounce beeswax

¼ teaspoon lecithin

2 teaspoons Orange Flower water (or plain distilled water)

10 drops Rose essential oil

10 drops Melissa essential oil

In a stainless steel double boiler or a pot set in a pan of very hot water, add the first four ingredients and stir gently until melted. Exchange the water in the bottom of the double boiler or the water in the pan for cold water. Mix with an electric beater or vigorously by hand until the mixture starts to thicken. Once again exchange the water in the pan or bottom of double boiler for cold water. Continue mixing until the desired consistency is reached then add the essential oils. Pour into a sterilized container and keep in the refrigerator. The essential oils offer some preservative potential.

Deodorant

20 drops Lavender essential oil

40 drops Petitgrain essential oil

40 drops Sage essential oil

½ cup baking soda

Combine the essential oils in a spray bottle or spritzer. Spread the baking soda out in a pan and evenly mist the baking soda.

Shake the pan and continue misting until the baking soda has absorbed all of the oil. Store in an airtight container. Put a small amount (about the size of a quarter) in the palm of your hand and apply to the underarms.

Toothpaste

1 tablespoon powered Myrrh

1 tablespoon dried Sage

1 tablespoon Marsh Mallow leaves

10 drops of Peppermint essential oil

Grind the three herbs in a nut or coffee grinder until well ground. Sift through an extra fine sieve several times. Put in a bottle and add the essential oil. Shake well to mix thoroughly. Pour about ½ teaspoon into the palm of the hand and dip damp toothbrush into it and brush the teeth. Rinse and use remaining tooth powder in hand. Use a drop or two of Peppermint or Spearmint essential oil in 4 ounces of purified water as a rinse.

Lip Balm

1 teaspoon cold-pressed castor oil

1 teaspoon palm kernel oil

1 teaspoon avocado oil

¼ ounce cocoa butter

1/3 ounce beeswax

12 drops essential oil (your choice)

In a small stainless steel pot or stainless steel measuring cup set in a pan of water add the first five ingredients. When dissolved and melded together, remove from heat and pour into tiny cosmetic jars. Little tub jars work best for getting your finger into the bottom of the jar. Immediately add the essential oil or group of essential oils to the container and stir gently. Use the different scented lip balm according to your mood. The close proximity of the lips to the nose allows for a steady flow of essential oil essence to the olfactory nerves at the back of the nose. From the olfactory nerves to the limbic system of the brain it enters an area where many of our emotions are processed. And you thought this balm was just for lips!

Bath Soaks

Baths are a precious ritual if you do them right. Take the time to light some candles and play some soft background music (the sound of waves crashing against the shore or the sound of waterfalls or rain are great). Always, always, use the time to mellow out. Don't think about anything stressful – replace negative thoughts with pleasant ones. Escape to the visions your mind conjures up while the body eases into relaxation.

As a general rule you can use from ten to thirty drops of essential oil in your bath water. Mix the essential oils with a teaspoon of sulfonated castor oil, grain alcohol or vodka to help the oils disperse in water.

Create your own exotic combination or choose one of the following combinations:

Old Growth Forest

Soak in a hot tub of water while visualizing the sights of the forest and breathing the scents of the outdoors. This is a great bath for men who seldom get into a tub of water. Prepare this bath for the man in your life and observe his mood when he emerges. Mix any of the following oils together totaling 10 to 30 drops. Before adding to bath water, mix the oils in 1 teaspoon of sulfonated castor oil or 1 teaspoon of grain alcohol or vodka to help disperse the oils in water.

Cedarwood essential oil

Pine essential oil

Spruce essential oil

Cypress essential oil

Fir essential oil

The Wedding Day

For that special day. Or any special day for that matter. Pick a day that you deem special enough to deserve a leisurely afternoon getting ready for the occasion. Shop in advance to make sure that you have all the ingredients on hand. Here's what you need.

Pre-bath Rub Down

½ cup sea salt

¼ cup virgin (no pun intended) olive oil

10 drops Lemon essential oil

Combine all the ingredients in a bowl. Standing in a bathtub without water, put about a tablespoon of the mixture in your hand. Starting at the feet, rub the salt mixture over the body with a circular motion, working your way up the body. This will gently exfoliate your skin.

The Bath

Mix any of the following purification oils together totaling 10 to 30 drops. Before adding to the drawn tub of hot bath water, mix the oils in 1 teaspoon of sulfonated castor oil or 1 teaspoon of grain alcohol or vodka to help disperse the oils in water.

Mandarin essential oil

Orange essential oil

Peppermint essential oil

Melissa essential oil

Lime essential oil

Juniper essential oil

Hyssop essential oil

You may also add any of the following to activate your love potential.

Jasmine absolute essential oil

Caraway essential oil

Ylang-Ylang essential oil

Rose essential oil

Cardamom essential oil

Whimsical Delight

This is an invigorating bath that should not be used at bed-time. Mix any of the following oils together totaling 10 to 30 drops. Before adding to bath water, mix the oils in 1 teaspoon of sulfonated castor oil or 1 teaspoon of grain alcohol or vodka to help disperse the oils in water.

Ginger essential oil

Benzoin balm essential oil

Myrrh essential oil

Petitgrain essential oil

Vetiver essential oil

Rosemary essential oil

Brain and Braun (Mind and Muscles)

Mix any of the following oils together totaling 10 to 30 drops. Before adding to bath water, mix the oils in 1 teaspoon of sulfonated castor oil or 1 teaspoon of grain alcohol or vodka to help disperse the oils in water.

Melilot essential oil

Vetiver essential oil

St. John's Wort essential oil

Clove essential oil

Chamomile essential oil

Cypress essential oil

Birch essential oil

Angel Time

A children's bath to calm and sedate them when their daily pressures become too great. Now is the time to introduce and indoctrinate your children to the natural way of life. Brought up with a deep awareness of nature and the gifts it supplies, children will gravitate towards prevention and natural therapies. I cannot imagine a greater gift to give a child. Their world is tougher than the one we grew up in and they need to know the powers of the earth's offering. Blend special aromatic baths specifically for each of your children. Or make up sedating, stimulating, healing and purification bath tonics and use when needed.

> Violet essential oil
>
> Heliotrope essential oil
>
> Chamomile essential oil
>
> Rose geranium oil
>
> Frankincense essential oil

Tropical Island

Set the scene for this one! All these bells and whistles will transform your bath into a journey on a tropical island. You will need:

> Music (waves crashing against the beach or comparable music)
>
> Candles (beeswax only)
>
> A pitcher of fresh juice mixed with an equal amount of water (to drink!)
>
> One of your "for company only" glasses
>
> A pair of shorts and a tee-shirt (for after the bath), or a sarong
>
> An electric fan (optional)

Recipe

¾ of a cup of mixed oils. Avocado, apricot kernel, sweet almond, or jojoba oil.

½ teaspoon Coconut essential oil

½ teaspoon Ylang-Ylang essential oil

½ teaspoon Neroli essential oil

Instructions

With the music playing softly in the background, relax your body bit by bit. Starting at your toes, slowly relax them. Next your ankles, then your shins, then continue on up the body. Once relaxed, let your mind drift off to the far side of a tropical island. There is no one around to disturb your thoughts. Just you and the trees, sand and water. Envision yourself really there. See yourself in your shorts and tee-shirt or sarong. Feel the gentle breezes (the "quiet" electric fan does wonders here), smell the air, and listen to the waves crash against the shore. Spend a few minutes here using all your senses. Now, imagine that your body is immersed in the water of the gentle wave as it travels towards the beach. Feel what that water feels like. Now bring back the music, the smell and the breeze. Spend as much time as you desire in this exotic place. Turn your head to the direction of the candles and with your mind's eye imagine that you are seeing the sun set and your day at the beach on a tropical island is over. Slowly open your eyes and reorient yourself before stepping out of the tub. Put on your resort wear (shorts and tee-shirt or sarong) and stay in the mood for as long as you can to enhance the results.

A Women's Bath Powder

For some, the ritual of bath powder following a bath is a hard one to give up. You don't have to if you make up one like the recipe below.

¼ pound food grade cornstarch

¼ ounce powered Benzoin gum

1 ounce powdered Rose petals

20 drops Ylang-Ylang Essential oil

10 drops Rose Essential Oil

In a blender or food processor, add the first 3 ingredients leaving the essentials oils to be added later. Blend until well mixed; one minute in blender, thirty seconds in food processor. Drop the oil into a small vessel. An egg cup works well. Add about a teaspoon of the powder mixture to the oils. With the flat of a spoon, mash the combination together. Add another teaspoon of powder, mix well and add to the powder mixture. Pour into a container that is large enough to allow a few inches of empty space at the top so the mixture gets well blended when you shake it. If desired, you can use the blender or food processor to further blend.

These are just a few of the many recipes available. Please check your library or bookstore for herbal cosmetic making books that contain a wide variety of recipes.

ten

Glossary

This glossary will provide you with necessary product ingredient information. If the ingredient you are looking for is not listed, break down some of its components. For example, if you are looking for Phenylacetaldehyde, look up phenyl and acetaldehyde.

Many of the so-called plant derived ingredients are extracted from the plant by using chemical processes. Essential oils are mainly derived with propylene glycol. Also, many of the natural substances are mixed with chemicals.

The ingredients which have been labelled as carcinogenic, mutagenic, toxic or as causing adverse reactions have had studies done on them either through independent researchers and scientists, the EPA, OSHA, NIOSH, ACGIH, IARC and/or the NFPA. To cite the individual outcome of each and every report would double the size of this book, therefore each has been condensed to the aforementioned aphorism. Regardless of whether it is a carcinogen or just causes an adverse reaction—harm is harm.

The following definition of terms will help explain what the various descriptions mean.

ANTIMICROBIAL/PRESERVATIVE/DISINFECTANT: used in cosmetics to control the growth of micro-organisms and bacteria which may include pseudomonas, staphylococcus and streptococcus. Besides preventing the obvious health problems that can be caused by exposure to these bacteria, anti-microbials present in cosmetics can cause discolouration, bad odor and separation of emulsions in some cases.

ANTIOXIDANTS: preservatives used to prevent fats from spoiling or becoming rancid.

ANTI-PERSPIRANT/DEODORANT: a substance that changes the pH level in the area applied, thus inhibiting moisture. Deodorant may contain some anti-perspirant. A deodorant's function is to control the odor caused by the bacterial reaction to sweat by inhibiting the growth of the bacteria. Deodorants will also contain some fragrance to mask odors.

ANTI-CAKING AGENT: a substance added to a formula that prevents the clumping together of the ingredients.

BINDER: a substance which swells or absorbs water, increases consistency and holds ingredients together.

BUFFER: a solution with a relatively stable pH level (an equal ratio between acid and alkali) which can remain unchanged by the addition of comparatively large amounts of either acid or alkali.

CHELATING AGENT: a compound that binds and precipitates (separates out of a solution or suspension) metals.

COLOUR ADDITIVE: colour of both natural and synthetic origin used widely in cosmetics. The letters FD&C in front of a colour means it can be used in food, drugs and cosmetics. D&C means the colour can only be used in drugs and cosmetics and cannot be used in a cosmetic likely to be inadvertently ingested such as in lipsticks.

CONDITIONER, HAIR: contain humectants that try to pull moisture from their surroundings much the same way they do in a lotion or body cream. Conditioners may also contain finishing agents that leave a waxy film on the hair making it feel softer and look shinier. Some protein containing conditioners may make claims that they can replace lost protein in hair but according to the American Medical Association there is little evidence that this is true. So far there is little proof that conditioners can penetrate the hair and effect any reconstruction of the damaged hair shaft.

DETERGENT/SOAP: synthetic, organic, liquid or water soluble cleansing agents not prepared from fats and oils (soaps). Detergents may be made from petroleum derivatives. They are not inactivated by hard water and do not leave a hard water scum as would soap. They may contain wetting agents or surfactants. Some may also contain antibacterial agents particularly those designed for acne cleansers and surgical type scrubs.

SOAPS: usually a mixture of sodium salts and fatty acids. Soaps are found in toothpastes, tooth powders and shaving creams.

EMOLLIENT: most emollients are a mixture of oils used in cosmetics, particularly body creams and moisturizers to prevent moisture from leaving the skin. In cosmetics they provide the smooth feeling or *glide* in a product.

EMULSIFIER: an agent used to produce an emulsion or mixture of two non-mixable liquids such as water and oil. The emulsifier allows the two to appear to become blended or homogenized.

SURFACTANT: wetting agent that lowers the surface tension of water allowing it to spread out and penetrate more readily.

FILM FORMER: a substance that helps to fix the product after application and prevent smudging. As an example, a liquid eyeliner would contain a film former.

FOAMER/STABILIZER: a substance added to a product to give it a desired consistency. Foam stabilizers could be vegetable gums, used as liquid emulsions to thicken cosmetic products and make them creamy.

GROUP: used to indicate that all ingredients which contain the same chemical compounds are classified under the same description.

HUMECTANTS/MOISTURIZER: a substance used to preserve the moisture content of materials by preventing moisture or water from leaving the skin or from a cosmetic product. Basically, it keeps your cosmetics (lipsticks, cream blusher, lotions, etc.) from drying out.

PROPELLANT: for use in aerosols. Propellants are a compressed gas that expels or propels material from a container. Chloroflurocarbons (CFCs) were most commonly used in the past because they are flammable. However, since they've been linked to the depletion of the earth's ozone layer they have systematically been removed from the marketplace. Other propellants include hydrocarbon gases such as butane and propane, carbon dioxide and nitrous oxide.

SOLVENT: a liquid used in the dissolving or dispensing of one or more substances.

SUNSCREEN/UV INHIBITOR: used in some cosmetics as an additive to protect skin against the UVB rays from the sun.

THICKENER/GELLANT: substances used to add body to cosmetics such as lotions and creams.

SKIN PROTECTANT: water repellent or oil repellent creams that act as a barrier against irritating chemicals.

PLASTICIZERS: chemicals that when added to natural or synthetic resins and rubbers make them more flexible or workable without changing the basic chemical makeup of the material.

EXFOLIANT/ANTIWRINKLE: any product that removes or abrades the outer layer of skin in order to reduce signs of aging or to appear to cause the decrease of wrinkles.

SUDSER: a chemical that promotes sudsing particularly of use in hard water conditions.

Ingredients

1-OCTADECANOL: Carcinogenic, mutagenic, toxic or causes adverse reactions. (See definition at beginning of glossary.)

1-TETRADECANOL: Carcinogenic, mutagenic, toxic or causes adverse reactions. (See definition at beginning of glossary.)

1,1,2,2-TETRACHLOROETHANE: Carcinogenic, mutagenic, toxic or causes adverse reactions. (See definition at beginning of glossary.)

1,1,2-TRICHLORO-1,2,2 TRIFLUOROETHANE: Carcinogenic, mutagenic, toxic or causes adverse reactions. (See definition at beginning of glossary.)

1,1,2-TRICHLOROETHANE: Carcinogenic, mutagenic, toxic or causes adverse reactions. (See definition at beginning of glossary.)

1,2-DIAMINOETHANE: Carcinogenic, mutagenic, toxic or causes adverse reactions. (See definition at beginning of glossary.)

1,2-DIBROMO-2,4-DICYANOBUTANE: Carcinogenic, mutagenic, toxic or causes adverse reactions. (See definition at beginning of glossary.) Can cause contact eczema.

1,2-DICHLOROETHANE: Carcinogenic, mutagenic, toxic or causes adverse reactions. (See definition at beginning of glossary.)

1,2-PHENYLENEDIAMINE: Carcinogenic, mutagenic, toxic or causes adverse reactions. (See definition at beginning of glossary.)

1,2,3-PROPANETRIOL: Carcinogenic, mutagenic, toxic or causes adverse reactions. (See definition at beginning of glossary.)

1,2,4-TRICHLOROBENZENE: Carcinogenic, mutagenic, toxic or causes adverse reactions. (See definition at beginning of glossary.)

1,2-BUTYLENE OXIDE: Carcinogenic, mutagenic, toxic or causes adverse reactions. (See definition at beginning of glossary.)

1,2-DICHLOROBENZENE: Carcinogenic, mutagenic, toxic or causes adverse reactions. (See definition at beginning of glossary.)

1,2-DICHLOROETHANE: Carcinogenic, mutagenic, toxic or causes adverse reactions. (See definition at beginning of glossary.)

1,2-DICHLOROETHYLENE: Carcinogenic, mutagenic, toxic or causes adverse reactions. (See definition at beginning of glossary.)

1,2-DICHLOROPROPANE: Carcinogenic, mutagenic, toxic or causes adverse reactions. (See definition at beginning of glossary.)

1,2-DIHYDROXYBENZENE: Carcinogenic, mutagenic, toxic or causes adverse reactions. (See definition at beginning of glossary.)

1,2-DIPHENYLHYDRAZINE: Carcinogenic, mutagenic, toxic or causes adverse reactions. (See definition at beginning of glossary.)

1,2-OXATHIOLANE-2,2-DIIDE: Carcinogenic, mutagenic, toxic or causes adverse reactions. (See definition at beginning of glossary.)

1,3-BUTADIENE: Carcinogenic, mutagenic, toxic or causes adverse reactions. (See definition at beginning of glossary.)

1,3-BUTYLENE GLYCOL: A solvent and humectant used to prevent spoilage in cosmetics. (See Ethylene Glycols Group.)

1,3-DICHLOROBENZENE: Carcinogenic, mutagenic, toxic or causes adverse reactions. (See definition at beginning of glossary.)

1,3-DICHLOROPROPENE: Carcinogenic, mutagenic, toxic or causes adverse reactions. (See definition at beginning of glossary.)

1,4-DIETHYLENE DIOXIDE: Carcinogenic, mutagenic, toxic or causes adverse reactions. (See definition at beginning of glossary.)

1,4-DIOXANE DIETHYLENE ETHER: Carcinogenic, mutagenic, toxic or causes adverse reactions. (See definition at beginning of glossary.) 40 percent of commercial cosmetic products have been shown to contain up to 85 ppm (parts per million) of the carcinogen 1,4-dioxane.

1,4-DICHLOROBENZENE: Carcinogenic, mutagenic, toxic or causes adverse reactions. (See definition at beginning of glossary.)

1,4-DIOXANE: A reactant chemical found in some shampoos and bubble baths, especially those for babies. It seems to occur in non-ionic ethoxylated surfactants that use ethylene oxide to temper the irritation factor. Carcinogenic, mutagenic, toxic or causes adverse reactions. (See definition at beginning of glossary.)

1-AMINO-2-METHYLANTHRAQUINONE: Carcinogenic, mutagenic, toxic or causes adverse reactions. (See definition at beginning of glossary.)

1-HEXADECANOL, NORMAL: Carcinogenic, mutagenic, toxic or causes adverse reactions. (See definition at beginning of glossary.)

1-NAPTHYLAMINE: Carcinogenic, mutagenic, toxic or causes adverse reactions. (See definition at beginning of glossary.)

2-BROMO-2-NITROPROPANE-1,3-DIOL: Carcinogenic, mutagenic, toxic or causes adverse reactions. (See definition at beginning of glossary.)

2-CHLORO-P-PHENYLENEDIAMINE SULFATE: Carcinogenic, mutagenic, toxic or causes adverse reactions. (See definition at beginning of glossary.)

2-ETHOXYETHYL-P-METHOXY: Carcinogenic, mutagenic, toxic or causes adverse reactions. (See definition at beginning of glossary.)

2-ETHOXYETHYL-P-METHOXYCINNAMATE: Carcinogenic, mutagenic, toxic or causes adverse reactions. (See definition at beginning of glossary.)

2-HYDROXY-2-PHENYLACETOPHENONE: Carcinogenic, mutagenic, toxic or causes adverse reactions. (See definition at beginning of glossary.)

2-HYDROXY-4-METHOXYBENZO PHENONE: Carcinogenic, mutagenic, toxic or causes adverse reactions. (See definition at beginning of glossary.)

2-HYDROXYETHYLAMINE: Carcinogenic, mutagenic, toxic or causes adverse reactions. (See definition at beginning of glossary.)

2-METHOXY-5-METHYL-4-NITROBENZENAMINE: Carcinogenic, mutagenic, toxic or causes adverse reactions. (See definition at beginning of glossary.)

2-METHOXYANILINE: Carcinogenic, mutagenic, toxic or causes adverse reactions. (See definition at beginning of glossary.)

2-METHYL-4-ISOTHIAZOLIN-3-ONE: Carcinogenic, mutagenic, toxic or causes adverse reactions. (See definition at beginning of glossary.)

2-NITRO-4-PHENYLENEDIAMINE: Carcinogenic, mutagenic, toxic or causes adverse reactions. (See definition at beginning of glossary.)

2-NITROPROPANE: Carcinogenic, mutagenic, toxic or causes adverse reactions. (See definition at beginning of glossary.)

2-PHENOXYETHANOL: Carcinogenic, mutagenic, toxic or causes adverse reactions. (See definition at beginning of glossary.)

2-TERT-BUTYLHYDROQUINONE: Carcinogenic, mutagenic, toxic or causes adverse reactions. (See definition at beginning of glossary.)

2,4-DIAMINOANISOL: Carcinogenic, mutagenic, toxic or causes adverse reactions. (See definition at beginning of glossary.)

2,4-DIAMINOANISOLE SULFATE: Carcinogenic, mutagenic, toxic or causes adverse reactions. (See definition at beginning of glossary.)

2,4-DIAMINOTOLUENE: Carcinogenic, mutagenic, toxic or causes adverse reactions. (See definition at beginning of glossary.)

2,4-TOLUENEDIAMINE: Carcinogenic, mutagenic, toxic or causes adverse reactions. (See definition at beginning of glossary.)

2,4,5,7-TETRAIODOFLUORESCEIN DISODIUM SALT: Carcinogenic, mutagenic, toxic or causes adverse reactions. (See definition at beginning of glossary.)

2,4,6-TRICHLOROPHENOL: Carcinogenic, mutagenic, toxic or causes adverse reactions. (See definition at beginning of glossary.) Cytotoxicity and genotoxicity has been established.

2,4,6-TRINITROPHENOL: Carcinogenic, mutagenic, toxic or causes adverse reactions. (See definition at beginning of glossary.)

2,4-D: Carcinogenic, mutagenic, toxic or causes adverse reactions. (See definition at beginning of glossary.)

2,4-DIAMINOANISOLE SULFATE: Carcinogenic, mutagenic, toxic or causes adverse reactions. (See definition at beginning of glossary.)

2,4-DIAMINOANISOLE: Carcinogenic, mutagenic, toxic or causes adverse reactions. (See definition at beginning of glossary.)

2,4-DIMETHYLPHENOL: Carcinogenic, mutagenic, toxic or causes adverse reactions. (See definition at beginning of glossary.)

2,4-DINITROPHENOL: Carcinogenic, mutagenic, toxic or causes adverse reactions. (See definition at beginning of glossary.)

2,4-DINITROTOLUENE: Carcinogenic, mutagenic, toxic or causes adverse reactions. (See definition at beginning of glossary.)

2,5-DIAMINOANISOL: Carcinogenic, mutagenic, toxic or causes adverse reactions. (See definition at beginning of glossary.)

2-ACETYLAMINOFLUORENE: Carcinogenic, mutagenic, toxic or causes adverse reactions. (See definition at beginning of glossary.)

2-AMINOANTHRAQUINONE: Carcinogenic, mutagenic, toxic or causes adverse reactions. (See definition at beginning of glossary.)

2-AMINOETHANOL: Carcinogenic, mutagenic, toxic or causes adverse reactions. (See definition at beginning of glossary.)

2-BROMO-2-NITROPROPANE-1, 3-DIOL: Can form carcinogens in cosmetics or on the skin. Often used in shampoos and moisturizers; avoid products with this ingredient. Sometimes called BNPD. Causes allergic contact dermatitis.

2-ETHOXYETHANOL: Carcinogenic, mutagenic, toxic or causes adverse reactions. (See definition at beginning of glossary.)

2-METHOXYETHANOL: Carcinogenic, mutagenic, toxic or causes adverse reactions. (See definition at beginning of glossary.)

2-NAPHTHYLAMINE: Carcinogenic, mutagenic, toxic or causes adverse reactions. (See definition at beginning of glossary.)

2-NITROPHENOL: Carcinogenic, mutagenic, toxic or causes adverse reactions. (See definition at beginning of glossary.)

2-NITROPROPANE: Carcinogenic, mutagenic, systemic effects, causes adverse reactions or is toxic.

3-CARBETHOXYPSORALEN: Carcinogenic, mutagenic, phototoxin; reacts with UV radiation to yield genotoxin, causes adverse reactions or is toxic.

3-METHYL ISOTHIAZOLIN: Carcinogenic, mutagenic, May cause contact allergies, causes adverse reactions or is toxic.

3,3'-DICHLOROBENZIDINE: Carcinogenic, mutagenic, toxic or causes adverse reactions. (See definition at beginning of glossary.)

3,3'-DIMETHOXYBENZIDINE: Carcinogenic, mutagenic, toxic or causes adverse reactions. (See definition at beginning of glossary.)

3,3'-DIMETHYLBENZIDINE: Carcinogenic, mutagenic, toxic or causes adverse reactions. (See definition at beginning of glossary.)

3,7-DIMETHYL-7-HYDROXYOCTENAL: Carcinogenic, mutagenic, toxic or causes adverse reactions. (See definition at beginning of glossary.)

3-PHENYLPROPENAL: Carcinogenic, mutagenic, toxic or causes adverse reactions. (See definition at beginning of glossary.)

4-CHLORO-1,2-PHENYLENEDIAMINE: Carcinogenic, mutagenic, toxic or causes adverse reactions. (See definition at beginning of glossary.)

4-ISOPROPYL-DIBENZOYLMETHANE HEXACHLOROPHENE: Carcinogenic, mutagenic, toxic or causes adverse reactions. (See definition at beginning of glossary.)

4-METHOXY-3-PHENYLENEDIAMINE: Carcinogenic contaminants of cosmetic products.

4-METHOXY-M-PHENYLENE DIAMINE: Carcinogenic, mutagenic, toxic or causes adverse reactions. (See definition at beginning of glossary.)

4-METHOXYANILINE: Carcinogenic, mutagenic, toxic or causes adverse reactions. (See definition at beginning of glossary.)

4-METHYL-2,4-PENTANEDIOL: Carcinogenic, mutagenic, toxic or causes adverse reactions. (See definition at beginning of glossary.)

4-NITRO-O-PHENYLENEDIAMINE: Mutagenic, causes adverse reactions or is toxic.

4-NOPD: Carcinogenic, mutagenic, toxic or causes adverse reactions. (See definition at beginning of glossary.)

4,4'-THIODIANILINE: Carcinogenic, mutagenic, toxic or causes adverse reactions. (See definition at beginning of glossary.)

4,5,8-TRIMETHYLPSORALEN: Carcinogenic, mutagenic, toxic or causes adverse reactions. (See definition at beginning of glossary.)

4,6-DINITRO-O-CRESOL: Carcinogenic, mutagenic, toxic or causes adverse reactions. (See definition at beginning of glossary.)

4-AMINODIPHENYL: Carcinogenic, mutagenic, toxic or causes adverse reactions. (See definition at beginning of glossary.)

4-DIMETHYLAMINOAZOBENZENE: Carcinogenic, mutagenic, toxic or causes adverse reactions. (See definition at beginning of glossary.)

4-NITROBIPHENYL: Carcinogenic, mutagenic, toxic or causes adverse reactions. (See definition at beginning of glossary.)

4-NITROPHENOL: Carcinogenic, mutagenic, toxic or causes adverse reactions. (See definition at beginning of glossary.)

5-CHLORO-2-METHYL-4-ISO THIAZOLIN-3-ONE: Studies show that it may cause contact dermatitis.

5-CHLORO-3-METHYL ISOTHIAZOLONE: Studies show that it may cause contact dermatitis.

5-METHOXYPSORALEN: Phototoxic; reacts with UV radiation to yield gentoxin.

5,7-DIHYDROXY-4-METHYL COUMARIN: Found to be a skin sensitizer.

5,7-DIHYDROXYCOUMARIN: Found to be a skin sensitizer.

5-NITRO-O-ANISIDINE: Carcinogenic, mutagenic, toxic or causes adverse reactions. (See definition at beginning of glossary.)

6-METHYLQUINOPHTHALONE: Phototoxic; reacts with UV radiation to yield gentoxin.

7-METHYLPYRIDO[3,4-C]PSORALEN: Phototoxic; reacts with UV radiation to yield gentoxin.

8-METHOXYPSORALEN (METHOXSALEN): Phototoxic; reacts with UV radiation to yield gentoxin.

ABIETIC ACID: Used as a texturizer in soaps. It is extracted from pine rosin.

ACACIA: Used as a stabilizer in cosmetics. Extracted from the acacia tree. It can cause allergic reactions.

ACETALDEHYDE: Carcinogenic, mutagenic, toxic or causes adverse reactions. (See definition at beginning of glossary.)

ACETAMIDE MEA: A humectant, used in a product to retain moisture, i.e., cream blusher and lipsticks will contain a humectant to keep them from drying out. Carcinogenic, mutagenic, toxic or causes adverse reactions. (See definition at beginning of glossary.)

ACETAMIDE: Carcinogenic, mutagenic, toxic or causes adverse reactions. (See definition at beginning of glossary.)

ACETONE: Used in nail polish and polish removers. Carcinogenic, mutagenic, toxic or causes adverse reactions. (See definition at beginning of glossary.)

ACETONITRILE: A solvent, (also see Acetone in 20 Most Common Chemicals found in Fragrance section) is used to dissolve or dispense of one or more substances as in nail polish remover. Carcinogenic, mutagenic, toxic or causes adverse reactions. (See definition at beginning of glossary.)

ACETYL ETHYL TETRAMETHYL TETRALIN: Used in perfumes. Can produce hyperirritability and other system effects.

ACETYLATED LANOLIN ALCOHOL: Natural lanolin processed into a hypo allergenic state. Repels water and is used as a water-resistant film to reduce water loss through the skin. An emollient, emulsifier and base. Used in skin, hair and bath preparations. Derived from the sheep's wool and extracted without harm to the animal. (See Lanolin Alcohol.)

ACID BLUE 74: Suspected carcinogen, teratogen, or toxin.

ACID BLUE 9: Suspected carcinogen, teratogen, or toxin.

ACID BLUE AMMONIUM SALT: Suspected carcinogen, teratogen, or toxin.

ACID GREEN 5: Suspected carcinogen, teratogen, or toxin.

ACID RED 18: Suspected carcinogen, teratogen, or toxin.

ACID RED 27: Suspected carcinogen, teratogen, or toxin.

ACID RED 87: Suspected carcinogen, teratogen, or toxin.

ACID VIOLET 49: Suspected carcinogen, teratogen, or toxin.

ACID YELLOW 73 SODIUM SALT: Suspected carcinogen, teratogen, or toxin.

ACROLEIN: Carcinogenic, mutagenic, toxic or causes adverse reactions. (See definition at beginning of glossary.)

ACRYLAMIDE: Carcinogenic, mutagenic, toxic or causes adverse reactions. (See definition at beginning of glossary.)

ACRYLATES/C 10-30 ALKYL ACRYLATE CROSSPOLYMER: Emulsion stabilizer and viscosity increasing agent. Used in skin care products, moisturizer compounds or fragrance preparation. Synthetic.

ACRYLIC ACID: Carcinogenic, mutagenic, toxic or causes adverse reactions. (See definition at beginning of glossary.)

ACRYLONITRILE: Carcinogenic, mutagenic, toxic or causes adverse reactions. (See definition at beginning of glossary.)

AETT: Used in fragrances as a fixative. Animal studies show that it damages the brain, spinal cord and other neuropathological conditions and may lead to death. It is readily absorbed by the skin and may still be in use as it has not been banned.

ALBUMEN: A class of protein. It has a tightening and film-producing effect on the skin. Animal, fruit or vegetable derived.

ALCOHOL C-12: Carcinogenic, mutagenic, toxic or causes adverse reactions. (See definition at beginning of glossary.)

ALCOHOL C-16: Carcinogenic, mutagenic, toxic or causes adverse reactions. (See definition at beginning of glossary.)

ALCOHOL: Water and oil solvent, fast drying, carrying agent, antifoaming agent, cosmetic astringent (solvent) and viscosity decreasing agent. A long chained molecule does not penetrate the skin. When it is used with water it becomes somewhat water soluble. This would be used to condition and to hydrate. Some alcohols are moisturizing (fatty alcohols, etc.). Naturally derived from vegetable or grains or synthetically produced. Also called ethyl alcohol or ethanol. Carcinogenic, mutagenic, toxic or causes adverse reactions. (See definition at beginning of glossary.)

ALCOHOLS AND POLYOLS (GROUP): May cause contact dermatitis.

ALDRIN: Carcinogenic, mutagenic, toxic or causes adverse reactions. (See definition at beginning of glossary.)

ALFALFA EXTRACT: An ingredient used in face masks and in the treatment of skin damage. High in vitamins A, B, C, D and E. An anti-fungal. Contains saponins. Vegetable derived.

ALGAE EXTRACT: Rich in the same vital nutrients, trace elements and amino acids present in human blood plasma, allowing it to penetrate the skin more thoroughly than most other ingredients. It is said to help nourish and remineralize the skin although I have not been able to find any research to corroborate this.

ALGIN: A gelatinous substance derived from seaweed. It absorbs 300 times its weight in water. It acts as an emulsifier, stabilizer and thickening agent.

ALGINATE: (See Sodium Alginate.)

ALKANOAMIDES (GROUP): Nitrosamines can form in all cosmetic ingredients containing amines and amino derivatives with nitrogen compounds. Nitrosamines are known to be carcinogens, cause allergic reactions and contact dermatitis.

ALKOXYLATED ALCOHOLS (GROUP): May contain dangerous levels of dioxane, a potent toxin, as a manufacturing by-product.

ALKOXYLATED AMIDES (GROUP): Nitrosamines can form in all cosmetic ingredients containing amines and amino derivativs with nitrogen compounds. Nitrosamines are known to be carcinogens, cause allergic reactions and contact dermatitis.

ALKOXYLATED AMINES (GROUP): May contain dangerous levels of ethylene oxide and/or dioxane, both potent toxins, as a manufacturing by-product.

ALKOXYLATED CARBOXYLIC ACIDS (GROUP): May contain dangerous levels of ethylene oxide and/or dioxane, both potent toxins, as a manufacturing by-product.

ALKYL BENZENE SULFONATE: A sufactant that is not often used because of its inability to biodegrade. (See Benzene.)

ALKYL ETHER SULFATES (GROUP): Nitrosamines can form in all cosmetic ingredients containing amines and amino derivatives with nitrogen compounds. Nitrosamines are known to be carcinogens, cause allergic reactions and contact dermatitis.

ALKYL SULFATES (GROUP): May cause skin irritation and dermatitis.

ALKYL-PHENOL-ETHOXYLADES: Used in the production of many shampoos. This substance has been found to mimic estrogen. Carcinogenic, mutagenic, toxic or causes adverse reactions. (See definition at beginning of glossary.) (See Phenol and Ethylene Glycol.)

ALLANTOIN: Extracted from comfrey root wheat sprouts, tabacco seeds and sugar beets. May also be synthetically produced from uric acid. An anti-inflammatory and anti-irritant, healer and soothing emollient for skin. Helps promote cellular renewal by cleaning away necrotic tissue and hastening the growth of new healthy tissue. Widely used in cosmetics for its soothing and healing properties. Make sure the allantoin you buy is from a natural source.

ALLYL BUTYRATE: Used in cosmetics as an absorption base and as an emulsifier. Esters are derived from unsaturated fats. Vegetable glycerin, shea or cocoa butter, beeswax and jojoba are examples of fatty acid wax esters. Cetyl alcohol from coconut palm kernels is a fatty acid ester. May be synthetically produced.

ALLYL CAPRATE: Used in cosmetics as an absorption base and as an emulsifier. Esters are derived from unsaturated fats. Vegetable glycerin, shea or cocoa butter, beeswax and jojoba are examples of fatty acid wax esters. Cetyl alcohol from coconut palm kernels is a fatty acid ester. May be synthetically produced.

ALLYL CAPROATE: Used in cosmetics as an absorption base and as an emulsifier. Esters are derived from unsaturated fats. Vegetable glycerin, shea or cocoa butter, beeswax and jojoba are examples of fatty acid wax esters. Cetyl alcohol from coconut palm kernels is a fatty acid ester. May be synthetically produced.

ALLYL CHLORIDE: Carcinogenic, mutagenic, toxic or causes adverse reactions. (See definition at beginning of glossary.)

ALMOND OIL: A nut oil high in linoleic, oleic and other fatty acids. Excellent for chapped or very dry skin. Healing and moisturizing. Nearly colorless and, odorless, almond oil is used in soaps, moisturizers and creams. If the almond oil is a synthetic then it is known as benzaldehyde. Benzaldehyde is carcinogenic, mutagenic, toxic or causes adverse reactions. (See definition at beginning of glossary.)

ALOE/ALOE EXTRACT/ALOE POWDER/ALOE VERA: A rich emollient known to promote healing to damaged or dry hair and skin. Extracted from the Aloe Vera plant. One of the oldest medicinal plants known. It is a natural oxygenator (drawing and holding oxygen to the skin) and acts as a surfactant, emollient, astringent, moisturizer, mild wound healer, skin soother and nutrient. It is also a skin protectant. Externally used for skin diseases, burns, bruises, eczema, sunburns and helps prevent scar tissue. Also helps to avoid infection and helps to regenerates skin tissue with no scarring and normal pigmentation of the skin returns.

ALPHA-HYDROXYTOLUENE: Carcinogenic, mutagenic, toxic or causes adverse reactions. (See definition at beginning of glossary.)

ALPHA-METHYLQUINOLINE): Carcinogenic, mutagenic, toxic or causes adverse reactions. (See definition at beginning of glossary.)

ALPHA-PINENE: Carcinogenic, mutagenic, toxic or causes adverse reactions. (See definition at beginning of glossary.)

ALPHA-HYDROXY ACIDS: An exfoliant, anti-wrinkle product, found in cosmetics—from skin care to hair products. It strips the outer layer of skin to produce a smoother finish. This may be caused because it acts as an irritant which causes the skin to puff, up thus temporarily filling out lines and wrinkles. More testing for safety and efficacy needs to be done. FDA warns that strengths over 3 percent may thin the skin over time. Practically all fruit acids are purchased from one chemical supplier who holds the patent on Alpha-hydroxyl Acids. Originally, it was used as a solvent in cleaning compounds and for tanning leather in the U.S. The exception to this is the natural sugar cane glycolics. Less irritation was found with the natural ingredients, perhaps because of the synergistic effect of the other compounds found in the natural source.

ALUMINUM CHLOROHYDRATE: Used in antiperspirants, it acts by altering the pH level of the skin on which it is applied, thereby retarding the flow of perspiration. Aluminum itself is listed as carcinogenic, mutagenic or toxic.

ALUMINUM HYDRATE or ALUMINA: A filler or binder used in foundations. It is a natural or synthetic form of aluminum found in bauxite and corundum. It can be irritating to the respiratory tract if inhaled. Aluminum itself is listed as carcinogenic, mutagenic or toxic.

ALUMINUM OXIDE: Carcinogenic, mutagenic, toxic or causes adverse reactions. (See definition at beginning of glossary.)

ALUMINUM POWDER: For external use only, including eye area. A colour additive in cosmetics. Iridescent colours in eyeshadows are achieved by adding pure aluminum. It has received FDA approval for use in cosmetics. Aluminum itself is listed as carcinogenic, mutagenic or toxic.

ALUMINUM STEARATE: A thickener and gellant used to add body to a substance. Aluminum itself is listed as carcinogenic, mutagenic or toxic.

ALUMINUM ZIRCONIUM TETRACHLOROHYDREX GLY: Used in anti-perspirants. Aluminum itself is listed as carcinogenic, mutagenic or toxic.

ALUMINUM: Carcinogenic, mutagenic, toxic or causes adverse reactions. (See definition at beginning of glossary.)

AMINE (GROUP): Nitrosamines can form in all cosmetic ingredients containing amines and amino derivativs with nitrogen compounds. Nitrosamines are known to be carcinogens, cause allergic reactions and contact dermatitis.

AMINOFORM: Carcinogenic, mutagenic, toxic or causes adverse reactions. (See definition at beginning of glossary.)

AMINOMETHYL PROPANOL: A nitrogen compound used to make hair fixatives soluble in water. A pH adjuster for hair and skin cleansing products. Used as an emulsifying agent for cosmetic creams and lotions. Avoid.

AMMONIA: Carcinogenic, mutagenic, toxic or causes adverse reactions. (See definition at beginning of glossary.)

AMMONIUM CHLORIDE: Used in permanent waves solutions and in some facial washes. Carcinogenic, mutagenic, toxic or causes adverse reactions. (See definition at beginning of glossary.)

AMMONIUM COCOYL ISETHIONATE: Surfactant and cleaning agent. Extra gentle.

AMMONIUM LAURETH SULFATE: Used in hair products and bubble baths. Has a small molecular weight and is readily absorbed by the skin. Laureth means that it contains ether which is listed as carcinogenic, mutagenic, toxic or causes adverse reactions. (See definition at beginning of glossary.)

AMMONIUM LAURYL SULFATE: Used mainly in shampoo, it has a high molecular weight and has the ability to bind on to dirt like a magnet which is then rinsed from the hair scalp. Apparently many manufacturers shy away from using it because of formulation difficulties and expense.

AMMONIUM NITRATE: Carcinogenic, mutagenic, toxic or causes adverse reactions. (See definition at beginning of glossary.)

AMMONIUM STEARATE: An ester of a fatty acid. Esterfication of fatty acids is a condensation reaction in which the molecule of acid unites with a molecule of alcohol with the elimination of a molecule of water.

AMMONIUM THIOGLYCOLATE: Used in permanent wave solutions. It has been found to be a mutagen. (See mutagen.)

AMPHOTERIC-6: An emulsifier and surfactant found in shampoos and conditioners. It is one of four types of sodium lauryl sulfate. Sodium lauryl sulfate has been found to be a mutagen. (See sodium lauryl sulfate.)

ANGELICA: Used in health oriented skin care products. This herb (Angelica archangelica) is said to soothe the nerves of the skin.

ANILINE: Carcinogenic, mutagenic, toxic or causes adverse reactions. (See definition at beginning of glossary.)

ANIONIC: A form of surfactant (negatively charged) used primarily in shampoos and conditioners due to its relative mildness, its foaming properties and low cost. It is an emulsifier and surfactant, also one of the four categories of SLS. Sodium lauryl sulfate has been found to be a mutagen.

ANNATTO: A naturally occurring red-yellow dye derived from the dried pulp of the Bixa orellana fruit.

ANTHANTHRENE: Carcinogenic, mutagenic, toxic or causes adverse reactions. (See definition at beginning of glossary.)

ANTHIUM DIOXIDE: A stable form of chlorine dioxide. Safe, mild to delicate tissue. Breaks down food film so bacteria have nothing to feed on. Neutralizes *sulfur-type* compounds which produce bad breath. It also breaks down the thin protein layer that clings to the enamel on the teeth. Because this layer is sticky it attracts food stains. Removing this layer produces whiter teeth. It has been clinically proven to aid in the arrest of gingivitis.

ANTHRACENE: Carcinogenic, mutagenic, toxic or causes adverse reactions. (See definition at beginning of glossary.)

ANTIMONY LACTATE: Carcinogenic, mutagenic, toxic or causes adverse reactions. (See definition at beginning of glossary.)

ANTIMONY PENTACHLORIDE: Carcinogenic, mutagenic, toxic or causes adverse reactions. (See definition at beginning of glossary.)

ANTIMONY PENTAFLUORIDE: Carcinogenic, mutagenic, toxic or causes adverse reactions. (See definition at beginning of glossary.)

ANTIMONY POTASSIUM TARTRATE: Carcinogenic, mutagenic, toxic or causes adverse reactions. (See definition at beginning of glossary.)

ANTIMONY TRIBROMIDE: Carcinogenic, mutagenic, toxic or causes adverse reactions. (See definition at beginning of glossary.)

ANTIMONY TRICHLORIDE: Carcinogenic, mutagenic, toxic or causes adverse reactions. (See definition at beginning of glossary.)

ANTIMONY TRIFLUORIDE: Carcinogenic, mutagenic, toxic or causes adverse reactions. (See definition at beginning of glossary.)

ANTIMONY TRIOXIDE: Carcinogenic, mutagenic, toxic or causes adverse reactions. (See definition at beginning of glossary.)

ANTIMONY: Used in the past for making of kohl (black eye coloring). Today, most kohl is made with chemicals. Carcinogenic, mutagenic, toxic or causes adverse reactions. (See definition at beginning of glossary.)

APPLE CIDER VINEGAR: Found in toners; may be used with water as an *acid rinse* to adjust the skin's own pH if it has being altered by harsh cleansers.

APRICOT KERNEL OIL: Natural oil from apricot pits, also known as persic oil. An emollient similar in composition to almond oil, it has a softening effect on the skin.

ARABIC GUM: An plant gum used as a thickener and emulsifier in creams and lotions and as a hair set in styling gels and sprays. (See Acacia)

ARNICA EXTRACT: Used in hair, scalp and skin care products. It is a skin freshener, soother, cleansing agent and moisturizer. It is derived from dried flower heads, roots or rhizomes of Arnicamontana. Rich in fatty acids and vitamins A, B, C and D.

ARSENIC ACID: Carcinogenic, mutagenic, toxic or causes adverse reactions. (See definition at beginning of glossary.)

ARSENIC PENTOXIDE: Carcinogenic, mutagenic, toxic or causes adverse reactions. (See definition at beginning of glossary.)

ARSENIC TRICHLORIDE: Carcinogenic, mutagenic, toxic or causes adverse reactions. (See definition at beginning of glossary.)

ARSENIC TRIOXIDE: Carcinogenic, mutagenic, toxic or causes adverse reactions. (See definition at beginning of glossary.)

ARSENIC: Carcinogenic, mutagenic, toxic or causes adverse reactions. (See definition at beginning of glossary.)

ASBESTOS: Although it is not listed on the label it may be a contaminant in talc. It is a proven carcinogen.

ASCORBIC ACID: Generally called Vitamin C. It is used in shampoos, conditioners, hair sprays, skin care and bath products. It is an antioxidant that is also used as a pH adjuster and as a preservative in cosmetics.

ASCORBYL METHYLSILANOL PECTINATE: Used as an antioxidant and a viscosity agent in personal care products. Pectin is reacted with Ascorbic acid.

ASCORBYL PALMITATE: An ester of ascorbic acid. An antioxidant for oils and fats; keeps products fresh and prevents color change. See Ascorbic acid. The palmitates are considered to be carcinogenic, mutagenic, causing adverse reactions or is toxic.

AURAMINE: Carcinogenic, mutagenic, toxic or causes adverse reactions. (See definition at beginning of glossary.)

AVOCADO OIL: An easily absorbed, nonocclusive, natural oil from avocados that is rich in vitamins A, D and E, amino acids, minerals and sterols. An excellent skin conditioner and moisturizer that is recommended for chronic eczema and other skin disorders. Known to accelerate healing.

AZULENE: An essential oil derived from German chamomile. It works as an anti-inflammatory, analgesic and detoxifier. It calms and soothes the skin.

BALSAM: Mildly antiseptic with somewhat large amounts of cinnamic or benzoic acid. Used in hair conditioners, soaps, creams and lotions for their anti-microbial properties and agreeable fragrance.

BARIUM AZIDE: Carcinogenic, mutagenic, toxic or causes adverse reactions. (See definition at beginning of glossary.)

BARIUM BROMATE: Carcinogenic, mutagenic, toxic or causes adverse reactions. (See definition at beginning of glossary.)

BARIUM CHLORATE: Carcinogenic, mutagenic, toxic or causes adverse reactions. (See definition at beginning of glossary.)

BARIUM CYANIDE: Carcinogenic, mutagenic, toxic or causes adverse reactions. (See definition at beginning of glossary.)

BARIUM HYPOCHLORITE: Carcinogenic, mutagenic, toxic or causes adverse reactions. (See definition at beginning of glossary.)

BARIUM NITRATE: Carcinogenic, mutagenic, toxic or causes adverse reactions. (See definition at beginning of glossary.)

BARIUM PERCHLORATE: Carcinogenic, mutagenic, toxic or causes adverse reactions. (See definition at beginning of glossary.)

BARIUM PERMANGANATE: Carcinogenic, mutagenic, toxic or causes adverse reactions. (See definition at beginning of glossary.)

BARIUM: Carcinogenic, mutagenic, toxic or causes adverse reactions. (See definition at beginning of glossary.)

BASIC ORANGE 2: Suspected carcinogen, teratogen, or toxin.

BASIC VIOLET 1: Suspected carcinogen, teratogen, or toxin.

BASIC VIOLET 10: Suspected carcinogen, teratogen, or toxin.

BASIC VIOLET 3: Suspected carcinogen, teratogen, or toxin.

BASIL OIL: An essential oil found in health oriented personal care products. This essential oil contains linalool, thymol, tannins, pinene and camphor, making it excellent for healing and soothing the skin. It has a stimulating effect on the skin's circulation and the oil glands and is also balancing.

BEE POLLEN: Used in skin, hand and body care products. Although it is an effective source of pantothenic acid it is not beneficial when applied topically.

BEESWAX: Natural wax produced by bees. Used in a wide variety of cosmetics as an emulsifier, thickener or stiffening agent. Can clog pores or prevent the skin from breathing if used as a primary ingredient in a formulation.

BENTONITE: A binder, bentonite a naturally occurring mineral (clay) found in western U.S and Canada. Used in a slurry mixture (water and clay) to smother forest fires. Used in facial masks, foundation make-up and oil-absorbing face powders. In make-up it can smother skin and prevent respiration. In facial masks it is said to draw out toxins. It is generally thought of as non-toxic but rats died when injected with it.

BENZAL CHLORIDE: Carcinogenic, mutagenic, toxic or causes adverse reactions. (See definition at beginning of glossary.)

BENZALDEHYDE: Artificial essential oil of almond. Used for its fragrance in many cosmetics. Central nervous system depressant.

BENZALKONIUM CHLORIDE: Hazard: highly toxic.

BENZAMIDE: Carcinogenic, mutagenic, toxic or causes adverse reactions. (See definition at beginning of glossary.)

BENZAMIDINES (GROUP): Causes facial dermatoses and contact dermatitis.

BENZENE: Used in chemical combinations in many personal care product formulations. It is a known bone-marrow poison. Carcinogenic, mutagenic, toxic or causes adverse reactions. (See definition at beginning of glossary.)

BENZENECARBOXYLIC ACIPHENYLFORMIC ACID: Carcinogenic, mutagenic, toxic or causes adverse reactions. (See definition at beginning of glossary.)

BENZIDINE: Carcinogenic, mutagenic, toxic or causes adverse reactions. (See definition at beginning of glossary.)

BENZO-A-PYRENE: Carcinogen contaminant in mineral oil.

BENZO-B-FLUROANTHENE: Carcinogen contaminant in mineral oil.

BENZOATES (GROUP): Carcinogenic, mutagenic, toxic or causes adverse reactions. (See definition at beginning of glossary.)

BENZOCAINE (ETHYL-P-AMINOBENZOATE): Carcinogenic, mutagenic, toxic or causes adverse reactions. (See definition at beginning of glossary.)

BENZOIC ACID N-ALKYL ESTERS: Causes inflammatory reactions.

BENZOIC ACID: Used as a anti-bacterial and anti-microbial agent in cosmetics. Brain damage, neurological disorders and cancer occurred in laboratory mice when fed small amounts of benzoic acid. Benzoic acid may be naturally derived from gum benzoin or from balsam in which case it is safe for use. Check the rest of the ingredients in the formulation and see if they are plant derived. The synthetic form is carcinogenic, mutagenic, toxic or causes adverse reactions. (See definition at beginning of glossary.)

BENZOIN GUM, BENZOIN BARK: Used as a natural preservative in hair grooming products including shampoo. A plant derived antiseptic and astringent with antioxidant and preservative properties. Healing agent.

BENZOIN: In its synthetic form (bitter almond oil camphor) it is highly toxic.

BENZOPHENONE: A sunscreen or skin care ingredient, it is a UVA blocker. Protects against ultraviolet light from sunlight and fluorescent sources. (Also see section on sunscreens for more information.) It is known to cause contact dermatitis.

BENZOPHENONES (GROUP): Can cause severe contact dermatitis.

BENZOPYRONE: Carcinogenic, mutagenic, toxic or causes adverse reactions. (See definition at beginning of glossary.)

BENZOTRICHLORIDE: Carcinogenic, mutagenic, toxic or causes adverse reactions. (See definition at beginning of glossary.)

BENZOYL CHLORIDE: Carcinogenic, mutagenic, toxic or causes adverse reactions. (See definition at beginning of glossary.)

BENZOYL PEROXIDE: Used in acne preparations in varying concentrations. It is a plasticizer and may be added to a natural or synthesized resin to make it more flexible. It is toxic when inhaled and certain concentrations found in acne products have also been found to be toxic.

BENZOYLPHENYL CARBINOL: Carcinogenic, mutagenic, toxic or causes adverse reactions. (See definition at beginning of glossary.)

BENZYL ALCOHOL: It is said to be natural and derived from herbs such as cherry laurel leaves, cassie absolute, balsam peru, jasmine, etc. It is used as a solvent in cosmetics. It is carcinogenic, mutagenic, toxic or causes adverse reactions. (See definition at beginning of glossary.)

BENZYL BENZOATE: Known to cause allergic reactions.

BENZYL CHLORIDE: Carcinogenic, mutagenic, toxic or causes adverse reactions. (See definition at beginning of glossary.)

BENZYLPARABEN: Preservative shown to have low sensitizing potential at low concentrations. (See Methylparaben and Propylparaben.)

BERGAMOT OIL: An essential oil widely used in massage oils and some skin care products. May cause contact dermatitis if used undiluted.

BERYLLIUM CHLORIDE: Carcinogenic, mutagenic, toxic or causes adverse reactions. (See definition at beginning of glossary.)

BERYLLIUM FLUORIDE: Carcinogenic, mutagenic, toxic or causes adverse reactions. (See definition at beginning of glossary.)

BERYLLIUM NITRATE: Carcinogenic, mutagenic, toxic or causes adverse reactions. (See definition at beginning of glossary.)

BERYLLIUM OXIDE: Carcinogenic, mutagenic, toxic or causes adverse reactions. (See definition at beginning of glossary.)

BERYLLIUM: Carcinogenic, mutagenic, toxic or causes adverse reactions. (See definition at beginning of glossary.)

BETA-CAROTENE: Used as a coloring agent, it has no restrictions. (See Carotene.)

BETAINE: Used in shampoos, facial cleansers and bath preparations. It is a surfactant, viscosity builder and foam booster.

BETA-PROPIOLACTONE: Carcinogenic, mutagenic, toxic or causes adverse reactions. (See definition at beginning of glossary.)

BHA (BUTYLATED HYDROXYANISOLE): A synthetic antioxidant used to prevent oxidation of oils in cosmetics. Some reports of allergic reaction. Derived from petroleum. Causes allergic contact dermatitis. Toxic by ingestion.

BHT (BUTYLATED HYDROXYTHALUENE): A synthetic antioxidant used to prevent oxidation of oils in cosmetics. Some reports of allergic reaction.

BIOTIN: Used in hair products to add body and shine. One of the Vitamin B complexes. Helps prevent hair loss and promotes growth.

BIS (2-CHLOROETHYL) ETHER: Carcinogenic, mutagenic, toxic or causes adverse reactions. (See definition at beginning of glossary.)

BIS (2-ETHYLHEXYL) ADIPATE: Carcinogenic, mutagenic, toxic or causes adverse reactions. (See definition at beginning of glossary.)

BIS (2-ETHYLHEXYL) PHTHALATE: Carcinogenic, mutagenic, toxic or causes adverse reactions. (See definition at beginning of glossary.)

BISABOLOL: Used in skin care products as an anti-inflammatory agent. It is derived from chamomile or yarrow.

BISMUTH CITRATE: A preservative for hair dye only (0.5 percent w/v maximum.)

BISMUTH OXYCHLORIDE: A synthetic agent derived from the mineral bismuth used to impart a slight sheen in face powders and eyeshadows. Can cause skin irritation.

BISMUTH: Causes intellectual impairment and memory loss punctuated by periods of confusion, tremulousness clumsiness, difficulty in walking and myclonic jerks.

BITTER ALMOND-OIL CAMPHOR: Highly toxic.

BIXANE HERB: Used in health oriented personal care products as an astringent and also as a natural colourant. It is derived from the seeds of a South American shrub. It is a natural reddish brown color but when mixed with an acid it becomes a deep red. (See Annatto.)

BLADDERWRACK: A type of seaweed. Abundant in the same trace minerals, amino acids and other vital nutrients present in human blood plasma. High in alginates. Balances and remineralizes the skin.

BLUE CAMOMILE: Used in shampoos and hair treatments for its softening and emollient properties. It is also used in skin care products for its anti-inflammatory and anti-microbial ability.

BLUE MALLOW: It is an emollient with skin-softening properties making it a useful addition to creams, lotions and masks. It is used for dry skin and inflammations, as well as an eye wash for swollen, irritated eyes.

BLUE NO. 99: Known to cause contact dermatitis.

BLUEBOTTLE: Used as a skin conditioner and moisturizer. Derived from the Centaures cyanus herb.

BNPD (2-Bromo-2-nitropropane-1, 3-diol): Not listed on the label but it forms when certain chemicals are combined. Often used in shampoos and moisturizers; avoid products with this ingredient. Listed as a formaldehyde-releasing preservative. It is a carcinogen.

BORAGE OIL: An anti-inflammatory, soothing oil high in linolenic acid. Highly beneficial to the skin. Used in many of the natural skin care products.

BORANES (GROUP): May cause contact allergies.

BORAX: Used as an alternative to shampoo by some health oriented individuals. Severe poisonings have resulted when applied to abraded skin. Avoid using this on the body.

BORIC ACIDS (GROUP): This ingredient should not be used in personal care products. It is toxic at doses of 1-3g for babies, 5g for children and 15-20g for adults. Causes fetal malformations and fetal death in mice.

BORNELONE: Carcinogenic, mutagenic, toxic or causes adverse reactions. (See definition at beginning of glossary.) May cause contact allergies.

BROMELAIN: An enzyme derived from pineapples. Digests dead protein, as in surface skin cells.

BROMOFORM: Carcinogenic, mutagenic, toxic or causes adverse reactions. (See definition at beginning of glossary.)

BRONOPOL: Used in a wide variety of facial creams, hair preparations, bath products and mascara. It is an alcohol. It is a known skin irritant at concentrations as low as 0.25 percent. May cause contact allergies.

BRONZE POWDER: A natural colourant used with no FDA restrictions.

BURDOCK: An antiseptic and antibacterial used topically in the treatment of eczema and other skin irritations. Used internally as a detoxifier. A common herb used in China for skin problems.

BUTANE: A propellant, hydrocarbon gas used to propel substances. May be narcotic when inhaled in large doses. Inflammable.

BUTANOL: Carcinogenic, mutagenic, toxic or causes adverse reactions. (See definition at beginning of glossary.) Causes skin and eye irritation.

BUTRYIC ACID: Used in cosmetics, it is naturally derived from plants, fruit and wormseed oil. Carcinogenic, mutagenic, toxic or causes adverse reactions. (See definition at beginning of glossary.)

BUTYL ACETATE: A solvent used to thin out substances or remove substances commonly found in nail care products. Found in other personal care preparations. It is derived from petroleum. Causes skin and respiratory irritations. It is highly toxic.

BUTYLACRYLATE: Carcinogenic, mutagenic, toxic or causes adverse reactions. (See definition at beginning of glossary.)

BUTYL ALCOHOL: Causes skin and eye irritation.

BUTYL BENZOATE: Carcinogenic, mutagenic, toxic or causes adverse reactions. (See definition at beginning of glossary.)

BUTYL ESTERS OF PVM/MA COPOLYMER: An ingredient that makes substances more flexible. It is a plastic made from vinyl methyl ether and maleic anhydride. It has an unknown history but the names butyl and esters certainly have some derogatory implication.

BUTYL LACTATE: An emulsifier used in preparations to produce a *rich* feel. (See Butyl Alcohol.)

BUTYL MYRISTATE: An emulsifier used in preparations to produce a *rich* feel. Carcinogenic, mutagenic, toxic or causes adverse reactions. (See definition at beginning of glossary.)

BUTYL OLEATE: An ester of butyl alcohol and oleic acid used as an emulsifier in preparations to produce a *rich* feel. (See butyl alcohol and oleic acid.)

BUTYL STEARATE (BUTYL OCTADECANOATE): Used as an emulsifier and humectant in many body lotions and creams. Derived from petroleum. Shown to have comedogenic (acne producing, acne promoting) properties.

BUTYLATED HYDROXYANISOLE (BHA): May cause allergic contact dermatitis.

BUTYLATED HYDROXYANISOLE (GROUP): Carcinogenic, mutagenic, toxic or causes adverse reactions. (See definition at beginning of glossary.) Causes allergic reactions.

BUTYLATED HYDROXYTOLUENE (GROUP): Carcinogenic, mutagenic, toxic or causes adverse reactions. (See definition at beginning of glossary.)

BUTYLENE GLYCOL: A solvent used in skin and hair preparations as a humectant, stabilizer and viscosity control agent. It is used to enhance other preservatives in preparations. Can be irritating if used as more than five percent of a formulation. (See 1,3-Butylene Glycol.)

BUTYLHYDROXYANISOL: May cause allergic reactions.

BUTYLPARABEN (N-BUTYL HYDROXYBENZOATE): Used as an anti-bacterial and anti-microbial in personal care products. Derived from petroleum or from gum benzoin. One of the most common preservatives used in cosmetics. Nonirritating at 0.05 of 1 percent. It is a skin sensitizer.

BUTYRALDEHYDE: Carcinogenic, mutagenic, toxic or causes adverse reactions. (See definition at beginning of glossary.)

C 12-15 ALCOHOLS BENZOATE: Used as an emulsion stabilizer and viscosity increasing agent in skin and hair conditioners and moisturizers. It is a mixture of synthetic aliphatic alcohols with 12-15 carbons in the alkyl chain (fatty alcohols). Carcinogenic, mutagenic, toxic or causes adverse reactions. (See definition at beginning of glossary.)

CA 24: Used a preservative and anti-microbial in shampoo and bath preparations. It contains 70 percent chloroacetamide and 30 percent sodium benzoate. It is used in concentrations up to 3 percent although as little as 0.1 percent has caused adverse reactions. (See Chloroacetamide.)

CACAO, BUTTER OF (THEOBROMA OIL, COCOA BUTTER: Causes follicular hyperkeratosis (chemically induced acne).

CADMIUM ACETATE: Carcinogenic, mutagenic, toxic or causes adverse reactions. (See definition at beginning of glossary.)

CADMIUM BROMIDE: Carcinogenic, mutagenic, toxic or causes adverse reactions. (See definition at beginning of glossary.)

CADMIUM: Carcinogenic, mutagenic, toxic or causes adverse reactions. (See definition at beginning of glossary.)

CAJEPUT OIL: Used in skin care products as an antiseptic and anti-viral agent. Its function is to cleanse and drain toxins and excess oil from the skin. Distilled from the flowers and leaves of the Melaleuca leucadendra tree which grows in Malaysia.

CALAMINE: Used in lotions to combat itching. A blend of zinc oxide (see zinc oxide) and a small amount of ferric oxide. Used in skin lotions. Some products may also contain phenols which are toxic. Carcinogenic, mutagenic, toxic or causes adverse reactions. (See definition at beginning of glossary.)

CALCIUM ALGINATE: Used as an emulsifier, stabilizer and film former especially in facial peel-off masks. Commonly used in the food industry.

CALCIUM CARBONATE: Used as a colouring agent in make-up. It is a natural occurring salt from chalk or limestone. Recent studies show that most calcium sources contains high levels of lead.

CALCIUM CHLORIDE: Used as an emulsifier and texturizer in cosmetics. Although the toxicity of its use in cosmetics is unknown, internal ingestion can cause digestive complaints. If breathed it can cause lung problems. It is used in antifreeze.

CALCIUM CYANAMIDE: Carcinogenic, mutagenic, toxic or causes adverse reactions. (See definition at beginning of glossary.)

CALCIUM SILICATE: Used in make-up as an anti-caking and opacifying agent. It acts as an absorbent. Used in face powders, blushers and bath salts.

CALENDULA EXTRACT: Extracted from the common Marigold flower. It is frequently used as a carrier oil for essential oils. Used in salves and cosmetics. Can also be used as a natural yellow color. Causes irritant dermatitis from plant and tincture.

CAMOMILE: Extracted from the flowers of several varieties of camomile. Used to treat skin problems since ancient times. Used as a softening agent for chapped or irritated skin. Reduces inflammation, itching and swelling. Also found in hair products.

CAMPHOR: Distilled from the wood of the camphor tree. It is a natural antiseptic and analgesic that helps to calm the skin and reduce redness. It is reported as having caused poisonings through skin absorption.

CANDELILLA WAX: Used in lipsticks and facial creams to thicken the consistency. It is an herbal hard wax obtained from the candelilla plant. Used as an occlusive and binder in lipsticks and creams. May seal the skin and prevent it from breathing.

CANOT OIL: Natural extract of carrot used as a colorant. High in beta-carotene; healing and soothing to the skin.

CANTHAXANTHIN: Causes fatal aplastic anemia.

CAPRIC ACID: A fatty acid derived from plants. Plant derived or synthetically produced.

CAPRIC TRIGLYCERIDES: Skin protectant and conditioner, water sealer, emulsifier. Used to moisturize. Oily liquid from plants, vegetable oils, dairy fats and sweat. Synthesized from coconut oil or palm kernel oil or synthetically produced.

CAPRYLIC ACID: A fatty acid derived from plants, palm and coconut oils. Plant derived or synthetically produced.

CAPSICUM OLEORESIN: Used in some hair tonics to promote hair growth presumably by stimulation. It is an oil from the pepper species. It may cause allergic reactions in some people.

CAPTAN: An anti-microbial, preservative and disinfectant. Used in soaps. Also used in agriculture as a fungicide. Carcinogenic, mutagenic, toxic or causes adverse reactions. (See definition at beginning of glossary.)

CARAMEL: A natural colourant with no FDA restrictions.

CARBA-MIX: Studies show that it may cause contact dermatitis.

CARBARYL: Carcinogenic, mutagenic, toxic or causes adverse reactions. (See definition at beginning of glossary.)

CARBOMER 934,940,941,960,961: Used as a thickener and stabilizers in creams, moisturizers, toothpastes, eye make-up and bathing products. They are high molecular weight cross-linked polymers. They can be an irritants. Avoid the eye area as they may cause irritation.

CARBON DISULFIDE: Carcinogenic, mutagenic, toxic or causes adverse reactions. (See definition at beginning of glossary.)

CARBON TETRACHLORIDE: Carcinogenic, mutagenic, toxic or causes adverse reactions. (See definition at beginning of glossary.)

CARBONYL SULFIDE: Carcinogenic, mutagenic, toxic or causes adverse reactions. (See definition at beginning of glossary.)

CARBOXBENZENE: Carcinogenic, mutagenic, toxic or causes adverse reactions. (See definition at beginning of glossary.)

CARCINOGEN: A substance that causes cancer. In personal care products two chemicals could react and produce a carcinogenic substance.

CARMINE: A natural red pigment derived from the dried female insect, the Cochineal, which feeds on the cactus plant. Used as dye or colour additive in cosmetics.

CARNAUBA: From the Brazilian wax palm. Used as a barrier agent and texturizer in lipsticks, deodorant sticks and depilatories.

CAROTENE (BETA-CAROTENE): Present in quantity in a variety of orange/yellow fruits and vegetables, such as carrots, cantaloupe and papaya. Carotene has an orange color that oxidizes (fades) when exposed to sunlight. It is converted into vitamin A by the body and is used for its cellular renewal and healing abilities. Antioxidants help fight free radicals. A skin conditioning agent and moisturizer. (See Carotene Derivatives.)

CAROTENE DERIVATIVES, NON-PROVITAMIN A: Studies show it to cause a reduction in red blood cells. May cause irreversible damage to the retina of the eyes.

CAROTENE, SYNTHETIC (PROVITAMIN A): Causes fatal aplastic anemia.

CARRAGEEN: A seaweed high in sulfur and said to be nourishing to the skin. A natural stabilizer, binding agent and emulsifier. Also known as Irish Moss or *red algae* it has been used in food and medicines in India for hundreds of years. It is similar to fucus and other seaweeds in fragrance and color.

CARROT EXTRACT: Acts as a photosensitizer.

CARROT OIL: Rich in beta carotene and vitamins A and E. Highly beneficial to hair and skin. Topical application of this oil promotes the formation of new cells and stimulates the production of sebum in dry, scaly scalps and skin. (See Carrot Extract.)

CASEIN: Hair and skin conditioning agent. Also used in bubble bath. Used in protective creams and as a protein in hair preparations to make the hair thicker and more manageable. A phosphoprotein from milk protein.

CASTOR OIL (RICINUS OIL): From the castor bean. Acts as a barrier agent, emollient and lubricant. Used in lipsticks and moisturizers. If the castor oil has been cold-pressed there will be some very advantageous healing and detoxification benefits. May cause allergic reactions when used in lipsticks.

CATIONIC: One of the four types of sodium lauryl sulfate, a surfactant, which can cause irritation and dryness as well as damage to eyes, especially in the young. Found in some shampoos and bubble baths.

CEDARWOOD OIL: From red cedar. It is a strong antiseptic and has a calming effect on the skin. It should not be used on people with high blood pressure or those sensitive to cedar.

CELLULOSE GUM: Used as an emulsifier and thickening agent in make-up, skin care, hair grooming and suntan preparations. It is a non-digestible carbohydrate found in the outer layer of vegetables and fruits. Some manufacturers combine it with various synthetic chemicals although a few use the completely natural source. Inhaling the powder during manufacturing or processing can be harmful to the lungs.

CERESIN WAX: Used as an emulsifier, hair conditioner and thickener. Derived from ozokerite by bleaching and refining. Although said to be naturally occurring, it is a hydrocarbon from petrochemicals.

CETEARETH-20: Used as an emollient and emulsifier in hair conditioners and cleansing products. It is made from stearyl alcohol (solid alcohols mixed with stearol, a derivative of stearic acid) and coconut or palm oil. Can be plant derived although manufacturers use synthetic versions.

CETEARTH-3: Used in cosmetics as an emulsifier. It is known to dry out the skin and causes many allergic reactions.

CETEARYL ALCOHOL: Used in cleansing and hair preparations. It is used as a carrying agent and thickener in lotions and other personal care products. It is a mixture of two fatty alcohols, cetyl and stearyl alcohol. It may be naturally derived or it may be produced synthetically. May cause contact sensitivity and dermatitis.

CETEARYL OCTANOATE: An ester used as an emollient and texturizer in personal care products. It is a wax made by combining fatty alcohols from vegetable sources. (See Esters.)

CETEARYL PALMITATE: An ester used as an emollient and texturizer in personal care products. It is a wax made by combining fatty alcohols from vegetable sources. (See Esters and Palmitates.)

CETETH-N (1-45): May contain dangerous levels of ethylene oxide and/or dioxane, both potent toxins, as a manufacturing by-product.

CETRIMONIUM CHLORIDE: An anti static agent, surfactant and emulsifier and moisturizer. Used in hair conditioners and other hair grooming aids and hand and body preparations. It is a synthetic quaternary compound. Toxic.

CETYL ACETATE: Skin conditioning agent, moisturizer and emollient. Used in make-up, skin care and cleansing, hair shampoos and grooming products and nail polish removers.

CETYL ALCOHOL: Widely used in make-up, skin care, hair conditioning and shampoos, cleanser and tanning preparations. It is an emollient and emulsion stabilizer, foam booster and viscosity increasing agent. It is a palmitic oil derived from coconuts. Causes contact eczema.

CETYL DIMETHICONE COPOLYOL: Skin protectant and conditioner, water sealer, emulsifier. Used to moisturize. It is a silicon of high molecular weight. (See Dimethicone and Alcohols and Polyols.)

CETYL ESTERS: Used in skin, body and hair products as an emollient, thickener and gellant. It is a wax made by combining fatty alcohols from vegetable sources. (See Esters.)

CETYL LACTATE: Used as an emollient and texturizer in cosmetics. May be natural or synthetic.

CETYL MYRISTATE: Used as an emollient and texturizer in cosmetics. May be natural or synthetic. (See Myristate.)

CETYL OCTANOATE: An ester used as an emollient and texturizer in personal care products. It is a wax made by combining fatty alcohols from vegetable sources. (See Esters.)

CETYL PALMITATE: An emollient and texturizer used in cosmetics. May be natural or synthetic. (See Palmitates.)

CETYL RICINOLEATE: An ester used as an emollient and texturizer in personal care products. It is a wax made by combining fatty alcohols from vegetable sources. (See Esters.)

CETYL STEARATE: An ester used as an emollient and texturizer in personal care products. It is a wax made by combining fatty alcohols from vegetable sources. (See Esters.)

CETYLIC ACID: Carcinogenic, mutagenic, toxic or causes adverse reactions. (See definition at beginning of glossary.)

CETYLIC ALCOHOL: Carcinogenic, mutagenic, toxic or causes adverse reactions. (See definition at beginning of glossary.)

CETYLPYRIDINIUM CLORIDE: Used as an antiseptic in personal care products. Carcinogenic, mutagenic, toxic or causes adverse reactions. (See definition at beginning of glossary.)

CETYL-STEARYLALCOHOL: A fatty acid used in a wide array of personal care products. It acts as an emollient. Studies show that it may cause contact dermatitis.

CHAMOMILE EXTRACT: May cause allergic dermatitis when used in creams.

CHERRY BARK EXTRACT: Used in skin care products for its astringent and healing properties.

CHINALDINE: Carcinogenic, mutagenic, toxic or causes adverse reactions. (See definition at beginning of glossary.)

CHLORACETAMIDE: Carcinogenic, mutagenic, toxic or causes adverse reactions. (See definition at beginning of glossary.)

CHLORAMBEN: Carcinogenic, mutagenic, toxic or causes adverse reactions. (See definition at beginning of glossary.)

CHLORAMPHENICOL: Carcinogenic, mutagenic, toxic or causes adverse reactions. (See definition at beginning of glossary.)

CHLORDANE: Carcinogenic, mutagenic, toxic or causes adverse reactions. (See definition at beginning of glossary.)

CHLORINE DIOXIDE: Carcinogenic, mutagenic, toxic or causes adverse reactions. (See definition at beginning of glossary.)

CHLORINE: Carcinogenic, mutagenic, toxic or causes adverse reactions. (See definition at beginning of glossary.)

CHLOROACETIC ACID: Carcinogenic, mutagenic, toxic or causes adverse reactions. (See definition at beginning of glossary.)

CHLOROBENZENE: Carcinogenic, mutagenic, toxic or causes adverse reactions. (See definition at beginning of glossary.)

CHLOROBENZILATE: Carcinogenic, mutagenic, toxic or causes adverse reactions. (See definition at beginning of glossary.)

CHLOROBUTANOL: Used as an anti-microbial, preservative and anti-bacterial. It is a very common preservative used in cosmetics. It is a central nervous system depressant and hypnotic, although with no known skin toxicity.

CHLOROFORM: Carcinogenic, mutagenic, toxic or causes adverse reactions. (See definition at beginning of glossary.)

CHLOROMETHYLISOTHIAZOLINONE: Studies have shown that it can cause contact dermatitis.

CHLOROPHYLL: The green component of plants used as a natural colorant in deodorants, creams and toothpaste. Antiseptic, anti-fungal, odor-absorbing.

CHLOROPRENE: Carcinogenic, mutagenic, toxic or causes adverse reactions. (See definition at beginning of glossary.)

CHLOROPROMAZINE (GROUP): Causes cutaneous phototoxicity reactions.

CHLOROTHALONIL: Carcinogenic, mutagenic, toxic or causes adverse reactions. (See definition at beginning of glossary.)

CHLOROXYLENOL: Cosmetic biocide and deodorant agent. Used in personal cleanliness products and in skin and hair care. Is a germicide and fungicide. Has no apparent irritating effects, although it does penetrate the skin. It is a halogenated phenolic compound. (See Phenols.)

CHOLECALCIFERAL: Used as a skin conditioner, moisturizer. Also used for the protective, corrective and renewal processes of hair and skin. Vitamin D 3.

CHOLESTEROL: Used in products to help hold the moisture in the skin. Found in all body tissues, the sebum is especially plentiful of cholesterol. Derived from cocoa beans and myrrh or from sheep's wool. Acts as an emulsifying and lubricating agent in cosmetics.

CHOLETH-N: May contain dangerous levels of ethylene oxide and/or dioxane, both potent toxins, as a manufacturing by-products.

CHONDROITIN SULFATE: A factor of the hyaluronic acid complex that is bioengineered (grown in a yeastlike culture in a laboratory).

CHROMATES: Contact allergens. Studies show that they may cause contact dermatitis.

CHROMIC ACETATE: Carcinogenic, mutagenic, toxic or causes adverse reactions. (See definition at beginning of glossary.)

CHROMIC ACID: Carcinogenic, mutagenic, toxic or causes adverse reactions. (See definition at beginning of glossary.)

CHROMIC SULFATE: Carcinogenic, mutagenic, toxic or causes adverse reactions. (See definition at beginning of glossary.)

CHROMIUM (III) OXIDE: Carcinogenic, mutagenic, toxic or causes adverse reactions. (See definition at beginning of glossary.)

CHROMIUM (VI) OXIDE: Carcinogenic, mutagenic, toxic or causes adverse reactions. (See definition at beginning of glossary.)

CHROMIUM HYDROXIDE GREEN: A colouring agent for cosmetics only, not food sor drugs.

CHROMIUM NITRATE: Carcinogenic, mutagenic, toxic or causes adverse reactions. (See definition at beginning of glossary.)

CHROMIUM OXIDE GREENS: A colouring agent for cosmetics, including eye area.

CHROMIUM OXYCHLORIDE: Carcinogenic, mutagenic, toxic or causes adverse reactions. (See definition at beginning of glossary.)

CHROMIUM: Carcinogenic, mutagenic, toxic or causes adverse reactions. (See definition at beginning of glossary.)

CINNAMALDEHYDE: Carcinogenic, mutagenic, toxic or causes adverse reactions. (See definition at beginning of glossary.)

CINNAMATE (CINOXATE): Studies show that it may cause contact dermatitis.

CINNAMATES (GROUP): Causes stinging sensations and adverse effects.

CINNAMIC ALDEHYDE: Studies show that it may cause contact dermatitis.

CINNAMYL ALDEHYDE: Studies show that it may cause contact dermatitis.

CINOXATE: Causes photosensitivity.

CIS-9-OCTADECENOIC ACID: Carcinogenic, mutagenic, toxic or causes adverse reactions. (See definition at beginning of glossary.)

CITRIC ACID: Used in hair conditioners, skin care, cleansers, bubble baths, make up, hair aids, tanning products, breath fresheners, aftershaves, colognes and toilet water. A preservative, stabilizer, buffer and chelating agent, found widely in plants, citrus fruits and in animal tissues. Adjusts pH and acts as an antioxidant.

CITRONELLA: An herb most commonly used as an insect repellent. In skin care, the essential oil is used to calm sebaceous glands.

CITRONELLAL HYDRATE: Carcinogenic, mutagenic, toxic or causes adverse reactions. (See definition at beginning of glossary.)

CITRUS OIL EXTRACT: A combination of grapefruit, orange and lemon oils used in health oriented personal care products.

CITRUS SEED EXTRACT: Natural preservative. Uses grapefruit seed extract, often combined with vitamins A, C and E to enhance effectiveness.

CLEMATIS (ARISTOLOCHIA CLEMATIS): Anti-inflammatory known for its healing and soothing properties on the skin. It dilates blood vessels. The oil from this herb is known for its skin rejuvenation qualities.

CLOFLUCARBAN: Used in personal care products as an anti-microbial, preservative and disinfectant. It is a toxic carbanilide compound.

CLOVE OIL (CARYOPHYLLUS OIL): Weak sensitizer.

COAL TAR DERIVATIVES (GROUP): Shown to have comedogenic (acne producing) properties, is a human carcinogen and is toxic by inhalation.

COAL TAR PITCH VOLATILES: Carcinogenic, mutagenic, toxic or causes adverse reactions. (See definition at beginning of glossary.) Shown to have comedogenic (acne producing) properties, is a human carcinogen and is toxic by inhalation.

COBALT NAPHTHENATE: Carcinogenic, mutagenic, toxic or causes adverse reactions. (See definition at beginning of glossary.)

COBALT: Studies show that it may cause contact dermatitis.

COCAMIDE DEA (COCOMIDE DIETHANOLAMINE): Used in hair, skin and personal care products. Coconut oil and diethamolamine combination used for cleaning, thickening and as a foam booster. Nitrosamines can form in all cosmetic ingredients containing amines and amino derivatives with nitrogen conmpounds. When DEA is applied to skin known carcinogens can form. Avoid.

COCAMIDE MEA (COCAMIDE MONOETHANOLAMINE): Appears most often in shampoos; can be mildly irritating depending on the formulation. Nitrosamines can form in all cosmetic ingredients containing amines and amino derivatives with nitrogen conmpounds. Nitrosamines are known carcinogens. Studies show that it may cause contact dermatitis and allergic reactions. Avoid.

COCAMIDOPROPYL BETAINE: Used as a subsidiary surfactant in shampoos in conjunction with other more powerful surfactants. Used in shampoos as a foaming anti-static, surfactant, thickener, hair and skin conditioning agent. It is a synthetic fatty acid although it is often listed as "coming from coconuts." Causes eyelid dermatitis.

COCAMIDOPROPYL HYDROXYSULTAINE: Used in hair and skin conditioners. It is an anti-static agent, surfactant, cleansing agent, foam booster and thickener. It is a synthetic chemical derived from coconut oil.

COCOA BUTTER: A saturated fat extracted from the seeds of the Theobroma cacao plant. Heavy emollient properties makes it unsuitable for facial skin. May produce contact sensitivities. Has been shown to promote acne.

COCOAMPHODIACETATE: An emulsifier and surfactant found in shampoos. (See Coconut Oil.)

COCOAMPHODIAPROPINATE: A surfactant found in shampoos. (See Coconut Oil.)

COCONUT OIL: A saturated fat naturally converted into soap by reacting it with salt. The fat molecules are large, making the oil *too heavy* for use on facial skin. Contains skin irritants.

COCONUT FATTY ALCOHOLS: The fatty alcohols from coconut palm kernels, which are natural emollients. The natural version is better than the synthetic but it is hard to tell who is using what.

COLAMINE: Carcinogenic, mutagenic, toxic or causes adverse reactions. (See definition at beginning of glossary.)

COLLAGEN: A humectant and moisturizer in cosmetics. Originally derived from animal products, bovine (cows) or avian (bird), now can be synthesized from plant proteins. According to cosmetic chemist, Aubrey Hampton, the plant-derived collagen must be carefully formulated (with correct percentages) without the presence of any petrochemicals or hydrocarbons. Properly structured, the collagen may be able to arrest or compensate for collagen loss. Collagen makes up the fibrous support system from which skin is made.

COLLOIDAL SULFUR: Sulfur is a naturally occurring material. Colloidal sulfur is a mixture of sulfur and gum acacia, derived from the African acacia tree. Known for its ability to calm the skin and sebaceous glands. Found in a wide variety of acne preparations, it helps reduce inflammation and swelling.

COLOPHONY (SYNONYM FOR ROSIN): Causes eyelid dermatitis.

COLOUR ADDITIVES: A colour additive can be defined generally as any material that will impart colour to either a product or the human body. Around the world the list of approved colours varies to a great degree. In the E.U. (European Union) for example, the list of approved colours for cosmetics include some that are not approved for use in cosmetics in the U.S. CI73015, the equivalent of FD&C No. 2 in U.S., along with seven others, have been delisted in the U.S. for use in cosmetics yet are still approved for use in the E.U. To add to the confusion, most of the colours in the E.U. and the U.S. are known by different names so it is even more difficult for the consumer to decipher labels that list colour additives. It seems necessary that, in this age of global marketing, manufacturers need to decide on universal standards and nomenclature for colours. According to the U.S. Food and Drug Administration, color additives should not be exposed to oxidizing or reducing agents that may affect the integrity of the color additives. Amounts of color additives used in cosmetic products are restricted to levels consistent with good manufacturing practice (unless the regulation specifies a maximum level).

COLTSFOOT: High in silicic acid and the amino acid cystine. Present in the hair protein, keratin. Cystine, applied topically, is known to help strengthen the hair and promote growth.

COMFREY EXTRACT: Used as a healing agent in skin care products. It is a source of mucopolysaccharides and allantoin. European studies show that some alkaloids in the comfrey are toxic. Leaves have irritant properties.

CORNFLOWER: Used in health oriented skin care products as a moisturizing agent.

COPPER CHLOROPHYLLIN: A colourant with a restricted concentration: 0.1 percent maximum. Restricted to specified combination with specified substances.

COPPER CYANIDE: Carcinogenic, mutagenic, toxic or causes adverse reactions. (See definition at beginning of glossary.)

COPPER POWDER: A colourant in cosmetics. The FDA has listed it as being unrestricted. (See Copper.)

COPPER: Carcinogenic, mutagenic, toxic or causes adverse reactions. (See definition at beginning of glossary.)

CORIANDER EXTRACT: Used in personal care products as a safe deodorizer. Excellent in skin care products to remove impurities.

CORN OIL (MAIZE OIL): Not widely used in cosmetics as it may promote acne.

CORNFLOWER DISTILLATE: Causes allergy and photosensitivity.

CORNFLOWER EXTRACT: Used in skin care as an anti-inflammatory agent. Extracted from the bachelor's button flower. Contains allantoin. Often used as an eye compress. May cause allergy and photosensitivity.

CORNSTARCH: A starchy white powder derived from corn that is very soothing to the skin. A safe alternative to face powder. Can also be used as an absorbent agent for underarms. If you are allergic to corn, you may also be allergic to cornstarch. Causes allergy and photosensitivity.

COUMARIN (GROUP): Found to be a skin sensitizer.

CRESYLIC ACID: Carcinogenic, mutagenic, toxic or causes adverse reactions. (See definition at beginning of glossary.)

CROSS-LINKED ELASTIN: Small enough (456 molecular weight) to penetrate the skin. Polypeptides, Desmosine and

Iso-Desmosine improves the flexibility, softness and elasticity of the skin. Wrinkled skin is deficient in these two amino acids.

CUCUMBER: Used in facial creams, lotions and cleansers for its anti-inflammatory, astringent, soothing and cooling properties on the skin.

CUMENE HYDROPEROXIDE: Carcinogenic, mutagenic, toxic or causes adverse reactions. (See definition at beginning of glossary.)

CUMENE: Carcinogenic, mutagenic, toxic or causes adverse reactions. (See definition at beginning of glossary.)

CUPFERRON: Carcinogenic, mutagenic, toxic or causes adverse reactions. (See definition at beginning of glossary.)

CUPRIC NITRATE: Carcinogenic, mutagenic, toxic or causes adverse reactions. (See definition at beginning of glossary.)

CUPRIC SULFATE: Carcinogenic, mutagenic, toxic or causes adverse reactions. (See definition at beginning of glossary.)

CYANIDE (GROUP): Causes poisoning from a cosmetic nail remover.

CYCLOHEXANE: Carcinogenic, mutagenic, toxic or causes adverse reactions. (See definition at beginning of glossary.)

CYCLOHEXIMIDE: Inhibits skin cell metabolism (lips).

CYCLOMETHICOME: Silicone oil, emollient, conditioner and solvent for skin and hair. Used in moisturizers and cleansers. No known toxicity when used externally.

CYPRESS OIL: Used in skin care preparations to reduce overactive sweat and oil glands. Distilled from the bark of the cypress tree, it is a natural astringent and said to be restorative. As a vasoconstrictor it also helps to shrink capillaries and calm the skin.

CYSTEINE: An amino acid obtained through fermentation. It is said to normalize sebaceous secretions.

D&C BLUE NO. 1: ALUMINUM LAKE: External use only, except eye area. Suspected carcinogen, teratogen, or toxin.

D&C BLUE NO. 2 ALUMINUM LAKE: External use only, except eye area. Suspected carcinogen, teratogen, or toxin.

D&C BLUE NO. 4 ALUMINUM LAKE: External use only, except eye area. Provisionally listed with FDA. Suspected carcinogen, teratogen, or toxin.

D&C BLUE NO. 4: External use only, except eye area. Suspected carcinogen, teratogen, or toxin.

D&C BROWN NO. 1: External use only, except eye area.

D&C GREEN NO. 3 ALUMINUM LAKE: External use only, except eye area.

D&C GREEN NO. 5: Permitted in drugs and cosmetics, except eye area. Known as Acid Green 25. Provisionally listed with FDA.

D&C GREEN NO. 6 LAKE: External use only, except eye area. Provisionally listed with FDA.

D&C GREEN NO. 6: External use only, except eye area.

D&C GREEN NO. 8: External use only, except eye area. Restricted concentration: 0.01 percent maximum.

D&C ORANGE NO. 10 LAKE: External use only, except eye area.

D&C ORANGE NO. 10: External use only, except eye area.

D&C ORANGE NO. 11 LAKE: External use only, except eye area.

D&C ORANGE NO. 11: External use only, except eye area.

D&C ORANGE NO. 17 LAKE: External use only, except eye area. Restricted concentrations: Lip products 6 percent maximum.

D&C ORANGE NO. 4 LAKE: External use only, except eye area. Provisionally listed with the FDA.

D&C ORANGE NO. 4: External use only, except eye area. Known as Acid Orange 7.

D&C ORANGE NO. 5 LAKE: External use only, except eye area. Can be toxic if ingested in large quantities. Restricted concentrations: Lip products 5 percent maximum. Mouthwashes/dentifrices (GMP).

D&C ORANGE NO. 5: External use only, except eye area. Can be toxic if ingested in large quantities. Restricted concentrations:

Lip products 5 percent maximum. Mouthwashes/dentifrices (GMP).

D&C RED NO. 17 LAKE: External use only, except eye area. Provisionally listed with FDA.

D&C RED NO. 17: External use only, except eye area. Suspected carcinogen, teratogen, or toxin.

D&C RED NO. 19 ALUMINUM LAKE: External use only, except eye area. Suspected carcinogen, teratogen, or toxin.

D&C RED NO. 19 ZIRCONINUM LAKE: External use only, except eye area. Suspected carcinogen, teratogen, or toxin.

D&C RED NO. 19: External use only, except eye area. Also known as Basic Violet 10. Suspected carcinogen, teratogen, or toxin.

D&C RED NO. 19 BARIUM LAKE: External use only, except eye area. Suspected carcinogen, teratogen, or toxin.

D&C RED NO. 21 LAKE: Permitted in drugs and cosmetics, except eye area. Provisionally listed with FDA.

D&C RED NO. 21: Permitted in drugs and cosmetics, except eye area. Also known as Solvent Red 43.

D&C RED NO. 22 LAKE: Permitted in drugs and cosmetics, except eye area. Provisionally listed with FDA.

D&C RED NO. 22: Permitted in drugs and cosmetics, except eye area. Suspected carcinogen, teratogen, or toxin.

D&C RED NO. 27 LAKE: Permitted in drugs and cosmetics, except eye area. Provisionally listed with FDA.

D&C RED NO. 27: Permitted in drugs and cosmetics, except eye area.

D&C RED NO. 28 LAKE: Permitted in drugs and cosmetics, except eye area. Provisionally listed with FDA.

D&C RED NO. 28: Permitted in drugs and cosmetics, except eye area.

D&C RED NO. 3 ALUMINUM LAKE: Permitted in drugs and cosmetics, except eye area. Made from FD&C Red No. 3—a mutagen. (See FD&C Red No. 3.)

D&C RED NO. 30 LAKE: Permitted in drugs and cosmetics, except eye area. Provisionally listed with FDA.

D&C RED NO. 30: Permitted in drugs and cosmetics, except eye area.

D&C RED NO. 31 LAKE: External use only, except eye area. Provisionally listed with FDA.

D&C RED NO. 31: External use only, except eye area.

D&C RED NO. 33 LAKE: External use only, except eye area. Restricted concentrations: Lip products 3 percent maximum. Mouthwashes/dentifrices (GMP). Provisionally listed with FDA.

D&C RED NO. 33: External use only, except eye area. Restricted concentrations: Lip products 3 percent maximum. Mouthwashes/dentifrices (GMP).

D&C RED NO. 34 LAKE: External use only, except eye area. Provisionally listed with FDA.

D&C RED NO. 34: External use only, except eye area.

D&C RED NO. 36 LAKE: External use only, except eye area. Restricted concentrations: Lip products 3 percent maximum. Provisionally listed with FDA.

D&C RED NO. 36: External use only, except eye area. Restricted concentrations. Lip products 3 percent maximum.

D&C RED NO. 4: Permitted in drugs and cosmetics, except eye area. Suspected carcinogen, teratogen, or toxin.

D&C RED NO. 4: Permitted in drugs and cosmetics, except eye area.

D&C RED NO. 6 LAKE: Permitted in drugs and cosmetics, except eye area. Provisionally listed with FDA.

D&C RED NO. 6: Permitted in drugs and cosmetics, except eye area.

D&C RED NO. 7 LAKE: Permitted in drugs and cosmetics, except eye area. Provisionally listed with FDA.

D&C RED NO. 7: Permitted in drugs and cosmetics, except eye area.

D&C RED NO. 9 BARIUM LAKE: Permitted in drugs and cosmetics, except eye area. Suspected carcinogen, teratogen, or toxin.

D&C RED NO. 9 STRONTIUM LAKE: Permitted in drugs and

cosmetics, except eye area. Suspected carcinogen, teratogen, or toxin.

D&C RED NO. 9 ZIRCONINUM LAKE: Permitted in drugs and cosmetics, except eye area. Suspected carcinogen, teratogen, or toxin.

D&C RED NO. 9: Permitted in drugs and cosmetics, except eye area. Suspected carcinogen, teratogen, or toxin.

D&C VIOLET NO. 2: External use only, except eye area.

D&C YELLOW NO. 10: Permitted in food, drugs and cosmetics, except eye area. Known as Acid Yellow 3. Certain manufacturing processes may contaminate this colour with the carcinogen beta-naphthylamine.

D&C YELLOW NO. 11: External use only, except eye area. Also known as Solvent Yellow 33. A known allergen.

D&C YELLOW NO. 5 ALUMINUM LAKE: External use only, except eye area.

D&C YELLOW NO. 6 ALUMINUM LAKE: External use only, except eye area. Suspected carcinogen, teratogen, or toxin.

D&C YELLOW NO. 7: External use only, except eye area.

D&C YELLOW NO. 8: External use only, except eye area. Suspected carcinogen, teratogen, or toxin.

DEA-CETYL PHOSPHATE: Used in personal care products as an emulsifier and surfactant. Recent studies suggest that when DEA comes in contact with skin, nitrosamines are formed. Nitrosamines are carcinogens. Avoid.

DEA (DIETHANOLAMINE): This ingredient is widely used in many shampoo preparations. When DEA is applied to skin known carcinogens can form. Avoid.

DEA CETYL PHOSPHATE: Recent studies suggest that when DEA comes in contact with skin, nitrosamines are formed. Nitrosamines are carcinogens. Avoid.

DEA DIHYDROXYPALMITYL PHOSPHATE: Studies show that it may cause contact dermatitis.

DEA LAURYL SULFATE: Used in many shampoos. Recent studies suggest that when DEA comes in contact with skin, nitrosamines are formed. Nitrosamines are carcinogens. Avoid.

DEA LINOLEATE: An ester found in personal care products. An ester is a product of a condensation reaction in which a molecule of an acid unites with a molecule of alcohol and eliminates a molecule of water. Recent studies suggest that when DEA comes in contact with skin, nitrosamines are formed. Nitrosamines are carcinogens. Avoid.

DEA METHOXYCINNAMATE: Can cause cancer causing nitrosamines in sunlight (phototoxin) Recent studies suggest that when DEA comes in contact with skin, nitrosamines are formed. Nitrosamines are carcinogens. Avoid.

DEA MYRISTATE: An ester found in personal care products. An ester is a product of a condensation reaction in which a molecule of an acid unites with a molecule of alcohol and eliminates a molecule of water. (See DEA and Myristate.) Recent studies suggest that when DEA comes in contact with skin, nitrosamines are formed. Nitrosamines are carcinogens. Avoid.

DECYL OLEATE: An ester found in personal care products. An ester is a product of a condensation reaction in which a molecule of an acid unites with a molecule of alcohol and eliminates a molecule of water. Has comedogenic (acne producing) properties.

DEHYDROACETIC ACID: Used in personal care products as an anti-microbial, anti-fungal, preservative and disinfectant.

DEIONIZED WATER: *Deionization* means that all the ions of soluble salts have been removed. Calcium, magnesium, sulfur, etc., can interfere with formulations and *deactivate* active ingredients.

DI TETROSODIUM EDTA: (See TETROSODIUM EDTA) *DI* indicates two or double molecules.

DIALLATE: Carcinogenic, mutagenic, toxic or causes adverse reactions. (See definition at beginning of glossary.)

DIAMINE (HYDRAZINE): Harzardous, toxic by ingestion, inhalation and skin absorption. Also, a strong irritant to skin and eyes.

DIAMINES (GROUP) (HYDRAZINE): Carcinogenic, mutagenic, toxic or causes adverse reactions. (See definition at beginning of glossary.)

DIAMMONIUM DITHIODIGLYCOLATE: Carcinogenic, mutagenic, toxic or causes adverse reactions. (See definition at beginning of glossary.)

DIAZOLIDINYL UREA: Anti-microbial, preservative and disinfectant. It is a protein by-product preservative derived from urine or synthetically produced. Acts as a moisturizer for hair preparations, cleansing products, skin care and make-up products, suntan aids and bathing preparations. May cause contact dermatitis.

DIAZOMETHANE: Carcinogenic, mutagenic, toxic or causes adverse reactions. (See definition at beginning of glossary.)

DIBENZOPYRAN: Carcinogenic, mutagenic, toxic or causes adverse reactions. (See definition at beginning of glossary.)

DIBROMOCYANOBUTANE (TEKTAMER 38): Causes adverse reactions or is toxic, causes allergic contact dermatitis.

DIBUTYL ADIPATE: An ester found in personal care products. An ester is a product of a condensation reaction in which a molecule of an acid unites with a molecule of alcohol and eliminates a molecule of water.

DICAPRYL ADIPATE: An ester found in personal care products. An ester is a product of a condensation reaction in which a molecule of an acid unites with a molecule of alcohol and eliminates a molecule of water.

DICEYLDIMONIUM CHLORIDE: Hair conditioning and anti-static agent. Used in many hair shampoo or grooming products. Also used in deodorants, lotions, mouthwashes and cuticle softeners. Diluted solutions are used in medicine to sterilize the skin and mucous membranes. It is a quaternary compound. (See Quaternary Compounds.) Concentrated solutions should not be used.

DICHLOROBENZYL ALCOHOL: A broad spectrum anti-fungal. Studies on mice and rats shows it to be toxic.

DICHLORO-M-XYLENOL: An anti-microbial, preservative and disinfectant found in personal care products and many baby products. It is toxic.

DICHLOROPHEN: Carcinogenic, mutagenic, toxic or causes adverse reactions. (See definition at beginning of glossary.)

DICHLORVOS: Carcinogenic, mutagenic, toxic or causes adverse reactions. (See definition at beginning of glossary.)

DICOFOL: Carcinogenic, mutagenic, toxic or causes adverse reactions. (See definition at beginning of glossary.)

DIEPOXYBUTANE: Carcinogenic, mutagenic, toxic or causes adverse reactions. (See definition at beginning of glossary.)

DIETHANOLAMINE: Generally known as DEA, it is widely used in many shampoo preparations. Recent studies suggest that when DEA comes in contact with skin, nitrosamines are formed. Nitrosamines are carcinogens. Avoid.

DIETHYLADIPATE: An ester found in personal care products. An ester is a product of a condensation reaction in which a molecule of an acid unites with a molecule of alcohol and eliminates a molecule of water.

DIETHYL PHTHALATE: Phthalates are recognized as being hormone mimicking. (See section on xeno-estrogens.) Carcinogenic, mutagenic, toxic or causes adverse reactions. (See definition at beginning of glossary.)

DIETHYLSULFATE: Carcinogenic, mutagenic, toxic or causes adverse reactions. (See definition at beginning of glossary.)

DIETHYLENE GLYCOL MONOSTEARATE: A nonionic surfactant used in shampoo and cleansing preparations. Ethylene Glycol groups are carcinogenic, mutagenic, causing adverse reactions or are toxic.

DIETHYLENE OXIDE: Carcinogenic, mutagenic, toxic or causes adverse reactions. (See definition at beginning of glossary.)

DIETHYLNITROSAMINE: Carcinogenic contaminant that can readily pass through the skin.

DIGALLOYLTRIOLEATE: Causes photosensitivity.

DIGLYCOL OLEATE PALMITATE; STEARATE: Esters found in personal care products. An ester is a product of a condensation reaction in which a molecule of an acid unites with a molecule of alcohol and eliminates a molecule of water. (See Oleic Acid, Palmitates, Glycols.)

DIHYDROXYACETONE: The *tanning agent* in many self-tanning formulas. It is actually a keto sugar that reacts with protein on the surface of the skin to create the look of a tan. The molecules in this ingredient are too large to penetrate the skin any deeper than the top layer. Since it is unable to react in any way with the melanin in the skin this ingredient does not afford the protection from sun that a real tan would. Studies show that it may cause contact dermatitis.

DIISOPROPANOLNITROSAMINE: Carcinogenic, mutagenic, toxic or causes adverse reactions. (See definition at beginning of glossary.)

DIMETHICONE: Used in many skin care preparations to help the cream glide. It is known to cause various adverse reactions both topically and internally. Avoid this ingredient.

DIMENTHICONE COPOLYOL: An oil derived from silicone (silica) to aid in the smooth application of a product. Also a thickener and anti-foam agent and emollient. Used as a conditioner in skin and hair products, for cleansers, foundations, aftershaves, bath soaps and suntan products. This is a safer, modified version of dimethicone.

DIMETHICON: Found to cause tumors and mutations in lab animals. (See Dimethicone.)

DIMETHICONOL: (See Dimethicone.)

DIMETHYLAMINE: Made from methanol and ammonia. It is used in soaps and detergents (and weed killers). Irritating to skin and mucous membranes. Nitrosamines can form in all cosmetic ingredients containing amines and amino derivatives with nitrogen compounds. Nitosamines are known carcinogens.

DIMETHYL LAURAMINE: Nitrosamines can form in all cosmetic ingredients containing amines and amino derivatives with nitrogen compounds. Nitosamines are known carcinogens.

DIMETHYL PHTHALATE: Contains phthalates which mimic estrogen. (See section on xeno-estrogens.) Carcinogenic, mutagenic, toxic or causes adverse reactions. (See definition at beginning of glossary.)

DIMETHYL STEARAMINE: Carcinogenic, mutagenic, toxic or causes adverse reactions. (See definition at beginning of glossary.) Nitrosamines can form in all cosmetic ingredients containing amines and amino derivatives with nitrogen compounds. Nitosamines are known carcinogens.

DIMETHYLSULFATE: Carcinogenic, mutagenic, toxic or causes adverse reactions. (See definition at beginning of glossary.)

DIMETHYLANILINE: Carcinogenic, mutagenic, toxic or causes adverse reactions. (See definition at beginning of glossary.)

DIMETHYLCARBAMOYL CHLORIDE: Carcinogenic, mutagenic, toxic or causes adverse reactions. (See definition at beginning of glossary.)

DIMETHYLNITROSAMINE: Carcinogenic, mutagenic, toxic or causes adverse reactions. (See definition at beginning of glossary.)

DI-N-BUTYLPHTHALATE: Contains phthalates which mimic estrogen. (See section on xeno-estrogens.) Carcinogenic, mutagenic, toxic or causes adverse reactions. (See definition at beginning of glossary.)

DI-N-OCTYLPHTHALATE: Contains phthalates which mimic estrogen (See section on xeno-estrogens) Carcinogenic, mutagenic, toxic or causes adverse reactions. (See definition at beginning of glossary.)

DIOCTYL ADIPATE: Used as a buffering agent in personal care products. It is a component of a group of esters designed to penetrate the skin. May be derived from beets or synthetically produced. (See esters.) It has been found to be lethal to rats in high doses but not toxic to humans.

DIOXANE (1,4-DIOXANE): A contaminant found in high levels in cosmetic raw materials and off-the-shelf products especially baby shampoo and bubble baths. It is a known carcinogen. (See section on Baby Products.)

DIOXYBENZONE (BENZOPHENONE-N (1-12)): Studies show that it may cause contact dermatitis.

DIOXYETHYLENE ETHER: Contains ethers. Carcinogenic, mutagenic, toxic or causes adverse reactions. (See definition at beginning of glossary.)

DIPHENYL: Carcinogenic, mutagenic, toxic or causes adverse reactions. (See definition at beginning of glossary.)

DIPHENYLKETONE: Carcinogenic, mutagenic, toxic or causes adverse reactions. (See definition at beginning of glossary.)

DIRECT BLACK 131: Suspected carcinogen, teratogen, or toxin.

DIRECT BLACK 38: Carcinogenic, mutagenic, toxic or causes adverse reactions. (See definition at beginning of glossary.)

DIRECT BLACK 38: Suspected carcinogen, teratogen, or toxin.

DIRECT BLUE 6: Carcinogenic, mutagenic, toxic or causes adverse reactions. (See definition at beginning of glossary.)

DIRECT BLUE 6: Suspected carcinogen, teratogen, or toxin.

DIRECT BROWN 1: Suspected carcinogen, teratogen, or toxin.

DIRECT BROWN 12: Suspected carcinogen, teratogen, or toxin.

DIRECT BROWN 154: Suspected carcinogen, teratogen, or toxin.

DIRECT BROWN 2: Suspected carcinogen, teratogen, or toxin.

DIRECT BROWN 31: Suspected carcinogen, teratogen, or toxin.

DIRESORCINOLPHTHALEIN: Carcinogenic, mutagenic, toxic or causes adverse reactions. (See definition at beginning of glossary.)

DISODIUM EDTA: Used for hair, skin and personal products. A chelating agent (a compound that binds and precipitates— separates out of a solution or suspension—metal or mineral ions). Nitrosamines can form in all cosmetic ingredients containing amines and amino derivatives with nitrogen compounds. Nitosamines are known carcinogens.

DISODIUM EDTA-COPPER: For use in shampoo only. (See Disodium EDTA.)

DISODIUM LAURAMIDO MEA-SULFOSUCCINATE: Used in shampoos. Surfactant (cleansing agent) and foam booster. Surfactants are wetting agents that lower water surface tension, permitting water to spread and penetrate more easily. (See MEA)

DISODIUM LAURETH SULFOSUCCINATE: Used in shampoos as a detergent, soap, emulsifier and surfactant. Made with fatty, sodium and sulfosuccinic acids. Studies show that products with this ingredient may contain dangerous levels of ethylene oxide, a potent toxin with NIOSH exposure limit of 1 ppm. An irritant to skin and eyes. A suspected human carcinogen.

DISODIUM OLEAMIDO PEG: Studies show that products with this ingredient may contain dangerous levels of ethylene oxide, a potent toxin with NIOSH exposure limit of 1 ppm. An irritant to skin and eyes. A suspected human carcinogen.

DISODIUM RICINOLEAMIDO MEA SULFOSUCCINATE: Used in cleansing preparations. It is a surfactant (cleansing agent), foam booster and moisturizer. (See MEA.)

DISODIUM SALT: May contain dangerous levels of nitrosamines (a potent carcinogen) as a by-product of manufacturing.

DISPERSE YELLOW 3: Suspected carcinogen, teratogen, or toxin.

DMDM HYDANTOIN: Used as a preservative in personal care products. It may release formaldehyde which is a suspected carcinogen. Hydantoin caused cancer when injected into rats.

DODECYL ALCOHOL: Carcinogenic, mutagenic, toxic or causes adverse reactions. (See definition at beginning of glossary.)

DOWICIL: May cause allergic reactions.

EDTA (ETHYLENE DIAMINE TETREACETIC ACID): A synthetic chemical that acts as a chelating agent (a compound that binds and precipitates—separates out of a solution or suspension-metal or mineral ions.) Also acts as an anti-microbial. Concentrations should be limited to 5 percent maximum in a formulation. Nitrosamines (a potent carcinogen) can form in all cosmetic ingredients containing amines and amino derivatives with nitrogen compounds.

ELASTIN: Protein found in the dermal layers of skin that functions to maintain skin elasticity. When applied topically, there appears to be no research proving that this highly insoluble protein has the ability to improve the elasticity of the skin.

ELDER BLOSSOMS/BERRIES: A mild astringent. Essential oil is high in fatty acids (66 percent) and very beneficial to the hair and skin.

ENZYMES: (See Plant Enzymes.)

EPICHLOROHYDRIN: Carcinogenic, mutagenic, toxic or causes adverse reactions. (See definition at beginning of glossary.)

EPOXYETHANE: Carcinogenic, mutagenic, toxic or causes adverse reactions. (See definition at beginning of glossary.)

ERGOCALCIFEROl: Used in hair products to help repair split ends. A form of Vitamin D.

ERYTHROSINE SODIUM: A coal tar derivative, it is used in rouge. Carcinogenic, mutagenic, toxic or causes adverse reactions. (See definition at beginning of glossary.)

ESCIN/B SITOSTEROL: Used in skin, body and hand preparations, contains protein and fatty oils. Used topically, it acts as a protectant due to its insolubility in water. Derived from the seed of the horse chestnut tree.

ESSENTIAL FATTY ACIDS: Therapeutic organic oils that moisturize the skin and hair. Sometimes known as vitamin F. These saturated (palmitic and stearic acids) or unsaturated fats (oleic, linoleic and linolenic acids) are found in vegetable and animal fats.

ESSENTIAL OILS: Aroma constituents from plants. Extraction processes vary according to the company who is doing the extraction process. Expression is the simplest and most natural process. It is used mainly for citrus fruits. Enfleurage is an extraction process that uses oils to soak up the plant oil. It is labour intensive and costly and reserved for the tuberose. Maceration involves the use of solvents to extract the oil but it also extricates waxes and other compounds which need to be removed through further processing. Another process involves using volatile solvents and then removing them through low pressure distillation. The most popular methods of extraction is through water or steam distillation. Most of the supposedly pure essential oils are now produced synthetically. Linalyl acetate and linalool produces the nature identical to lavender.

ESTERS: an ester is formed by combining alcohol and a acid and eliminating the water. Toxicity depends on the individual ester.

ETHANOL: Widely used in cosmetics, in after shaves bubble baths, deodorants, hair preparations, suntan and skin care lotions, mouthwash, colognes and perfumes. It is derived from the fermentation of sugar and starch or from grains. It is an alcohol from hydrocarbons. At concentrations of 15 to 20 percent it acts as a preservative and at concentrations of 60 to 70 percent it acts as a bactericidal. More than 80 g per day would be toxic. The acceptable dose would be 7 g per day. Mouthwashes that contain more than 25 percent alcohol are suspected of causing esophageal cancer. Provokes a late allergic reaction in some people when used topically. Taken orally, ethanol is toxic in doses above 80 g. Ethanol is often purposely made poisonous by the addition of methanol and it is then known as SD (especially denatured alcohol). Check to see where it is listed on the product label. If it is close to the bottom then low concentrations have been used.

ETHANOLAMIDE OF LAURIC ACID: A surfactant used in shampoo.

ETHANOLAMINE: Carcinogenic, mutagenic, toxic or causes adverse reactions. (See definition at beginning of glossary.)

ETHANOLAMINES (GROUP): Nitrosamines can form in all cosmetic ingredients containing amines and amino derivatives with nitrogen compounds. Nitosamines are known carcinogens.

ETHERS (GROUP): Causes adverse reactions or is toxic. Studies show that it may cause contact dermatitis.

ETHIODIZED OIL: Natural oil form Poppy seed (Fatty acids) with Iodine. It is used as an antiseptic, anesthetic, germicide and expectorant.

ETHOXYDIGYCOL: Used as a solvent for oil and water. It is an emulsifier and is used for decreasing viscosity. Used in cleansing products, skin care, moisturizers, hair shampoos and conditioners. Used as a solvent and thinner in nail enamels. It is said to be non-irritating and non penetrating when applied to human skin but all ethoxylated ingredients should be avoided. (See Section on Hormones.)

ETHOXYETHYL-METHOXY CINNAMATE: Carcinogenic, mutagenic, toxic or causes adverse reactions. (See definition at beginning of glossary.)

ETHOXYLATED LANOLINS: Carcinogenic, mutagenic, toxic or causes adverse reactions. (See definition at beginning of glossary.)

ETHYLACETATE: A solvent used in nail products. May depress the central nervous system. Considered toxic.

ETHYLACRYLATE: Carcinogenic, mutagenic, toxic or causes adverse reactions. (See definition at beginning of glossary.)

ETHYL ALCOHOL (ETHANOL): Colorless, vaporizable liquid. Has a burning taste. Well-known us as the active ingredient in alcoholic beverages. Commonly called simply *alcohol*, although there are many other kinds of alcohols. Ethanol is widely used in cosmetics as a solvent and as an antibacterial agent. As a preservative, it is effective at concentrations of 15 percent to 20 percent. It's a antitoxin in concentrations of 60 percent to 70 percent, with a bactericidal effect within 45 seconds. It's also used in acne treatments and in rinses for oily hair. Ethanol absorbs water and thus can be very drying in fast-drying skin lotions (at concentrations of 15 percent); the lotions need to include glycerols and vegetable oils to minimize the drying effect. Causes systemic eczematous contact dermtitis.

ETHYL BENZENE: Carcinogenic, mutagenic, toxic or causes adverse reactions. (See definition at beginning of glossary.)

ETHYL BENZOATE: Causes inflammatory reaction.

ETHYL CAPRATE/CAPROATE: An ester found in personal care products. An ester is a product of a condensation reaction in which a molecule of an acid unites with a molecule of alcohol and eliminates a molecule of water.

ETHYL CARBANATE: An ester found in personal care products. An ester is a product of a condensation reaction in which a molecule of an acid unites with a molecule of alcohol and eliminates a molecule of water.

ETHYL CHLORIDE: Carcinogenic, mutagenic, toxic or causes adverse reactions. (See definition at beginning of glossary.)

ETHYL CHLOROFORMATE: Carcinogenic, mutagenic, toxic or causes adverse reactions. (See definition at beginning of glossary.)

ETHYL CINNAMATE: An ester found in personal care products. An ester is a product of a condensation reaction in which a molecule of an acid unites with a molecule of alcohol and eliminates a molecule of water. (See Cinnamates Group.)

ETHYL ESTER OF HYDROLYZED ANIMAL PROTEIN: A conditioner, humectant, moisturizer and film-former in cosmetics. Aids in the comb out of hair tangles.

ETHYL ESTER OF PVM/MA COPOLYMER: A fixative in hair spray. It is a vinyl polymer made from a reaction between acetylene and certain compounds such as alcohol, phenol and amines. (See Esters and Phenol.)

ETHYL HEXYL: An ester found in personal care products. An ester is a product of a condensation reaction in which a molecule of an acid unites with a molecule of alcohol and eliminates a molecule of water.

ETHYL MYRISTATE: An ester found in personal care products. An ester is a product of a condensation reaction in which a molecule of an acid unites with a molecule of alcohol and eliminates a molecule of water. (See Myristate.)

ETHYL OLEATE: An ester found in personal care products. An ester is a product of a condensation reaction in which a molecule of an acid unites with a molecule of alcohol and eliminates a molecule of water. (See Oleic Acid.)

ETHYLPARABEN: Used as a preservative with anti-microbial and preservative qualities. This ingredient, along with butylparaben and propylparaben, may be irritating to the skin if more than 5 percent is present in a formulation. Many commercially made cosmetics contain a higher percentage. It is believed to be a sensitizer and may cause contact dermatitis. Check to see where it is listed on the label. (See methylparaben.)

ETHYL-P-HYDROXYBENZOATE: Has low sensitizing potential.

ETHYL PALMITATE/STREARATE: An ester found in personal care products. An ester is a product of a condensation reaction in which a molecule of an acid unites with a molecule of alcohol and eliminates a molecule of water.

ETHYLENE ALCOHOL: Carcinogenic, mutagenic, toxic or causes adverse reactions. (See definition at beginning of glossary.)

ETHYLENE DIBROMIDE: Carcinogenic, mutagenic, toxic or causes adverse reactions. (See definition at beginning of glossary.)

ETHYLENE GLYCOL DISTEARATE: A nonionic surfactant used in shampoo. (See Ethylene Glycols Group.)

ETHYLENE GLYCOL MONOPHENYL ETHER: Carcinogenic, mutagenic, toxic or causes adverse reactions. (See definition at beginning of glossary.)

ETHYLENE GLYCOL MONOSTEARATE: A nonionic surfactant used in shampoo. (See Ethylene Glycols Group.)

ETHYLENE GLYCOLS (GROUP): toxic by ingestion and inhalation. Induces allergic reactions and has been known to cause chemically induced contact dermatitis.

ETHYLENE OXIDE: Potent toxin with NIOSH exposure limit of 1 ppm. It is a skin and eye irritant and a suspected human carcinogen.

ETHYLENE THIOUREA: Carcinogenic, mutagenic, toxic or causes adverse reactions. (See definition at beginning of glossary.)

ETHYLENE: Carcinogenic, mutagenic, toxic or causes adverse reactions. (See definition at beginning of glossary.)

ETHYLENEDIAMINES (GROUP): Causes facial dematoses and contact dermatitis.

ETHYLENEDIAMINETETRAACETIC ACID: Carcinogenic, mutagenic, toxic or causes adverse reactions. (See definition at beginning of glossary.)

ETHYLENEIMINE: Carcinogenic, mutagenic, toxic or causes adverse reactions. (See definition at beginning of glossary.)

ETHYLHEXYL p-METHOXYCINNAMATE: An ingredient used in sunscreens. Absorbs UV rays.

EVENING PRIMROSE OIL: A source of essential fatty acids, particularly gamma-linolenic acid. Helps to regenerate skin cells. A healing agent for dry and damaged skin.

EVERGREEN OIL: An oil used in skin care products for its cooling, soothing and astringent effect. Extracted from evergreen magnolia leaves.

EXT.D&C VIOLET NO. 2: Colourant for external use only, except eye area.

EXT.D&C YELLOW NO. 7: Colourant for external use only, except eye area.

FAMESOL: A sesquiterpene alcohol, occurring naturally in many essential oils such as chamomile, rose, citronella, sandalwood and lemon grass. Deodorant and bacteriostat.

FATTY ACIDS: Widely used in cosmetics. Some are unsaturated such as oleic, linolenic and linoleic or saturated such as palmitic and stearic. Obtained by hydrolysis or produced synthetically. Found to be contaminated with N-nitroso-N-methylalkylamines.

FATTY ALCOHOLS (GROUP): Used in skin and hair care products. Cetyl lauryl, oleyl and stearyl fatty acids are examples of fatty alcohols. They can be naturally derived or synthetically produced. May cause cosmetic allergies.

FATTY AMINE OXIDES: Nitrosamines can form in all cosmetic ingredients containing amines and amino derivatives with nitrogen compounds. Nitrosomines are known carcinogens.

FATTY ACID ESTERS: Used in cosmetics as an absorption base and as an emulsifier. Esters are derived from unsaturated fats. Vegetable glycerin, shea or cocoa butter, beeswax and jojoba are examples of fatty acid wax esters. Cetyl alcohols from coconut palm kernels is a fatty acid ester. (See Fatty Acids.)

FD&C BLUE NO. 1 ALUMINUM LAKE: Permitted in food, drugs and cosmetics, except eye area. Known as Acid Blue No. 9. Suspected carcinogen, teratogen, or toxin.

FD&C BLUE NO. 1: Permitted in food, drugs and cosmetics, except eye area. Suspected carcinogen, teratogen, or toxin.

FD&C BLUE NO. 2: Permitted in food, drugs and cosmetics, except eye area. Suspected carcinogen, teratogen or toxin.

FD&C BLUE NO. 2 ALUMINUM LAKE: Permitted in food, drugs and cosmetics, except eye area. Suspected carcinogen, teratogen, or toxin.

FD&C GREEN NO. 3 LAKE: Permitted in food, drugs and cosmetics, except eye area. Provisionally listed with FDA.

FD&C GREEN NO. 3: Permitted in food, drugs and cosmetics, except eye area. Suspected carcinogen, teratogen, or toxin.

FD&C RED NO. 3: Permitted in food, drugs and cosmetics, except eye area. Also known as Acid Red. Suspected carcinogen, teratogen, or toxin. Has been found to: (1) cause human breast cells to grow, (2) mimic the effect of natural estrogen at the molecular level, (3) damage the genetic material of human breast cells. This colour agent is acting as an environmental estrogen and by damaging cellular DNA may be a major factor that contributes to breast cancer.

FD&C RED NO. 4: External use only, except eye area. No longer available for use in foods because of possible threats to the adrenal glands and urinary bladder. Suspected carcinogen, teratogen, or toxin.

FD&C RED NO. 40, ALUMINUM LAKE: Permitted in food, drugs and cosmetics including the eye area. Provisionally listed with FDA. Suspected carcinogen, teratogen, or toxin.

FD&C YELLOW NO. 5 ALUMINUM LAKE: Permitted in food, drugs and cosmetics, except eye area. Provisionally listed with FDA.

FD&C YELLOW NO. 5: Permitted in food, drugs and cosmetics, except eye area.

FD&C YELLOW NO. 6 ALUMINUM LAKE: Permitted in food, drugs and cosmetics, except eye area. Provisionally listed with FDA. Suspected carcinogen, teratogen, or toxin.

FD&C YELLOW NO. 6: Permitted in food, drugs and cosmetics, except eye area. Suspected carcinogen, teratogen, or toxin.

FENUGREEK EXTRACT: An emollient, anti-inflammatory and healing agent used for treating skin.

FERRIC AMMONIUM FERROCYANIDE: Used in cosmetics as a colour additive. It is extremely toxic.

FERRIC AMMONIUM: Ferrocyanide. A colourant for external use only including eye area. It is very toxic.

FERRIC FERROCYANIDE: A colourant for external use only including eye area. It is very toxic.

FLUOMETURON: Carcinogenic, mutagenic, toxic or causes adverse reactions. (See definition at beginning of glossary.)

FLUORANS: Shown to have comedogenic (acne producing) properties.

FLUORANTHENE: Carcinogenic, contaminant found in mineral oils and waxes.

FLUORESCEINS (GROUP): Studies show cytotoxicity and genotoxicity.

FLUORIDE: Used in most toothpastes to prohibit enzyme production. Although it is promoted to stop tooth decay, it is toxic to the body.

FLUOROCARBONS: A component of aerosols that destroys the ozone layer of the atmosphere.

FORMALDEHYDE (GROUP): It can be found in a wide variety of cosmetics and personal care products from toothpaste to hair care products to lipsticks and body lotions. It is an anti-microbial, preservative and disinfectant. Unfortunately, it is hidden in many chemical combinations. For instance, DMDM Hydantoin and MDM Hydantoin may contain formaldehyde freed during the manufacturing process. Formalin is a trade name for formaldehyde. It is severely toxic when inhaled or swallowed. Forty-four percent of all people whose skin is exposed to it get an irritating reaction. It is used in shampoos at concentrations of 0.1 percent to 0.2 percent. Methanol is sometimes added to formaldehyde at a 15 percent concentration to prevent polymerization. It is extremely toxic, a suspected carcinogen and is strongly linked to cancer.

FORMIC ALDEHYDE: Carcinogenic, mutagenic, toxic or causes adverse reactions (See definition at beginning of glossary.)

FRAGRANCES (GROUP): Used in practically all personal care products to mask the smell of the ingredients. (See Section on Fragrance.) Practically all fragrances contain toxic ingredients. A safe fragrance would be a natural scent from plant or from essential oil.

FRUCTOSE: Used in personal care products as a humectant. It is a sugar found in honey and fruits.

FRUIT ACIDS: Used as an exfoliant in most cosmetics or as a collagen stimulant in others (depending on the concentration—see Alpha Hydroxy Acids.)

FUCUS: Its essential oil is a stimulant often used in massage lotions, anti-cellulite preparations and some hair care products for its ability to increase blood circulation to the skin or scalp. A seaweed rich in alginic acid, amino acids, polysaccharides, minerals and vitamins.

FUROCOUMARIN-PLUS-UVA: A known phototoxin that reacts with UV radiation to yield a genotoxin.

GERANIOL: A natural component of many essential oils and used as an ingredient in perfume. Causes pigmented contact dermatitis.

GERANIUM OIL: Used in skin care products for its ability to balance sebum production and to promote healing. The fragrance is used as an anti-depressant. Causes pigmented contact dermatitis.

GINGER: Used in skin care and bath products. A stimulant and anti-irritant, its warming, soothing properties are very beneficial to the skin. Sometimes used as a fragrance. In both powdered and liquid form it is used in bath oils and other cosmetics.

GINKGO BILOBA: Used in some health oriented skin and hair care products. It is an astringent and improves the circulation. The Chinese have used this herb for close to 5,000 years to slow the aging process.

GINSENG: An important tonic herb for anti-wrinkle creams and other hair and skin care products.

GLYCERETH: Used in skin care preparations, it is a synthetic form of glycerin made with polyethylene glycol ether. (See Glycols and Ethers.)

GLYCERIN: Used in a great deal of skin and body care products, it acts as a humectant—a water-attracting/binding ingredient. Since it acts as a water-attracting agent it can actually draw moisture from the skin leading to long-term moisture loss. Sweet, syrupy alcohol that can be produced artificially from propylene alcohol or naturally derived from vegetable oils .The most prevalent source is an animal source but it is generally mixed with vegetable oils when used in cosmetics. A strictly plant source is available in some products which appears to be uncontaminated. For the most part it is carcinogenic, mutagenic, toxic or causes adverse reactions. (See definition at beginning of glossary.)

GLYCEROL MONOSTEARATE: A nonionic surfactant found in shampoos and cleansing products. Causes skin allergies.

GLYCEROL: Carcinogenic, mutagenic, toxic or causes adverse reactions. (See definition at beginning of glossary.)

GLYCERYL COCOATE: Used in cosmetics as an emulsifier and surfactant, it is a glycerin by-product of coconut oil. (See Glyceryl Esters.)

GLYCERYL DILAURATE: Largely artificial chemical with a drop or two of some natural fatty acid. Used as a texturizer and as a opacifying agent in shampoos, lotions and creams. (See Glyceryl Esters.)

GLYCERYL ERUCATE: Largely artificial chemical with a drop or two of some natural fatty acid. Used as a texturizer and as a opacifying agent in shampoos, lotions and creams. (See Glyceryl Esters.)

GLYCERYL ESTERS (GROUP): Studies show that it may cause contact dermatitis.

GLYCERYL HYDROXYSTEARATE: Largely artificial chemicals with a drop or two of some natural fatty acid. Used as a texturizer and as a opacifying agent in shampoos, lotions and creams. (See Glyceryl Esters.)

GLYCERYL MONOGLYCERIDE: Used in cosmetics as an anti-microbial and preservative. (See Glyceryl Esters.)

GLYCERYL MONOLAURATE (GLYCEROL MONO-LAURATE): Causes irritation.

GLYCERYL MONOSTEARATE: Largely artificial chemicals with a drop or two of some natural fatty acid. Used as a texturizer and as a opacifying agent in shampoos, lotions and creams. Carcinogenic, mutagenic, toxic or causes adverse reactions. (See definition at beginning of glossary.)

GLYCERYL MYRISTATE: Largely artificial chemicals with a drop or two of some natural fatty acid. Used as a texturizer and as a opacifying agent in shampoos, lotions and creams. (See Glyceryl Esters.) Causes skin allergy.

GLYCERYL OLEATE: Largely artificial chemicals with a drop or two of some natural fatty acid. Used as a texturizer and as a opacifying agent in shampoos, lotions and creams. (See Glyceryl Esters.)

GLYCERYL OLEATE: Used in cosmetics. Contact with eyes may cause irritation. Causes skin allergies.

GLYCERYL PABA: Causes photosensitivity.

GLYCERYL RICINOLEATE: Largely artificial chemicals with a drop or two of some natural fatty acid. Used as a texturizer and as a opacifying agent in shampoos, lotions and creams. (See Glyceryl Esters)

GLYCERYL STEARATE SE: Used in shampoos as a pearlizing agent also as an opacifier in lotions. It is an emulsifier. (See Glyceryl Esters)

GLYCERYL STEARATE: Used as an emulsifier and surfactant, hair conditioner. Made by combining glycerin and stearic acid. It helps combine oils and water. Causes skin allergies.

GLYCERYL THIOGLYCOLATE: Studies show that it may cause contact dermatitis.

GLYCERYL TRIMYRISTATE: Largely artificial chemicals with a drop or two of some natural fatty acid . Used as a texturizer and as a pacifying agent in shampoos, lotions and creams. (See Glyceryl Esters.)

GLYCINE: Used in skin care preparations as a texturizer. It is an amino acid.

GLYCOL DISTEARATE: Skin conditioning agent and viscosity increasing agent. Used in shampoos and conditioners, cleansing products and bath preparations.

GLYCOL STEARATE: Used in shampoos as a pearlizing agent also as an opacifier in lotions. It is an emulsifier. (See Glycols Group.)

GLYCOL, 1,2-ETHANEDIOL: Carcinogenic, mutagenic, toxic or causes adverse reactions. (See definition at beginning of glossary.)

GLYCOLIC ACID: A fruit acid that can be chemically produced or may be obtained from sugar cane. Depending on its concentration, it is often used for exfoliation. (See Alpha-Hydroxy Acids.)

GLYCOLS (GROUP): Used as a humectant in all sorts of personal care products. Propylene glycol, for instance, has been shown to cause liver abnormalities and kidney damage in laboratory animals. Ethylene glycol is a suspected bladder carcinogen. Diethylene glycol and carbitol are considered toxic. Carcinogenic, mutagenic, toxic or causes adverse reactions. (See definition at beginning of glossary.)

GLYCOSAMINOGLYCANS: Used as a humectant and skin softener in cosmetics. It is also known as mucopolysaccharides which is a basic component of the skin. It is a gelatinous material that cements cells together and helps to maintain a moist environment for collagen, elastin and dermal cells and provides support for connective tissue and mucous membrane. They are said to minimize wrinkles.

GLYCYLALCOHOL: Carcinogenic, mutagenic, toxic or causes adverse reactions. (See definition at beginning of glossary.)

GOLDENSEAL EXTRACT: Used in personal care products as a healing agent and antiseptic. Derived from plant.

GOTU KOLA EXTRACT: A healing herb (Centella asiatica) used as a healing agent in skin care products.

GRAIN ALCOHOL: May cause systemic eczematous contact dermatitis.

GRAPE SEED EXTRACT: Used in skin care products as an anti oxidant because of its ability to neutralize free radicals. Its capacity to prevent oxidation from occurring makes it an excellent prevention ingredient.

GRAPE SEED OIL: Used in skin care products and as a carrier oil for essential oils (aromatherapy).

GRAPEFRUIT SEED EXTRACT: Used in personal care products as an anti-microbial, anti-fungal and preservative. Often mixed with propylene glycol. (See Propylene Glycol.)

GREEN CHROMOXIDE: A colourant used health oriented products.

GREEN TEA: Used for its healing effects in skin care products, it has been documented as having anti-carcinogenic abilities. Also known as Camellia Sinensis. It protects the skin from the damaging UVB rays.

GUAIAZULENE: Used in skin care products as a healing agent for soothing and calming irritated skin. Generally called azulene, it comes from the German chamomile plant. Used as a colourant for external use only, except eye area.

GUANINE: Used in skin care products and make-up. It imparts a luminescence to the product. It is derived from fish scales, sugar beets, yeast and clover seed.

GUAR GUM: Naturally occurring resin from seeds of an Asian tree. Used as a thickener and emulsifier.

GUMS: Used in hair gels and setting lotions. They are naturally derived polysaccharides of high molecular weight that are dispersed in water. (See Gums.)

HAIR KERATIN AMINO ACIDS: Hair and skin conditioners. (See Hydrolyzed Hair Keratin.)

HAMAMELIS WATER: Used as an astringent in skin care products. It is a witch hazel extract. Contains alcohol. Witch hazel causes adverse reactions. (See definition at beginning of glossary.) (See Witch Hazel.)

HECTORITE: Naturally occurring clay used in facial masks to draw out oil. May also draw moisture from skin. Gelling agent and thickener. Derived from bentonite clay.

HEMATITE: A natural mineral used as a color in face powders and make up.

HENNA: Used in shampoos and as a rich conditioner for hair. It is anti-fungal and anti-bacterial. Some natural hair colouring hennas may actually contain synthetic colours.

HEPTACHLOR: Carcinogenic, mutagenic, toxic or causes adverse reactions. (See definition at beginning of glossary.)

HEXACHLOROBENZENE: System toxin in infants.

HEXAMIDINE DIISETHIONATE: Causes facial dermatoses and contact dermatitis.

HEXYL LAURATE CAPRYLIC: Skin protectant and conditioner, water sealer, emulsifier. Used to moisturize. May be derived from plant or synthetically produced.

HEXYLENE GLYCOL: A humectant, moisturizer, solvent and plasticizer found in hair and skin care products. Toxic by ingestion and inhalation, irritant to skin, eyes and mucous membranes.

HMTA: Carcinogenic, mutagenic, toxic or causes adverse reactions. (See definition at beginning of glossary.)

HOMESALATE (HOMOMENTHYL SALICYLATE): Artificial chemical that is used to replace the phenolic compounds that are used in sunscreens. Causes follicular eruption.

HONEY: Used in many personal care products it acts as an emollient, humectant and anti-bactericide.

HOPS EXTRACT: Used in skin care products as a skin softener. Extracted from the flowers of the Hop Vine.

HORSE CHESTNUT EXTRACT: An anti-irritant and calming substance used in skin care creams for problem skin. Often used in anti-cellulite creams or lotions. Research shows that it aids in the removal of excess fluids.

HORSETAIL EXTRACT: Used in skin care products for its softening and smoothing ability and also for its astringent effect. It also helps to strengthen vein and capillary walls.

HUMECTANT: Used to retain moisture in the skin. May actually pull moisture from the underlying layers up to the surface robbing the immature cells of vital nutrients.

HYALURONIC ACID: A protein occurring in the skin, it moisturizes and conditions the skin. Known as a water binder, it is able to bind 1000 times its weight in water. It is an enzyme with capabilities of hydrolyzing mucopolysaccharides.

HYALURONIDASE: (See Hyaluronic Acid.)

HYDANTOINS (GROUP) (GLYCOLYLUREA): Used as a preservative in personal care products. It may release formaldehyde which is a suspected carcinogen. Hydantoin caused cancer when injected into rats. It can also cause dermatitis.

HYDOROLYZED HAIR KERATIN: Strengthens the hair shafts and helps prevent split ends and breakage. Used as both a hair and skin conditioner. It is a protein derivative.

HYDREATED SILICA: A mild abrasive material in the base of the toothpaste. An absorbent and thickening agent. Also found in cleansing products, manicuring products and bath preparation. An anti-caking agent to keep loose powders free flowing. (See Silica.)

HYDROCARBONS (GROUP): Studies show that it causes dermatitis, chemically induced acne, contains carcinogen contaminant.

HYDROCORTISONE: Used in skin care preparations for skin disorders. It is an adrenal gland hormone that has been synthesized for medicinal use. It can adversely affect the skin by damaging the collagen of the connective tissues.

HYDROCOTYL EXTRACT: Used in skin care products for its ability to balance and calm the skin. Acts as an anti-inflammatory agent.

HYDROFLUOROCARBON 152A: Used in hair spray, it acts as a propellant. It is also used in many hair preparations. Derived from petroleum, natural gas or coal. (See Hydrocarbons Group.)

HYDROG TALLOWETH-60 MYRISTYL GLYCOL: Used in cosmetics as an emulsifier and stabilizer. (See Glycols.)

HYDROGEN PEROXIDE: Studies have shown it to cause tumors and it is a cancer causing agent.

HYDROGENATED VEGETABLE OIL: Used in a wide variety of personal care products, it acts as an emollient, thickener and gellant. Hydrogenated means that hydrogen has been added to the oil to change it to a solid. The essential fatty acids in the oil are destroyed through this process.

HYDROLYZED ANIMAL PROTEIN: Used in many hair care preparations to help repair split ends and hold moisture in the hair. A by-product of the beef industry. It provides sheen to the hair.

HYDROLYZED MUCOPOLYSACCHARIDES: Used in skin and hair care products for its water binding (moisture holding) ability. (See Mucopolysaccharides.)

HYDROLYZED WHOLE WHEAT PROTEIN: Used in hair care products to help retain the moisture. Imparts shine and luster to dull hair.

HYDROQUINOL: Carcinogenic, mutagenic, toxic or causes adverse reactions. (See definition at beginning of glossary.)

HYDROQUINONE: Used as a skin bleaching agent and as an antioxidant to prevent rancidity. Causes sensitivity to sunlight.

Causes hyperpigmentation (brown globules). Toxic if taken internally. Linked to cancer, see section on sunscreens.

HYDROQUINONES (GROUP): Carcinogenic, mutagenic, toxic or causes adverse reactions. (See definition at beginning of glossary.)

HYDROXY CITRONELLAL: Studies show that it may cause psoriasis on the face.

HYDROXY PROPYLMETHYL CELLULOSE: Mild eye and skin irritant.

HYDROXYBENZOIC ACIDS: Studies show that it may cause contact dermatitis.

HYDROXYCITRONELLA: Causes allergies and contact dermatitis.

HYDROXYCOUMARINS: Found to be a skin sensitizer.

HYDROXYETHYLCELLULOSE: Used in hair conditioners, shampoos, eye make-up and skin cleansers as a binder, viscosity increaser, emulsion stabilizer and film former. It is an artificial polymer.

HYDROXYPROPYL AMINOBENZOATE: Carcinogenic, mutagenic, toxic or causes adverse reactions. (See definition at beginning of glossary.)

HYDROXYPROPYL GUAR: Used in hair and skin care products as a foaming agent and stabilizer. Used to reduce the amount of other surface surfactants in the formula.

HYDROXYPROPYL METHYLCELLULOSE: Used in shampoos, cleansing products, skin care deodorizers and indoor tanning products. It is a moisturizer, binder, emulsion, stabilizer, film former and thickener. (See Hydroxypropylcellulose.)

HYDROXYPROPYLCELLULOSE: Found to be a mild irritant.

IMIDAZOLIDINYL UREA: A preservative used in shampoos as bactericide. May be derived from either methanol (wood alcohol or allantoin) or from a bovine source. If heated to high temperatures, such as over the boiling point, it does produce formaldehyde. It is known to cause dermatitis.

INDIGOIDS: Shown to have comedogenic (acne producing) properties.

INOSITOL: A B vitamin used in shampoos or scalp conditioners. Aids cell respiration and it helps strengthen the scalp.

IODIDES: A compound containing iodine, naturally occurring in plants that grow in the sea. Applied topically, it is an excellent antiseptic.

IRGASAN DP-300: An anti-microbial and preservative. It is a biphenyl derived from coal tar. Biphenyls can mimic estrogen in the body.

IRON OXIDE: A colour additive, inorganic pigment compound of iron and oxygen found in a wide range of colors from black to yellow. Used as a natural colorant. No restrictions by FDA. Suspected carcinogen, teratogen or toxin.

ISOBUTANE: Used in aerosol sprays it acts as a propellant. A hazard to the environment.

ISOCETYL PALMITATE: Largely artificial chemical with a drop or two of some natural fatty acid. Used as a texturizer and as a opacifying agent in shampoos, lotions and creams. (See Palmitates.)

ISOCETYL STEARATE: Shown to have comedogenic (acne producing) properties.

ISOEUGENOL: Studies show that it may cause contact dermatitis.

ISOPARRAFIN (C13-16): Mixtures of aliphatic hydrocarbons. (See Hydrocarbons.)

ISOPROPANOLAMINE: A buffering agent used in cosmetics. (See Amines Group.)

ISOPROPYL ALCOHOL: Used as an astringent and oil dissolving agent in skin care products. It is a synthetic solvent made from propylene. Used in nail products and rubbing alcohol. Can be drying to the skin if used as a primary ingredient in a formulation. Isopropyl alcohol was found to collect in body organs. Avoid this ingredient.

ISOPROPYL-HYDROXYPALMITYL-ETHER: May cause contact allergies.

ISOPROPYL ISOSTEARATE: Used in skin care products. It is made by combining various fatty acids with isopropyl alcohol. Has comedogenic (acne producing) properties.

ISOPROPYL LANOLATE: An emollient that acts as a wetting agent for cosmetic pigments. Used as a binder for pressed powders and as a lubricant in lipsticks. It is made by combining various fatty acids with isopropyl alcohol. (See Isopropyl Alcohol.)

ISOPROPYL MYRISTATE (AND ITS ANALOGS): Used as an emollient, plasticizer and lubricant in preshaves, aftershaves, shampoos, bath oils, antiperspirants, deodorants and various creams and lotions. It helps to reduce the greasy feel of the oils in the product. Part natural and part synthetic. Can cause skin irritation and clog pores. Has comedogenic (acne producing) properties.

ISOPROPYL PALMITATE: Used in many moisturizing creams. It forms a thin layer on the skin and easily penetrates. Causes skin irritation and dermatitis.

ISOPSORALEN: Causes cutaneous phototoxicity reactions.

ISOSTEARAMIDE DEA: Nitrosamines can form in all cosmetic ingredients containing amines and amino derivatives with nitrogen compounds. Nitosamines are known carcinogens. (See Diethanolamine.)

ISOSTEARETH-N: May contain dangerous levels of ethylene oxide and dioxane, both potent toxins, as a manufacturing by-product.

ISOSTEARYL NEOPENTANOATE: Has comedogenic (acne producing) properties.

ISOTHIAZOLINONE: Studies show that it may cause contact dermatitis.

IVY EXTRACT: Used in skin and body preparations and bubble baths. It soothes and calms the skin. It is found in anti-cellulite lotions for its skin-toning properties. Contains saponins. Plant derived. Can cause irritant and allergic dermatitis.

JC RED NO. 6: Suspected carcinogen, teratogen, or toxin.

JOJOBA BUTTER: A natural butter made from Jojoba Oil. A good skin emollient.

JOJOBA MEAL: High in protein and natural fibers, this by-product of the oil-rich jojoba plant contains 17 amino acids. Its mild, exfoliating properties help wipe away dead skin cells and nourish and deep-cleanse the skin without drying it out.

JOJOBA OIL: Used in skin and hair care products. It aids in cellular renewal and helps the skin retain water. It is extracted from the beans of a desert shrub.

JOJOBA WAX: A natural wax made from Jojoba Oil.

KAOLIN: A white Chinese clay used to give color and *slip* to powders. It also helps to gently absorb oil on the surface of the skin. Used in make-up, it may prevent the skin from breathing. Used in clay masks, it may be drying to the skin.

KARITE BUTTER: Used in hair care, skin care, cleansers, suntan preparations and lipsticks. It soothes, smoothes, conditions and moisturizes skin. It contains the natural fats and oils from the fruit of the Karite tree. (See Shea Butter.)

KELP: Used as a healer, soother and tissue regenerator, also a conditioner, thickener and moisturizer. Used in bath preparations and shampoos. With its iodine content, it acts as an antiseptic for wounds. Derived from seaweed.

KOHL (COLORING COMPOUND): Causes lead and antimony poisoning.

KOLA NUT EXTRACT: (See COCA EXTRACT.)

KUKUI NUT OIL: The natural oil extracted from the kukui nut from Hawaii, which is often blended with other oils in skin formulations. A natural moisturizer, astringent, soother and mild cleanser.

LACTALBUMIN: A natural milk protein high in lactic acid and containing the eight amino acids, it has a tightening and film-producing effect on the skin. Animal, fruit or vegetable derived.

LACTIC ACID: Used as an exfoliant, it is a class of AHA (See Alpha-hydroxy Acids.) Produced by bacterial fermentation.

LACTOYL METHSILANOL ELASTINATE: Used for skin and hair conditioning. It is a protein derivative.

LAMINARIA: A seaweed whose essential oil helps attract and retain moisture on the skin. An excellent humectant and nutrient.

LANETH-10 ACETATE: Used in skin care products as an emulsifier and minor humectant. It is a derivative of lanolin. (See Lanolin Group.)

LANOLIN (GROUP): An oil extracted from the wool of sheep without causing any harm to the animal. It is one of the oils closest to human sebum, making it an excellent moisturizing ingredient. Lanolin is a natural emulsifier and humectant that absorbs water and holds it to the skin to help prevent dryness. There may be a difference in the quality of the raw material used but it is listed as toxic. Also has comedogenic (acne producing) properties.

LANOLIN ACID: Used in skin care products as an emulsifier, thickener and gellant. It is a derivative of lanolin. (See Lanolin Group.)

LANOLIN ALCOHOL: Used as an emulsifier and thickener for shampoos and bath gels. It is the fatty alcohol from lanolin. Has comedogenic (acne producing) properties. (See Lanolin Group.)

LANOLIN AND LANOLIN DERIVATIVES: Causes adverse skin reactions, has comedogenic (acne producing) properties. (See Lanolin Group.)

LANOLIN, ACETYLATED: Studies show that it may cause contact dermatitis. (See Lanolin Group.)

LANOLIN, ETHOXYLATED: Ethoxylation may render the ingredient a xeno-estrogen. Also can cause contact dermatitis. (See Lanolin Group.)

LAPPA EXTRACT: Used in hair care products it is anti inflammatory, reduces infection and clears toxins and dissipates swelling. It promotes tissue repair and benefits dry, scaly skin. It helps with eruptions, eczema, psoriasis, sores, boils and carbuncles.

LAURAMIDE DEA: Used as a foaming agent, thickener, stabilizer and gellant in shampoos and bath products. It is a nonionic surfactant. May be drying to the skin. Depending on overall formulation and the quality of the raw materials, it may be contaminated with nitrosamines.

LAURAMIDOPROPYL DIMETHYLAMINE: May cause contact allergic reactions.

LAUREL EXTRACT: Used in personal care products as an anti-bacterial. (See Laurel Oil.)

LAUREL OIL: Causes severe allergies.

LAURETH-N: Carcinogenic, mutagenic, toxic or causes adverse reactions (See definition at beginning of glossary.) May contain dangerous levels of ethylene oxide and/or dioxane, both potent toxins, as a manufacturing by-product.

LAURETH-23: A nonionic surfactant and foaming agent found in shampoos. It is a polyethylene glycol of lauryl alcohol. (See Lauryl Alcohol and Glycols.)

LAURYL ALCOHOL: This fatty alcohol, often derived from coconut oil, is used to make anionic surfactants. It may be natural or man-made. It may cause acne.

LAVENDER OIL: A widely used oil in health oriented skin care products. It is used for its healing agents and ability to balance the skin. It helps to reduce scarring and also stimulates the growth of new cells. May cause contact allergies and photosensitivity.

LEAD: Carcinogenic, mutagenic, toxic or causes adverse reactions. (See definition at beginning of glossary.)

LEAD ACETATE: Scalp hair dye only. (0.6 percent pb w/v maximum). Suspected carcinogen, teratogen or toxin but is still found in hair dyes, especially the ones that turn your hair dark over time.

LEAD CHROMATE: Carcinogenic, mutagenic, toxic or causes adverse reactions (See definition at beginning of glossary.)

LEAD DIOXIDE: Carcinogenic, mutagenic, toxic or causes adverse reactions. (See definition at beginning of glossary.)

LEAD FLUOBORATE: Carcinogenic, mutagenic, toxic or causes adverse reactions. (See definition at beginning of glossary.)

LEAD SULFIDE: Carcinogenic, mutagenic, toxic or causes adverse reactions. (See definition at beginning of glossary.)

LEAD SULPHATE: Carcinogenic, mutagenic, toxic or causes adverse reactions. (See definition at beginning of glossary.)

LECITHIN: Used as an emulsifier, antioxidant and surfactant in many personal care products. It is often obtained from common egg yolk, soybeans, sunflower seeds and some vegetables but may also come from an animal source. It is a phospholipid that has the ability to bind 300 times its weight in water. It contains stearic, palmitic and oleic acid compounds.

LEMON EXTRACT: Citrus fruit extract used as an acidifier (pH adjuster), astringent and moisturizer. Used in skin and body products, shampoos and other hair grooming preparations, cleaning and fresheners, suntan products and bubble baths. Juice can cause dermatitis.

LEMON GRASS: Used in health oriented products. It is anti-microbial and analgesic with antioxidant properties. Its fragrance is used in products to impart a safe aroma.

LEMON OIL: An oil obtained from the outer rind of lemons. It is used as astringent antiseptic and bactericide with the ability to stimulate the white corpuscles that defend the body. Can cause phototsensitivity.

LEMON PEEL OIL: Can cause photosensitivity.

LEMON PEEL: Studies show that it causes dermatitis.

LINALOL, 3,7-DIMETHYL-1,6-OCTADIEN-3-OL: Causes facial psoriasis.

LINALOOL: Carcinogenic, mutagenic, toxic or causes adverse reactions. (See definition at beginning of glossary.)

LINDANE: Carcinogenic, mutagenic, toxic or causes adverse reactions. (See definition at beginning of glossary.)

LINEOLEAMIDE DEA: Nitrosamines can form in all cosmetic ingredients containing amines and amino derivatives with nitrogen compounds. Nitrosamines are known carcinogens.

LINOLEAMIDOPROPYL ETHLY DIMONIUM ETHO-SULFATE: Nitrosamines can form in all cosmetic ingredients containing amines and amino derivatives with nitrogen compounds. Nitrosamines are known carcinogens.

LINOLEIC ACID/LINOLENIC ACID: Used as a surfactant, hair and skin conditioner, cleanser and moisturizer. For hand and body products, hair conditioners, cleaning agents, tanning products and lipsticks. It is a polyunsaturated essential fatty acid. It is one of the most beneficial skin care ingredients.

LINSEED OIL (FLAXSEED OIL): Shown to promote acne.

M-DIAMINOBENZENE: Carcinogenic, mutagenic, toxic or causes adverse reactions. (See definition at beginning of glossary.)

MAGNESIUM ALUMINUM SILICATE: A naturally occurring mineral that is commonly used to emulsify, thicken and color cosmetics. Especially used in antiperspirants, creams and shaving creams. (See Aluminum.)

MAGNESIUM CARBONATE: Found in powders and make-up covering preparations. It is an anti-caking and binding agent.

MAGNESIUM CITRATE: Used in hair conditioner. It acts as a humectant in that it tries to pull moisture from surroundings. It can actually cause dryness and brittleness in hair.

MAGNESIUM LAURETH SULFATE: May contain dangerous levels of ethylene oxide and/or dioxane, both potent toxins, as a manufacturing by-product.

MAGNESIUM OLETH SULFATE: May contain dangerous levels of ethylene oxide and/or dioxane, both potent toxins, as a manufacturing by-product.

MAGNESIUM SILICATE: (See Talc.)

MAGNESIUM STEARATE: Used as a colouring and filler agent in cosmetics. Recent research shows that if ingested it can damage the T cells. It is a compound of magnesia and stearic acid. (See Stearic Acid Groups.)

MAGNESIUM: A mineral used as an anti oxidant, thickener, skin conditioner, moisturizer and cleanser. Found in a wide variety of personal care products. It is said to help regulate the oil production of the skin and scalp.

MALLOW EXTRACT: Used in skin care as a softener and soother. It has anti inflammatory and anti-irritant properties.

MANGANESE VIOLET: An inorganic pigment colour additive, considered safe for use around the eyes.

MANGANESE: Used in skin care and make-up products. It is said to be calming and soothing to the skin. Carcinogenic, mutagenic, toxic or causes adverse reactions. (See definition at beginning of glossary.)

MARITIME PINE BARK EXTRACT OPC: (See Grape Seed Extract.)

MATRICARIA EXTRACT: Used in skin care, shampoos as a cleanser and moisturizer and eye make-up. Used externally to treat wounds and inflammation. It is antiseptic and anti-microbial. Extracted from the flower heads of German chamomile. For the treatment of dry, reddened, burned or sensitive skin.

MENTHOL: Frequently used as an antiseptic and topical anesthetic in skin lotions and tonics and shave creams. Can cause adverse reactions when applied in high concentrations to the skin.

MERCURIC AMMONIUM CHLORIDE: Highly toxic. Poses a considerable health risk and is a systemic poison.

MERCURIC CHLORIDE (GROUP): Highly toxic. Poses considerable health risk and is a systemic poison.

MERCURIC CHLORIDE, AMMONIATED: Highly toxic. Poses considerable health risk and is a systemic poison.

MERCURIC CYANIDE: Highly toxic. Poses considerable health risk and is a systemic poison.

MERCURY BICHLORIDE: Highly toxic. Poses considerable health risk and is a systemic poison.

MERCURY CHLORIDE, AMMONIATED: Studies show that it causes dermatitis.

MERCURY CHLORIDE: Highly toxic. Poses considerable health risk and is a systemic poison.

METALS (GROUP): Studies show that it may cause contact dermatitis on hands.

METHACRYLATE COPOLYMER: Film-former hair fixative, suspending agent. A synthetic polymer.

METHANAL: Carcinogenic, mutagenic, toxic or causes adverse reactions. (See definition at beginning of glossary.)

METHANINIE (QUATERNIUM 15): Causes induced contact dermatitis.

METHANOL: Carcinogenic, mutagenic, toxic or causes adverse reactions. (See definition at beginning of glossary.)

METHENAMINE (GROUP): Skin irritant, flammable, dangerous fire risk.

METHOXSALEN: Causes burns by photosensitation.

METHOXY PEG-100: Used in cosmetics as a humectant and solvent and as an emulsifier and stabilizer. PEG is the abbreviation for polyethylene glycol, polyoxethylene, polyglycol and polyether glycol. (See Glycols Group and PEG.)

METHOXY PEG-17 DODECYL GLYCOL: Used in cosmetics as a humectant and solvent and as an emulsifier and stabilizer.

PEG is the abbreviation for polyethylene glycol, polyoxethylene, polyglycol and polyether glycol. (See Glycols Group and PEG.)

METHOXY PEG-22 DODECYL GLYCOL COPOLYMER: Used in cosmetics as a humectant and solvent and as an emulsifier and stabilizer. PEG is the abbreviation for polyethylene glycol, polyoxethylene, polyglycol and polyether glycol. (See Glycols Group and PEG.)

METHYL ACETATE: Synthetic chemical used as an aromatic and solvent. It can cause dryness.

METHYL ALCOHOL (GROUP): Causes contact eczema.

METHYL-ALPHA-D-GLYCOPYRANOSIDE: Studies show that it causes dermatitis.

METHYLANTHRANILATE: Used in sunscreen products. (See Section on Sunscreens.) May cause an allergic reaction. Can be found in makeup and body lotions as well as products labeled as sunscreens.

METHYL BENZOATE: Carcinogenic, mutagenic, toxic or causes adverse reactions. (See definition at beginning of glossary.)

METHYL CHLORIDE: Carcinogenic, mutagenic, toxic or causes adverse reactions. (See definition at beginning of glossary.)

METHYL CHLOROFORM: Carcinogenic, mutagenic, toxic or causes adverse reactions. (See definition at beginning of glossary.)

METHYL CHLOROISOTHIAZOLININE: Carcinogenic, mutagenic, toxic or causes adverse reactions. (See definition at beginning of glossary.)

METHYL ESTER: Carcinogenic, mutagenic, toxic or causes adverse reactions. (See definition at beginning of glossary.)

METHYL ETHYL KETONE: Carcinogenic, mutagenic, toxic or causes adverse reactions. (See definition at beginning of glossary.)

METHYL GLUCETH: May contain dangerous levels of ethylene oxide and/or dioxane, which are both potent toxins, as a manufacturing by-product.

METHYL GLUCETH-10: Used in skin and hair care products because of its moisture retentive qualities. Used because it is a freezing point depressant. (See Methyl Gluceth.)

METHYL GLUCETH-20: Skin conditioner and humectant, moisturizer and cleanser. Used in skin care, cleansing and bath products and manicuring preparations. (See Methyl Gluceth.)

METHYL GLUCOSE SESQUISTEARATE: Used as an emulsifier, surfactant, humectant and moisturizer. Carcinogenic, mutagenic, toxic or causes adverse reactions (See definition at beginning of glossary.)

METHYL GLUCOSIDE DIOLEATE: Studies show that it causes dermatitis.

METHYL GLUCOSIDE: Studies show that it causes dermatitis.

METHYL HYDRAZINE: Carcinogenic, mutagenic, toxic or causes adverse reactions. (See definition at beginning of glossary.)

METHYL IODIDE: Carcinogenic, mutagenic, toxic or causes adverse reactions. (See definition at beginning of glossary.)

METHYL ISOBUTYL KETONE: Carcinogenic, mutagenic, toxic or causes adverse reactions. (See definition at beginning of glossary.)

METHYL ISOCYANATE: Carcinogenic, mutagenic, toxic or causes adverse reactions. (See definition at beginning of glossary.)

METHYL METHACRYLATE : A solvent used in the nail industry (artificial nail, polish, glues etc.). See section on nail products for more cautions regarding fumes. Highly flammable, dangerous fire risk, explosive limits in air 2.1-12.5 percent.

METHYL METHACRYLATES (GROUP): See section on nail products for more cautions regarding fumes. Highly flammable, dangerous fire risk, explosive limits in air 2.1-12.5 percent.

METHYL OLEATE: Has acne producing properties.

METHYL-P-HYDROXYBENZOATE: Carcinogenic, mutagenic, toxic or causes adverse reactions. (See definition at beginning of glossary.)

METHYL SALICYLATE: Used in skin care products as an anti-microbial and preservative. It is the main component of wintergreen oil. It is also used as a topical anesthetic and anti-inflammatory agent. Can be irritating to mucous membranes.

May be derived from wintergreen oil, birch oil or made synthetically.

METHYL VIOLET: A colourant used in semi-permanent hair dyes. Although banned by the FDA, a recent report showed that two products still contained it. Carcinogenic, mutagenic, toxic or causes adverse reactions. (See definition at beginning of glossary.)

METHYLCELLULOSE: Mild eye and skin irritant.

METHYLCHLOROISOTHIAZOLINONE: Causes cosmetic allergies.

METHYLDIBROMO GLUTARONITRILE (TEKTAMER 38): Causes allergic contact dermatitis.

METHYLENE BROMIDE: Carcinogenic, mutagenic, toxic or causes adverse reactions. (See definition at beginning of glossary.)

METHYLENE CHLORIDE: A solvent used in skin and nail care products. It is damaging to the liver. It is highly absorbable and turns to carbon monoxide in the body which can stress the cardiovascular system.

METHYLISOTHIAZOLININE: Causes cosmetic allergies.

METHYLPARABEN: Used in a wide variety of personal care products as a preservative. It is derived from Parahydrorbenzoic acid and gum benzoic from sytoc tree. Found in skin, hair, make-up, baby products, deodorants, cleansers and bath items, dental products, shaving creams, nail polish and foot talcs. Used as a preservative with anti-microbial qualities. This ingredient, along with butylparaben and propylparaben, may be irritating to the skin if more than 5 percent is present in a formulation. Many commercially made cosmetics contain a higher percentage. Most health oriented manufacturers use 0.15 of 1 percent. Check to see where it is listed on the label. Also, problems associated with these parabens stem from improper formulating. The pH level of the other ingredients must be between 4.5 and 5. All synthetic preservatives are cellular toxins.

METHYLSILANOL CARBOXYMETHYL THEOPYLLINE: Cellulite energy molecule algesium c. It is a high performance cellulite botanical ingredient.

METHYLSILANOL MANNURONATE: Used in skin care products as a skin conditioner.

METHYSILANOL CARBOXYMETHLY THEOPHYLLINE ALGINATE: Reaction product of methysilanol hydroxyproline and aspartate acid (amino acids) skin conditioning agent.

METHYSILANOL HYDROXYPROLINE ASPARTATE: Reaction product of methysilanol hydroyproline and aspartate acid (amino acids) skin conditioning agent.

MICA: Used as a natural colour additive this inorganic mineral has a natural iridescence and varies in color from brownish green and blue to colorless. It is used to impart a sparkle in cosmetics.

MICHLER'S KETONE: Carcinogenic, mutagenic, toxic or causes adverse reactions. (See definition at beginning of glossary.)

MICROCRYSTALLINE WAX: Used as a stiffening and opacifying agent in skin and hair care products.

MINERAL OIL: Used in a wide variety of skin care products as an emollient. It is a petro chemical by-product. It seals the skin and floods it with moisture and prevents the skin's natural respiration process. It is extremely comedogenic (acne producing) when used as a primary ingredient in moisturizers, liquid foundation and other cosmetics. May contain polycyclic aromatic hydrocarbons (PAH) which is mutagenic and the carcinogen anthanthrene.

MIPA: Causes severe eye and skin irritations.

MODULAN: Has caused skin irritation and histological changes in rabbits.

MOLYBDENUM TRIOXIDE: Carcinogenic, mutagenic, toxic or causes adverse reactions. (See definition at beginning of glossary.)

MONOAZOANILIES: Shown to have comedogenic (acne producing) properties.

MONOETHANOLAMINE SULFITE: Causes allergic reactions and contact dermatitis. Nitrosamines can form in all cosmetic ingredients containing amines and amino derivatives with nitrogen compounds. Nitrosamines are known carcinogens.

MONOETHANOLAMINE: Liquid amino alcohol that is used as a humectant and emulsifier in cosmetics. Carcinogenic. See nitrosamines note in Monoethanolamine sulfite.

MONOISOPROPANOLAMINE: Carcinogenic, nitrosamines can form in all cosmetic ingredients containing amines and amino derivatives with nitrogen compounds. Nitrosamines are known carcinogens.

MONOSTEARIN: Carcinogenic, mutagenic, toxic or causes adverse reactions. (See definition at beginning of glossary.)

MONOTERTIARY BUTYL HYDROQUINONE: Carcinogenic, mutagenic, toxic or causes adverse reactions. (See definition at beginning of glossary.)

MOSKENE: Causes pigmented contact dermatitis.

MTD: Carcinogenic, mutagenic, toxic or causes adverse reactions. (See definition at beginning of glossary.)

M-TOLUENEDIAMINE: Carcinogenic, mutagenic, toxic or causes adverse reactions. (See definition at beginning of glossary.)

MUCOPOLYSACCHARIDES: Used as a humectant and skin softener in cosmetics. It is a basic component of the skin. It is a gelatinous material that cements cells together and helps to maintain a moist environment for collagen, elastin and dermal cells and provides support for connective tissue and mucous membrane. They are said to minimize wrinkles.

MUSK AMBRETTE: Causes pigmented photoallergic contact dermatitis.

MUSK MOSKENE: Causes pigmented contact dermatitis.

MUTAGEN: A substance that is capable of changing the genetics within the cell.

MYRISTAMIDOPROPYL DIMETHYLAMINE: May cause contact allergic reactions.

MYRISTATES (GROUP): May be synthetic or natural. Found to have comedogenic (acne producing) properties and is toxic.

MYRISTIC ACID: A fatty acid used in skin, body and hand preparations. (See Myristates.)

MYRISTYL ALCOHOL: Used in skin, body and hand preparations. It is a fatty alcohol derived from myristyl acid. It is an emulsion stabilizer, emollient, surfactant, foam booster, thickener and moisturizer. Causes cosmetic allergies

MYRISTYL MYRISTATE : Has comedogenic (acne producing) properties.

MYRISTYL PROPIONATE: Skin conditioning agent and emollient and moisturizer. Prepared from fatty acids. It gives lotions and creams a smooth velvety feel. Has comedogenic (acne producing) properties.

MYRRH EXTRACT: Used in skin care and dental products. In skin care it is used to revitalize aging and wrinkling skin. It is an anti-inflammatory, disinfectant and astringent and restrains infection. Its mild anti-microbial action is recommended for sensitive skin. It promotes tissue repair and is used for circulatory problems. Extracted from Myrrh gum tree.

N-NITROSO COMPOUNDS: The literature says its mild anti-microbial action is recommended for sensitive skin. However, studies show it to be a carcinogen contaminant.

N-NITROSO-N-METHYLALKYLAMINES: The literature says its mild anti-microbial action is recommended for sensitive skin. However, studies show it to be a carcinogen contaminant of fatty amine oxides.

N-NITROSO-N-METHYLTETRADECYL AMINE:) (See N-Nitroso Compounds.)

N-NITROSOALKANOLAMINES: (See N-Nitroso Compounds.)

N-NITROSOBIS (2-HYDROXYPROPYL)AMINE: (See N-Nitroso Compounds.)

N-NITROSODIMETHYLAMINE: Carcinogenic contaminant in cosmetics.

N-NITROSOMORPHOLINE: Carcinogenic contaminant in cosmetics.

N-OCTADECANOIC ACID: Carcinogenic, mutagenic, toxic or causes adverse reactions. (See definition at beginning of glossary.)

N-PROPYL BENZOATE: Causes inflammatory reactions.

N-PROPYLAMINES: Hazard, strong irritant to skin and tissue.

N,NITROSO-N-ETHYLUREA: Carcinogenic, mutagenic, toxic or causes adverse reactions. (See definition at beginning of glossary.)

NAPHTHALENE: Hazard, toxic by inhalation.

NAPHTHALENES (GROUP): Toxic, can produce hypeirritability and other system effects.

NAPHTHOQUINONE: Hazard, irritant.

NAPHTOL: Causes severe eye and skin irritation.

NAPHTOQUINONES (GROUP): Causes adverse effects such as contact dermatitis.

NATURAL FRAGRANCES: Used in health oriented products. Scents are from the essential oils or from the essences of fruit.

N-BUTYL ALCOHOL: Carcinogenic, mutagenic, toxic or causes adverse reactions. (See definition at beginning of glossary.)

N-BUTYL BENZOATE: Carcinogenic, mutagenic, toxic or causes adverse reactions. (See definition at beginning of glossary.)

N-DODECANOL: Carcinogenic, mutagenic, toxic or causes adverse reactions. (See definition at beginning of glossary.)

NEOCHROMIUM: Carcinogenic, mutagenic, toxic or causes adverse reactions. (See definition at beginning of glossary.)

NEOMYCIN: Studies show that it may cause contact dermatitis.

NEOPENTYL GLYCOL DICAPRYLATE/DICAPRATE: Used as a lubricant; soothing and softening to the skin. It is a compound of neopentyl glycol, which is derived synthetically and dicaprylate/dicaprates, which are derived from coconut. Caprylates are in the glyceride family and are found in human sebum.

NEROLI: Used in health oriented personal care products. Used for dry or sensitive skin. It is the essential oil distilled from the flowers of the bitter orange tree.

NETTLE: Used in skin, hair and scalp preparations it is known to stimulate the circulation. It is said to stimulate hair growth and skin and softens hair. High in phosphates and trace minerals and plant hormones.

NIACIN: Vitamin B-3. (See Vitamin B.)

NIACINAMIDE: Hair conditioning and skin conditioning agent used in skin care products and shampoos. It is a skin stimulant. It is from Niacin (vitamin B-3). It is necessary for healthy condition of all tissue cells.

NICKEL: Causes adverse reactions such as contact dermatitis. The OSHA lists it as a carcinogen. Causes eyelid dermatitis— found in eyelash curler. May cause contact allergies and eczema.

NICKEL AMMONIUM SULFATE: Carcinogenic, mutagenic, toxic or causes adverse reactions. (See definition at beginning of glossary.)

NICKEL CARBONYL: Carcinogenic, mutagenic, toxic or causes adverse reactions. (See definition at beginning of glossary.)

NICKEL CYANIDE: Carcinogenic, mutagenic, toxic or causes adverse reactions. (See definition at beginning of glossary.)

NICKEL HYDROXIDE: Carcinogenic, mutagenic, toxic or causes adverse reactions. (See definition at beginning of glossary.)

NICKEL SULFATE: Causes facial contact dermatitis.

NIOBE OIL: Carcinogenic, mutagenic, toxic or causes adverse reactions. (See definition at beginning of glossary.)

NITRILES (GROUP): Causes allergic reactions, contact eczema and causes chemically induced contact dermatitis.

NITRILOTRIACETIC ACID: Found to be carcinogenic.

NITROBENZENES (GROUP): Carcinogen contaminant found in cosmetics.

NITROCELLULOSE: Flammable, man-made substance. Used as an emulsifier and plastic protective film in cosmetics, especially nail polish.

NITROFEN: Carcinogenic, mutagenic, toxic or causes adverse reactions. (See definition at beginning of glossary.)

NITROGEN MUSTARD: Carcinogenic, mutagenic, toxic or causes adverse reactions. (See definition at beginning of glossary.)

NITROGLYCERIN: Carcinogenic, mutagenic, toxic or causes adverse reactions. (See definition at beginning of glossary.)

NITROSAMINES: Cancer causing contaminant found in cosmetics.

N-NITROSODIETHANOLAMINE: Carcinogenic, mutagenic, toxic or causes adverse reactions. (See definition at beginning of glossary.)

N-NITROSODIETHYLAMINE: Carcinogenic, mutagenic, toxic or causes adverse reactions. (See definition at beginning of glossary.)

N-NITROSODIMETHYLAMINE: Carcinogenic, mutagenic, toxic or causes adverse reactions. (See definition at beginning of glossary.)

N-NITROSODI-N-BUTYLAMINE: Carcinogenic, mutagenic, toxic or causes adverse reactions. (See definition at beginning of glossary.)

N-NITROSODI-N-PROPYLAMINE: Carcinogenic, mutagenic, toxic or causes adverse reactions. (See definition at beginning of glossary.)

N-NITROSODIPHENYLAMINE: Carcinogenic, mutagenic, toxic or causes adverse reactions. (See definition at beginning of glossary.)

N-NITROSOMORPHOLINE: Carcinogenic, mutagenic, toxic or causes adverse reactions. (See definition at beginning of glossary.)

N-NITROSO-N-METHYLUREA: Carcinogenic, mutagenic, toxic or causes adverse reactions. (See definition at beginning of glossary.)

N-NITROSONORNICOTINE: Carcinogenic, mutagenic, toxic or causes adverse reactions. (See definition at beginning of glossary.)

NONOXYNOL COMPOUNDS: Synthetic ethoxylated alkyl phenols used as dispersing agents to solubilize essential oils. Ethoxylated ingredients pose a high risk of being xeno-estrogenic.

NONYLPHENOL: Causes skin irritation and dermatitis.

NOVOCAIN (TM FOR A BRAND OF PROCAINE HYDRO-CHLORIDE): Studies show that it causes dermatitis.

N-PHENYLENEDIAMINE: Carcinogenic, mutagenic, toxic or causes adverse reactions. (See definition at beginning of glossary).

O-BENZENE DICARBOXYLIC ACID: Carcinogenic, mutagenic, toxic or causes adverse reactions. (See definition at beginning of glossary.)

O-NITRO-P-AMINOPHENOL: Carcinogenic, mutagenic, toxic or causes adverse reactions. (See definition at beginning of glossary.)

O-PHENYLENEDIAMINE: Carcinogenic, mutagenic, toxic or causes adverse reactions. (See definition at beginning of glossary.)

OAK MOSS: Causes allergies and skin irritations.

O-ANISIDINE HYDROCHLORIDE: Carcinogenic, mutagenic, toxic or causes adverse reactions. (See definition at beginning of glossary.)

O-ANISIDINE: Carcinogenic, mutagenic, toxic or causes adverse reactions. (See definition at beginning of glossary.)

OCTACHLORONAPHTHALENE: Carcinogenic, mutagenic, toxic or causes adverse reactions. (See definition at beginning of glossary.)

OCTADECYL ALCOHOL: Carcinogenic, mutagenic, toxic or causes adverse reactions. (See definition at beginning of glossary.)

OCTYL DIMETHYL PABA: A sunscreen agent. (See the section on sunscreens and see PABA.)

OCTYL METHOXCINNAMATE: Used in skin care and sunscreen products. Extracted from cinnamon or cassia oil. It keeps excessive ultra violet radiation (UVB) from penetrating the skin by absorbing the ultraviolet light. Also a moisturizer and a hair protectant.

OCTYL PALMITATE: A surfactant, emulsifier, moisturizer, cleansing agent used in shampoos, cleansing products, shaving creams, for hand and body products and mascara. It occurs naturally in seasonings such as allspice, anise and celery seed and is obtained from palm oil, Japan wax or Chinese vegetable tallow. It is an acne producing ingredient.

OCTYL SALICYLATE: Ultraviolet light absorber and moisturizer, for skin care, make up and tanning preparations. Used also in antiseptics.

OCTYL STEARATE: Skin emollient and conditioner and moisturizer. For skin care, make-up, cleansing products and indoor tanning preparations. Also in deodorants and protective creams. It is a natural fatty acid used to make bar soap, lubricants, to soften chewing gum and suppositories. The ester of 2-ethylhexyl alcohol, a fatty alcohol. Octyl stearate may be derived from tallow or vegetable oils. It is an acne producing ingredient.

OCTYLACRYLATES COPOLYMERS: Used in hair preparations as a plasticizer.

OCTYLDODECANOL: Used in emollient, solvent, plasticizer. (See Stearyl Alcohol.)

OCTYOXYNOL-N: Used as an emulsifier and dispersing agent. It is a non-ionic detergent that may be slightly sensitizing. As a by-product of manufacturing, it may contain hazardous levels of ethylene oxide and/or dioxane. Toxic.

OIL OF MIRBANE: Carcinogenic, mutagenic, toxic or causes adverse reactions. (See definition at beginning of glossary.)

OIL OF PURCELLIN: Causes skin irritation and dermatitis.

OLEAMIDOPROPYL DIMETHYLAMINE: May cause contact allergic reactions, contact dermatitis.

OLEIC ACID: A surfactant, cleansing agent used in soft soap, skin and shave creams, nail polish and lipsticks, liquid make-up, lip rouge, shampoos and pre-shave lotions. It is a common constituent of many animal and vegetable fats. It is an unsaturated fatty acid. Depending on concentration, it can be mildly irritating and is acne producing.

OLETH-N: As a by-product of manufacturing, it may contain hazardous levels of ethylene oxide and/or dioxane. Toxic.

OLETH-2 THROUGH OLETH-50: These polyethylene glycol ethers of oleic alcohol are used as surfactants. (See Oleic Acid and PEG and Glycols Group.)

OLEYL ALCOHOL: Found in fish oils it is used as an emollient. It has softening and lubricating qualities and is used to make surface-active agents.

OLIBANUM EXTRACT: Used in skin care to promote blood circulation. It helps to regenerate the skin tissues. Also used as a fragrance component. A distilled oil from the gum resins of a plant found in Ethiopia, Egypt and Arabia.

OLIVE OIL CASTILE: Saponified with sodium hydroxide, it becomes soap. (See Sodium Hydroxide.)

OLIVE OIL: Natural oil used as an emollient in soaps, cleansers and shampoos. Has acne promoting properties.

O-PHENYLPHENOL: Carcinogenic, mutagenic, toxic or causes adverse reactions. (See definition at beginning of glossary.)

OSMIUM TETROXIDE: Carcinogenic, mutagenic, toxic or causes adverse reactions. (See definition at beginning of glossary.)

O-TOLUIDINE HYDROCHLORIDE: Carcinogenic, mutagenic, toxic or causes adverse reactions. (See definition at beginning of glossary.)

O-TOLUIDINE: Carcinogenic, mutagenic, toxic or causes adverse reactions. (See definition at beginning of glossary.)

OXIRANE: Carcinogenic, mutagenic, toxic or causes adverse reactions. (See definition at beginning of glossary.)

OXYBENZONE: A sunscreen or skin care ingredient, it is a UVA blocker. Protects against ultraviolet light from sunlight and fluorescent sources. (Also see section on sunscreens for more information.) Can cause contact dermatitis.

OXYMETHYLENE: Carcinogenic, mutagenic, toxic or causes adverse reactions. (See definition at beginning of glossary.)

P-AMINOBENZOIC ACID: (See PABA.)

P-DIAMINOBENZENE: Carcinogenic, mutagenic, toxic or causes adverse reactions. (See definition at beginning of glossary.)

P-DOHYDROXYBENZENE: Carcinogenic, mutagenic, toxic or causes adverse reactions. (See definition at beginning of glossary.)

PABA (P-AMINOBENZOIC ACID): A common sunscreen agent. Product labels will list PABA as para-aminobenzoic due to recent FDA regulations. Possibly phototoxic and photoallergenic and a common sensitizer.

PALM OIL: Used as a high-sudsing cleansing agent and texturizer in soaps. Extracted from the oil of an African palm nut.

PALMAROSA OIL: Used in skin care as a cellular regenerator. Works on problem skin, acne or dry skin. From the essential oil of palmarosa grass.

PALMITATE: Used as an oil in many cosmetics especially in baby oils, bath oils, eye creams, hair conditioners and moisturizers. It is the salt of palmitic acid. (See Palmitic Acid.) It can cause allergic reactions in some people. May cause adverse reactions or dermatitis.

PALMITATES (GROUP): Studies show that they may cause contact dermatitis.

PALMITIC ACID: Used in shampoos, cleansing products, shaving creams, for hand and body products and mascara as a surfactant, emulsifier, moisturizer, cleansing agent. It occurs naturally in many of our seasonings such as allspice, anise and celery seed and is obtained from palm oil, cottonseed, peanuts, Japan wax or Chinese vegetable tallow. May cause adverse reactions or dermatitis.

PALMITIC ACIDS (GROUP): Studies show that they may cause contact dermatitis.

PALMITYL CETYL STEARYL ALCOHOL: Carcinogenic, mutagenic, toxic or causes adverse reactions. (See definition at beginning of glossary).

PANTHENOL: Used in hair grooming aids, make-up, skin care cleansers, bath products, suntan preparations and nail polish and removers. It is a component of Vitamin B-5, yeast and wheat germ. A nutrient cell proliferater, hair protectant and thickener. Acts as a healing agent in skin care and helps prevent split ends and smoothes the cuticle of hair. Actually increases the hair's diameter for fuller, thicker hair.

PAPAIN: Used in skin care products as an exfoliant to dissolve dead skin cells. Always test on a piece of cardboard before using. Several brands actually dissolved the cardboard it was rubbed on to. (See section on Exfoliants—Facial Scrubs.)

PARABENS: Trademarked name for the methyl, propyl, butyl and ethyl esters of p-hydroxybenzoic acid. Used in a wide variety of personal care product formulations as broad-spectrum preservatives. They are derived from Parahydrorbenzoic acid.

Found in skin, hair, make-up, baby products, deodorants, cleansers and bath items, dental products, shaving, nail polish and foot talcs. Used as a preservative with anti-microbial qualities. These ingredients, methylparaben, butylparaben and propylparaben, may be irritating to the skin if more than 5 percent is present in a formulation. Many commercially made cosmetics contain a higher percentage. Most health oriented manufacturers use 0.15 of 1 percent. Check to see where it is listed on the label. Also, problems associated with these parabens stem from improper formulating. The pH level of the other ingredients must be between 4.5 and 5. May cause allergic reactions. Effective against bacteria, fungus, yeast and mold.

PARAFFIN: Used in cosmetics as a thickener or gellant in creams and lotions. It is a mixture of hydrocarbons and is derived from petroleum. It is known to be contaminated with the carcinogens, benzo-a-pyrene and benzo-b-fluroanthene.

PARAPHENYLENEDIAMINE DIHYDROCHLORIDE: Carcinogenic, mutagenic, toxic or causes adverse reactions. (See definition at beginning of glossary.)

PARAPHENYLENEDIAMINE: Carcinogenic, mutagenic, toxic or causes adverse reactions. (See definition at beginning of glossary.)

PARATHION: Carcinogenic, mutagenic, toxic or causes adverse reactions. (See definition at beginning of glossary.)

PARSLEY SEED OIL: May cause irritation and/or allergic dermatitis.

P-BENZOQUINONE: Carcinogenic, mutagenic, toxic or causes adverse reactions. (See definition at beginning of glossary.)

P-CRESIDINE: Carcinogenic, mutagenic, toxic or causes adverse reactions. (See definition at beginning of glossary.)

PEANUT OIL: An emollient often found in some skin care products and massage oils. Many individuals react negatively to peanuts and may also react to peanut oil. Contamination of pesticide residue and fungal infestation may also be in the peanut oil.

PECTIN: Used as a thickening agent in natural cosmetics. Obtained from the cell walls of plants, the peel of citrus and apple pomace.

PEG 100 STEARATE: It is an emulsifier and surfactant. Polyethylene glycol combined with stearic acid to form a water-soluble ester used as an emulsifier and emollient; has a softening effect on the skin. (See PEG and Stearates Group.)

PEG: Numbers 4 to 200. Abbreviation for polyethylene glycol; polyoxethylene; polyglycol; polyether glycol. Used in a wide variety of personal care products as a humectant, moisturizer, emulsifier, emollient, binder and solvent. They are synthetic polymers. Higher numbers indicate more PEG chains are present in the molecule. (See Ethers and Glycols Group.) As a manufacturing by-product dangerous levels of the toxin, dioxane has been found.

PEG-200 GLYCERYL TALLOWATE: A hair conditioning agent, surfactant, cleansing agent. This is a mixture of triglycerides (fats) derived from tallow (animal fat).

PEG-22 DODECYL GLYCOL COPOLYMER: Carcinogenic, mutagenic, toxic or causes adverse reactions. (See definition at beginning of glossary.)

PEG-40 CASTOR OIL: A compound made from polyethylene glycol (PEG) and castor oil, an extract of the castor bean. This ingredient is used as a solvent to help disperse other ingredients in a solution. (See PEG.)

PEG-40 STEARATE: A surfactant, cleansing agent and moisturizer. Used for skin, hand and body care, deodorants, some items in the make-up line, indoor tanning preparations and hair conditioner. A widely used emulsifying agent. (See PEG.)

PEG-5 CETETH-10 PHOSPHATE: A compound of polyethylene glycol, ceteth (from coconut fruit) and ethylene oxide, with phosphoric acid (which is produced synthetically). Used as an emulsifier. (See PEG.)

PEG-7 GLYCERYL COCOATE: A combination of polyethylene glycol and glyceryl cocoate to form a type of sucrose (sugar) extract. It is a mild cleansing agent and emollient that breaks up fat on the skin's surface without stripping the skin's natural oils or causing dryness. (See PEG.)

PEG-8: A polymer of ethylene oxide. Acts as an emollient, plasticizer and softener for cosmetics creams and shampoos. Ethylene oxide may mimic estrogen in the body, a xeno-estrogen. (See Ethylene Oxide.)

PENTACHLOROPHENOL: Carcinogenic, mutagenic, toxic or causes adverse reactions. (See definition at beginning of glossary.)

PEPPERMINT FLAVOR: Extract of aromatic peppermint plant used in mouthwashes and breath fresheners, toothpaste, skin fresheners, bubble baths, shave creams, cleansing products and body and hand preparations. Astringent and skin stimulator anesthetic, germicide, decongestant and cleanser.

PEPPERMINT OIL: An essential oil containing menthol that has a cooling effect on the skin. Used as an antiseptic. May be irritating to mucous membrane.

PEPTIDES: Natural or synthetic peptides are comprised of amino acids linked by peptide bonds. When peptide bonds in the hair are broken, the result is damaged hair.

PER-14M: A polymer used as a binder, emulsion stabilizer and thickener in shampoos, conditioners, bath products, mascara and shaving preparations.

PERFLUOROPOLYMETHYLISOPROPYL ETHER: Non-irritating and non-sensitizing ingredient that has shown to resist the penetration of acids, alkalis, aromatic solvents and other aggressive agents. Protects against water and oil soluble substances. Also used as a skin conditioning agent. It is used in barrier creams.

PEROXYACETIC ACID: Carcinogenic, mutagenic, toxic or causes adverse reactions. (See definition at beginning of glossary.)

PERSULPHATES, ALKALINE: Causes asthma in hairdressers.

PERYLENE: Carcinogenic contaminant in mineral oil and waxes.

PETROLATUM: Used in skin and hand care products to form an occlusive barrier on the skin. Prevents the skin from taking in oxygen and respiring out waste. Highly comedogenic (acne producing) ingredient. It is a petrochemical. May contain two well known carcinogens, benzo-a-pyrene and benzo-b-fluroanthene.

PETROLEUM DISTILLATE: A solvent used in skin care products. It is a petroleum derivative. Avoid this ingredient as it may be a xeno-estrogen.

PHBS: These are preservatives widely used in many cosmetics and shampoo. Another name for parabens. (See Parabens.)

PHENACETIN: Carcinogenic, mutagenic, toxic or causes adverse reactions. (See definition at beginning of glossary.)

PHENOL CARBOLIC ACID: Used as an anti-microbial and preservative in cosmetics. (See Phenol.)

PHENOL: Used in many ingredient combinations that are used in personal care product formulations. Fatal poisonings care occur through skin absorption.

PHENOXYETOL: A preservative used in skin care, cleansing products, many make-up products, shampoos, conditioners and other hair grooming aids, bubble baths, foot powders, indoor and outdoor tanning products and cuticle softeners. Also used as a fixative for perfumes and bactericides, insect repellents and as topical antiseptics. Carcinogenic, mutagenic, toxic or causes adverse reactions. (See definition at beginning of glossary.)

PHENYL MERCURIC ACETATE: Used as a preservative and anti-microbial in shampoos and eye cosmetics. It is made by heating benzene with mercuric acetate. It is highly toxic if inhaled or swallowed and can enter the body through the eyes or surrounding skin. Causes skin irritation.

PHENYL TRIMETHICONE: Used in hair preparations to aid in wet comb-out. Forms a moisturizing barrier between the surface cells of hair and skin without build-up. Reduces friction and static while it adds shine to the hair.

PHENYLBENZIMIDAZOLE SULFONIC ACID: Functions as an ultraviolet light absorber in sunscreens, cleansing products, hand and body preparations. An organic compound. (See section on sunscreens.)

PHENYLBENZOYL CARBINOL: Carcinogenic, mutagenic, toxic or causes adverse reactions. (See definition at beginning of glossary.)

PHENYLCARBINOL: Carcinogenic, mutagenic, toxic or causes adverse reactions. (See definition at beginning of glossary.)

PHENYLENEDIAMINES (GROUP): Studies show it to cause facial dermatitis.

PHENYLMETHANOL: Carcinogenic, mutagenic, toxic or causes adverse reactions. (See definition at beginning of glossary.)

PHOSGENE: Carcinogenic, mutagenic, toxic or causes adverse reactions. (See definition at beginning of glossary.)

PHOSPHOLIPIDS: A group of organic compounds ideal for nourishing the skin. It is a true anti-aging ingredient that strengthens and repairs the epidermis by topical application. Phospholipid molecules consist of one part that attracts water (hydrophillic) and two more parts that are attracted to lipid substances (lipophillic)—very similar to an emulsifier. The hydrophillic part consist of a phosphate ester with two lipophillic essential fatty acid chains attached.

PHOSPHORIC ACID: Inorganic phosphate based acid. Used in pH balancing many personal care, hair care, skin and body care and cleaning products. Also used as a solvent in detergents. It is used as a metal ion sequestrant. It is very destructive to the skin if used in high concentrations.

PHOSPHOROUS (YELLOW): Carcinogenic, mutagenic, toxic or causes adverse reactions. (See definition at beginning of glossary.)

PHTHALATES (GROUP): Used as plasticizers in cosmetics, especially in nail products. They are well recognized as xeno-estrogens and are testicular toxins.

PHTHALIC ACIDS (GROUP): (See Phthalates Group.)

PHTHALIC ANHYDRIDE: Carcinogenic, mutagenic, toxic or causes adverse reactions. (See definition at beginning of glossary.)

p-HYDROXYBENZOIC ACID: An anti-microbial and preservative in personal care products. (See Benzoic Acid.)

PHYTANTRIOL: Used as an emollient and protective shield in skin care products. Current research not available.

PINENE: (See section on fragrance.) Studies show that it may cause contact dermatitis.

PLANT ENZYMES: Used in health oriented skin care lines. The proteolytic enzymes (papain) are free-radical scavengers. They are said to have the ability to digest protein and selectively digest only the dead skin cells without harming the living ones.

PLANTAIN EXTRACT: Used in skin and hair care products for its antiseptic, soothing and astringent properties. It has a healing affect on sores and ulcers and is good for eczema.

P-NITROSODIPHENYLAMINE: Carcinogenic, mutagenic, toxic or causes adverse reactions. (See definition at beginning of glossary.)

POLYAMINOPROPYL BIGUANIDE: A synthetically derived preservative. It was originally developed by Bausch and Lomb for use in eye products worn by contact lens wearers. It is said to be one of the most gentle, yet effective, anti-microbial preservatives available. Amino derivatives may contain or may form nitrosamines as a result of manufacturing.

POLYCYCLIC AROMATIC HYDROCARBONS (PAH): Found in mineral oils (even highly refined mineral oil) and petrolatum. It is a carcinogen.

POLYETHOXYLATED COMPOUNDS: Forty-eight percent of cosmetic products containing polyethoxylated surfactants were found to contain 7.3-85.9 ppm of 1,4 dioxane, a potent carcinogen.

POLYMERS: Used in cosmetics to keep sunscreens from washing off, in hair-setting products and as binders in skin creams. Plastic fingernails are also produced by polymerization.

POLYOXYETHYLENE SORBITAN MONOOLEATE: Studies show that it may cause contact dermatitis.

POLYPROPYLENE GLYCOL: Known as PPG. Used in many personal care products. Studies show it to cause skin irritation and dermatitis.

POLYQUATERNIUM (1 THRU 14): Used in a wide array of hair products as an anti-microbial, preservative, emulsifier, surfactant and an agent to control static. (See Quaternium.)

POLYSORBATE 20: Used in hair shampoos, conditioner, tonics and other grooming aids, skin care, cleanser, fresheners, make-up, bath aids, tanning preparation, baby products, shave cream and cuticle softener. It is a fatty acid ester used as an emulsifier, surfactant and an anti-irritant in shampoos. It is extracted from the myrrh gum tree. Some allergic reactions reported. May cause sensitivity and irritation.

POLYSORBATE 60: Used in shampoos, conditions and other hair grooming products, skin care aids, eye make-up, bubble baths and cleansing agents, baby products, deodorants and tanning preparations. Extracted from myrrh gum tree. Used for fragrance, disinfectant and astringent. A oil and water emulsifier and a cell re-normalizer. Emulsifies hormones that stop hair growth. May cause sensitivity and irritation.

POLYSORBATE 80: Used for hair products, skin preparations, mouthwashes, breath fresheners, baby products, suntan aids, make up, bathing items and shave creams. Extracted from myrrh gum tree. Used for fragrance, disinfectant and astringent. Oil and water emulsifier. May cause sensitivity and irritation.

POLYSORBATE NUMBERS 20-85: Fatty acid esters. Used in many cosmetics as emulsifiers. Polysorbates are assigned different numerical values according to their formulas and whether they're intended to be used in foods or cosmetics. Causes sensitivity and irritation.

POLYVINYLPYRROLIDINE (PVP): Used as a plasticizer in hairsprays and sometimes in make-up, shampoo and facial cream. Used because it imparts a hard, transparent, lustrous film. Reports show that it may cause harm if the particles are breathed. Modest intravenous doses administered to rats caused tumors.

POTASSIUM CHROMATE: Carcinogenic, mutagenic, toxic or causes adverse reactions. (See definition at beginning of glossary.)

POTASSIUM HYDROXIDE: Used in the manufacturing of liquid soaps and bleaches. It is commonly called lye and is used as an alkalizer in cosmetics. Shown to cause extreme eye and skin irritation. Carcinogenic, mutagenic, toxic or causes adverse reactions. (See definition at beginning of glossary.)

POTASSIUM SALT OF IODEOSIN: Carcinogenic, mutagenic, toxic or causes adverse reactions. (See definition at beginning of glossary.)

POTASSIUM SODIUM COPPER CHLOROPHYLLIN: A natural colorant derived from chlorophyll.

POTASSIUM SODIUM: Used in toothpastes.

POTASSIUM SORBATE: Used in personal care products as a mold and yeast inhibitor.

PPG-2-ISODECETH-4: Carcinogenic, mutagenic, toxic or causes adverse reactions. (See definition at beginning of glossary.)

PPG-M CETETH-N: Carcinogenic, mutagenic, toxic or causes adverse reactions. (See definition at beginning of glossary.)

PPG: (See polypropylene glycol.)

PPG-10 METHYL GLUCOSE ETHER: A humectant and moisturizer found in skin care products. (See Ethers Group and PPG.)

PPG-15 STEARYL ETHER: Found in bath preparations, cleansing products, personal cleanliness aids, foundations, colognes and toilet waters. Skin conditioning agent, moisturizer and emollient. (See Ethers Group.)

P-PHENYLENEDIAMINE: Used as an intermediate in hair dyes, it is the main component in permanent hair dyes. (See section on hair dyes.)

PRIMARY ALCOHOL FROM C8 TO C20: Carcinogenic, mutagenic, toxic or causes adverse reactions. (See definition at beginning of glossary).

PRIMARY HEXADECYLALCOHOL: Carcinogenic, mutagenic, toxic or causes adverse reactions. (See definition at beginning of glossary.)

PROCAINE (GROUP): Toxic, in creams it causes dermatitis.

PROCAINE HYDROCHLORIDE (PROCAINE): Causes systemic eczematous contact-type dermatitis.

PROPANEDIOLS (GROUP): Causes delayed contact allergy. Causes unilateral mydriasis.

PROPANTHELINE BROMIDE: Causes unilateral mydriasis.

PROPOLIS (BEESWAX): Causes hypersensitivity and irritation.

PROPOXUR: Carcinogenic, mutagenic, toxic or causes adverse reactions. (See definition at beginning of glossary.)

PROPYL ALCOHOL: (See Isopropyl Alcohol.)

PROPYL GALLATE: Used as an anti-oxidant and preservative in cosmetics. It is a known irritant and can cause allergic reactions.

PROPYLAMINES (GROUP): (See Amines Group.)

PROPYLENE CARBONATE: A solvent used in cosmetics.

PROPYLENE GLYCOL: Used in the great majority of personal care products. It is used as a humectant, surfactant and solvent. Besides cosmetics it is used as anti-freeze. It can be irritating to the skin if more than 5 percent is used in a formulation. With its small molecular weight, it can enter into the body. It has been shown to cause liver abnormalities and kidney damage in laboratory animals. See section on body care products for more cautions. Toxic.

PROPYLENE GLYCOL-2 MYRISTYL PROPIONATE: Shown to have comedogenic (acne producing) properties.

PROPYLENE GLYCOL BUTYL ETHER: Propylene glycol is used in antifreeze. It has shown to cause liver abnormalities and kidney damage. Toxic. (See Propylene Glycol and Ethers Group.)

PROPYLENE GLYCOL CETETH-N: May contain dangerous levels of dioxane a potent toxin, as a manufacturing by-product.

PROPYLENE GLYCOL MONOLAURATE: A non-ionic surfactant used in shampoos. Toxic.

PROPYLENE GLYCOL MONOSTEARATE: A non-ionic surfactant used in shampoos. Toxic.

PROPYLENE GLYCOL STEARATE: Functions as an emollient, thickener and emulsion stabilizer in creams and lotions. Toxic.

PROPYLENE IMINE: Carcinogenic, mutagenic, toxic or causes adverse reactions. (See definition at beginning of glossary.)

PROPYLENE OXIDE: Carcinogenic, mutagenic, toxic or causes adverse reactions. (See definition at beginning of glossary.)

PROPYLENE: Carcinogenic, mutagenic, toxic or causes adverse reactions. (See definition at beginning of glossary.)

PROPYLPARABEN (PROPYL-P-HYDROXYBENZOATE): Found in many personal care products, it is a common preservative. It is an effective preservative, bacteria and fungus killer and active against other organisms. It was developed in Europe. (See Parabens.)

PSEUDOCUMENE: Carcinogenic, mutagenic, toxic or causes adverse reactions. (See definition at beginning of glossary.)

PSORALEN (FUROCOUMARINES): A phototoxin that reacts with UV radiation to proiduc genotoxin.

PSORALENS (GROUP): Causes cutaneous phototoxicity reactions.

PURCELLIN, OIL OF: Causes skin irritation.

PVM/MA COPOLYMER: Used in cosmetics as a thickener, dispersing agent and stabilizer. It gives shampoo its soapy feel. Highly irritating to eyes, skin and mucous membrane.

PVP/EICOSENE COPOLYMER: A synthetic polymer, binder, film former, thickener, suspending agent and non-surfactant used in mascara and suntan preparations. (See Polyvinylpyrrolidine.)

PYRIDAXINE-ALPHA-KETOGLUTARATE: Hair and skin conditioning agent. In skin cleansers and fresheners and many hair grooming aids. Carcinogenic, mutagenic, toxic or causes adverse reactions. (See definition at beginning of glossary.)

PYRIDINE: Used in cosmetics as a solvent. It is a skin irritant and it is toxic.

PYROPHYLLITE: A colourant for external use only, except eye area.

QUATERNARY AMMONIUM COMPOUND: (See Quaternary Ammonium Salts.)

QUATERNARY AMMONIUM SALTS: Used as water repellents, fungicides, emulsifiers, paper and fabric softeners, antistatic agents and corrosion inhibitors. Their use in cosmetics, especially in hair conditioners and creme rinses, came from the paper and fabric industries. Studies show that it may cause fatal drug allergy (anaphylactic shock) in susceptible people.

QUATERNIUM -15: Used as an anti-microbial and preservative in a number of products. It is a formaldehyde releasing preservative. It is toxic, avoid.

QUATERNIUM: With any number they are carcinogenic, mutagenic, toxic or causes adverse reactions. (See definition at beginning of glossary.)

QUINALDINE: Strong irritant to mucous membranes.

QUINAZOLINE YELLOW: Studies show that it causes dermatitis.

QUINOL: Carcinogenic, mutagenic, toxic or causes adverse reactions. (See definition at beginning of glossary.)

QUINOLINE: Causes allergic contact dermatitis.

QUINOLINES (GROUP) (CHINOLINE): Causes allergic contact dermatitis.

QUINOPHTHALONE (YELLOW NO, 33): Causes allergic contact dermatitis.

QUINTOZENE: Carcinogenic, mutagenic, toxic or causes adverse reactions. (See definition at beginning of glossary.)

RASPBERRY EXTRACT: Used as a skin moisturizer, it contains Vitamin C & A, calcium, phosphorous, iron and trace minerals. It strengthens, restores and promotes tissue repair.

RED DYES (GROUP): (See Colour Additives) All D&C red dyes tested to date are shown to have comedogenic (acne producing) properties; causes adverse reactions or is toxic. (See FD&C Red #3.)

RED OIL: Carcinogenic, mutagenic, toxic or causes adverse reactions. (See definition at beginning of glossary.)

RED PETROLATUM (SEE ALSO PETROLATUM): Causes adverse reactions or is toxic; causes discoloration of skin and extremities.

RESINS (GROUP): Causes adverse reactions or is toxic. Studies show that it may cause contact dermatitis on hands, causes eyelid dermatitis and other adverse effects including allergic reactions.

RESORCINOL: Used as an anti-dandruff agent because of its antiseptic properties. It is irritating to the skin and mucous membrane. Also can be found in mouth wash and toothpaste. It can cause a blood disorder (methemoglobinemia), convulsions and death.

RESORCINOLPHTHALEIN: (See Resorcinol.)

RETINOIC ACID (RETIN-A): Vitamin A acid. A prescription chemical skin exfoliant. May irritate skin and cause sun sensitivity.

RETINYL PALMITATE POLYPEPTIDES: Used for cleansing and bath aids, skin care, hair care, make-up preparations, suntan products, after shave lotion and nail care. It is a Vitamin A from a plant source. Used for its antioxidant, conditioning, emollient and moisturizing effects. A rare water soluble form of Vitamin A and protein enzymes. Gives elasticity to skin.

RETINYL PALMITATE: A humectant and topical form of a Vitamin A derivative. A primary antioxidant vitamin, free-radical scavenger and cellular renewal ingredient (healer). It is on the toxic list.

RHODAMINE B: A colourant used in semi-permanent hair dyes. Although it was banned by the FDA, a recent report showed that two products still contained it. Used in lipstick it decreases the collagen content on the fibroblast cell layer of the human lip. Can also impair the formation on extracellular matrix which is important for the maintenance of the lip tissue.

RHODAMINES (GROUP): Can hinder skin cell metabolism.

RIBOFLAVIN (VITAMIN B-2): Used in indoor tanning preparations. It produces and improves melanin production and it is also a skin conditioning and moisturizing agent used in skin care, hair care, cleansing and bathing, make-up, after shaves and nail creams.

RICE BRAN OIL: Used as an emollient in skin care products. Rich in vitamin E and derived from the bran of rice. It easily penetrates the skin because it has a small molecular weight.

RICE POWDER: A safe and effective alternative to talc for face powders.

RICINOLEAMIDOPROPYL DIMETHYLAMINE LACTATE: Has been shown to cause contact allergic reactions.

RICINOLEIC ACID: May cause dermatitis.

ROSA MOSQUETA: (See Rose Hip Seed Oil.)

ROSE GERANIUM OIL: Used in skin care products for its ability to balance sebum production and to promote healing. The fragrance is used as an anti-depressant. Rose geranium has been shown scientifically to alter brain waves producing a more relaxed state.

ROSE HIP SEED OIL: A unique oil extracted from a rare mountain rose that grows in Chile. An extremely functional, high quality lipophilic EFA compound. Very high GLA and other extraordinary ingredients. Very high in vitamin E and C. It acts as an astringent, soother, mild cleanser and pore refiner. Studies show that it reduces wrinkles and smoothes the skin.

ROSEMARY EXTRACT: Used in shampoos, conditions, skin cleansing, freshening and general care for skin stimulation and regeneration. High in GLA. It is a toner and purifier, with anti-microbial properties. May cause irritation. Allergic dermatitis and photosensitivity.

ROSEWOOD OIL: Used in skin care or massage oils as an antiseptic. It is distilled from the bark of a Amazon rain forest tree. It is high in linalool (70 percent), making it balancing and healing.

ROSIN: May cause allergic reactions.

SACCHARIN: Carcinogenic, mutagenic, toxic or causes adverse reactions. (See definition at beginning of glossary.)

SAFROLE: Carcinogenic, mutagenic, toxic or causes adverse reactions. (See definition at beginning of glossary.)

SAGE EXTRACT: Used in shampoos, conditioners and other hair grooming aids, skin cleansing and care, fresheners and after shaves and anti-perspirants. It is a bacteria fighter and very good on wounds. Sage will help hair re-grow if the roots are not permanently damaged and will remove dandruff.

SALICYLIC ACID: Used in skin and body care products as a fungicide, sunscreen and anesthetic. It is used in some preparations as a mild exfoliant. Generally, it is a synthetic chemical but it can also be derived from plant.

SANDALWOOD OIL: Used as an antiseptic as well as a skin soother. It aids the skin in holding water. Derived from a small Indian evergreen tree.

SARSAPARILLA ROOT: A mild organic detergent and skin purifier. Contains saponins.

SCOPARONE: Carcinogenic, mutagenic, toxic or causes adverse reactions. (See definition at beginning of glossary.)

SD ALCOHOL: Specially denatured ethyl alcohol, treated to become unfit for oral consumption. Used as a solvent and astringent in toners, deodorants, mouthwashes and hairsprays. Also used as a preservative. Very drying to the skin. (See Alcohol.)

SEC-BUTYL ALCOHOL: Carcinogenic, mutagenic, toxic or causes adverse reactions. (See definition at beginning of glossary.)

SECONDARY AMINES: Carcinogenic, mutagenic, toxic or causes adverse reactions. (See definition at beginning of glossary.) Recommended not to be used in Europe.

SELENIUM: A yellowish or brown mineral discovered in the earth's crust in 1807, it is used as a dandruff treatment in shampoos. Carcinogenic, mutagenic, toxic or causes adverse reactions. (See definition at beginning of glossary.)

SESQUITERPENE (GROUP): Carcinogenic, mutagenic, toxic or causes adverse reactions. (See definition at beginning of glossary.) Causes severe allergies.

SESQUITERPENE LACTONE: Carcinogenic, mutagenic, toxic or causes adverse reactions. (See definition at beginning of glossary.) Causes severe allergies.

SHEA BUTTER: Used in skin care products because of its activity on cell regeneration and capillary circulation. This favours the healing of small wounds, cracks, crevices, skin ulcers and reduces the signs of aging. It has restructuring effects on the epidermis, also on dry and fragile hair. It has an anti-elastase characteristic which makes it a good active ingredient against stretch marks. It is derived from the fruit of the Karite tree.

SILICA (SILICON DIOXIDE): An anti-caking, thickener, suspending agent and non-surfactant. Also a moisturizer used for make-up, personal cleansing and deodorizing, skin care, hair care and nail polish or enamels. Used as an absorbent material in toilet preparations and is a particularly good skin protectant in creams. A naturally occurring colorless crystal or white powder commonly found in a variety of rocks. High in various minerals, silica helps to remineralize the skin and it also has a softening effect. It is toxic by inhalation and chronic exposure to dust may cause silicosis.

SILICONE: A group of inorganic compounds of silicon and oxygen. A clear liquid used to produce slip and richness. They provide a mesh-like coating to the skin allowing skin respiration to take place while holding the moisture in. Used as a substitute for oil in many types of products. Examples include dimethicone, dimethicone copolyol, simethicone and cyclomethicone.

SILK AMINO ACIDS: Moisturizer and hair conditioner. Skin is softened and protected. Used in hair conditioners, shampoos and other hair grooming products. Also used in mascara.

SILK POWDER: A by-product of the silk industry used in face powders to gently absorb excess oil that may be present on the surface of the skin. Obtained from silk, it is high in amino acids. As a make-up powder, it leaves skin soft and smooth. (See Silk.)

SILK: Can cause contact urticaria.

SILVER: Nail polish only. Restricted concentration: 1 percent maximum. Carcinogenic, mutagenic, toxic or causes adverse reactions. (See definition at beginning of glossary.)

SILVER NITRATE: Carcinogenic, mutagenic, toxic or causes adverse reactions. (See definition at beginning of glossary.)

SIMETHICONE: A silicone oil. This clear liquid is used as an antifoaming agent, ointment base and as a hair and skin protectant.

SKARALKONIUM CHLORIDE: Used in hair products as an effective hair conditioner and softener.

SOAP BARK EXTRACT: A bark derived from the Quillaja Saponaria tree native to South America. The bark is actually a mild soap with astringent and stimulatory properties.

SOAPSTONE: Carcinogenic, mutagenic, toxic or causes adverse reactions. (See definition at beginning of glossary.)

SODIUM ALGINATE: Natural compound. Mostly used as a thickener and emulsifier in foods, pharmaceuticals and cosmetics. It is a natural compound.

SODIUM ASCORBATE: Used in cosmetics as an antioxidant and preservative.

SODIUM BENZOATE: Common preservative. Referred to as a benzoic acid with sodium bicarbonate (baking soda). It is a moisturizer, used in hair care, skin care, cleansers, dental products and eye make-up. Also is an antiseptic. It may cause allergic reactions, use in food limited to 0.1 percent.

SODIUM BISULPHITE: Artificial chemical that is used as a hair relaxer and a preservative. Carcinogenic, mutagenic, toxic or causes adverse reactions. (See definition at beginning of glossary.)

SODIUM BORATE: Preservative, pH adjuster and moisturizer used in skin care, hair care, make-up, personal care, cleansing and freshening, suntan preparation, nail creams bath salts. An astringent, expectorant, antiseptic and eye wash. Applied to wounds and injuries, it prevents putrefaction. A detergent builder, emulsifier and preservative in cosmetics. Caution—ingestion of 5 to 10 grams by young children can cause severe vomiting, diarrhea and death.

SODIUM C12-15 PARTHE-15 SULFONATE: A fatty alcohol used in shampoo as a surfactant and cleansing agent. Also used in skin care preparation.

SODIUM C14-16 OLEFIN SULFONATE: Emulsifier and cleaner and surfactant used in soaps, shampoos and bubble baths. Comes from a mineral source.

SODIUM CARBOMER 941: Used as a thickener and stabilizer in creams, moisturizers, toothpastes, eye make-up and bathing products. Depending on overall formulation, it can be an irritant. Avoid the eye area as it may cause irritation. (See Carbomers.)

SODIUM CARBONATE: Used in cosmetics as a humectant and an alkalizer.

SODIUM CHLORIDE: Table salt used as a thickener in skin and hair preparations.

SODIUM CITRATE: Crystalline salt. Used in cosmetics as a sequestrant and an alkalizer and in foods as a buffering agent. It is a crystalline salt.

SODIUM COCOYL ISETHIONATE: A mild coconut derived surfactant that is mixed with chemicals.

SODIUM CYANIDE: Carcinogenic, mutagenic, toxic or causes adverse reactions. (See definition at beginning of glossary.)

SODIUM DEHYROACETATE: Preservative and moisturizer used in skin care, make up, suntan preparations, cleansers and cuticle softeners. It is used as a fungicide and anti-bacterial.

SODIUM DODECYL SULFATE: Carcinogenic, mutagenic, toxic or causes adverse reactions. (See definition at beginning of glossary.) Causes contact eczema.

SODIUM DODECYLBENZENE SULFONATE: Surfactant and cleansing agent. For use in bubble bath, soaps, eyeliner and personal care products. (See Benzene.)

SODIUM FLUORIDE: (See Fluoride.)

SODIUM HEXAMETAPHOSPHATE: Used in shampoos, bath salts and bubble baths. It is an emulsifier, texturizer and sequestering agent.

SODIUM HYALURONATE: Hyaluronic acid. A cellular renewal ingredient and healing agent that is found in all human cells. Although this ingredient was originally extracted for commercial use from roosters' combs, it is now also produced synthetically and at least two manufacturers use a form derived from plant that closely resembles that in human skin.

SODIUM HYDROXIDE: Used to alter the pH in personal care products. It is used as the base alkali of soap manufacturing. Also used in oven cleaners and liquid drain cleaners. Varying degrees of skin and eye irritation.

SODIUM LACTATE: Used in skin care products as a alternative to glycerin.

SODIUM LAURETH SULFATE: An ionic (negatively charged) surfactant. Used in shampoos as it is milder than sodium lauryl sulfate. It does, however, have an ether added. It is toxic. (See Ether Group.)

SODIUM LAUROYL SARCOSINATE: Surfactant, cleansing and conditioning. Used for shampoos and hair conditioner, cleansing and bathing preparations and foundations. Is a long chain chemical compound which makes it mild. A mild cleansing agent derived from coconut oil. Appropriate for use in shampoos; may be too drying for use on the skin.

SODIUM LAURYL SULFATE: Very popular ingredient. Used as a detergent, emulsifier and surfactant in over a thousand cosmetic products. This includes shampoos, toothpaste, lotions and creams. Used as an emulsifier and a detergent. Strongly degreases and dries the skin. Japanese studies show that it damages the DNA (the genetic code) within the cells.

SODIUM OLETH SULFATE: May contain dangerous levels of ethylene oxide and/or dioxane, both potent toxins, as a manufacturing by-product.

SODIUM PCA (NAPCA): Conditioner for skin and hair, a moisturizer and humectant. For skin and hair care, cleaning and bathing and suntan products. It is a naturally occurring component of human skin that is believed to be in part responsible for its moisture binding capacity. Its highly water absorbing and at a high humidity dissolves in its own water hydration. The sodium salt of pyroglutamic acid. The synthetic version can seriously dry the skin and cause allergic reactions.

SODIUM PCA METYLSILANOL: (See SODIUM PCA.)

SODIUM STEARATE: Used in deodorant sticks, shaving creams, toothpastes and shampoos.

SODIUM THIOGLYCOLATE: A chemical used in permanents as a hair relaxer. Is a primary irritant.

SOLUBLE COLLAGEN: This dermal protein makes up 70 percent of the body's connective tissue. Applied topically, pure soluble (non-cross-linked) collagen is readily absorbed by the skin and helps retain moisture and elasticity. (See Collagen.)

SORBIC ACID (2,4-HEXADIENOIC ACID): Organic acids used as a preservative in skin and hair products for babies and adults. Obtained from the berries of the mountain ash. It is a humectant and a mold and yeast inhibitor used as a replacement for glycerin, a binder for toilet preparations. Can cause redness and a slight burning sensation for some people. Known to cause urticaria.

SORBITAN LAURATE: An emulsifier and stabilizer for cosmetics. Known to cause urticaria.

SORBITAN MONOPALMITATE: A nonionic surfactant used in skin and hair care products. (See Palmitates and Sorbitan Palmitate.)

SORBITAN MONOSTEARATE: A nonionic surfactant used in skin and hair care products. (See Stearates.)

SORBITAN OLEATE: Studies show that it may cause contact urticaria.

SORBITAN PALMITATE: Studies show that it may cause contact dermatitis.

SORBITAN SESQUIOLEATE: Studies show that it may cause contact dermatitis.

SORBITAN STEARATE: Studies show that it may cause urticaria.

SORBITOL: A solid, white crystalline substance very much like sugar but more than twice as sweet. It is derived from fruits such as apples, berries, cherries, pears and plums; it may also be derived from corn syrup. It is a humectant (water-attracting/binding) ingredient as well as an emollient. Used in dental preparations, skin and hair care and cleansing, deodorants, colognes, eye make-up and suntan preparations.

SOY OIL: An oil from the soybean used in skin care products. It has a small molecule, which allows it to easily penetrate the skin. Consists of mostly glycerides of linoleic, oleic, linolenic and palmitic acids. With the genetic altering of soy beans it may be wise to avoid products with soy in them unless you can ascertain that the source is pure.

SOYA PROTEIN: Vegetable protein from soy. Applied topically, it is an excellent hydrator, readily absorbed by the skin for improved texture and resiliency. In hair formulas, it combines with fatty acids and amino acids to coat porous or damaged hair and help repair split-ends. (See also Vegetable Protein.)

SOYAMIDE DEA: A synthetic ingredient. (See DEA.)

SOYBEAN OIL: (See Soy Oil.)

SPEARMINT OIL: Derived from Mentha spicata, this essential oil is high in menthol, limonene and bisabolol, as well as flavonoids, tocopherols, betaine, choline, azulene, tannin and rosemaric acid. Milder than its cousin peppermint, it is antiseptic, anti-parasitic and anti-inflammatory. Because of the menthol it contains, it is cooling and soothing to the skin and helps to increase circulation.

SPIRAEA EXTRACT (SPIRHEA): Used as freshener due to its sweet fragrance. Has anti-inflammatory properties and pain relief. Extracted from flowers of Spiraea ulmaria. Not for use if pregnant or nursing.

SQUALANE: A nutrient-rich oil present in human sebum (the skin's own moisturizer) and involved in the process of cell growth. Squalane can be created synthetically or obtained from either the liver of the rare Japanese azame shark or olive oil or wheat germ oil. It is more stable against oxidation than Squalene. It is also a natural bactericide and healer. It spreads evenly along the surface of the skin to coat all of its contours, nonocclusively, to protect it. Squalane is also able to penetrate deeper and more readily than most other oils.

SQUALENE: Squalene is the edible form. (See Squalane.)

ST. JOHN'S WORT: An emollient and skin softener. Used in skin care products as a healing agent for chapped, dry, wrinkled or irritated skin and in suncare and after-sun products. Also very beneficial to damaged or dry hair and scalp.

STEARALKONIUM CHLORIDE: Used almost universally in hair conditioners. It was originally developed by the textile industry for use as a fabric softener. It also has anti-static properties.

STEARAMIDOETHYL DIETHYLAMINE PHOSPHATE: Can cause allergic contact dermatitis.

STEARAMIDOPROPYL DIMETHYLAMINE: Hair conditioning agent derived form hydrolyzed vegetable protein, anti-static and moisturizing. It can cause allergic dermatitis and has carcinogenic properties.

STEARAMIN OXYD: May be contaminated with nitrosamines. A known carcinogen.

STEARETH (PLUS #): Used as an emulsifier in lotions. May contain hazardous levels of ethylene oxide and/or dioxane which are potent toxins.

STEARIC ACID: An emollient, surfactant, moisturizer, cleansing agent and emulsifier. Found mainly in the natural fatty acids in plants and vegetables. Used in skin care, hair care, cleansing, bathing and deodorant products, make-up, tanning products, baby care products, shaving preparations and colognes, etc. May cause allergic reactions and other adverse effects.

STEARIC ACIDS (GROUP): (See Stearic Acid.)

STEARYL ALCOHOL: Pearlizing agent, lubricant and antifoam agent used in cosmetics. Studies show that it may cause contact dermatitis and allergies.

STEATITE: Carcinogenic, mutagenic, toxic or causes adverse reactions. (See definition at beginning of glossary.)

STYRENE MONOMER: Carcinogenic, mutagenic, toxic or causes adverse reactions (See definition at beginning of glossary).

STYRENE OXIDE: Carcinogenic, mutagenic, toxic or causes adverse reactions. (See definition at beginning of glossary.)

SUCROSE COCOATE: A very gentle cleansing agent in the form of a sugar derived from coconut oil. Non-stripping and non-drying to the skin, it solubilizes and washes off completely with water.

SUGAR CANE EXTRACT / SUGAR CANE GLYCOLIC EXTRACT: Mixed fruit or extracts are buffered. Dissolves glue-like substances that hold dead skin cells around eyes. (See Alpha Hydroxy Acids.)

SULFATE: Artificial liquid. Made with sulfated oils. Used to make manufactured soaps and detergents. Harmful to marine life and the environment.

SULFURIC ACID: Carcinogenic, mutagenic, toxic or causes adverse reactions. (See definition at beginning of glossary.)

SULISOBENZONE (BENZOPHENONE-4): May cause photo-sensitivity.

SUNFLOWER OIL: An emollient extracted from the seeds of the sunflower. Rich in essential fatty acids, it is a good base for massage oils and lotions.

SUPEROXIDE DIMUTASE (SOD): Powerful enzyme of the body for neutralizing free radicals; also a reducing agent. Anti-aging, tremendously potent anti-oxidant, keeps the membranes fluid, tissues and muscles supple. It is protective to our cells and it safeguards their energy making processes. It is a protein.

SWEET ALMOND OIL: Emollient, solvent, skin conditioner and moisturizer. Significantly aids in maintaining the delicate balance of the skin's natural oils. Highly effective in skin care and cleansing, foundations and eye make-up, hair care, bathing aids and tanning products.

TALC (MAGNESIUM SILICATE): A natural mineral. Adheres to skin; used in makeup, powders and foundation; produces slip and coloring. A lung irritant when used in powder form. (See Section on babies.) Carcinogenic, mutagenic, toxic or causes adverse reactions. (See definition at beginning of glossary.) Toxic by inhalation, some talc found to contain amphibole particle distribution typical of asbestos.

TALLOW AMIDOPROPYL DIMETHYLAMINE: May cause contact allergic reactions.

TAR CAMPHOR: Carcinogenic, mutagenic, toxic or causes adverse reactions. (See definition at beginning of glossary.)

TEA (TRIETHANOLAMINE): Raises the pH in formulas. A natural colorer taken from natural inorganic crystals. Also used in skin and personal care products, in make up of all types. May contain nitrosamines, a known carcinogen, as a by-product of manufacturing.

TEA CARBOMER: May contain nitrosamines, a known carcinogen, as a by-product of manufacturing.

TEA-COCO HYDROLYZED PROTEIN: May contain nitrosamines, a known carcinogen, as a by-product of manufacturing. Has be shown to cause serious facial dermatitis.

TEA COCOYL GLUTAMATE: May contain nitrosamines, a known carcinogen, as a by-product of manufacturing. Has be shown to cause serious facial dermatitis.

TEA DODECYLBENZENESULFONATE: Surfactant, cleansing agent, used in shampoos and hair dyes. Used as an emulsifier and wetting agent and are effective in hard or soft water. May contain nitrosamines, a known carcinogen, as a by-product of manufacturing.

TEA LAURYL SULFATE: A common high-foaming surfactant found in shampoos. A combination of triethanolamine and the salt of lauryl sulfuric acid. May contain nitrosamines, a known carcinogen, as a by-product of manufacturing.

TEA SALICYLATE: A phototoxin that can cause cancer in sunlight.

TEA STEARATE (TRIHYDROXYETHYLAMINE STEARATE): Can cause serious facial dermatitis. May contain nitrosamines, a known carcinogen, as a by-product of manufacturing.

TEA TREE OIL (MELALEUCA): Distilled from the leaves of the Australian tree Melaleuca alternifolia. Used for its germicide, fungicide and antiseptic properties. This oil is commonly used for treating acne, cuts, burns and insect bites.

TERATOGEN: A harmful substance that has the ability to pass through the placenta to the unborn child.

TEREPHTHALIC ACID: Carcinogenic, mutagenic, toxic or causes adverse reactions. (See definition at beginning of glossary.)

TERPENES (GROUP): May cause psoriasis on the face.

TERT-BUTYL ALCOHOL: Carcinogenic, mutagenic, toxic or causes adverse reactions. (See definition at beginning of glossary.)

TERTIARY AMMONIUM COMPOUNDS: Can cause fatal allergic reaction (anaphylactic shock). May also cause an increase in sensitivity to muscle relaxants resulting in anaphylactic shock. Causes contact dermatitis.

TETRACHLOROETHYLENE: Carcinogenic, mutagenic, toxic or causes adverse reactions. (See definition at beginning of glossary.)

TETRACHLORVINPHOS: Carcinogenic, mutagenic, toxic or causes adverse reactions. (See definition at beginning of glossary.)

TETRAETHYL LEAD: Carcinogenic, mutagenic, toxic or causes adverse reactions. (See definition at beginning of glossary.)

TETRAHYDRONAPHTHALENE: An irritant to eyes and skin.

TETRAHYDRONAPHTHALENES (GROUP): Can produce hyperirritability and other system effects. May contain nitrosamines, a known carcinogen, as a by-product of manufacturing.

TETRASODIUM EDTA: A chelating agent that bonds mineral ions in shampoos and conditioners and other hair grooming products, cleansing products including bath aids in personal care, make-up, tanning products, baby shampoos, shave creams and make-up removal preparations. Prolonged skin contact may cause irritation, possibly even a mild burn.

TETRASODIUM SALT: Carcinogenic, mutagenic, toxic or causes adverse reactions. (See definition at beginning of glossary.)

THALLIUM: Carcinogenic, mutagenic, toxic or causes adverse reactions. (See definition at beginning of glossary.)

THEOBROMA OIL: Carcinogenic, mutagenic, toxic or causes adverse reactions. (See definition at beginning of glossary.)

THIAZOLES (GROUP): A known mutagen that can also cause allergic reactions, contact allergy and dermatitis.

THIOACETAMIDE: Carcinogenic, mutagenic, toxic or causes adverse reactions (See definition at beginning of glossary).

THIOGLYCOLATES: Carcinogenic, mutagenic, toxic or causes adverse reactions. (See definition at beginning of glossary.)

THIOMERSAL: Carcinogenic, mutagenic, toxic or causes adverse reactions. (See definition at beginning of glossary.) Causes dermatitis.

THIOUREA: Carcinogenic, mutagenic, toxic or causes adverse reactions. (See definition at beginning of glossary.)

THYME EXTRACT: May cause contact allergy in some individuals.

THYME LEMON OIL: An essential oil belonging to the medicinal labiate family of plants; distilled from the wild-crafted herb collected in Spain. It is balancing and it strengthens the immune system and aids cellular renewal.

TIN OXIDE: A brownish black colouring agent used in make-up.

TITANIUM DIOXIDE: Used in make-up, skin care and cleansing products, dental products, deodorants and nail polishes and enamels. It is mainly used as a white pigment and opacifier in make-up and sunblock products. Its reflecting qualities reduces the effects of UVA and UVB rays. No known toxicity when used externally. Not for internal use.

TISSUE RESPIRATORY FACTORS: Used in skin care products as an anti-inflammatory and moisturizer. Commonly known as live yeast cell extract, it has been found to work with the skin stimulating the living cells into producing protective substances. It is a glyconucleopeptide.

TITANIUM TETRACHLORIDE: Carcinogenic, mutagenic, toxic or causes adverse reactions. (See definition at beginning of glossary.)

TOCOPHEROL: Used in skin care products for its ability to act as an anti-oxidant, skin conditioner, cleanser and moisturizer. Used in make up, skin preparations, hair care and suntan aids, fresheners, shaving creams and after shave lotions. Obtained by the vacuum distillation of edible vegetable oil used as a dietary supplement. It helps protects fat in the body's tissues from abnormal breakdown. It can cause contact dermatitis.

TOCOPHERYL ACETATE: A synthetic form of Vitamin E. It acts as an antioxidant, conditioner, moisturizer and promoter of skin growth. Used in make-up, skin care, hair care, indoor tanning aids, cleansing and bath products, nail polish and enamels, shaving creams and after shave lotion.

TOLUENE: Used as a solvent in cosmetics, especially nail polish and also dyes. It is used in pharmaceuticals and gasoline as a blending agent. It is toxic and narcotic in high concentrations.

TOLUENE-2,4-DIAMINE: Carcinogenic, mutagenic, toxic or causes adverse reactions. (See definition at beginning of glossary.)

TOLUENE SULFONAMIDE: Formaldehyde resin. Used as a plasticizer in nail polishes; a strong sensitizer.

TOLUENE-2,4-DIISOCYANATE: Carcinogenic, mutagenic, toxic or causes adverse reactions. (See definition at beginning of glossary.)

TOLUENESULFONAMIDE FORMALDEHYDE RESIN: Carcinogenic, mutagenic, toxic or causes adverse reactions. (See definition at beginning of glossary.) Can cause contact dermatitis.

TONKA BEAN CAMPHOR: Carcinogenic, mutagenic, toxic or causes adverse reactions. (See definition at beginning of glossary.)

TOXAPHENE: Carcinogenic, mutagenic, toxic or causes adverse reactions. (See definition at beginning of glossary.)

TOXIN: A poisonous substance that causes pathology in the body.

TRAGACANTH: Herbal gum. Used as a thickener in cosmetics and in hair care products as a hairspray or setting-lotion ingredient.

TRETINOIN (VITAMIN A RETINOIC ACID, RETIN-A): (See Retinoic Acid.)

TRICHLORFON: Carcinogenic, mutagenic, toxic or causes adverse reactions. (See definition at beginning of glossary.)

TRICHLOROETHYLENE: Carcinogenic, mutagenic, toxic or causes adverse reactions. (See definition at beginning of glossary.)

TRICLOSAN: A bactericide with very high percutaneous absorption. Can cause liver damage; an eye irritant.

TRICYCLIC: Carcinogenic, mutagenic, toxic or causes adverse reactions. (See definition at beginning of glossary.)

TRIDECYL STEARATE (STEARIC ACID): (See Stearic Acid.)

TRIETHANOLAMINE (TEA): An alkalizing agent in cosmetics, used to adjust pH balance. Can cause irritation and sensitivity if more than 5 percent is used in a formulation. May contain nitrosamines, a known carcinogen, as a by-product of manufacturing.

TRIETHANOLAMINE DODECYLBENZENE SULFONATE: (See TEA and Dodecylbenzene Sulfonate.)

TRIETHANOLAMINE SALTS: Can cause serious dermatitis on the face.

TRIETHYL CITRATE: Used as a film former in hair products.

TRIFLURALIN: Carcinogenic, mutagenic, toxic or causes adverse reactions. (See definition at beginning of glossary.)

TRIMETHYL BENZENE: Carcinogenic, mutagenic, toxic or causes adverse reactions. (See definition at beginning of glossary.)

TRIS (2,3-DIBROMOPROPYL) PHOSPHATE: Carcinogenic, mutagenic, toxic or causes adverse reactions. (See definition at beginning of glossary.)

TURPENTINE OIL: Studies show that it may cause contact dermatitis.

TYROSENE: Used as a tanning accelerator. It is an amino acid that plays a part in the production of melanin, a dark pigment found in the skin.

ULTRAMARINE BLUE: A natural colouring pigment used in health oriented personal care products. Safe for use on skin.

ULTRAMARINE GREEN: Carcinogenic, mutagenic, toxic or causes adverse reactions. (See definition at beginning of glossary.)

ULTRAMARINE PINK: A natural colouring pigment used in health oriented personal care products. Safe for use on skin.

ULTRAMARINE VIOLET: A natural colouring pigment used in health oriented personal care products. Safe for use on skin.

ULTRAMARINES (blue, green, pink, red, violet): The FDA allows external use only, including eye area.

UREA (GROUP) (CARBAMIDE): Studies show that it may cause contact dermatitis.

UREA: Research shows that it can damage skin function, thinning of the top layer of the skin (epidermis) and cause changes in the skin when used in high concentrations.

URETHANE: Carcinogenic, mutagenic, toxic or causes adverse reactions. (See definition at beginning of glossary.)

UROCANIC ACID: A phototoxin.

VALERATES (GROUP): Studies show that it may cause contact dermatitis and it is a suspected carcinogen.

VANADIUM: Carcinogenic, mutagenic, toxic or causes adverse reactions. (See definition at beginning of glossary.)

VEGETABLE GLYCERINE: A rich humectant, emollient and lubricant naturally extracted from vegetable oils, glycerine has been used in cosmetic formulations for thousands of years. Synthetic glycerine, derived from propylene alcohol, is highly irritating to the skin and scalp and should be avoided.

VEGETABLE PROTEIN: Used in skin and hair care products as a source of amino acids. The molecule is too big to enter skin unless it has undergone a process to cleave the size or is wrapped in a lyposome. Applied topically, vegetable protein acts as a humectant, drawing moisture up from the lower levels of the skin. In hair formulas, it combines with fatty acids and amino acids to coat porous or damaged hair and help repair split-ends.

VETIVER OIL (VETIVERT): An essential oil similar to lemon grass and citronella that grows in India and other tropical climates. It is also acts as a humectant.

VINYL ACETATE: Carcinogenic, mutagenic, toxic or causes adverse reactions. (See definition at beginning of glossary.)

VINYL BROMIDE: Carcinogenic, mutagenic, toxic or causes adverse reactions. (See definition at beginning of glossary.)

VINYL CHLORIDE: Carcinogenic, mutagenic, toxic or causes adverse reactions. (See definition at beginning of glossary.)

VINYLIDENE CHLORIDE: Carcinogenic, mutagenic, toxic or causes adverse reactions. (See definition at beginning of glossary.)

VITAMIN A: Used topically as a skin treatment. Beneficial for rough, scaly, dry or damaged skin and it has been shown to clear up some forms of acne and to relieve symptoms of psoriasis and other skin disorders. It is often found in sun protection creams for its healing and hydrating properties. A vitamin A deficiency reduces the mucopolysaccharides in the skin, which accelerates the skin's aging process.

VITAMIN B-5: (See Panthenol.)

VITAMIN B-COMPLEX: Water soluble vitamins that, when applied topically, help control excess oil secretion and reduce enlarged pores. Recommended for rough, scaly skin and blemishes. Since B vitamins are the regulators of the metabolic functions of our body and are constituents of the prosthetic groups of enzymes, they are important to skin cell respiration.

VITAMIN D: One of three vitamins able to be absorbed by the skin and the only one that the body is able to manufacture (when exposed to ultraviolet light). This vitamin is necessary for the building of new skin cells, as well as bones, teeth and hair.

VITAMIN E: A natural cellular renewal (healing) ingredient and antioxidant. In its pure form, the oil is too heavy for daily use on the face. However, it makes an excellent ingredient in moisturizers, eye treatment preparations and facial masks. In its pure form, it may be used for healing cuts, abrasions and burns.

VITAMIN F: Fatty Acids are known in Europe as Vitamin F. It consists of linoleic, linolenic and arachidonic acids, the three essential fatty acids. Vitamin F acts as a skin protector against infection, eczema and other skin conditions. Used in moisturizers, it helps rebuild rough, dry or damaged skin and hair. (See Fatty Acids.)

VITAMIN H: Also known as Biotin, it is an important factor in the growth of tissue and for the correct composition of sebaceous gland secretion. A deficiency of vitamin H leads to dry skin and seborrheic dermatitis, which in turn leads to the formation of dandruff and crusts on the scalp. Vitamin H is vital for the maintenance of a normal fat metabolism and also protects from hair loss.

WATER: Purified water, demineralized water and mineral water are forms of water used in health oriented products.

WATERCRESS EXTRACT: Used in skin and hair care products for its stimulatory properties. It is extracted from the flowers and leaves of nasturtium officinalis.

WHEAT GERM EXTRACT: Used as a tissue respiratory agent and its ability to oxygenate. Extracted from the core of the wheat kernel. It is a protein and high in vitamin E, thiamine and B6.

WHEAT GERM GLYCERIDES: Used in moisturizers and lotions, it is derived by pressing wheat germ.

WHEAT GERM OIL: A skin nourisher that also acts as a natural preservative because of its high vitamin E content. It is a natural source of vitamins A, E and D and squalane.

WHEAT PROTEIN: (See Vegetable Protein.)

WILLOW BARK: Used topically as an antiseptic and astringent. It is used externally for eruptions, sores, burns and wounds as it reduces inflammation.

WITCH HAZEL/WITCH HAZEL DISTILATE/WITCH HAZEL EXTRACT: Often called Hamamelis Water. Used in skin care and aftershave products as a toner, astringent and soothing cleanser. It is extracted from the alder bush. It helps to restore correct pH balance without stinging. Helps combat blemish causing bacteria and refines pores. Extracted from bark and leaves of the plant. Witch hazel water is 15 percent alcohol. It may cause allergic contact dermatitis.

WOOD ALCOHOL (METHYL ALCOHOL): It has been found to be a animal mutagen. It can cause systemic poisoning in the body. It can also cause facial contact dermatitis.

XANTHAN GUM: A thickener, binder and emulsion stabilizer. Used in skin and hair care products, make-up, cleansers, indoor and outdoor tanning products, deodorants, shave creams and bathing preparations. This is a common stabilizer taken from the fermentation of carbohydrates along with the lantlomanous canapiatirs plant.

XANTHENE This ingredient inhibits cell metabolism. It has also shown to have comedogenic (acne producing) properties.

XYLENES: Carcinogenic, mutagenic, toxic or causes adverse reactions. (See definition at beginning of glossary.)

YEAST MUCOPROTEIN: A nutrient from grain and other natural sources. It is a skin oxygenator. Yeast is a fungi that is a dietary source of folic acid (B12). It produces enzymes that will convert sugar into alcohol and carbon dioxide.

YELLOW NO. 11: Studies show that it may cause contact dermatitis.

YLANG-YLANG OIL: Extracted from the flower of the ylang-ylang tree. It is used in cosmetics as a fragrance.

ZINC OXIDE: Widely used in powders and creams to help cosmetics adhere to the skin. A natural, physical sun-blocking ingredient. Carcinogenic, mutagenic, toxic or causes adverse reactions. (See definition at beginning of glossary.)

ZINC POTASSIUM CHROMATE: Carcinogenic, mutagenic, toxic or causes adverse reactions. (See definition at beginning of glossary.)

ZINC STEARATE: Widely used in powders and creams to help cosmetics adhere to the skin. May be harmful if inhaled; has an effect on the lungs similar to asbestos. Carcinogenic, mutagenic, toxic or causes adverse reactions. (See definition at beginning of glossary.)

ZINC: Mineral essential for growth and cell regeneration and to promote healing. It is often prescribed orally to help control some forms of acne. Zinc helps to remineralize and calm the skin. Carcinogenic, mutagenic, toxic or causes adverse reactions. (See definition at beginning of glossary.)

ZINEB: Carcinogenic, mutagenic, toxic or causes adverse reactions. (See definition at beginning of glossary.)

Appendix A

Suggested Reading

Being Beautiful—Deciding for Yourself, Center for the Study of Responsive Law, P.O. Box 19367, Washington DC 20036.

Cosmetics Buying Guide, Andrew Scheman and David Severson, Consumer Reports Books.

Creating Your Own Cosmetics—Naturally, Nikolaus Smeh, Alliance Publishing Company.

Nontoxic, Natural, & Earthwise, Debra Lynn Dadd, Jeremy P. Tarcher, Inc.

Take Care of Your Skin, Elaine Brumberg, Harper & Row.

What's in Your Cosmetics?, Aubrey Hampton, Odonian Press.

Safe Shopper's Bible, David Steinman and Samuel Epstein, McMillian.

Appendix B

Dear Sirs,

    In accordance with my desire to know what I am putting on my body, I am writing to request a list of the ingredients that your company uses in the following products:

* See Note	facial cleanser	shampoo
	moisturizer	conditioner
	toner	setting gel
	sunscreen	hairspray
	lipstick	deodorant
	mascara	toothpaste
	eyeshadow	mouthwash
	eyeliner	lip-balm
	foundation	shaving cream
	blush	nail products

    Failure to meet with my request will result in my choosing products from a manufacturer that wishes to inform the consumer about the ingredients that they are using. I do not wish to have the list sent to my doctor, as is the usual procedure, but wish to have the information myself so that I can make informed choices.

    Thank you for your cooperation. It is greatly appreciated.

NOTE: Request the ingredient information only on the products that you are using or intend to use. Requesting a full set of ingredient lists is costly to the manufacturer and may result in non-compliance.

How to Stay in Touch

Some of you may want to be kept abreast of ongoing changes in cosmetic formulating. We can expect to see changes as the industry begins to understand our stance on integrity of ingredients, efficacy in design and surety of safety. The *Cosmetic Health Report* will keep you apprised of the following:

- critiques on cosmetic manufacturing companies
- articles on cosmetic reformulation
- product spotlights
- legal and lobbying updates
- cosmetic recipes
- seminar and workshop dates and locations

Visit our website at:
http://www.cosmetichealthreport.com
or write to:
The Cosmetic Health Report, Inc.
342-1482 Gulf Road
Point Roberts, WA 98281

Bibliography

Alpha hydroxy acid-based cosmetics, DCI, Jan. 1995.

Alzheimer's Disease and Aluminum. Public Health Reports, Nov/ Dec., 1993.

Alzheimer's Disease Is It Aluminum? Lisa Poniatowski Easley, Harvard Health Letter, Oct. 1990, Vol. 15.

Alzheimer's Stepchild. Peter Radetsky, Discover, Sept. 1992.

Analysis of Cosmetics with Regard to Legislation, Liem, D.H., Wagenigen, 1976.

Artificial Fingernail Products. A Guide to Chemical Exposures in the Nail Salon.

Baby's New Bottle, edited by Barbara Wickens, Maclean's, Jan. 16, 1995.

Bailey Issues Sternest AHA Warning to Date, DCI, May 1994.

Beach Bummer, Michael Castleman, Kerry Laureman, Mother Jones, May/June 1993.

Beauty News, "Talc," Longevity, Aug. 1994.

Being Beautiful—Deciding for Yourself Selected Readings. Washington, DC: Center for the Study of Responsive Law, 1986.

Bone Cancer Incidence Rates in New York State: Time Trends and Fluoridated Drinking Water, Martin C. Mahoney, Philip C. Nasca et al American Journal of Public Health, Vol. 81, No.4. April, 1991.

Brief Original Contributions A case-control study of borderline ovarian tumors: the influence of perineal exposure of talc, Bernard L. Harlow and Noel S. Weiss, American Journal of Epidemiology, The Johns Hopkins University School of Hygiene and Public Health, Vol. 130, No. 2, 1989.

Carcinogenic Effect of Sequential Artificial Sunlight and UV-A Irradiation in Hairless Mice, Bent Staberg, MD et al, Arch Dermatol - Vol. 119, 1983.

Chromosomes changes with time in lymphocytes after occupational exposure to toluene, E. Schmid, M. Bauchinger and R. Hauf, Mutation Research, Elsevier, 142(1985) 37-39.

Chronic Sunscreen Use Decreases Circulating Concentration of 25-Hydroxyvitamin D, Lois Y. Matsuoka, MD et al, Department of Dermatology Medical College, April 1988.

Citizens for a Toxic-Free Marin, Making Sense of Scents, Compiled by Julia Kendal

Color Cosmetic, Market is Impacted Heavily by Nature, Lisa Kintish, Soap/Cosmetic/Chemical/Specialities May 1990.

Color it Temporary, Susan Jaques, American Health, Nov. 1991.

Consumer Health and Product Hazards Cosmetics and Drugs, Pesticides, Food Additives

Cosmetic Additives An International Guide, Flick, Ernest W. Noyes Publications, Park Ridge, New Jersey: 1991.

Cosmetic and Toiletry Formulations, 2nd Edition, Flick, Ernest W. Noyes Publications, Park Ridge, New Jersey: 1989.

Cosmetic Bench Reference, Allured Publishing Corporation, Wheaton, Illinois: 1988

Cosmetic Colors Status in the US and in the European Union, James M. Akerson, Consultant, DCI Oct. 1994.

Cosmetic Science, Vol. 1, Edited by Breuer, M.M., Biomedical Department, Gillette Research Institute, Academic Press Inc., (London) Rockville, Maryland: 1978.

Cosmetic Talc and Ovarian Cancer, D.L. Longo, R.C. Young, The Lancet, Aug. 18, 1979.

Cosmetics and the Skin, Wells, F.V., Lubowe, Irwin I., MD, Reinhold Publishing Corporation, New York, Chapman & Hall Ltd., London: 1964.

Culture Shock, Michael McDermott, Cosmetic & Drug Marketing.

Dangerous Beauty—Scientists Warn of Harmful Ingredients in Our Shampoos and Cosmetics, New Health and Longevity, Feb., 1994.

Dangerous Cosmetics, Carola Barczak, MA, RMT, Health Naturally, Oct/Nov. 1994.

Decoding the Cosmetic Label, Judith E. Foulke, FDA Consumer, May 1994.

Dioxin via skin: A hazard at low doses?, Science News, March 4, 1989.

Dioxin's Other Face, Karen F. Schmidt, Science News, Vol. 141, Jan. 11, 1992.

Disarming the Armpit, American Health, Dec. 1990 (p.16).

Do Estrogen-Imitators Wreak Reproductive Havoc? Lani Sinclair, Safety and Health, Aug. 1994.

Don't Drink the Water? Brush your teeth, but the fluoride from your tap may not do much good and may cause cancer. Saron Begley, Newsweek, Feb. 5, 1990.

Dox, Ida G., Melloni, B. John, Eisner, Gilbert M. Harper Collins Illustrated Medical Dictionary, Harper Collins, New York: 1993.

Edited by Epstein, Samuel S. And Grundy, Richard D., Volume 2 of the Legislation of Product Safety. Cambridge, Massachusetts: The M.I.T. Press, 1974.

Efficacy survey on wrinkle treatment products for Narhex Australia Pty. Ltd., Dr. Vyt Garnys, Ph.D., Cetec Pty. Ltd. Consulting Enterprises in Technology

Environmental toxins suspected in breast cancer, The London Free Press, Canadian Press, Thursday, Sept. 29, 1994.

EPA Scrutiny of Phthalates May Hurt DEP, Chemical Marketing Reporter, May 8, 1989.

EPA: Dioxins are more than carcinogens, J. Raloff, Science News, Sept. 17, 1994.

Evaluation of Preservatives For Cosmetic Products, John R. Sabourin, DCI, Dec. 1990.

FDA Airs Agenda On Regulation of Cosmetics At CTFA Conference, by Donald A. Davis, Editor, DCI, May 1990.

Fluoride Update, Bill McCord, Health Freedom News, Feb. 1992.

Fragrances Come Alive, Anthony Floreno, Chemical Marketing Reporter, May 8, 1995.

Glenn, William. Dangerous Chemicals In The Workplace. Don Mills, Ontario: Occupational Health and Safety Canada, Corpus Information Services, 1988.

Good News For Kids Who Hate Baths, Lab Notes by Jerry E. Bishop. The Wall Street Journal, Jan. 11, 1988.

Group feels no scent is good sense, Susan Leblanc (Halifax Chronicle—Herald), Vancouver Sun, Mon. March 13, 1995.

Guide for labeling of cosmetics, Health and Welfare Canada, Canadian Government Publishing Centre Supply and Services Canada, Ottawa, 1988.

Hair Dye Genotoxicity, D.J. Kirkland MD, et al, American Heart Association Journal, Vol. 98, No. 6, Dec. 1979.

Hair Dye Use and Risk of Leukemia and Lymphoma, Kenneth Cantor, Ph.D., et al, American Journal of Public Health, Vol. 78, No. 5. May 1988.

Hair Dye Use in White Men and Risk of Multiple Myeloma, Linda Morris Brown M.P.H. et al, American Journal of Public Health, Dec. 1992.

Hair Scare, Natalie Angier and Rick Weiss, Mademoiselle, Feb. 1993.

Hairy Portals for Toxic Chemicals, J. Raloff, Science News, Vol. 133 June 25, 1988.

Harry's Cosmeticology, 7th Edition, Edited by Wilkinson, J. B., M.A., Bsc., Cchem, FRSC, Moore, R. J., Bsc. Cchem, MRSC, MIInfSc., Chemical Publishing Company Inc., New York: 1982.

Hazard Evaluation System and Information Service, California Occupational Health Program, Berkeley, CA. Prepared by Susan Quenon, RN, BS, Nov. 1989.

Help or Hype. The truth about skin care products. Jami Laughridge, WD Your Body Your Health, Jan. 1992.

Hot Field: Neurotoxicity, Richard Stone, Science, Vol. 259, Mar. 5, 1993.

Hot Lips, Consumer Report, Nov. 1992.

Hydroxy Acids and Skin Aging, Walter P. Smith, Soap/Cosmetics/Chemical Specialities, Sept. 1993.

Hydroxy Acids and Skin Aging, Walter P. Smith, Vol. 109, Cosmetics and Toiletries Magazine, Sept 1994.

In Vitro Percutaneous Absorption, Scientifically Speaking, Anne Wolven Garret, DCI, June 1989.

Is Aluminum a Dementing Ion? The Lancet, Mar. 21, 1992.

John Peters, MD, American Journal of Industrial Medicine, 3:169-171, Sept. 1982.

Kerney Levenstein, Mary. Everyday Cancer Risks And How To Avoid Them. Garden City Park, New York: Avery Publishing Group Inc., 1992.

Kilgour, Q.F.G., McGarry, Marguerite. Complete Hairdressing Science. Heinemann Professional Publishing, 1989.

Lawson, Lynn, Staying well in a Toxic World, Noble Press Inc., Chicago: 1993.

Long wave Ultraviolet Radiation and Promotion of Skin Cancer, Mary Steidl Matsui, Cold String Harbour Laboratory Press, Jan, 1991.

Malignant Mimicry. False Estrogens May Cause Cancer and Lower Sperm Counts, John Rennie, Scientific American, Sept. 1993.

Mena, I., MD and Villanueva-Meyer, J., MD, The Clinical and Scientific Basis of M.E./CFS., The Nightingale Research Foundation, Ottawa: 1992.

Milder Listerine Announced Following Cancer Report, Ron Winslow, Wall Street Journal, April 23, 1991.

Mixed news on hair dyes and cancer risk, K.A. Fackelmann, Science News, Vol. 145, Feb. 1994.

Mouth cancer from a morning gargle? Marjory Roberts, US News and World Report, July 1, 1991.

Mouthwash Use in the Risk of Oral and Pharyngeal Cancer, Department of Health and Human Services,

National Institute of Health, National Cancer Institute, Bethesda Maryland, April 1991.

Multiple Chemical Sensitivity Patients Show Poor Visual and Verbal Skills, Pippa Wysong, The Medical Post, Sept. 27, 1994.

Multiple Myeloma in Cosmetologist, Sylvanna Guidotti B.A., William E. Wright MD,

Murray, J. J., Rugg-Gunn, A.J., Jenkins, G.N., Fluorides in carries prevention, 3rd. Edition, Butterworth-Heinemann Ltd., Oxford: 1991.

Natural Beauty, Natural Colors, Natural Looks, Joni Laughran, L.C., Ph.D., Let's Live, Nov. 1992.

Natural Body Care Products A Glossary of Terms and Ingredients. Feather River Co., 1992

Neglected Neurotoxicants, Sarah Williams, Science, Vol. 248, May 25, 1990.

Neurotoxicology: New Marker for Nerve Damage, Richard Stone, Science, Vol. 259, March 12, 1993.

Neurotoxins: At Home and the Workplace. Report to the Committee on Science and Technology US House of Representatives. Ninety-ninth Congress, Second Session, June 1986. US Government Printing Office, Washington, DC., 1989.

New Contaminant Found in Many Shampoos, Keeping Posted, Drug and Cosmetic Industry, Nov. 1992.

Newburger's Manual of Cosmetic Analysis, 2nd Edition, Edited by Senzel, Alan J., Published by the Association of Official Analytical Chemists, Inc., Washington, DC: 1977.

Nitrosamines Reexamined, Food For Thought Beatrice Trum Hunter, Consumers' Research, Jan., 1988.

Nontoxic, Natural, & Earthwise, Debra Lynn Dadd, Jeremy P. Tarcher, Inc.

Not So Fertile Ground, Michael D. Lemonick, Time, Sept. 19, 1994.

Null, Gary, Ph.D., The 90's Healthy Body Book, Health Communications, Inc. Deerfield Beach, Florida: 1994.

Openshaw, F., B.Sc., M.I.T. Hairdressing Science. Longman Group Limited, 1978.

Ovarian Cancer and Talc A Case-Control Study, Daniel W. Cramer MD, et al. Cancer, July 15, 1982.

Ovarian Cancer. New Ways to Reduce Your Risk, Randi Londer Gould, Redbook, Vol. 184, Mar. 1995.

Perfume Expose, Richard H. Conrad Ph.D., Environmental Consultant, Oct. 23, 1994.

Perfume Protest at Fairmont Hotel, Carl Nolte, San Francisco Chronicle, Tues. Oct. 25, 1994.

Personal Care With Principle. Chicago: The National Anti-Vivisection Society, 1993.

Plasma Humain et Plasma Marin, Human Plasma and Marine Plasma, Passebecq, Andre Ph. D, M.D, and Soulier, Jean-Marc Ph.D, pharmacist, Nouvelles Presses Interntionales, Vallesvilles: 1991.

Polycyclic Musks to Grow On Strength of Lower Prices, Matthew Gallagher, Chemical Marketing Reporter, June 21, 1993.

Possible Morbidity In Women From Talc on Condoms, Journal of American Medical Association (JAMA), March 15, 1995.

Proctor, Nick H., Ph.D. , Hughes, James P., MD, F.A.C.P. , Fishchman, Michael L., MD, M.P.H. Chemical Hazards of the Workplace, 2nd Edition. New York: Van Nostrand Reinhold, 1989.

Propylene Glycol—Material Safety Data Sheet, ARCO Chemical Company.

RACHEL'S Environmental & Health Weekly #499, Chemicals and the Brain, Peter Montague, June 20, 1996

The Erice Statement was signed by:

Dr. Enrico Alleva (Head, Section of Behavioral Pathophysiology; Institute of Neurobiology; Rome, Italy); Dr. John Brock (Chief -PCBs and Pesticides Laboratory; Center for Environmental Health; Centers for Disease Control; Atlanta, Georgia); Dr. Abraham Brouwer (Associate Professor and Toxicology and Research Coordinator; Department of Toxicology; Agricultural University; Wageningen, The Netherlands); Dr. Theo Colborn (Senior Program Scientist; Wildlife and Contaminants Project; World Wildlife Fund; Washington, DC.;) Dr. M. Cristina Fossi (Professor, Department of Environmental Biology; University of Siena; Siena, Italy); Dr. Earl Gray (Section Chief;

Developmental and Reproductive Toxicology Section; US Environmental Protection Agency [EPA] Research Triangle Park, North Carolina); Dr. Louis Guillette (Professor; Department of Zoology; University of Florida; Gainesville, Florida); Peter Hauser, MD (Chief of Psychiatry Service [116A]; Baltimore Veterans Administration Medical Center; 10 North Greene Street; Baltimore, Maryland); Dr. John Leatherland (Professor, Chair; Department of Biomedical Sciences; Ontario Veterinary College; University of Guelph; Guelph, Ontario, Canada); Dr. Neil MacLusky (Professor; Director of Basic Research; Division of Reproductive Science; Toronto Hospital; Toronto, Ontario, Canada); Dr. Antonio Mutti (Professor; Laboratory of Industrial Toxicology; University of Parma Medical School; Parma, Italy); Dr. Paola Palanza (Researcher; Department of Biology and Physiology; University of Parma; Parma, Italy); Dr. Susan Porterfield (Associate Professor and Associate Dean of Curriculum; Medical College of Georgia; Augusta, Georgia); Dr. Risto Santti (Associate Professor; Department of Anatomy; Institute of Biomedicine; University of Turku; Turku, Finland); Dr. Stuart A. Stein (Associate Professor of Neurology, Medicine, Pediatrics, OB-GYN, and Molecular and Cellular Pharmacology; University of Miami School of Medicine; Miami, Florida; and Chief of Neurology Children's Hospital of Orange County, Orange, California); Dr. Frederick vom Saal (Professor; Division of Biological Sciences, University of Missouri; Columbia, Missouri); Dr. Bernard Weiss (Professor, Department of Environmental Medicine; University of Rochester School of Medicine and Dentistry; Rochester, New York).

Red No. 3 and Other Colorful Controversies, Dale Blumenthal, FDA Consumer, May 1990.

Rethinking Retin-A, Leslie Vreeland, Allure, Nov. 1991.

Rogers, Sherry A., MD, Tired or Toxix? A Blueprint for Health. Syracuse, New York: Prestige Publishing, 1990

Safety evaluation of barrier creams, B.N. Gupta, Ravi Shanker et al, Contact Dermatitis, (1987) 17:10-12.

Scary Beauty, Meryl Gordon, Allure, Nov. 1992.

Sensitivity to Sunscreens, J.S.C. English, I.R. White, and E. Cronin, Contact Dermatitis, 1987:17:159-162.

Sick Sense. Perfumes that Stink, Jill Sharer, LA Weekly, June 25-July 1, 1993.

Skin Cancer Statistics. Self, July 1992 (p.125).

Skin Care Products Can Harm Babies, Your Health, Feb. 25, 1992.

Sunscreens and Hydroquinone. Scientifically Speaking, Anne Wolven Garrett, DCI, March 1989.

Suppression of in vivo Growths of Human Cancer Solid Tumor Xenografts by 1,25 Dihydroxyvitamin D3, John Eisman, et al, Garavan Institute of Medical Research Jan. 1987.

Surfactants: Evolution or Revolution. Anita Hipius Shaw, Soap/Cosmetics/Chemical Specialities, Sept 1992.

The AHA Phenomenon, Jean Godfrey-June, Longevity, Sept. 1993.

The Anti-Wrinkle Revolution, Leslie George, Self, Nov. 1992.

The Chemistry and Manufacture of Cosmetics, de Navarre, Maison G., Ph.C., B.S., MS. Vol. IV, Second Edition. Continental Press, Orlando, Florida: 1975.

The Aromatherapy Book, Jeanne Rose, Herbal Studies Course/Jeanne Rose and North Atlantic Books, Berkeley, CA, 1992

The Eyes Have It, Scientifically Speaking, Anne Wolven Garret, DCI, Aug. 1989.

The Fraud of Fluoridation review by Jule Klotter, Townsend Letter for Doctors, Aug/Sept. 1995.

The Molecular Basis of Skin Irritation, C. Prottey, Unilever Research Laboratory, Cosmetic Science, 1978.

The Problem with Packaging, Rebecca Johnson

The Trouble with Packaging, Allure Magazine, August, 1991.

The Wall Street Journal (October 13, 1992)

Tooth Whiteners: They Work But Questions Remain About Long-Term Safety. Health Facts, Centre for Medical Consumers, March 1992.

Toxicity of Ethylene Glycol, Diethylene Glycol and Propylene Glycol to Human Cells in Culture, Kyo Mochida and Manabu Goymyoda, Bulletin of Environmental Contamination and Toxicology (1987) 38:151-153.

Toxicity Testing: Strategies to Determine Needs and Priorities. Washington, D.C.: National Research Council: National Academy Press, 1984.

Twenty Most Common Chemicals Found in Thirty-One Fragrance Products, 1991 EPA Study, Compiled by Julia Kendal

Update on Color Regulations Worldwide, Soap/Cosmetics/Chemical Specialities, Dec. 1989.

Update: Alzheimer's/Aluminum. University of California, Berkeley Wellness Letter, April 1993.

Updates: Hair Dye Study, FDA Consumer, May, 1994.

Updating Preservatives, Alan Binenstock, Soap/Cosmetics/Chemical Specialities, May 1990.

Urinary Mutagens in Cosmetologist and Dental Personnel, J.G. Babish et al, Journal of Toxicology and Environmental Health, 34(2):197-206.

Water Worries. Mark Nichols, Dan Hawaleshka, Macleans, April 10, 1995.

What Price, Beautiful Skin, Claire Kowalchik, Rodale's Healthy Woman.

What's in that red stuff, anyway? Consumer Reports, February 1988. (P.77).

When the immune system goes awry, Nancy Monson, Glamour, Jan. 1994. p. 20.

Why Women Believe In Miracles, Judy Bachrach, Allure Oct. 1993.

Winter, Ruth, MS. A Consumer's Dictionary of Cosmetic Ingredients. New York: Crown Trade Paperbacks, 1994.

Winter's Skin, The Lancet, Vol. 335 No. 8684, Feb. 3, 1990.

Women's Health Update, Tori Hudson, ND, Townsend Letters For Doctors, Oct. 1994.

"Yuppie Flu" is Dead CDC: Chronic Fatigue Syndrome is Widespread, Severe. Townsend Letter for Doctors, Aug./Sept. 1995.

Index

A

B

C

F

Fatigue 43, 45
Feingold Association 25
Fibroblasts 19
Fluoride 30-32
Fluorosis 30
Formaldehyde 11, 13, 27, 30, 32, 47, 53, 71
Foundation 17, 25-26, 33
Fragrance 10, 21, 25, 27, 33, 39-40, 42-43, 45-47, 58, 69, 71, 74, 76, 100

G

g-Terpinene 45
Glycerin 8, 24, 33, 99
Glycol ethers 51, 52

H

Hair dye 12-16, 65, 75
Hair follicles 9-10, 86-88
Hairspray 43-45
Hand lotion 33, 44
Headaches 25, 49, 53
Heavy metals 28
Hepatocellular neoplasm 39
Hormone disrupters 59, 61
Hormone mimick 62
Hormones 11, 18, 59, 60, 61, 86
Humectants 28, 30, 33, 55, 70
Hydrocarbon 29, 56, 100
Hydroquinone 39
Hypodermis layer 81, 83, 88
Hypoxia 53

I

Immune system 31, 45, 86, 90

K

Kaolin 26

L

M

N